MIAOW

BENITO PÉREZ GALDÓS

Translated from the Spanish by
MARGARET JULL COSTA

NEW YORK REVIEW BOOKS

New York

THIS IS A NEW YORK REVIEW BOOK
PUBLISHED BY THE NEW YORK REVIEW OF BOOKS
207 East 32nd Street, New York, NY 10016
www.nyrb.com

AC/E   This publication is supported in part by a grant from Acción
ACCIÓN CULTURAL   Cultural Española (AC/E), a state agency.
ESPAÑOLA

Library of Congress Cataloging-in-Publication Data
Names: Pérez Galdós, Benito, 1843–1920, author. | Costa, Margaret Jull,
   translator.
Title: Miaow / by Benito Pérez Galdós; translated by Margaret Jull Costa.
Other titles: Miau. English
Description: New York: New York Review Books, 2025. | Series: New York
   Review Books classics |
Identifiers: LCCN 2025004194 (print) | LCCN 2025004195 (ebook) |
   ISBN 9781681379470 (paperback) | ISBN 9781681379487 (ebook)
Subjects: LCGFT: Novels.
Classification: LCC PQ6555.M513 2025 (print) | LCC PQ6555 (ebook) |
   DDC 863/.5—dc23/eng/20250303
LC record available at https://lccn.loc.gov/2025004194
LC ebook record available at https://lccn.loc.gov/2025004195

ISBN 978-1-68137-947-0
Available as an electronic book; ISBN 978-1-68137-948-7

The authorized representative in the EU for product safety and
compliance is eucomply OÜ, Pärnu mnt 139b-14, 11317 Tallinn, Estonia,
hello@eucompliancepartner.com, +33 757690241.

Printed in the United States of America on acid-free paper.
10 9 8 7 6 5 4 3 2 1

I

AT FOUR o'clock in the afternoon, the kids from the school on Plazuela del Limón erupted out of the classroom, making the very devil of a racket. No hymn to liberty, of the many composed in various countries, is quite as beautiful as that intoned by those oppressed by elementary education as they throw off the shackles of school discipline and emerge onto the street chirruping and skipping. The insane frenzy with which they throw themselves into the most perilous of acrobatics, the havoc they wreak on some poor peaceful passerby, the delirium of individual freedom that sometimes ends in blows, tears, and bruises, all seem like a first draft of the revolutionary triumphs celebrated by men in unhappier times . . . As I said, they burst onto the street, with the last eager to be first, the smaller kids screaming louder than the bigger ones. Among them was a boy of diminutive stature, who left the herd in order to make his way home alone and in silence. As soon as his classmates saw what seemed to them less like a parting of the ways and more like a retreat, they set off in hot pursuit, assailing him with mocking comments and cruel jokes, not all of them in the best taste. One grabbed his arm, another rubbed his face with his "innocent" hands, which were, in fact, covered with an amalgam of all the muck in the world; the boy, however, managed to free himself and to flee . . . well, what else are feet for? Then two or three of his more shameless pursuers pelted him with stones, shouting "Miaow, Miaow, Miaow"; and then the whole lot of them repeated that infernal refrain: "Miaow, Miaow, Miaow."

The poor object of this mockery was called Luis Cadalso, and he was a rather small, pale, timorous lad, about eight or possibly ten years old and so timid that he avoided the friendship of his fellows, fearful of their jokes and too slow-witted to come up with a suitable riposte. He was always the last to be involved in any pranks, the slowest and clumsiest in any games, and the best-behaved pupil in class, albeit one of the least outstanding, perhaps because his shyness prevented him from revealing what he knew or concealing what he didn't know. As he turned the corner of Comendadoras de Santiago to go to his house, which was in Calle de Quiñones, opposite the women's prison, he was joined by one of his classmates, a boy weighed down with books, with his slate slung over his shoulder, and wearing trousers made nearly entirely of patches, shoes that let in the daylight, and a blue beret perched on his shaven head, a boy with a distinctly rat-like face. His name was Silvestre Murillo, who was the hardest-working student at school and Cadalso's best friend there. His father, the sacristan at the Montserrat church, intended him to study law, because he had got it into his head that, one day, this snot-nosed brat would be "someone," possibly a famous orator, or, why not, a minister. The future celebrity spoke thus to his friend:

"Listen, Cadalso, if they made jokes like that about me or roughed me up, I'd give as good as I got. You're just not brave enough. I don't reckon they should give people nicknames. D'you know who started it? Joker, the pawnbroker's son. Yesterday, he was saying that, according to his mother, your grandmother and your aunts are called the Miaows because of their faces, because they look like cats. He said they were given that name by the other regulars in the gods at the Teatro Real, and that when people see them arrive, the whole audience says: 'Here come the Miaows.'"

Luis Cadalso blushed scarlet. He felt too indignant, too shocked and ashamed to defend his family's wounded dignity.

"Joker is a pleb and a nobody," added Silvestre, "and calling people names is what plebs do. His father's a pleb, and so are his mother and his aunts. They live by sucking the blood out of poor people, and you know what, if someone can't afford to redeem a cloak, they simply fleece them—by which I mean, they sell the cloak and leave them to freeze to death. My mama calls them harpies. Have you ever seen them out on their balcony airing the cloaks? They're all as ugly as sin, and my papa says you could make a pair of table legs out of their noses and still have wood to spare...Joker is a right one too, always messing around and clowning about like he was at the circus. And, of course, since *he's* been given a nickname, he wants to have his revenge by giving you one too. He won't try it out on me though, because he knows I can turn nasty, very nasty indeed...But because you're so small and timid, and you don't bite back when they have a go at you, that's why they don't respect you, like."

Stopping outside his house, Cadalso gazed sadly at his friend, but Silvestre gave him a nudge and said:

"Don't worry, I won't ever call you Miaow, not ever," and he raced off toward the Montserrat church.

In the hallway of the house where Cadalso lived was the office of a public scribe. The screen or partition—lined with marbled paper imitating the various colors of jasper—concealed the space reserved for that office or agency which was constantly engaged in matters of great importance. The multiplicity of these matters was set out on the handwritten notice pinned to the street door. It was given in the form of an index and read thus:

Marriages—Wedding banns cheaply and promptly arranged.
Maids—Supplied.
Waiters—Provided.
Cooks—Procured.
Accordion teacher—Recommended.
Note—One desk reserved solely for ladies.

Still absorbed in his own thoughts, Cadalso was walking past the screen when these words emerged from behind it:

"Luisito, you silly boy, it's me."

The boy turned, and a very large, stout woman reached out from behind the screen to take him fondly in her arms:

"You silly billy! Fancy walking straight past without a word. I have your teatime treat right here. Mendizábal had some business to deal with and left me here to keep an eye on things, in case any clients should appear. You can keep me company."

Mendizábal's wife was so huge that when she was in the office, it was as if a cow had entered the room and settled its vast hindquarters on the bench, with all the remaining space occupied by the super-abundant volume of its front half. She had no children, and was fond of all the neighborhood kids, especially Luis, who deserved to be pitied and fussed over because he was so sweet and humble, and, more than that, because in his household, or so she said, there was never enough to eat. She always had some treat for him when he came home from school. That afternoon, it was a sticky bun, which she had placed on the top of the sander, leaving the sugary coating slightly gritty, not that Luis noticed as he bit greedily into it.

"You'd better go upstairs now," said the concierge-cum-scribe while he was still devouring the bun with its coating of sand. "Up you go, sweetheart; you don't want your grandmother to tell you off, but leave your books there and then you can come down later to keep me company and play with Canelo."

The boy raced up the stairs, where a door was opened by a lady whose face could easily have given rise to numismatic controversies, just as certain coins do where the lettering has worn away, because sometimes, if you saw her in profile and in a certain light, you would think she was at least sixty, while at others, even an expert would say she was a well-preserved forty-eight or fifty.

She had fine, dainty features, the sort people describe as "child-like," and she still had a rosy complexion; her hair was an almost alchemical ash-blond and fell in effusive waves about her forehead. Twenty-odd years before the time we're speaking of here, a hack journalist in charge of reporting alternately on society gossip and on the price of flour used these words to describe that same lady when she appeared in the salons of the governor of a third-rate province: "Who is this figure straight out of a painting by Fra Angelico, who arrived wrapped in vaporous clouds and clothed in the golden aura of fourteenth-century iconography?" The "vaporous clouds" were the little gauze dress that Señora de Villaamil had ordered to be sent from

Madrid for the occasion, and I wouldn't be at all surprised if by "golden aura" he meant those effusive waves of hair, which must have been blond at the time and, therefore, on a par, in literary terms, with the gold of Arabia.

Twenty or twenty-five years after her elegant success in that provincial town, whose name we need not mention, the lady, Doña Pura by name—wearing a rather grubby dressing gown, some rather ancient felt slippers, and a loose, green tartan housecoat—was opening the door to her little grandson and saying:

"Ah, it's you, Luis. I thought it was Ponce with the tickets for the Teatro Real. And he promised he would come at two o'clock! Young people nowadays are so unreliable!"

At this point, another lady appeared, very similar to the first in her short stature, childlike features, and the enigmatic matter of her age. She was wearing a threadbare jacket—the remote descendant of a man's overcoat—and a long apron made of sacking, as worn in kitchens everywhere. She was Doña Pura's sister, and her name was Milagros. In the dining room, where Luis went to leave his books, a young woman was busy sewing, sitting right by the window to make the most of the fading light, which was as short-lived as on a February day. She too bore a resemblance to the other two women, except as regards age. She was Abelarda, Doña Pura's daughter and Luis Cadalso's aunt. Luis's mother, Luisa Villaamil, had died when he was barely two years old. We will speak of his father, Víctor Cadalso, later.

The three women pecked away at the extraordinary fact that Ponce (Abelarda's titular fiancé, who provided the family with tickets to the Teatro Real) usually brought them their tickets promptly at two but had still not arrived at half past four.

"When it's all so up in the air, and we have no idea whether we're going to the theater or not, it's just impossible to know what to do or to make plans for the evening. What a laggard the fellow is!" said Doña Pura scornfully, and her daughter replied:

"It's still not too late, Mama. There's plenty of time. You'll see, he'll bring the tickets."

"Yes, but with performances like tonight's, when the tickets are so scarce you really need an insider to get them for you, it's very cruel to keep us on tenterhooks like this."

Meanwhile, Luis was looking at his grandmother, at his older aunt and his younger aunt, and comparing their physiognomies with that of the cat who was also in the dining room, asleep at Abelarda's feet, and he thought the resemblance quite perfect. His lively imagination immediately suggested to him that the three women were two-legged cats dressed as people, like the ones in that book *The Animals as Painted by Themselves*; and this hallucination led him to wonder if he too was a two-legged cat and if, when he spoke, he miaowed. He moved rapidly on from this to thinking that the nickname given to his grandmother and his aunts in the gods at the Teatro Real really was the most accurate and most reasonable in the world. All this appeared in his mind in a flash, with the clarity and speed of a brain still practicing its powers of observation and reason. However, he went no further in his feline cogitations because his grandmother, placing one hand on his head, said:

"Didn't Paca give you your usual afternoon treat?"

"Yes, she did, Mama, and I've already eaten it. She told me to bring my books upstairs and then go down and play with Canelo."

"Off you go then, and be quick, and you can stay there for a while if you like. Ah, no, now I remember . . . come back soon, because your grandfather needs you to run an errand for him."

She was just saying goodbye to the boy at the front door when, from a room just off the hallway, there came a cavernous, sepulchral voice:

"Puuura, Puuura."

She opened a door on the left and went into the so-called office, a room of about seven square feet, with a window that opened onto a gloomy courtyard. Given that there was already so little daylight, you could barely see anything in there apart from the luminous rectangle of the window, against which was silhouetted a long, thin, shadowy figure who, as he was getting up from his chair, appeared to be gradually unfolding himself, and who stretched and yawned, before saying in a hoarse, timorous voice:

"Didn't it even occur to you to bring me a light? You know I'm in here writing and that it gets dark earlier than one would like, and here I am ruining my eyesight writing on this dreadful paper."

Doña Pura went into the dining room, where her sister was already lighting an oil lamp, and soon reappeared before her husband, lamp in hand. The tiny room and its inhabitant emerged out of the darkness like something rising up from the void.

"I'm absolutely frozen," said Don Ramón Villaamil, Doña Pura's husband, who was a tall, thin man with large, rather frightening eyes, long transparent ears that fitted closely to his skull, and yellow skin so deeply lined that the shadows cast by the folds resembled dark stains. His short, sparse, bristly beard was sprinkled with gray hairs, which formed drifts of white among the black; his smooth skull was the color of a recently disinterred bone, as if he had just plucked it from an ossuary to cover his brains. The strength of his jaw and the size of his mouth, the combination of those three colors—black, white, and yellow—plus those fierce dark eyes, all invited comparisons with the face of an old, consumptive tiger who had once dazzled the audiences of traveling menageries but whose garishly striped skin was all that remained of his former beauty.

"So, who have you written to?" she asked, turning down the flame of the lamp, which was sticking its smoking tongue out of the glass chimney.

"To the head of personnel, to Señor de Pez, to Sánchez Botín, and to anyone who can get me out of this mess. First and foremost, though (and here he gave a deep sigh), I've decided to go back to my friend Cucúrbitas. He's the only truly Christian person among my so-called friends, a gentleman and an honest fellow, who understands the needs of others. Unlike the rest of them! You saw what that ignoramus, Rubín, did to me yesterday. I explained our situation to him and had to stoop to begging him for a mere nothing, a small advance and . . . God knows the bitter gall I had to swallow while I waited for him to decide, I mean, the indignity of it . . . anyway, that ungrateful, forgetful wretch, who I took on as a scribe in my office when I was chief clerk, fourth class, that shameless devil, who, thanks to his sheer effrontery, was promoted over my head to become a governor no less, that man had the rank indelicacy to give me two and a half pesetas."

Villaamil sat down and struck the desk so hard that the letters he had written jumped into the air, as if terrified and eager to escape. When he heard his wife sigh, he raised his yellow face and continued in a sorrowful voice:

"This world is nothing but egotism and ingratitude, and the more infamous things you see, the more there are waiting to appear... Like that idler Montes, who owes his whole career to me, because I put his name forward to be promoted to the Central Accounts Office. Do you know, he won't even deign to say hello to me now? He acts as if he were the minister himself... And there's no stopping the man. They've just raised his salary to fourteen thousand. Every year, it's another promotion, up and up. That's the reward you get for being a toady and a lickspittle. He doesn't know a thing about administration, all he does is talk to the director about hunting, greyhounds and birds and I don't know what... A dog could spell better than him; he writes 'accommodate' with one 'c' and 'acquittal' with none. But let's forget about such knaves. As I was saying, I've decided to turn to our friend Cucúrbitas again. True, I've already been to him a few times for help, but I just don't know what else to do. Cucúrbitas understands what it means to be down on your luck, and he feels sorry for those who are, because he's been down on his luck too. I knew him when he had holes in his pants and two inches of grease on his hat... And he knows how grateful I am. Do you think his generosity will have run dry? God have mercy on us if it has, because if that friend turns his back on us, we'll all have to throw ourselves off the viaduct."

Villaamil gave another long sigh and stared down at the ground. The ailing tiger was transfigured. He now wore the sublime expression of an apostle being martyred for his faith, rather like Saint Bartholomew in that Ribera painting after he had been hung from a tree then flayed alive by those villainous gentiles as if he were a goat. We should point out that regular attendees at certain cafés had nicknamed Villaamil "Ramses II."

"Well, give me the letter for Cucúrbitas," said Doña Pura, who was accustomed to such jeremiads and considered them perfectly natural and normal. "The boy will run all the way there. Put your trust in Providence, dear, like me. Don't be discouraged. (She said this in a tone of cheerful optimism.) I have a feeling... and you know I'm rarely wrong... I have a feeling that you'll have another job before the month is out."

2

"A JOB!" cried Villaamil, pouring heart and soul into that one word. His hands waved around for a while above his head, then dropped like lead onto the arms of his chair. By this time, though, Doña Pura was no longer there, for she had taken the letter and was already calling down the stairs to her grandson, who was still in the porter's lodge.

It was nearly six when Luis set off on his errand, after making a brief stop in the scribe's office.

"Goodbye, my dear," said Paca, kissing him. "You'd better go so that you're home in time for supper. (She read the name on the envelope.) It's quite a walk from here to Calle del Amor de Dios. Do you know the way? You won't get lost?"

Lost! How could he possibly get lost when he had been to the house of Señor Cucúrbitas more than twenty times before, as well as to the houses of other gentlemen, bearing messages, both verbal and written! He was the bearer of his grandfather's terrible anxieties, sadnesses, and impatiences; he it was who delivered to various parts of the city that poor unfortunate man's requests for help or for a letter of recommendation. And in his role as courier, he had acquired such a thorough topographical knowledge of the city that he could navigate every district and never get lost; and although he knew perfectly well the shortest route to his destination, he usually took the longer one, out of habit, but also because he loved both walking and looking, taking immense pleasure in studying shopwindows, in listening—never missing a word—to the patter of the sundry mountebanks selling elixirs or performing feats of prestidigitation. He would often come across a monkey sitting astride a dog, or else manipulating the stirrer on the hot chocolate stand just like a "real person"; or it might be a poor scrawny bear in chains, or else Italians, Turks, or fake Moors doing all kinds of tricks to beg for money. He also enjoyed watching fancy funerals, water carts hosing down the streets, soldiers marching along to a band, blocks of stone being hoisted up onto a building under construction, a Viaticum accompanied by many candles, the replacement horses waiting for the trams, trees being dug up and transplanted, and whatever other diversions the streets had to offer.

"Wrap up warm," said Paca, giving him another kiss and tying the scarf around his neck more tightly. "They should buy you some woollen gloves. Your little hands are frozen *and* you've got chilblains. You'd be so much happier with your Auntie Paca! Give Mendizábal a kiss, and off you go! Canelo will go with you."

A dog appeared from under the table; he had a fine head, short legs, a curly tail, fur the color of an ice cream wafer, and he trotted happily ahead of Luis. Paca accompanied them to the street door, watched them leave, then, returning to the narrow office, resumed her knitting, saying to her husband:

"Poor boy! They send him out at all hours delivering their letters. The latest begging letter is to the same fellow they've been pestering for days. That poor man has a lot to put up with! Those Villaamils are worse than the plague. And I bet you anything you like that, tonight, those three fine ladies will go gadding off to the theater and won't be home until the small hours."

"Families these days don't know the true meaning of Christian virtue," said Mendizábal gravely and sententiously. "It's all show."

"They're up to their eyes in debt too. (Furiously wielding her needles.) The butcher says he'll be hanged if he lets them run up any more credit with him, the greengrocer's put his foot down too, and so has the baker... If those flibbertigibbets managed their affairs better, they could make do with a dish of potatoes, if they had any... But oh no! Potatoes? Not them! The poor things! Whenever they do get some money, even if it's only given out of charity, they're off living the high life, no expense spared. Tarting up the few clothes they have to look like they're the very height of fashion, and I don't know how many times Doña Milagros has revamped her one-and-only dress, the one that's the color of a mustard plaster. And that unpleasant daughter of hers is forever stitching bits of leather to her hat, adding old ribbons or a chicken feather, or one of those golden-headed nails they use to hang pictures on."

"Pretension upon pretension . . . The dire consequences of materialism," said Mendizábal, who was in the habit of repeating turns of phrase from the newspaper to which he subscribed. "There's no such thing as modesty any more, no simplicity. Whatever happened to the honest poverty of our parents . . . (here he failed to recall the next phrase) to that . . . oh, you know . . ."

"Well, when poor Don Ramón does close his eyes for the last time, he'll go straight to heaven. He's a saint and a martyr. Believe me, if I could give him a job, I would. I feel so sorry for him! He looks at people as if he was about to eat them, poor man, and he *would* eat you, not out of malice, but out of sheer hunger. (Sticking the fourth knitting needle in her hair.) It's positively frightening. When the minister sees him come into the office, I don't know why he doesn't die of fright and give him a job just to be rid of him."

"Villaamil," said Mendizábal smugly, "is an honest man, and the government now is full of rogues. There's no honesty, no Christian feeling, no justice. What is there instead? Thievery, irreligiosity, shamelessness. That's why they won't give him a job, and they won't until the one man arrives who can bring justice. Whenever Don Ramón pops in for a chat, I always say to him: 'Don't bother your head about it, Señor Don Ramón, it's freedom of worship that's to blame. Because as long as we have rationalism, my friend, as long as no one is crushing the serpent's head, and . . .' (Losing the thread of what he's saying and having no idea where he was going.) And so on . . . I mean . . . (Reverting to his original theme.) There's no proper Christian feeling anymore."

Meanwhile, Luis and Canelo were following their usual itinerary, walking down Calle Ancha and from there turning into Calle del

Pez. Whenever they became separated, the dog would stop and look back, his tongue hanging out. Luis would pause to look in shopwindows and occasionally say to his companion something along the lines of: "Hey, Canelo, look at these beautiful trumpets." The dog would then place his two front paws on the edge of the window but, clearly having little interest in trumpets, would soon head off again. Finally, they reached Calle del Amor de Dios. Ever since the occasion when Canelo had a barking match with another dog who lived in the Cucúrbitas household, he always adopted a very prudent attitude now and waited for his friend outside in the street. Luis would go up to the second floor, where his grandfather's tireless protector lived, but the servant who opened the door that evening greeted him with a scowl. "The master isn't in." But Luis, who had been told what to do should his victim be absent, said he would wait. He knew that, at seven o'clock on the dot, Señor Don Francisco Cucúrbitas would, infallibly, return home for supper. He sat down on the bench in the hall. His feet didn't touch the floor, and he swung them back and forth to distract himself from the tedium of that long wait. The imitation oak coat stand—complete with gold hooks for hats, a mirror, and special holes for umbrellas—that had once provoked his admiration now left him unmoved. Not the cat, though, who would usually appear from inside the apartment to welcome him and rub against his legs. That evening, the cat clearly had other things to do, because he failed to put in an appearance; on the other hand, Luis did see the Cucúrbitas girls, two pretty young things, who, although they usually came over to observe him with a mixture of pity and disdain, had never once said a civil word to him. Señora de Cucúrbitas—who, being fat and round, seemed to Luis like a human version of Pizarro the elephant, a beast very popular among Madrid's children at the time—would also put in an appearance, and Luis was already familiar with her slow, heavy steps. She would appear at the corner where the right-hand corridor met the hall, and from there, she would eye the messenger suspiciously, then, without a word, withdraw. As soon as he heard her coming, he would leap to his feet like a doll on springs, remembering the etiquette lessons given him by his grandfather.

"How are you? How do you do?" But the hulk, who rivalled even Paca in size, never deigned to answer him, and left, making the floor-boards tremble, like the steamroller Luis had seen at work in the streets of Madrid.

That night, the respectable Señor Cucúrbitas was unusually late for supper, and Luis could see that the girls were growing impatient, the reason being that they were going to the theater and wanted to dine early. Finally, the doorbell rang, and the servant scurried over to open the door while the two young things, recognizing their father's footsteps and his ring, ran off down the corridor together, calling for supper to be served. When Señor Cucúrbitas came in and saw Luis, it was clear from the expression on his face that he was not best pleased. The boy stood up and fired off his greeting at point-blank range, but Cucúrbitas went straight into his office without even responding. Luis waited to receive his usual summons and saw the girls go in, urging their father to make haste, and heard him say: "I'll be there in a moment . . . tell them to serve the soup," and Luis could not help imagining how delicious that soup would be. He was still thinking this when one of the girls came out of the office and said: "You can come in now." He entered, cap in hand, and repeated his words of greeting, to which Don Francisco now deigned to reply in a fatherly tone. Believing Don Francisco to be a very kindly man, Luis failed to understand the slight frown on the prudent functionary's plump face and assumed that he would do as he had on all the other evenings. Luis knew the routine by heart: Señor Cucúrbitas would read the letter from Villaamil, then write a reply or simply take a green or a red note out of his wallet, put it in an envelope, and hand it to him, saying: "There you are, lad, off you go." It was also quite common for him to take a few coins from his pocket and put them in a small screw of paper, which he would then give to Luis, accompanying this with the same words or else saying: "Be careful now, don't lose it and don't let anyone steal it from you. Put it in your trouser pocket . . . There you are, my fine boy. And may God go with you."

That night, alas, as he stood next to the "ministerial" desk, Luis watched as Don Francisco, his bushy eyebrows knit into a frown, wrote a letter, then sealed it without including any notes or coins. Luis also noticed that as he signed the letter, Don Francisco uttered a heartfelt sigh and gave him a look of genuine compassion.

"God bless you, sir," Luis said, taking the letter; and the kind gentleman placed one hand on his head. Then, as he bade Luis farewell, he put two large coins in his hand, adding these magnanimous words to that generous action: "Buy yourself some cakes." Filled with gratitude, the boy left . . . But, as he went down the stairs, he was assailed by a sad thought: "He didn't put any money in with the letter." This was indeed the first time he had failed to do so. It was also the first time that Don Francisco had given him coins for his private purse and encouraged the vice of eating cakes. He noticed all this with the penetrating intelligence provided by his long experience of carrying those messages. Then, reverting to his childish innocence, he thought: "But who knows, maybe the letter says that he can start work tomorrow . . ."

Canelo, who was growing impatient, met him at the door. They set off again, and at a cake shop in Calle de las Huertas, Luis bought two cakes for ten *céntimos* each. The dog ate one, and Luis the other. Then, still licking their lips, they hurried on, taking the shortest route through that same labyrinth of streets and small squares, some brightly lit and packed with people, others not at all. Here there was gaslight, there utter gloom; here there were crowds, there solitude or just a few stray figures. They walked down streets in which there was barely room for the hurrying hordes, and down others where they saw more women than lights, and still others where there were more dogs than people.

3

WHEN HE reached Calle de la Puebla, Luis was already feeling so weary that he paused to rest a little and sat down on the steps leading up to one of the three iron-grilled doors that belonged to the Convento de Don Juan de Alarcón. And no sooner had he taken a seat on the cold steps than he was overwhelmed by sleep . . . Or, rather, it was more like a fainting fit, a not unfamiliar phenomenon, and one that never occurred without him first becoming aware of the strange preceding symptoms: "Oh no!" he thought, greatly alarmed. "I'm going to have one of those things . . . one of those . . ." In fact, Luis did sometimes experience something very odd, a funny turn, which began with a heaviness in the head, a drowsiness, cold shivers down the spine, and ended with a complete loss of sensation and consciousness. That night, in the brief interval between thinking he was about to faint and completely losing his senses, he recalled a poor man who used to sit on that very step to beg for alms. He was an ancient blind man with a long white beard tinged with yellow, who would sit wrapped in an ample brown cloak, patched and dirty, that hung about him in heavy folds; with his white head bare, his hat in one hand, only his attitude told you he was begging, for he never once opened his lips to speak. This venerable figure filled Luis with respect, and on the very rare occasions that he had money to spare, he would throw a *céntimo* into the man's hat.

Anyway, as we were saying, the boy sank into a profound state of lethargy, his head lolling, and then he realized that he was not alone. Beside him sat an older man. Was it the blind beggar? For a moment, Luis thought that it was, because the man also had a thick, white beard and was wearing a cloak or cape…Then Luis began to pick out the differences and similarities between the beggar and this other person, for while the latter was looking at him with eyes like stars, his nose, mouth, and forehead were identical to those of the beggar, his beard the same length, although whiter, far whiter. And the cloak was both the same and different; the long folds were the same, as was the way in which the man wore it wrapped about him; however, the color was quite different, although Luis struggled to put a name to it. Was it white or blue, what the devil was that color? It was full of soft shadows, dappled with bright rays, like the shafts of light that shine down from between the clouds. Luis thought that he had never seen anything lovelier. From among the folds of his cloak, the man held out an exquisite white hand. Luis had never seen such a hand, strong and manly, but also fine and white as a lady's hand…The man was looking at him in a benign, fatherly way and then he said:

"Don't you recognize me? Don't you know who I am?"

Luis looked at him hard, too shy to actually respond. Then the mysterious gentleman, smiling the way bishops do when they give a blessing, said:

"I am God. Don't you recognize me?"

Luis then felt not only shy, but so afraid that he could hardly breathe. Unable to believe what he had heard, he tried to pluck up enough courage to blurt out:

"*You* are God? Ah, if only you were…"

And the apparition, for what else can we call him, responded kindly to good little Luis's incredulity and, smiling still more fondly, said again:

"Yes, I am God. You seem frightened, but please don't be. I love you, I love you very much…"

Luis began to feel less afraid. He was so moved he could have wept.

"I know where you've just come from," the apparition continued. "Señor Cucúrbitas gave you nothing tonight. Well, he can't always help. As he would say: There are so many needs to satisfy!"

Giving a deep sigh, so as to return his breathing to normal, Luis regarded the handsome old man, who—one elbow on his knee, resplendent beard resting on his hand, head turned slightly to one side in order to look at the boy—clearly considered this conversation to be of great importance:

"You and yours must be patient, my friend, very patient."

Luis sighed even more loudly, and feeling that his soul was now free of fear and, at the same time, full of initiative, he managed to say:

"But when will my grandfather find another job?"

The sublime person with whom Luis was speaking stopped looking at him for a moment and, gazing down at the ground, appeared to be thinking hard. Then he again turned to look at the boy and with a sigh—yes, he too sighed!—spoke these grave words:

"Consider the situation. For every vacancy there are two hundred applicants. It's driving the ministers crazy, because they don't know who to give which job. They have so many obligations to so many people that I really don't know how the poor men stand it! Be patient, my child, be patient, for the letter of appointment will come when the moment is right... For my part, I will do something for your grandfather too... How sad he'll be tonight when he reads that letter! Be sure not to lose it. Now, you're a good boy, but you need to study harder. You didn't know your grammar today. You made so many mistakes that the whole class laughed, and quite right too. What madness made you say that 'the participle expresses the idea of the verb in the abstract'? You were confusing it with the 'gerund,' and then you made a complete hodgepodge of 'moods' and 'tenses.' Your problem is that you don't concentrate, and when you're supposed to be studying, you're really just daydreaming..."

Luis blushed scarlet and, putting his hands between his knees, squeezed them hard.

"It's not enough to be well-behaved in class, you have to study, to focus on what you're reading and memorize it. If not, you and I really can't be friends. I'll get annoyed with you, and then there'll be no point in you coming to me later, asking why your grandfather can't find a job... While we're here, though, I have to say that you're quite right to complain about that boy Joker. He's a common, ill-mannered lout, and the next time he calls you 'Miaow,' I'll rub his tongue with a chili pepper. But this business of nicknames is something you'll just have to put up with, and when anyone calls you 'Miaow,' just say nothing and accept it. There are worse names."

Luis was very grateful, and although he knew God was everywhere, he was amazed that he should be so well-informed about what went on at school. Then he burst out with:

"If I ever catch him again…"

"Look, my friend," his companion said in a stern, fatherly voice, "don't play the strong man with me. You're no match for your schoolmates when it comes to fighting. They're too tough. Do you know what you should do? When Joker calls you 'Miaow,' tell the teacher, and you'll see, he'll punish him by making him kneel on the floor with his arms outspread and stay there for a whole half an hour."

"I wish he would, or even better, for a whole hour."

"Your grandmother and your aunts were given that nickname in the gods at the Teatro Real because they really do resemble three cats, always so neat and well-groomed. It's quite a funny nickname really."

Luis felt his pride wounded, but said nothing.

"I happen to know that they're going to the theater again tonight," added the apparition. "That Ponce fellow delivered the tickets a while ago now. Why don't you ask them to take you as well? You'd really enjoy the opera. It's such a wonderful spectacle!"

"They never want to take me…(Said in a mournful voice.) You tell them, sir."

Even though we address God familiarly as "Our Father" in prayers, it seemed rude to be so familiar when face to face with him.

"Me? No, I don't want to get involved in that. Besides, tonight they're all going to be in a very bad mood. Your poor grandfather! When he opens that letter…You haven't lost it, have you?"

"No, sir, I have it here," said Luis, taking it out of his pocket. "Would you like to read it?"

"No, silly. I know exactly what it says. Your grandfather will be most upset, but he just has to accept it. These are very difficult times, very difficult."

The sublime image repeated "very difficult" two or three times, sadly shaking his head, then, fading fast, he vanished. Luis rubbed his eyes. He knew he was awake, and he knew which street he was in. Opposite him was the basket-maker's shop, and there, above the door, were two wickerwork bull's heads, a favorite plaything among children in Madrid. He also recognized the wineshop, with its window full of bottles; the passersby all looked perfectly normal, and Canelo, who was still at his side, seemed like a real dog. He glanced around him, to see if there was any trace left of that marvelous vision, but there was nothing. "It was that 'thing' again," thought Luis, not knowing how else to describe it, "but this time it was different."

When he got up, his legs felt so weak he could barely stand. He patted his jacket, afraid he might have lost the letter, but it was still there in his pocket. Goodness! He'd had that funny turn before but had never actually seen someone so ... so ... well, he didn't know how to describe him, really. And he was absolutely sure that he *had* seen him and spoken to him. A great gentleman like that! Was he really the Eternal Father in the flesh? Or was it the old blind man playing a trick on him?

Absorbed in these thoughts, Luis hurried home as fast as his weak legs would allow. He was feeling dizzy, and the coldness he had felt lingered in his spine however quickly he walked. Canelo seemed somehow jittery too ... Had he seen something? What a shame he couldn't speak and bear witness to the truth of that wonderful vision! Because Luis recalled how, during their conversation, God had stroked the dog's head several times, and Canelo had looked up at him, tongue hanging loose ... So, Canelo could have testified ...

He reached home, and Abelarda, hearing him coming up the stairs, opened the door to the apartment before he even knocked. His grandfather appeared too, anxious to see him, and the boy, without a word, placed the letter in his hands. Don Ramón went to his office, feeling the envelope before he actually opened it, and, at the same moment, Doña Pura called Luis to come and eat, because the family had nearly finished their meal. They hadn't waited for him because he had taken such a long time, and the ladies had to rush off to the theater to get a good place up in the gods before it became too crowded.

Two covered plates, one on top of the other, contained the boy's soup and stew, both of which were cold by the time he began eating; not that he noticed, he was too hungry.

Doña Pura was still tying the three-week-old napkin around her grandson's neck when Villaamil returned to the room for his "dessert." In times of trouble, his face took on an expression of bloodthirsty ferocity, for when that saintly man, who wouldn't harm a fly, was weighed down by some sorrow, he looked as if he were chewing on raw human flesh, seasoned with bitter aloes instead of salt. Doña Pura had only to glance at him to know that the letter had brought nothing. The poor man began mechanically shelling the two withered walnuts on his plate. His sister-in-law and her daughter were also watching him, reading on his face—the face of a decrepit old tiger— the pain eating him up inside. To try and add a cheery note to that sad scene, Abelarda suddenly said:

"Ponce says that La Pellegrini will get all the applause tonight."

"That seems most unfair to me," said Doña Pura with great feeling. "It's simply a way of humiliating La Scolpi Rolla, who does a fairly good job in the role of Amneris. True, her success is in large part due to her fine figure and to her showing her legs, but La Pellegrini, for all her airs and graces, is really nothing to write home about."

"Nonsense, girl," retorted Milagros authoritatively. "The other night she sang the *fuggi fuggi, tu sei perdutto* as we haven't heard it sung since the days of Rossina Penco. She does wave her arms about rather too much, and, frankly, opera should be about singing not arm-waving."

"Anyway, no dawdling," said Pura. "On nights like tonight, any dawdlers will be left standing on the stairs."

"Don't be silly. Guillén and the medical students will be sure to save us seats."

"You can't rely on that, so let's go, we don't want a repeat of the other night. Why, if it hadn't been for those nice pharmacy students, we would have been left standing outside like fools."

Villaamil, who heard none of this, ate a dried fig, possibly swallowing it whole, and strode back to his office like someone about to commit some terrible deed. His wife followed him, saying fondly:

"What's wrong? Did that nonentity send you nothing at all?"

"Nothing," said Villaamil in a voice that seemed to emerge from the bowels of the earth. "As I said: He's had enough of me. You can't keep asking day after day… He's done me so many favors, so many, that asking for more is sheer impudence. I really shouldn't have written to him again!"

"The blackguard!" cried Doña Pura furiously, this being the term, and others far worse, that she applied to any friends who swerved to avoid the sword thrust.

"No, he's not a blackguard," declared Villaamil, who even in times of greatest difficulty would not allow his "donors" to be insulted. "It's simply that he's not always in a position to help his fellow man. He's not a blackguard though. When it comes to ideas, he hasn't a single one in his head and never has had, but that doesn't take away from the fact that he's one of the most honest men in the department."

"He's not so very honest (said with genuine anger), not when he shows his true colors. Remember when he worked with you in the Central Accounts Office. He was the stupidest man there. Everyone knew it, and whenever some gross error came to light, they would all say: 'Cucúrbitas.' And yet he's never once been without a job, and he's always being promoted. And why is that? Well, he may be very stupid, but he's better than you at using his position. Do you really believe that he doesn't happily have people grease his palm to get their business dispatched more quickly?"

"Be quiet, woman."

"You're such an innocent! That's why you're in the situation you're in now, forgotten and poor, because you haven't got a sly bone in your body, and because you're such a devotee of Saint Scrupulous. Believe me, that's not honesty, it's stuff and nonsense. Take a good look at Cucúrbitas; he may be a complete idiot, but you watch, he'll rise to be director and then, who knows, a minister. You'll never be anything, and if they do give you a job, they'll pay you a pittance, and we'll still be in the same mess. (Growing more heated.) And all because of your priggishness, your refusal to assert yourself, because, as you well know, Father Modest was never made Prior. If I were you, I'd go to the newspapers and tell them all the scandalous goings-on that even I know about in that department, all the dirty schemes engaged in by many of those who are now at the top of the tree. Yes, sing out, and see what happens...unmask all those rogues...That would hit them where it hurts. Then you'd see how quickly they found a position for you, how the director himself would come here, hat in hand, begging you to accept a post."

"Mama, it's getting late," said Abelarda, putting on her scarf.

"I'm coming! You're too prim and proper, too respectful, too yes-sir-no-sir, always so polite and so honest, such a goody-goody, and what do you get in return? They treat you like a complete nobody. It's true (raising her voice), you should be director by now, that's as plain as day, but you're not because you're too spineless and too timid, because, let's be frank, you're utterly useless and haven't a clue about how the world works. Sighing and complaining will get you nowhere. If you want a job, you have to show your teeth, but you're too inoffensive, you don't bite, you don't even bark, you're a laughingstock. They say: 'Ah, Villaamil, he's so honest! Such a dependable employee.' Whenever anyone tells me how dependable someone is, I check to see how many patches he has on his jacket. In short, being so honest has been your downfall. Sometimes, saying someone is honest is tantamount to saying they're a fool. But that's not true. A man can have all the integrity in the world and still be able to look after himself and his family..."

"Oh, leave me in peace," muttered Villaamil glumly, sitting down in a chair that creaked beneath his weight.

"Mama," said Abelarda again, growing impatient.

"I'm coming, I'm coming."

"This is how God made me, and I can't be any other way," said poor Villaamil. "But it's not a question of me being this or that, it's a matter of earning our daily bread, tomorrow's bread. Things are certainly bad...and the prospects look bleak. Tomorrow..."

"God won't abandon us," said Pura, trying to boost his spirits and making an effort to instill him with hope, an effort that resembled the flounderings of a drowning man. "I'm so used to living on next to nothing that having too much of anything would be quite a shock, almost frightening...Tomorrow..."

She finished neither the sentence nor the thought. Her daughter and her sister were now so urgent in their pleas for her to make haste that she quickly got ready, and as she wrapped a blue scarf about her head, she gave this order to her husband:

"Put the boy to bed, and if he doesn't want to study, then don't make him. The poor little thing has enough to do, because I suppose, tomorrow, he'll be sent off to deliver another big batch of letters."

Good Señor Villaamil felt a great weight lifted off his soul when he saw them leave. His sorrows were more companionable than his family and offered more diversion and consolation than his wife's words, because his sorrows, while they may have weighed on his heart, didn't scratch his face, while Doña Pura, when she laid into him, was all beak and claws.

4

LUIS WAS sitting at the dining table, leaning on his elbows, his books spread out before him. There were so many of them that the young scholar felt proud to see them all lined up like that, and he did appear to be reviewing them, like a general reviewing his troops. The poor things were so battered they looked as if they had been used as projectiles in some furious battle; the pages were all dogeared, the corners of the covers bent or torn, the binding sticky with grime. On the first page of each and every one of them, however, was inscribed the owner's name, written in a hesitant hand, because it was of vital importance that it should be known that the books were the exclusive property of Luis Cadalso y Villaamil. He picked one up at random, to see which it would be. Oh no, it just had to be that wretched grammar book! He opened it cautiously and saw the swarm of words on the page lit by the lamp. They resembled a teeming cloud of mosquitoes caught in a ray of sunlight. Cadalso read a few lines. "What is an adverb?" The words of the answer declined to be read, running and jumping from one margin to the other. The adverb was clearly a very good thing, but Luis could still not understand why. He then read whole pages, their meaning never once penetrating his mind, which had still not recovered from the shock of that vision, nor had he yet shaken off the physical malaise, despite having eaten his supper with a hearty appetite; and, noticing that he felt worse when he concentrated on the book, he thought the best remedy would be to turn down the corners of each page, until the poor thing resembled nothing so much as a curly endive lettuce.

He was still busy with this task when he heard his grandfather leave his office, having extinguished the lamp for lack of oil, and even though he wasn't actually engaged in writing anything, the darkness had propelled him out of his lair and into the dining room. For some time, the poor, overwrought man paced up and down the room and the corridor, talking to himself and occasionally stumbling, because the mat was so uneven and full of holes that it was impossible to walk without tripping.

On other nights, when grandfather and grandson had been left alone, the old man would pick up Luis's lessons and drum them into him by sheer repetition. On that night, though, Villaamil was in no mood to do this, for which the boy was very grateful, and, in order to look as if he were actually doing something, he began to uncurl those tormented pages, smoothing them out with the palm of his hand. Not long afterwards, weary from studying and from visions, he used that same book as a soft cushion for his head and actually fell asleep on the definition of the adverb.

Villaamil was saying: "This is simply too much, Señor Almighty. What did I do so wrong that you should treat me thus? Why can't I find a job? Why do even my most trusted friends abandon me?" No sooner had the unfortunate man's spirits hit rock bottom than they once again flared up, and he imagined he was being pursued by secret enemies who had sworn their eternal hatred. "Who can it be? Who is this meddler who has declared war on me? Perhaps some ungrateful wretch who owes me his whole career?" To make matters worse, his own administrative career began to pass before him, a slow but honorable affair, with postings in both Spain and the colonies, beginning in 1841, when he was just twenty-four (when Señor Surra was secretary of the Treasury). Up until the terrible crisis in which we find him now, he had seldom been unemployed: four months during the time that Bertrán de Lis was in post, eleven months during the two years under the Progressive Party, and three and a half in Salaverría's day. After the Revolution, he moved to Cuba, then to the Philippines, until driven out by dysentery. He had now turned sixty and had spent thirty-four years and ten months as a civil servant. In another two months he could retire on a pension worth four-fifths of his regulation salary, the amount he had earned in the highest post he had occupied, that of head of department, third class. "What kind of world is this! It's so unfair! And then they're surprised when there are revolutions! All I'm asking for is two months' work so that I can retire on that four-fifths salary..." When his soliloquy was at its most passionate, he stumbled and collided with the door, which sent him rebounding against the edge of the table that shook under the impact. Luis woke with a start and heard his grandfather, as he found his feet again, uttering these words, which seemed to Luis the most terrifying he had heard in his entire life: "... in accordance with the Budgetary Law of 1835, duly modified in 1865 and 1868!"

"What is it, Grandpa?" he said in alarm.

"Nothing, child, it's nothing to do with you. Go to sleep. Not in the mood to study tonight? Quite right too. What's the point? The more stupid a man is, and the more of a rogue, the higher he rises... Come on, off to bed. It's getting late."

Villaamil looked around him, and although he managed to find a candleholder, he was hard pressed to find a candle. Finally, after much rummaging, he found two stubs in Pura's bedside table, and after lighting one of them, he began getting the boy ready for bed. Luis slept in the same "bedroom" as Milagros, which was, in fact, in the dining room itself and was furnished with a rather ancient dressing table—a pensioner with only four-fifths of its drawers—as well as various trunks and the two beds. With the exception of the living room, which still retained a certain elegance, the whole apartment bore witness to the poverty, neglect, and slow ruin that comes from failing to notice the ravages of time.

Villaamil started helping his grandson to undress, saying to him:

"Yes, my child, blessed are the stupid, for theirs is the kingdom... of the Administration."

And as he was unbuttoning Luis's jacket, he tugged so hard on the sleeves that the boy almost fell over.

"My child, learn this, learn this for when you become a man. No one remembers those who fall—instead, they kick them so hard they can never get up again... Because, in accordance with the Cánovas law of 1876, I should be head of department, second class, but here I am, almost starving... Letters of recommendation rain down on the minister, and nothing happens. They tell him: 'Just look at his record,' and nothing happens. Do you think he even bothers to examine my record? If only he would... All I get are promises and postponements: We will be in touch in due course; your request has been duly noted... The usual nonsense they spout in order to squirm out of any awkward situation... And yet I have always served loyally, worked like a black, never caused any trouble; and when I was working at the Secretariat, in 1852 or thereabouts, Don Juan Bravo Murillo took a real shine to me and called me into his office one day and said... well, out of modesty, I won't tell you what he said... Ah, if that great man could see me now... suspended! Why, in 1855, I drew up a budgetary plan that won the praise of Señor Don Pascual Madoz and Señor Don Juan Bruil, a plan that, after twenty years of thinking about it, I have since redrafted, as I set out in five memoranda that I have right here! And that was no easy task, I can tell you. Replacing all present-day contributions with income tax. Ah, income tax, that is my life's dream, the focus of many studies, and the result of long experience... They just don't understand, but that's what this country is like, namely on the road to ruin and growing poorer by the day, and with all sources of wealth drying up, it's simply tragic... My idea is to have just one tax, based on good faith, on the contributor's pride and social conscience, for that is the best remedy for the nation's poverty. Then there are import tariffs, which should be raised in order to protect national industries... And lastly, the overhaul of the national debt, reducing it to one kind of issue and one rate of interest..."

When he reached this point, Villaamil pulled so hard on Luis's trousers that the boy let out a cry:

"Grandpa, you'll pull my legs off if you're not careful!"

To which the irate old man merely replied:

"Yes, I must have some secret enemy, some good-for-nothing determined to destroy me, to dishonor me..."

Luis was finally tucked up in bed. It had become customary not to turn out the lamp until long after he had fallen asleep, because he suffered from nightmares and would feel afraid if he woke suddenly in the dark. Seeing that the first candle stub was burning out, Villaamil lit the other one and, sitting down beside the dressing table, he began reading the newspaper, *La Correspondencia*, which had just been slipped under the door. In his current febrile state, the poor unfortunate was eagerly reading the advertisements for jobs, and with fateful marksmanship, his eye instantly alighted on a piece of bad news. "Señor Montes has been appointed first official in the Tax Office … A royal decree has been issued, appointing Don Basilio Andrés de la Caña to the honorable post of Head of the Administration." "This is utterly scandalous, cronyism gone mad. It wouldn't even happen in a tribe in Africa. Our poor country, poor Spain! It makes my hair stand on end just to think what will come of this administrative mess … Basilio's a good man, but only yesterday—well, perhaps longer ago than that—he was working for me as a clerk, fourth class!" After grief came hope. "Staff will soon be appointed to form the new personnel at the Tax Office. It is said that among these will be several highly intelligent functionaries currently without posts."

For a moment, Villaamil's eyes danced over the page, leaping from word to word. His eyes grew moist. Would he be included among the new personnel? The friends who had recommended him to the Minister in that long, wearisome campaign would probably propose him for this next group of appointees. "Oh, if only I could be among those blessed few! When will they decide, though? Pantoja told me it would be in a matter of days."

And since hope was restoring life to his whole being and filling him with a terrible restlessness, he set off once more into the dark labyrinth of corridors. "Appointments … the new personnel … making way for highly intelligent functionaries, and not just intelligent, but experienced … Oh, dear God, please inspire them, shine your bright light into those empty noggins of theirs … let them see clearly … let them notice me and take proper note of my record of service. If they do, there's no question about it, they will appoint me … Or will they? Some secret voice is telling me they will. I feel hopeful. No, I won't let myself believe it, I won't give in to enthusiasm. Far better to remain pessimistic, very pessimistic, so that the opposite of what one fears will happen. I've noticed that whenever you feel confident that something will happen, fate will strike you down. We always get it wrong. Best not to hope for anything, to see the future as black as the blackest night, and then, suddenly... there is light! Yes, Ramón, tell yourself they will give you nothing, that there is no hope, and then, by believing that, the opposite will happen. Because that is how things work. Meanwhile, tomorrow, I will pull every string; I will write to a few friends and go and call on others, and what about the minister... with all those letters of recommendation... Now, that's an idea, why don't I write to the minister himself?"

As he said these words, he happened to turn to where Luis was sleeping and, as he watched him, he thought of all the walking the boy would have to do the next day delivering those letters. It's impossible to know how all this connected up with the images in the boy's head as he lay dreaming, but the fact is that, while his grandfather was observing him, Luis, deep asleep, was again seeing the white-bearded person from his vision, and, most strikingly of all, that person was sitting at a desk piled high with what Luis estimated to be at least two million trillion letters. The Lord was writing in what seemed to Luis the most perfect italic script imaginable. Not even Don Celedonio, his teacher at school, could have done better. When he had finished the letter, our Eternal Father put it in an envelope whiter than snow, held it to his mouth, from which emerged a good length of fine, pink tongue that quickly licked the seal; once this was done, he again took up the pen, which was—and this was even stranger—Mendizábal's pen, and dipped it in Mendizábal's inkpot, and began to write the address. Looking over his shoulder, Luis thought he saw that immortal hand writing the following words on the envelope:

For the attention of his Excellency the Secretary of the Treasury,
whoever he may be,
your ever humble servant,
God

5

THAT NIGHT, Villaamil slept for barely fifteen minutes. He would doze off for a moment, but then the thought of those imminent new appointments—as well as his self-imposed regime of pessimism, expecting the worst and hoping that, by doing so, good would triumph—would sow his bed with thorns and wake him up the instant he closed his eyes. When his wife returned from the theater, Villaamil shared a few extraordinarily distressing thoughts with her, something about the difficulty of buying food for the next day, for there was not a penny in the house, nor anything worth pawning; all their credit had been used up, as had the generosity and patience of their friends.

Although she affected serenity and hope, Doña Pura was actually deeply concerned, and she too spent a sleepless night, making calculations for the next day, which promised to be alarmingly grim. She no longer dared order goods on credit from any of the stores, because she met with nothing but frowns and rude, disrespectful comments, and not a day went by without some discourteous, demanding storekeeper coming to their door to berate her. Perhaps they could pawn something? Her mind made a rapid inventory of all the useful items already condemned to exile: jewellery, capes, cloaks, overcoats. They had reached the very limit of such, so to speak, bond issues, and there was no human way the whole family could be further stripped bare. There had been a large-scale pawnage the previous month (January 1878), on the very day King Alfonso married Queen Mercedes. And yet the three Miaows had missed not a single one of the public celebrations held on that occasion in Madrid. Illuminations, military parades, the wedding procession to the church of Atocha; they saw it all, and always from the best possible vantage point, elbowing their way through the crowds.

The living room, yes, surely they could pawn something from the living room! This thought always instilled terror in Doña Pura, sending shivers down her spine, because the living room was the room closest to her heart, the true symbolic expression of hearth and home. It contained some lovely, albeit rather antiquated pieces of furniture, witnesses to the past glory of the Villaamil family; two dark, marble-topped cabinets decorated with gold leaf and lacquer; damask-upholstered chairs, moquette carpets, and some silk curtains bought from the magistrate in Cáceres when he was transferred and had to move house. Those curtains were as dear to Doña Pura as the very fabric of her heart. And when the specter of need appeared to her and whispered the terrifying sums of money required for the next day's economic battles, Doña Pura would shudder, saying: "No, no, better the shirts off our backs than those curtains." Laying bare their bodies seemed a reasonable sacrifice, but laying bare the living room ... never! Despite Ramón's lack of employment and their subsequent social diminution, the family still received a number of visitors. What would those visitors say if they noticed the absence of the silk curtains, which were the envy of everyone who saw them! Doña Pura closed her eyes in an attempt to shut out this dreadful idea and go to sleep; but the image of the living room had become so firmly lodged in her mind that she kept seeing it all night long, so clean, so elegant ... None of their friends had such a living room. The carpet was so beautifully preserved that it seemed as if no human foot had ever trodden it, and this was because, during the day, they protected it by wearing soft cloth overshoes and took care to clean it regularly. The upright piano may have been out of tune, *very* out of tune, but it did have a magnificent rosewood case. There wasn't a stain on any of the chairs. The dressers glowed and the objects placed on them—the gilt clock that no longer worked, the candlesticks with their glass covers—were all exquisitely kept. And there was not a speck of dust on the many knickknacks that completed the décor: photographs in embroidered frames, old sweet boxes, little porcelain dogs, and an imitation Bohemian cut-glass decanter. Abelarda spent her idle hours dusting these trinkets as well as others as yet unmentioned. These were extremely fragile, delicate objects made of wood, the kind of thing that amuses aficionados of domestic marquetry. A neighbor had a special little machine and made endless lovely things, which he then gave to friends. There were baskets, tiny pedestals, Gothic chapels and Chinese pagodas, all very charming, very fragile, very look-don't-touch, and very difficult to dust.

Doña Pura turned over in bed, as if trying to vary her gloomy thoughts with a change of position. Instead, she succeeded only in summoning up an even clearer mental image of those sumptuous maroon curtains made from the kind of gorgeous silk "that you just can't find anymore." All the lady visitors would be sure to touch the incomparable fabric and rub it between their fingers to gauge its quality, but you really had to feel its weight to know how exceptionally fine it was. In short, Doña Pura felt that sending those curtains to the Monte de Piedad or to the pawnshop would be as painful as sending a child off on a ship to the Americas.

While that figure out of a painting by Fra Angelico lay tossing and turning on her narrow mattress (she slept in the little bedroom off the living room, while her husband, ever since he returned from the Philippines, slept in a bed in his office), she set about distracting herself and her sorrows by recalling the emotions of the opera and how well the baritone had sung the *rivedrai le foreste imbalsamate* ...

Meanwhile, Villaamil, alone, febrile, and sleepless, was thrashing about in the large matrimonial bed, the springs of whose mattress were in a pitiful state, some sunken and broken, others sticking bolt upright. The wool mattress on top was not much better, with large lumps here and hollows there, so that the bed could, with some justification, have been used in the Inquisition's dungeons to punish heretics. That bed was the external expression or mold of Villaamil's tortured soul, and so when his insomnia prompted him to turn over yet again, he would fall down a deep abyss, from which there arose, like a demonic hump, a huge spur that would stick in his ribs; and when he clambered out of the abyss, a hard fist of matted wool would punch him in the back.

Sometimes he would manage to sleep despite all those ups and downs, but that night, his brain was so overwrought that it exaggerated the unpredictable nature of the terrain; one moment, he thought he was about to plummet earthwards, feet in the air, the next he was poised on the very top of a hill or about to be carried off to the Philippines by a furious typhoon. "Let's be pessimistic,"—was his motto— "let's believe as vigorously as we can that I won't be included among those new appointments, then I can feel surprised when I am. I will not hope for that happy event, no, I won't, then it will happen. It's always the unexpected that happens. I will think the worst. They will not choose you, my poor Ramón. They will once again thwart your ambitions. But even though I am convinced, utterly convinced, that I will be given nothing, and no one can shift me from that belief, even though I know my enemies will not take pity on me, I will bring all my influences to bear on the minister and ask even the morning star to speak on my behalf. I am as sure of that as I am that this is night and not day. Abandon every last glimmer of credulity. No vain hopes, no 'Maybe yes, maybe no,' no optimistic foolery. You won't get it, you won't, however hard you try."

6

DOÑA PURA finally fell asleep and slept soundly until morning. Villaamil rose at eight without having slept a wink. When he left his room between eight and nine, after first splashing his face with a little cold water and running a comb through his sparse hair, no one else was up. Their straitened circumstances meant they could not afford to employ a maid, and the three women rather haphazardly shared out the household chores among them. Milagros, who was in charge of cooking, usually rose earlier than the other two, but she had gone to bed very late the night before, and when Villaamil left his room and headed for the kitchen, she had not yet appeared. He examined the unlit stove, the empty coal bunker, and in the closet that served as a pantry, he found a few crusts of bread, some greasy paper presumably containing a slice or two of ham or some other sort of cold meat, a dish containing a few chickpeas, a measly stump of sausage, an egg, and half a lemon. The tiger sighed and went into the dining room to check the drawer in the dresser, in which, among the knives and napkins, there were a few more bits of stale bread. Just then, he heard noises, the sound of running water, and then Milagros came into the kitchen, her feline face washed clean, her dressing gown unbuttoned, her hair in curling papers, and a white scarf over her head.

"Is there any hot chocolate?" Villaamil asked, without even bothering to wish her good morning.

"There's about half an ounce left," she replied, hurrying to open the drawer in the kitchen table. "I'll make you some straight away."

"No, it's not for me. Make some for the boy. I don't need any hot chocolate. I'm not in the mood. I'll just have a slice of dry bread and a little water."

"Fine. There's some over there. We have plenty of bread. And there's a small slice of ham in the pantry. The egg is for my sister, though. I'll light the fire. Would you mind chopping some wood while I go and see if I can find some matches?"

Once he had eaten some bread, Don Ramón picked up the axe and started chopping up a piece of wood, which happened to be an old chair leg, and with each blow, he gave a heavy sigh. The sound made by the wood as it split open seemed as much a part of Villaamil himself as if he were slicing off strips of his own lean, living flesh and splinters from his poor old bones. Meanwhile, Milagros was filling the stove with coal and kindling.

"Will we be having stew today?" she asked her brother-in-law in somewhat enigmatic tones.

Villaamil pondered this stark question.

"Possibly. Who knows?" he said, sending his imagination off into the unknown. "Let's wait until Pura gets up."

Pura was the one who resolved all conflicts, for, being a person of initiative, she was known for making unexpected decisions and finding prompt solutions. Milagros, on the other hand, was all passivity, modesty and obedience. She never raised her voice or commented on what her sister decided should be done. She worked for the other members of the family, driven by her own humble conscience and out of a habit of subordination. Although fatally bound all her life to the family's wretched fate and having shared all their vicissitudes, she never complained nor had she ever been known to bemoan her ill fortune. She considered herself to be a great artiste cut off in the first flower of youth, and all because of the circumstances into which she had been born; and when she saw that she would never succeed as a singer, that sadness outweighed all other sadnesses. It must be said that Milagros had indeed been born with a genuine talent as an opera singer. At twenty-five, she had a truly wonderful voice, took regular singing lessons, and was mad about music. Fate, though, did not allow her to launch herself into a career as a singer. Unfortunate love affairs, family problems, all intervened to delay her first much-awaited public appearance, and by the time those obstacles had vanished, it was too late, for Milagros had lost her beautiful voice. Even she had failed to notice how her artistic ambitions had slowly, gradually, given way to the precarious situation in which we see her now, nor how her dream of appearing on stage and triumphing as a singer had turned into this bare kitchen with no food in it. When she thought about the harsh contrast between her hopes and her eventual fate, she was incapable of measuring the steps leading her from the heights of poesy to the basements of banality.

Milagros was of a slender, delicate build, perfect for the roles of Margherita, Dinorah, Gilda, or La Traviata, and she had a high soprano voice. All this came to nothing, however, and she never enjoyed public acclaim. She had sung only once at the Teatro Real, in the part of Adalgisa, and this was thanks to the generosity of the company and because she was studying at the Conservatoire. She was over the moon, and all the newspapers had predicted a brilliant future for her. And at the Liceo Jover, before an invited and undemanding audience, she sang in *Sapho,* and in Bellini's *I Capuleti e i Montecchi,* and in the third act of an opera by Vaccai. The plan was that she would then go to Italy, but this plan had come to nothing because of a love affair and the hope of making a good marriage. However, relations between the young man and her family grew increasingly complicated, time passed, and all the singer's hopes came to nothing: She didn't go to Italy, she wasn't contracted to sing at the Teatro Real, and she didn't marry.

Doña Pura and Milagros were the daughters of an army doctor, Escobios by name, and the nieces of the bandmaster of the Infantry Regiment known as the *Inmemorial del Rey.* Their mother was a Muñoz, and they liked to think they were related to the Marqués de Casa-Muñoz. Indeed, when it was decided that Milagros would be an opera singer, they had considered Italianizing her surname and calling her La Escobini, but since her artistic career was nipped in the bud, that Italian stage name never appeared on any posters.

Before Señorita de Escobios's career was cut short, she enjoyed a brief period of success and acclaim in a third-class provincial capital, where she went with her sister, Villaamil's wife. Villaamil was chief clerk in the Finance Department, and, as was only natural, his family became friendly with the civil and military governors, who held gatherings attended by the town's crème de la crème. Milagros sang at the concerts put on by the brigadier's wife, and she proved to be a wild success, electrifying her audiences. She gained suitors by the dozen, as well as the envy of other women, which rather spoiled those moments of triumph. A young man from the town, a poet and journalist, fell madly in love with her. It was he who, in a review of one such soirée, had written in exalted fashion of Doña Pura, describing her as "a figure straight out of a Fra Angelico painting." He described Milagros in such hyperbolic terms that he provoked laughter, and the natives still recall some of the words he used to describe the young woman as she entered the room, walked over to the piano, and began to sing: "She is Modest Ophelia weeping for her failed love and celestially trilling a lament for its death." And here's the strange thing: the very man who wrote those words on page two of the newspaper was actually tasked—and indeed paid for—writing the commercial report on page one. This was another lament: "Flour. The price has pretty much stagnated this week. Only one thousand two hundred sacks were produced at twenty-two and three quarters. There were no buyers, and although yesterday two thousand sacks were on sale for twenty-two and a half, no one took up the offer." The following day, he was back with "Modest Ophelia, or the angel who brought some heavenly melodies to us down here on Earth." This was clearly not going to end well. In fact, the young man, growing ever more inflamed and ever madder when his love remained unrequited, one day dived headfirst into the millrace of a flour mill, and even though he was quickly dragged from the water, he was declared dead at the scene. Shortly after this unfortunate incident, which greatly shocked Milagros, she returned to Madrid, and this was the occasion of her debut at the Teatro Real, the concerts at the Liceo Jover, and everything else we described earlier. Add several more bleak years to this sad accumulation of events, years during which she aged rapidly and suffered a swift decline, and we find "Modest Ophelia" in the Villaamil kitchen, with the fire lit in the oven, but nothing to cook on it.

Abelarda emerged from a small dark room off the inner corridor. Rubbing her eyes, her hair all dishevelled, and trailing the grubby hem of an overlarge dressing gown that had been worn by her mother in happier times, she too made her way to the kitchen just as Villaamil was leaving it in order to go and wake his grandson and get him dressed. Abelarda asked if the baker was coming, a question Milagros was unable to answer, because she could not possibly form a judgement on so grave a matter without first consulting her sister.

"Go and get your mother up," she said in flustered tones, "and see what she says."

Shortly afterwards, a loud clearing of the throat could be heard coming from the bedroom in the living room, where Pura usually slept. Out of the small door that opened onto the hallway, opposite the study, came the lady of the house, wearing an old jacket belonging to Villaamil and radiating annoyance, with her hair in curling papers, her small face still red from the cold water she had just splashed it with, a shabby shawl wrapped about her, and, on her feet, a pair of voluminous slippers.

"Can't you do anything without me? You are a pair of ninnies. It's not that difficult. Have you made the boy's hot chocolate?"

Milagros brought the mug in from the kitchen, while Abelarda was sitting the boy down at the dining table and tying a napkin round his neck. Villaamil went to his study and, shortly afterwards, reappeared, inkpot in hand, saying:

"There's no ink, and today I have more than forty letters to write. Look, Luís, when you've finished your breakfast, go downstairs and ask our friend Mendizábal if he'd be so kind as to give me a drop of ink."

"I'll go," said Abelarda, taking the inkpot and going downstairs just as she was.

The two sisters, meanwhile, were whispering in the kitchen. About what? Presumably the impossibility of feeding the whole family with one egg, some stale bread, and a few bits of meat that weren't even enough for the cat. Pura was frowning and pursing her lips in such a strange way that they almost touched her nose, which itself seemed to grow longer. "Modest Ophelia" echoed that gesture of perplexity, and the two women looked so alike, they could almost have been one and the same. Villaamil distracted them from their meditations when he entered the kitchen, announcing that he had to go to the ministry and needed a clean shirt.

"Oh, good heavens!" cried Pura in despair. "The only clean shirt you have is in such a terrible state that it needs a complete overhaul."

Abelarda, however, undertook to have it ready and even ironed by midday—provided there was a fire lit. Don Ramón also made a few heartfelt pleas to her about the lapels of his overcoat, which were fraying and torn in parts, and begged her to apply her sewing skills to them as well. She told him not to worry, and the good man went back to his study. The secret conversation in the kitchen ended with Pura suddenly rushing into her bedroom to get dressed, then rushing out into the street. An immense idea had just exploded in that brain packed with gunpowder, as if set off by a spark from her eyes.

"Get a good blaze going and fill the saucepans with water," she said to her sister as she was leaving, then scampered off like a very sprightly squirrel.

At the sight of such determination, and knowing the head of the family as they did, Abelarda and Milagros stopped worrying about finding enough food for the day, and—one in the kitchen, the other in her bedroom—they launched into the duet from *Norma*: *in mia mano al fin tu sei*.

7

PURA RETURNED at around eleven o'clock, slightly out of breath and followed by an errand boy from the market in Plazuela de los Mostenses, who came slogging up the stairs carrying a heavy basket full of groceries. Milagros, who opened the front door, repeatedly crossed herself from shoulder to shoulder and from forehead to waist. She had seen her sister get out of all kinds of difficult situations before, thanks to her energy and initiative, but this morning's master stroke seemed to go above and beyond what one might expect even from such a determined woman. A quick review of the contents of the basket revealed various kinds of food—animal and vegetable—and all of excellent quality, more suited to the table of a director general than to that of a mere seeker after employment, but then this was Doña Pura through and through: You either went the whole hog or not at all. Milagros was even more amazed to see the bulging purse in her sister's hand.

"My dear," the lady of the house said in a confidential manner, having first dismissed the errand boy, "I had no alternative but to go begging to Carolina Lantigua, you know, Pez's wife. I could have died of embarrassment, but I simply had to close my eyes and jump in, like someone diving into the water. The shame of it! But I painted such a tragic picture of our situation that she was moved to tears. She's such a kind soul. She gave me ten *duros*, which I promised to repay her soon, and I will, yes, I will, because I'm sure Villaamil will be given a post in the next round of appointments. They can't possibly leave him out. I have absolute confidence now. Anyway, take this to the kitchen. I'll be right there. Is the water boiling?"

She went into the study to tell her husband that, for that day at least, the crisis was over, although without explaining how or why. They must also have talked about the likelihood of him being given a post, because Villaamil could be heard shouting angrily:

"Don't come to me with your foolish optimism. I've told you before and I'm telling you now: I will *not* be chosen. Believe me, I have absolutely no hopes, none at all. When you waltz in here with your silly hopes and illusions, with that mania of yours for seeing everything through rose-tinted glasses, you do me tremendous harm, because, afterwards, harsh reality always hits home, and the world goes dark again."

So immersed was the poor man in his pessimistic ponderings that, when he was summoned to the dining room and they placed before him a magnificent lunch, it didn't even occur to him to demand an explanation for an abundance completely at odds with their economic situation. He ate quickly, then dressed ready to go out. Abelarda had darned the lapels of his overcoat so perfectly—imitating the weft of the torn fabric and dabbing benzine on the collar—that she had made it look at least five years younger. Before he left, he charged Luis with the distribution of the letters he had written, setting out for him the most efficient route so that he could make the deliveries as methodically and quickly as possible. Luis could not have been more pleased, because this meant that he needn't go back to school that day and could spend the whole afternoon like a gentleman of leisure, out for a stroll with his friend Canelo the dog. Canelo was always very quick on the uptake when it came to food. He rarely bothered going up to the second-floor apartment because of the lack of things edible; however, thanks to his highly tuned instincts, he somehow knew about that splendid lunch, all the more splendid given its rarity. Whether he was on guard in the porter's lodge or inside the apartment or even asleep under the scribe's desk, he could always tell when provisions had been delivered to the Villaamil household. Quite how he knew this, no one can say, but the fact is that even the most vigilant of customs officers had nothing on him. He would then apply this knowledge and go upstairs to that place of abundance and spend the whole day there or even two, but as soon as he sensed scarcity, he would say to himself, "Hm, perhaps another day," and they wouldn't see hide nor hair of him. On that day, though, he went upstairs soon after he saw Doña Pura arrive with the errand boy; and because the three Miaows were always very good to Canelo and gave him treats, Luis found it very hard to persuade his canine friend to join him on his saunter round the streets. Canelo left very reluctantly and did so only out of a sense of social duty and to avoid giving rise to gossip.

That afternoon, the three Miaows were in fine spirits. They had the happy gift of living always in the present moment, never thinking of the morrow. It's a mental ability like any other, and a practical philosophy which, whatever you may think of it, and although many have railed against it, has not as yet been entirely discredited. Pura and Milagros were in the kitchen preparing the evening meal, which would have to be excellent, lavish, and made to the highest standards, as compensation for their disconsolate stomachs. Never stopping, with one skimming the soup or frying some meat, while the other was pounding away in the mortar to the rhythm of an *andante con espressione* or an *allegro con brio*, they were discussing the head of the household's probable or, rather, certain appointment. Pura talked of paying off all their debts and bringing home the various useful objects that were somewhere out there in the world, the captives of usurers.

Abelarda was in the dining room, her sewing basket before her, pinning a little brown dress on a tailor's dummy. She was neither strikingly pretty nor particularly ugly, and in a contest for insignificant faces, she would undoubtedly have won first prize. She had bad skin and dark eyes, but she bore a certain harmonious resemblance to her mother and her aunt, whence came their nickname. I mean, in isolation, the young woman's face was not particularly like that of a cat, but when seen alongside the other two she seemed to take from them certain physiognomic features, rather like a proof of pedigree or lineage, for they had the same small, slightly pouting mouth, the same indefinable line connecting nose and mouth, the same round, lively eyes, and the characteristically wild hair, which looked as if they had all been rolling around on the floor playing with a screwed-up piece of paper or a ball of wool.

That afternoon was full of pleasures, because they also had visitors, which Pura always greatly enjoyed. She quickly abandoned her culinary tasks to don a housecoat and smooth her hair before gaily entering the living room. The visitors were Federico Ruiz and his wife, Pepita Ballester. Ruiz, a distinguished "Thinker," was also unemployed and was having a terrible time of it, although his clothes bore more evidence of this than his wife's; nevertheless, he wore his unemployment lightly, or rather, he was, by nature, so optimistic that he even took a certain delight in it. He was always the same indefatigable man, with a finger in many pies, concocting plans to bring about literary or scientific revolutions, thinking up some new occupation that would never have occurred to anyone else. The dear man made one wonder if there was, indeed, some kind of national army of the arts.

He wrote articles about what should be done to make agriculture more productive, about the advantages of cremation, or a detailed account of life in the Stone Age as if it had happened only yesterday. His financial situation was always pretty precarious, because he lived by his pen. Very occasionally, once in a blue moon, he managed to get the Ministry of Public Works to buy a certain number of old publications or such utterly pointless books as *Communism in the Light of Reason*, *The Fire Services in the Various European Nations*, or *A Picturesque Study of Castles*. But his heart was so overflowing with good cheer that he had no need of Christian resignation in order to accept his misfortune. Feeling contented eventually became a matter of pride, and so as not to give way to despair, he managed, by dint of sheer imagination, to embrace the idea of poverty, reaching the absurd conclusion that the greatest pleasure in the world was having not a penny to one's name or any means of earning it. Having to scrape by in life, and setting off each morning wondering which editor of which ailing magazine or moribund newspaper would take the article he had written the previous night, contained a whole array of emotions that would remain forever unknown to the rich. And he did work really hard; indeed, beside him, the prolific theologian and writer Alonso Tostado was a laggard when it came to speed of writing. Yes, earning one's daily bread like that was an almost voluptuous pleasure. And he never lacked for bread. His wife was a real gem and helped him cope with that awkward situation. But it was his own nature that carried him through, his predisposition for optimism, his idealistic determination to turn bad things into good and grim poverty into happy abundance. Resignation brings no sorrows with it. Poverty is the beginning of wisdom, and you will find no happiness among the privileged classes. The "Thinker" would often quote from Luis de Eguílaz's play, in which the protagonist considers what fun it is to be poor, and says with great feeling:

I had just five duros on my wedding day.

And he would remember, too, how, in response, the upper circle would almost collapse beneath the audience's thunderous applause and enthusiastic stamping, proof of how popular being poor was among the moneyless classes. Ruiz had also once written a play in which he proved that to be honest and fair, it's essential to be out at the elbows, and that the rich always come to a sticky end. Needless to say, despite the idealism with which he gilded the copper of his dire economic circumstances, passing off his small change as gold, Ruiz was still doing all he could to find a new position. He was constantly pestering the Ministry of Public Works, and the Boards of Public Education and Agriculture all trembled whenever he made an appearance. If there was no actual post, he hoped to be given some small commission to study something or other, anything from literary copyright laws around the world to grain deposits in Spain.

8

DURING the visit, they spoke first about the opera, to which Ruiz, like the Miaows, often went as a regular member of the claque. Then the conversation turned to the subject of work.

"They won't keep Don Ramón waiting much longer," said Ruiz.

"He's going to be on the list of candidates they're putting together in the next few days," said Pura, beaming. "The only reason his name hasn't appeared as yet is because Ramón didn't want to accept a post outside of Madrid. The ministry was very keen to send him to a province where they need men like my husband, but Ramón has had enough of traveling. To be honest, I want him to be given a job so that he has something to do, that's all. You just can't imagine, Federico, how hard it is for my husband to be idle . . . it's just unbearable. I mean he's been working ever since he was a boy! Plus, being given a post would assure him a decent pension. Ramón only needs to work for another two months to be able to retire on four-fifths of his salary. If it weren't for that, he'd be better off at home. I say to him: 'Don't worry, dear, we'd have enough to live a modest life.' But no, that's not enough for him; he likes the office atmosphere and doesn't even really enjoy smoking his cigarettes unless he has a couple of files to study."

"Oh, I can quite believe that. He's such a fine man. And how is his health?"

"Well, his stomach's a little delicate, and I have to invent some new dish every day to tempt him. My sister and I do all the cooking now, just for something to do, and so that we don't have to employ a maid; well, maids always turn out to be a disaster anyway. We make something special for him every day . . . tidbits and tasty morsels. I sometimes have to go over to Plazuela del Carmen in search of things you can't find in Plazuela de los Mostenses."

"Well, at least that's something I don't have to worry about," said Ruiz's wife, "because my husband has a cast-iron stomach and a healthy appetite too. No need for tidbits to keep *him* going."

"Yes, thank God," said Ruiz jovially. "That's where I get my cheerful disposition from and my confidence in whatever the future might bring. Believe me, Doña Pura, there's nothing more important than a good digestive system. I am, as usual, resigned to my fate: If they give me a job, fine, if not, that's fine too. To tell the truth, I don't much like working in an office; I would prefer what the minister offered me yesterday: a commission to study pawnbroker's shops in Germany—a very important matter."

"Oh, very important. Imagine!" said Doña Pura, arching her eyebrows.

Just then, another visitor arrived. This was a friend of Villaamil's who lived in Calle del Acuerdo, a certain Guillén, who, as it happened, was lame and worked in the Internal Revenue Department. Having first greeted everyone, he announced that, just that afternoon, a colleague of his in Personnel had assured him that Villaamil would be on the next list of appointments. Doña Pura was equally sure of this, and Ruiz and his wife both seconded this hopeful prediction; and given the ensuing shower of congratulations, Doña Pura ended up offering her good friends a little glass of wine and some cakes. For, included in the basket of provisions on that happy day had been a three-peseta bottle of muscatel, which Doña Pura usually reserved for her husband as a post-prandial treat. Ruiz and Guillén clinked glasses and offered an affectionate toast to their dear friends. The sobriety of the "Thinker" was in marked contrast to Guillén's rather vulgar incontinence, for he begged Doña Pura not to take the bottle away and blithely helped himself to more wine, with the result that soon there was only just over half a bottle left.

By the time Villaamil arrived home, the lamps were lit, and the visitors had left. Doña Pura ran to meet him, pleased to see a hint of satisfaction on his fierce, tigerish face.

"What happened? What news?"

"Nothing," said Villaamil, who was already walling himself in behind a pessimism from which no one would be able to shift him. "Nothing as yet, only the usual empty, charming words."

"What about the minister? Did you see him?"

"Yes, and he received me very warmly," Villaamil allowed himself to say, thus unwittingly undermining his pretense at misanthropy. "Yes, very warmly indeed, almost as if... how can I put it... almost as if God had touched his heart, had spoken to him about me. He was the very soul of amiability... delighted to see me... so sorry not to have me by his side... determined to include me..."

"There, you see. How can you say that you have no hope?"

"None, woman, absolutely none (resuming his usual role). Nothing but empty words, you'll see. I should know. Believe me, they won't give me a job until Judgement Day, and then only late in the afternoon!"

"Honestly, that's like spitting in God's face. He might take umbrage, you know, and with good reason too."

"Don't talk nonsense—and if you will insist on hoping, then you're going to be disappointed. Since I choose not to be disappointed, I don't hope for anything. Then, when the blow falls, I won't even bat an eyelid."

While they were engaged in this heated discussion as to whether one should or shouldn't hope, Luis arrived and reported to them that he had delivered all the letters. He was cold and hungry and had a slight headache. On the way back, he had again sat down outside the same convent, but this time the "thing" didn't happen, and the vision refused to appear in any form at all. Canelo, meanwhile, did not leave Doña Pura's side for a moment, following her from the study to the kitchen and from there to the dining room, and when Villaamil was summoned to supper and was somewhat slow to respond, that very knowing dog went to fetch him, wagging his tail, as if to say: "If you're not hungry, just say so, but don't keep the rest of us hanging about."

They all ate with a reasonably hearty appetite and in a fairly good humor, and, afterwards, Villaamil savored every puff of the Havana cigar Señor de Pez had given him that afternoon. It was a very large cigar, and having first thanked his friend, he had told him that he would keep it for later. The cigar reminded him of more prosperous times. Was it perhaps a sign that those times were about to return? It was almost as if Villaamil were reading his good fortune in the spiraling blue smoke, because he sat staring at it foolishly as it curled elegantly upwards to the dining-room ceiling, forming a slight nimbus around the lamp.

That night, they had more visitors (Ruiz, Guillén, Ponce, Cuevas and his wife, and Pantoja and his family, of whom more later), and together they finalized a plan, already discussed the previous month, to put on a short play, because some of them had a rare gift for theatricals, especially comedies. Federico Ruiz agreed to choose a play, decide on the casting and direct the rehearsals. Abelarda would take one of the main roles and Ponce another, although, with praiseworthy modesty, he recognized that he didn't have an ounce of wit in him and would reduce the audience to tears in even the most comical of roles, and he therefore reserved for himself the role of the father, should there be such a character in the play.

Weary of such silliness, Don Ramón fled the living room for the dark interior of the apartment, in search of a gloom to match his pessimism. He chanced to go into Milagros's room, where she was getting Luis ready for bed. The poor boy had made a few vain attempts to study, but his head ached and he had a sense of fear and foreboding about that vision, which, although it had given him much pleasure, had also caused him a certain degree of anxiety. He was convinced that he might suffer another attack and again begin to see very strange things. When his grandfather entered the room, Luis was already in bed, and his aunt was making him recite the usual prayer, which he gabbled his way through: *Now I lay me down to sleep and pray the Lord my soul to keep*, etc. Then, interrupting the prayer, he suddenly turned to Villaamil and said:

"Grandpa, it's true, isn't it, that the minister gave you a very warm welcome?"

"Yes, my boy," said the old man, astonished at this remark and at the tone in which it was spoken. "Who told you?"

"Me? Oh, I just know."

Luis was looking at his grandfather with such a strange expression on his face that the poor man didn't know what to think. It was, he thought, the expression one might see on the face of the Infant Jesus; that is to say, one that combined the seriousness of a grown man with the charm of a child.

"I just know," Luis said again, fixing his grandfather with a look that rendered the man immobile. "And the minister is very fond of you ... because they wrote to him ..."

"Who wrote to him?" Villaamil asked eagerly, taking a step toward the bed, his eyes shining.

"They wrote to him about you," said Luis, feeling himself filling up now with a sense of dread that would not allow him to continue.

At that very same moment, Villaamil decided that this was all stuff and nonsense and, turning, he clapped one hand to his head, muttering:

"Really, the things the boy comes out with!"

9

STRANGELY enough, nothing happened to Luis that night; he neither felt nor saw anything, because, as soon as he lay down, he fell into a very deep sleep. So deep that, the following morning, it was hard to wake him. He felt completely exhausted, as if he had been walking for miles in some remote, unfamiliar place he could no longer recall. He went to school and, needless to say, didn't know his lessons. Indeed, he was so slow-witted that the teacher made fun of him in front of the other boys. It was very rare at the school for someone to be so utterly humiliated by a teacher, for, as punishment for his ignorance and lack of application, Luis was made to sit at the back of the class. At eleven o'clock, when they were given a writing task, Luis was sitting next to the mischievous, playful Joker, who was as wriggly and restless as a worm, for wherever he was there could be no peace. His real name was Paquito Ramos y Guillén, and his parents owned the pawnbroker's in Calle de Acuerdos. The lame and gainfully employed Guillén, whom we saw in the Villaamil apartment celebrating the imminent appointment of his friend with copious libations of muscatel wine, was the maternal uncle of the Joker, who owed his nickname to his mouse-like quickness and his brilliant imitations of the poses and gestures of the clowns and acrobats at the circus. Everything he did turned into a mime act, sticking out his tongue, flipping his eyelids inside out, and, when he could, putting his finger in the inkpot and daubing his face with black lines.

That morning, when the teacher wasn't looking, Joker opened his satchel, into which he and his friend Luis stuck their shaven heads to peruse its varied contents. The most striking thing was a collection of rings, glittering with gold and rubies. These were not, of course, made of metal, but of paper, the kind manufacturers wrap around mediocre cigars, hoping to pass them off as high quality. This treasure had come to Paquito Ramos thanks to a swap. They belonged originally to a boy called Polidura, whose father, a waiter in a café or a restaurant, used to pick up the cigar rings that smokers dropped on the floor and, for lack of anything better, give them to his son to play with. Polidura had collected more than fifty such rings of varying qualities. Some were printed with the words *Flor fina*, while others said *Selectos de Julián Álvarez*. Polidura eventually grew bored with his collection and, having first drawn up a contract in the presence of witnesses, swapped it with Joker for a spinning top still in good working order. Luis gave the new owner the ring from the cheap cigar that Señor de Pez had given to his grandfather, who had then smoked it so majestically after supper.

Joker's prank, faithfully copied by good little Luis, consisted in putting those unusual gems on their fingers two or three at a time and, when the teacher wasn't looking, raising their hands and showing them off to their fellow rapscallions. If the teacher turned round, they would immediately remove them and start writing as if nothing had happened. On one occasion, however, the teacher turned very suddenly and caught Luis with his hand in the air, distracting the whole class. The teacher was immediately transformed into a raging lion. He soon realized that the main villain was that rascal Joker, who had a whole stash of paper rings in his satchel, and having first snatched the cluster of jewels from their fingers, he then grabbed hold of the whole hoard and tore it into pieces, concluding this performance by boxing the ears of both boys. Joker burst into tears, saying:

"It wasn't me ... it was Miaow's fault."

And Miaow, as wounded by this calumny as by the use of that nickname, declared in stern, dignified tones:

"They all belonged to him. I only brought one with me ..."

"Liar."

"*He's* the liar."

"Miaow is a hypocrite," said the teacher, and Luis could not suppress the pain he felt at hearing that vile nickname in the mouth of Don Celedonio. He let out a disconsolate cry, and the whole class imitated him, repeating Miaow, Miaow, Miaow, until the teacher gave them all a good hiding, dealing out blows willy-nilly to backs and cheeks, like a fierce boatswain mercilessly flogging the galley slaves.

"I'll tell my grandfather," cried Luis, outraged, "and I won't come to this school ever again."

"Silence ... silence the lot of you," roared their executioner, threatening them with a ruler, the edges of which were sharp as a knife. "Now get writing, you scoundrels, and if I hear another peep out of one of you, I'll split your head open."

As he left the classroom, Luis was still furious with his friend Joker. The latter—a brazen creature, endlessly bold and impudent—gave Luis a shove, saying:

"It was your fault, idiot ... chump ... cat-face. If I ever catch you ..."

Luis spun round angrily, in the grip of an intense rage that turned him deathly pale and made his eyes flash.

"Do you know what I think? I don't think you have any right to call me names, you vulgar, common nobody!"

"Miaow!" miaowed Joker scornfully, sticking out his tongue and curling his fingers like claws. "Miaow, Miaow, pussycat ... Come here, pussycat ..."

For the first time in his life, Luis felt brave. Blind with fury, he hurled himself on his opponent, and would have done so even had his opponent been a grown man. Screams of savage, childish glee broke out all around them, and many of the other boys, seeing Luis, most unusually, on the attack, shouted:

"Go on, hit him ..."

Miaow fighting with Joker was a real novelty, provoking dramatic, unprecedented excitement, rather like seeing a hare turning on a ferret or a partridge viciously pecking a gundog. And Joker's defiant attitude was a fine sight too, for, after he received the first blow, he stood legs akimbo, the better to keep his balance, throwing down books and slate so as to have his hands free ... all the time muttering with a kind of mad sangfroid:

"Come on then, dammit, do your worst."

There then ensued one of those primitive, Homeric, hand-to-hand struggles, which are all the more interesting because of the lack of weapons, and which consist in the two opponents grappling with each other, pushing and shoving, butting heads together like rams, each doing his darnedest to topple the other. If Joker put up a brave fight, so did Luis. Murillito, Polidura, and the others watched and applauded, dancing around with the wild enthusiasm of a pagan tribe, athirst for blood. The teacher's daughter, a rather mannish young woman, happened to come out of her house at that point, and by administering a couple of hard slaps, she managed to pull them apart, saying:

"You should be ashamed of yourselves. Go home this instant, or I'll call the police and have you clapped in jail."

Both boys were red-faced, breathing heavily, and spewing forth crude insults worthy of the tavern, especially Joker, who was completely fluent in the language of the street.

"Come on now, lads," Murillito, the sacristan's son, was saying in conciliatory tones. "That's enough now, come on ... break it up, enough's enough."

As the mediator, though, he was clearly ready to give the participants a good swipe if either of them tried to resume the fight. A passing policeman broke up the crowd, and they headed off, shouting and running, some of them full of praise for Luis's show of courage. Luis, on the other hand, walked home in silence. His anger was gradually subsiding, although nothing could persuade him to forgive Joker for calling him by that nickname, and he could feel in his heart the first stirrings of heroic pride, an awareness that he was now ready for life, given his now proven ability to take on an opponent.

Since it was Thursday, there was no school that afternoon. Luis went home, and, over lunch, no one in the family noticed how upset he was. Afterwards, he went downstairs to spend some time in the company of his friends, Paca and Mendizábal, who would doubtless have some tidbit to offer him.

"It sounded like you were having a good time upstairs," Paca said. "Listen, has your grandfather been appointed to a new post yet? Because, by now, he really should be a minister or even an ambassador. That was certainly some shopping basket they brought home yesterday! Even bottles of muscatel, as if that were the most normal thing in the world. All very classy! But we are what we are, and now no one's going to be able to get Canelo to come downstairs again . . ."

Luis explained that his grandfather hadn't yet been given a post, but that it would happen any day now. As it was a really beautiful afternoon, Paca suggested to her young friend that they go and enjoy the sunshine in the esplanade outside the Conde-Duque military barracks, just a hop and a skip from Calle de Quiñones. The large lady donned her cloak, while Luis ran upstairs to ask permission, then they set off. It was three o'clock, and the vast area between the Paseo de Areneros and the barracks was flooded with sunlight and crowded with locals who had come there to stretch their legs. A large part of that terrace was then, as now, full of blocks of stone, tiles and cobbles, the detritus or the preparations for work to be carried out by the council, and, among all that stonework, the women who lived in the area were in the habit of erecting washing lines to dry their clothes. The one area that was obstacle-free was used by the soldiers to practice drills, and that afternoon, Luis watched the new cavalry recruits being trained by an officer, who, sword in hand and bellowing orders, was teaching them to march in step. Luis enjoyed watching them going back and forth and hearing the way they marched in unison, saying one, two, three, four, one, two, three, four, a low rumble that melded with the rhythmic sound of boots on the ground, like a vast drum being beaten by a giant. Among the people gathered there to enjoy the sun were vendors of peanuts and hazelnuts, languidly crying their wares. Paca bought Luis a few treats, then sat on a block of stone to gossip with various friends and neighbors. Luis ran after the soldiers, copying their movements; for a whole hour, he came and went in military fashion, keeping time with them—one, two, three, four, one, two, three, four—until, feeling weary, he sat down on a pile of flagstones. Then his head started to spin a little; the great bulk of the barracks seemed to sway from side to side, along with the Palacio de Liria, hidden behind the greenery of its garden, whose trees seemed to be stretching up into the air in order to breathe more freely outside the immense tomb in which they were planted. Luis felt the onset of one of those familiar funny turns of his; he became oblivious to everything around him, he grew dizzy, he fainted, he experienced the usual strange sense of shock, which was really a fear of the unknown, and resting his head on a nearby block of stone, he fell asleep like an angel. The vision he had seen at the convent door instantly appeared, as clear and palpable as a living being, sitting right opposite him, although he could not have said exactly where. The fantastic image had no backdrop, no perspective. It contained only that one sublime figure. It was the same person with the same long, white beard, wearing clothes impossible to describe, his left hand hidden among the folds of his cloak, his right hand raised, the hand of a person about to speak. However, the most surprising thing was that, before the Lord even said a word, he reached out that hand to him, and when Luis looked at it, he saw that the fingers were full of the same paper rings that had formed part of the Joker's large collection. The rings glittered on every finger—although not on the two fingers raised in blessing, the ones that had created the world in seven days—as if they were made of real gold and real precious stone. Luis was entranced. Then the Lord spoke:

"Look, Luis, these are the rings the teacher took away from you. Pretty, aren't they? I picked them up from the floor and immediately made them new again, just like that. Your teacher is a bully, and I'll teach him not to hit you boys so hard. As for Joker, he may be a real scamp, but he doesn't mean any harm. He's just been badly brought up. Decent boys don't give other boys nicknames. You were quite right to get angry, and you did well. I can see that you're a brave lad and can defend your honor."

Luis felt very pleased to hear himself described as "brave" by a person of such authority. He felt so much respect for him, though, that he didn't feel able to thank him; however, he was about to say something when the Lord wagged a disapproving finger at him—one of those heavily beringed fingers—and said sternly:

"But, my child, while, on the one hand, I'm very pleased with you, on the other, I'm afraid I must tell you off. You didn't know your lesson today. You didn't get a single right answer, not even by chance. You clearly hadn't opened your book all day (mortified, Luis opened his mouth as if about to offer an apology). Oh, I know what you're going to say. You were out late delivering letters and didn't get home until dark. But you still had time to do a little studying, so don't come to me with any lame excuses. And this morning, why didn't you at least cast an eye over the geography lesson? And the blunders you made in class today! Whatever gave you the idea that France is bordered to the north by the Danube, and that the Po passes through Pau? Honestly! Do you really think that I made the world just so that you and other snotty little kids like you could spend your time unmaking it?"

The august personage fell silent, his eyes fixed on Luis, who was turning every possible shade of red and saying nothing, overwhelmed, unable to look or stop looking at his interlocutor.

"You really must see things as they are," the Lord said at last, gesturing with his beringed hand. "How can you expect me to find a position for your grandfather if you won't study? You can see how depressed the poor man is, waiting for that appointment open-mouthed as if for the communion wafer. He's rapidly losing hope. And it's all your fault, because if you were to study hard . . ."

On hearing this, Luis felt as overcome by guilt as if he had a rope around his neck and was about to be garrotted. He tried to take a breath, but couldn't.

"You're not stupid, and I know you understand," said God. "Put yourself in my place, yes, put yourself in my place, and you'll see that I'm right."

Luis pondered all this. He had to admit that he was right, because the logic was irrefutable, as clear as day. If he didn't study, how then would his grandfather ever find another post? This seemed to him so true that his eyes welled up with tears. He tried to speak, to make a solemn promise that he would study, that he would work like a fiend, when he felt a hand on his neck.

"Sweetheart," Paca said to him, shaking him. "Don't go to sleep here, you'll catch cold."

Luis looked at her in bewilderment, and in his eyes, the lines of the vision became blurred for a moment with those of reality. The images soon grew clear again, although not his ideas; he saw the Conde-Duque barracks, and heard that one, two, three, four, one, two, three, four, as if it were emerging from beneath the ground. The vision, though, remained indelibly stamped on his soul. He couldn't doubt it when he recalled the beringed hand, the ineffable voice of the Father and Creator of all things. Paca helped him up and took him home. Then, removing from his pocket the peanuts she had given him earlier, she said:

"Don't eat too many of these, they're bad for your stomach. I'll look after them for you. We'd better go home, the dew is starting to fall."

But Luis wanted to go on sleeping; his brain felt dull, as if he had drunk too much; his legs were shaking, and his back felt terribly cold. As he walked home, he was filled with doubts as to the authenticity or the divine nature of that apparition. "Is he God or isn't he?" he wondered. "He seems to be, because he knows absolutely everything… On the other hand, he might not be, because he has no angels with him."

Once back from the walk, he stayed downstairs with his good friends, and Mendizábal, having finished his work, and after putting away his papers and cleaning his diligent pens, set about lighting the lamps on the stairway. Paca cleaned the glass panes on the lantern and lit the small oil lamp inside. The public scribe then took the lamp and, as solemnly as if he were lighting a procession accompanying the viaticum, went to hang it in its proper place, between the first and second floor. Villaamil, who happened to be coming up the stairs, stopped, as usual, to have a chat with the scribe.

"Congratulations, Don Ramón," said Mendizábal.

"Hush," replied Villaamil, adopting the pained expression of someone with a terrible toothache. "There's no call for congratulations yet, nor will there be ..."

"Ah, I thought ... Oh, they're a useless lot, Don Ramón. And they have the nerve to call themselves ministers! As I always say, we need a new broom to sweep 'em all out ..."

"Now, now, my friend," cried Villaamil with a certain air of governmental moderation, "you know I hate extreme views. Besides, your ideas are quite different from mine. What do you want? More religion? Well, fine, but what we don't want is obscurantism ... Let's not deceive ourselves. What we need here is administration, morality ..."

"But that's just the problem (spoken in a triumphant voice.) As long as there's no faith, morality is precisely what there won't be. Faith comes before everything, am I right?"

"You are, but, my friend, let's not exaggerate."

"Any society that loses its faith (spoken in the same triumphant tone) is heading straight for the abyss ..."

"That's all very well but ... there's morality and morality; as you sow, so shall ye reap, and so on, and we should leave it to the priests to deal with matters of conscience. Don't get the two things muddled up, my friend, government and religion."

"I'm not muddling anything up ... Anyway, you'll see. (Going down one step, while Villaamil went up one.) As long as there's all this freethinking, you'll be left without a post; yes, as long as there's no justice and no one gives a damn about merit. Anyway, goodnight."

And with that he went back down the stairs—that extraordinarily ugly, strange-looking man, whose eyes were so close together they seemed to become one whenever they fixed their gaze on something. His nose jutted out from his forehead, then immediately flattened and straightened, his wide nostrils splayed out above his upper lip, and his whole nose was so broad and large that it took up almost half his face. His mouth was large too, and the deep lines at each corner divided his sparse, gray beard into three flaccid compartments; he had a narrow forehead, enormous, hairy hands, a thick neck, a short, hunched body, as if he were a remnant of some race that was, until only recently, still walking on all fours. As he descended the stairs, gripping the banister, he seemed to be going down them on his hands. Yet despite this close affiliation with a gorilla, Mendizábal was a good man, his only fault being his loathing for freethinking. During the first civil war, he had traded in flints, spied for the rebels, and served as cook to Father Cirilo. He would often say: "I really should write my life story!" One final biographical detail: he had mended a wheel on the carriage belonging to the pretender Don Carlos when the latter landed at the port of La Rápita intending to stage a coup. The coup failed.

10

As he was returning home shortly after nightfall, Luis heard footsteps behind him, but did not turn round. However, when he was only a few steps from reaching the second floor, someone seized his head and squeezed it hard, preventing him from looking back. He feared he was being attacked by some ugly, bearded thief who was about to burgle the house and whose preliminary step was to take him captive. Before he had time to scream, though, the intruder lifted him up bodily and gave him a kiss. Then Luis saw the man's face, and when he recognized him, his unease in no way diminished. He had last seen that face some time before, he couldn't quite remember when, on a night of arguments and uproar, with everyone at home screaming. Abelarda had had a fit of hysteria, and his grandmother had called for help from the neighbors. This dramatic domestic scene had left an indelible impression on Luis, who had no idea why his aunts and his grandmother were so angry.

At the time, his grandfather had been working in Cuba, and the family wasn't living in Calle de Quiñones. He remembered too that the fury of the Miaows had all fallen on one person, who subsequently vanished from the house, never to return until the occasion described here. That man was his father. Luis dared not call him by that affectionate name and, instead, said in a surly manner: "Let me go!" The man then knocked on the door, and when Doña Pura opened it and saw who was there, accompanied by Luis, she looked for a moment like someone who quite simply could not believe her eyes. Her face took on an expression first of surprise and fear, then of annoyance. She murmured: "Víctor. Is it you?"

He went in, greeting his mother-in-law almost warmly, in a courteous, genuine manner. Villaamil, who had extremely keen hearing, shuddered when, from his office, he recognized the man's voice. "Víctor...Víctor here in this house again! He'll only bring disaster down on us again." And when his son-in-law went in to greet him, Don Ramón's tigerish face became positively alarming, and his carnivorous jaw trembled as if he were ready to pounce on the first prey that appeared before him. But all he said was: "What are you doing here? Have you been given leave?"

Víctor Cadalso sat down opposite his father-in-law. The oil lamp stood between them, and the light illuminating their faces emphasized the stark contrast between them. Víctor was the perfect example of manly beauty, one of those men who seem destined to preserve and pass on physical elegance to the human race, which, grown so disfigured by endless crossbreeding, very occasionally produces a single fine example, as if to enjoy the pleasure of gazing at itself in its own mirror and convince itself that archetypes of beauty do still exist despite its countless ugly progeny. The chiaroscuro of the lamp emphasized the young man's handsome features. His nose was perfection; his dark eyes, with their large pupils, could shift at will from the tenderest of emotions to the most serious. His pale brow had the smooth, perfectly honed lines which, in sculpture, indicates nobility. (This nobility depends on the equilibrium between the bones of the skull and the perfect harmony of lines.) His strong neck, his slightly ruffled jet-black hair, his short, dark beard, completed the beauty of that sculpted bust, more Italian than Spanish. He was of medium build, his body as graceful and well-proportioned as his head, and as for age, he must have been somewhere between thirty-three and thirty-five. Feeling unable to respond directly to his father-in-law's question, he hesitated for a moment, then got up the courage to say:

"No, not on leave...that is, I had a falling-out with my boss. I left without saying a word to anyone. You know what I'm like. I won't have anyone making a fool of me. I'll tell you the whole story later. On another matter: I arrived this morning on the eight o'clock train and took a room in a guesthouse in Calle del Fúcar. I thought I would stay there, but I'm in such a state that if you and Doña Pura wouldn't mind, I'd rather come here for a few days, no more than that, I promise."

Doña Pura shuddered and ran to pass on this dreadful news to her sister and her daughter. "That awful man is going to stay here! Whatever are we going to do?"

"Look, we're very cramped and crowded as it is," said Villaamil, his face growing ever fiercer and gloomier. "Why don't you go and stay with your sister Quintina?"

"Well, you know how it is," he said. "My brother-in-law and I don't exactly get along. I'd feel much more comfortable lodging with you. I promise to be quiet and reasonable and not mention certain minor matters."

"But do you or do you not still have your post in Valencia?"

"To be honest . . . (He mumbled the first few words, then managed to come out with an answer that disguised his own perplexity.) That boss of mine is an utter scoundrel . . . He's been trying to get rid of me and even tried to lodge a complaint against me, but he's no match for me."

Villaamil sighed, trying to read on his son-in-law's face the mystery that lay behind this untimely visit. Alas, he knew from long experience how inscrutable Víctor's face could be and that, being a consummate actor, he could use it to express whatever emotion best suited his ends.

"So, what do you think of your son?" Villaamil asked, seeing Pura come into the room with Luis. "He's certainly grown, and we're keeping a careful eye on his health. He's still rather delicate, which is why we don't nag him too much to study harder."

"He has time enough for that," said Víctor, embracing and kissing Luis. "He looks more and more like his mother, my poor Luisa, don't you think?"

Villaamil's eyes filled with tears. His daughter, who had died in the flower of youth, had been the very apple of his eye. On the day of her premature death, Villaamil had aged at least ten years. Whenever anyone mentioned her at home, the poor man felt again the same overwhelming grief, and hearing Víctor speak of her, that sorrow became mingled with the repugnance of hearing a murderer grieving for his victim once she is dead. Doña Pura's spirits also plummeted on seeing and hearing the man who had been the husband of her beloved daughter. Luis became sad too, more out of habit than anything, because he had noticed that whenever anyone mentioned his mother's name at home everyone sighed and grew serious.

Taking his son with him, Víctor went to greet Milagros and Abelarda. The former loathed him with all her heart and responded to his greeting with cold disdain. Abelarda, his sister-in-law, had immediately shut herself in her room when she heard his voice; when she came out, her color, which was never good, resembled that of a corpse. Her voice trembled, and she tried to affect the same disdain her aunt had shown toward Víctor when he shook her hand. "So, you've come back, you worthless good-for-nothing," she managed to stammer out; then, not knowing what else to do, she went back into her room.

Meanwhile, Villaamil, anxious and troubled, stretched out his arms as if he were being crucified and said to his wife:

"Mark my words, this man will bring misfortune on this house just as he always has. When I heard his voice, I thought hell was coming in through the front door. I curse the hour (here he grew more excited, thumping the desk hard with his two hands), I curse the hour that man entered my home for the first time; I curse the hour that our beloved daughter fell in love with him, and I curse the day we let her marry him . . . but there was no alternative. Ah, if only my daughter were alive today, even if she were disgraced! How ridiculous to marry off your daughter knowing nothing about the groom! Pura, be very wary of this trickster. He knows how to clothe his evil ways in captivating, seductive words. It won't work with me, oh no, he only deceived me that once. I soon got the measure of him, though, and now I'm on my guard, because that man is the most evil creature God ever set down on this earth."

"Hasn't he told you why he's come? Has he been suspended? He's probably been up to his old tricks, and he's hoping you'll cover up for him."

"Me? (Horrified, eyes wild.) That would be like covering up for the devil himself! Oh, no, if that's the case, he's come to the wrong place..."

When it was supper time, Víctor nonchalantly took his seat at the table and even made a few jocular comments. The others looked at him with hostile eyes, avoiding the cheerful topics he tried to bring up. He occasionally grew suspicious and sullen, but like an actor remembering the lines he had momentarily forgotten, he quickly resumed his role as the jolly, good-natured guest. Then the real difficulty resurfaced. Where would they put him? And overcome by the impossibility of giving lodgings to the intruder, Doña Pura said bluntly:

"No, it's just not possible, Víctor. As you can see, there's no way we can put you up here."

"Don't worry, Mama," he said, stressing that term of affection. "I'll be fine here on the sofa in the dining room. Give me a blanket and I'll sleep like a saint."

Given this show of humility, Doña Pura and the other Miaows could do nothing to oppose his suggestion. When their evening guests began arriving, Víctor said to Doña Pura:

"Look, Mama, I won't join you. I really don't want to see anyone, not at least for a few days. I think I heard Pantoja's voice. Don't tell him I'm here, will you?"

"Why all the mystery?" said his mother-in-law tartly. "Are you just going to stay here in the dining room? Well, if you must know, I'll be putting the water glasses on this table for anyone who's thirsty, and I warn you, Pantoja drinks about half a jug every night."

"I'll go to Luis's room, unless you could possibly put your 'watering hole' elsewhere."

"Where would you suggest?"

"No, don't worry, Mama, and please don't change your habits for my sake. You go back to the living room, where the crème de la crème are already waiting for you. Don't forget to leave a blanket for me here though. I'll fetch my luggage tomorrow."

When Doña Pura told her husband about Víctor's evident fear of being seen, he grew even more uneasy and heaped more curses on the intruder. When the tray with the glasses and the jug of water—the only liquid refreshment the family could afford to offer their friends—had been placed on the dining room table, Víctor was left alone for a while with his son, who was showing unusual dedication to his studies that night.

"Do you do a lot of studying?" Víctor asked, patting the boy's head.

Luis responded with a shy, embarrassed nod, as if studying were a crime. His father was like a stranger to him, and his shyness left him tongue-tied. The man's presence filled the poor child with a very odd mixture of respect and fear. He respected him because he was his father—a word that, to his tender soul, had its own natural value; and he feared him because at home he had heard him spoken of a thousand times in the most unfavorable terms. Víctor was the bad father, just as Villaamil was the good father.

Hearing the footsteps of some thirsty guest on their way to the watering hole, Víctor slipped into Milagros's room. From there he recognized the voice of Ponce, a theater critic and Abelarda's fiancé; he recognized another voice too, that of Pantoja, an Internal Revenue Department employee who was a friend of Villaamil's, and even of Víctor himself, although Víctor considered him to be the most miserable, useless human machine to be found in any office. He couldn't help noticing that Abelarda was one of the thirstiest people that night. She came out two or three times and volunteered to do her Aunt Milagros's usual job of putting Luis to bed. While she was thus engaged, Víctor came into the bedroom, fleeing another thirsty guest.

"Papa is very upset about you just turning up like this," Abelarda said, without actually looking at him. "You burst into our lives like Mephistopheles rising up through a trapdoor, alarming us all by the mere sight of you."

"Anyone would think I ate people," responded Víctor, sitting down on Luis's bed. "Besides, there's no mystery about my arrival; there's something that neither your father nor your mother will understand, but I know that you will once I've explained, because you've always been kind to me, Abelarda; you don't loathe me the way the others do, you know my misfortunes, you know my faults, and you feel sorry for me."

He said all this very sweetly, contemplating his now half-undressed son. Abelarda was avoiding looking at him. Luis, though, had fixed his gaze on his father, as if trying to decipher the meaning of his words.

"Me feel sorry for *you*?" said the insignificant Abelarda in a tremulous voice. "Wherever did you get that idea? Do you really think I believe a word you say? You might fool some women, but not me—I am my mother's daughter, after all!"

And when Víctor began a rather vehement response, Abelarda silenced him with a meaningful look. She was afraid someone might come in or that Luis would understand, and that look signaled a new stage in the dialogue.

"I don't want to know anything," she said, finally having the courage to look him in the eye.

"Well, who can I trust if not you, the one person who does understand me?"

"Go to church and kneel in the confessional . . ."

"The torch of faith burned out in me long ago. I am in darkness," declared Víctor, looking at the boy, who already had his hands pressed together to begin his prayers.

And when the boy had finished, Abelarda turned to his father and said earnestly:

"You're a very bad man, very bad. Turn to God, commend yourself to him, and . . ."

"I don't believe in God," said Víctor brusquely. "God only exists in dreams, and I woke up a long time ago."

Luis hid his face in the pillows, gripped by a sudden terrible chill, a great malaise, and all the usual early symptoms of the state in which his mysterious friend would appear to him.

11

AT MIDNIGHT, when the guests had gone, Víctor sat down on the sofa in the dining room and covered himself with the blanket Abelarda had given him. He didn't know that she'd given him her only blanket and would go to bed fully clothed that night. Everyone else had retired, everyone except Villaamil, who refused to go to bed until he'd had some explanation from his son-in-law. The lamp in the dining room was still lit, and when Villaamil went in, he found Víctor sitting up on his hard bed with the blanket wrapped about his lower half. Víctor realized at once that his father-in-law wanted to have it out with him, and he prepared himself for combat, easy enough for a quick-witted man like him with an equally quick tongue, always the right word at the right moment, as befitted a purebred southerner born on the Granada coast with the Alpujarras behind him and Morocco in front. "The fellow wants a fight. Well, so be it. Let battle commence. Like a toreador, I'll use my cape to draw him on."

"Now that we're alone," said Villaamil in a grave tone of voice that instilled fear, "you must be quite frank with me. You've obviously done something stupid, Víctor. I can see it in your face, although your face rarely shows your true feelings. Tell me the truth now and don't try to bamboozle me with some nifty footwork or with one of those strange ideas you're so very fond of."

"I'm not the one who has strange ideas, my dear Don Ramón. That's your privilege. One should judge a person's ideas by the success they bring him. By the way, have you been reappointed yet? I imagine not. And there you are innocently waiting for justice to be done—well, you might as well expect the moon to sing. As I've told you a thousand times, it's the state that insists we have a right to make a living. If the state never dies, then, at least in administrative terms, neither should civil servants. Let me tell you something: until you change your ways, they're not going to give you a post. You'll spend months and years living on nothing but illusions, trusting the flattering words and the treacherous smiles of those who, when faced by an idiot, puff themselves up and pretend to be his protectors."

A furious Villaamil said:

"Are you really fool enough to believe that *I* have any hopes? Wherever do you get the idea that I'm harboring even a thousandth of some wretched little hope? Me, get reappointed? The thought has never even occurred to me. I'm not hoping for anything. I'll go further: I feel positively offended that you should imagine that I'm just waiting to hear a few polite turns of phrase and some empty words."

"But I've always known you to be so trusting, so optimistic..."

"Optimistic? Me? (Feeling most put out.) Víctor, please, don't make a mock of these gray hairs of mine. Above all, don't change the subject. This isn't about me, but about you. I ask again: What have you done? Why are you here, and why are you avoiding people?"

"I just find such social gatherings tiresome, and you know how extreme I am in my dislikes. I'm not avoiding anyone, it's just that I don't want to see Ponce and his bleary eyes, or speak to Pantoja, whose breath, quite frankly, should carry a warning sign."

"It's nothing to do with Pantoja's breath, but the fact that you left your post under a dark cloud."

"No, no cloud at all, but if my boss ever says a word against me, I'll see him locked up. (Warming to his theme.) I'll have you know that I have been of such service to the state that, if it had one iota of gratitude, it would make me department head. But, as you well know, the state is an ungrateful beast and rarely hands out prizes. If an intelligent civil servant doesn't look out for himself, he's lost. If you must know, when I went to Valencia to take over the Estates and Tax Office, the place was on its knees. My predecessor was an actor who had lost his voice and was given the job as a sinecure on retiring from the stage. The poor fellow hadn't a clue. Then I arrived and, oh boy, did I get things moving. What a mess! They had completely failed to collect any personal contributions. And as for municipal taxes, it was a total disaster. I summoned the mayors, applied a little pressure, and generally put the wind up them. The result: I brought in a fortune for the Treasury, a fortune that would have been lost if it hadn't been for me...Then, I had a think, and I said to myself: 'What is the natural consequence of my service to the nation? Well, the natural, logical, inescapable consequence of defending the state against the taxpayer is the state's ingratitude. Let us then open our umbrellas to protect ourselves from such ingratitude, which is sure to bring us nothing but misery.'"

"So, what you're saying is that your hands are not exactly clean."

"No, sir, that's not what I'm saying at all. (Sitting up and gesturing energetically.) As the mediator between the taxpayer and the state, my job was to prevent the two from devouring each other. If I hadn't made peace between them, there would have been nothing left. I am part of the taxpaying community, which is the nation; as a civil servant, I am part of the state. Given this dual nature, I must safeguard my own life in order to avoid that fatal clash of interests between taxpayer and state."

"I don't understand you, and neither will anyone else. (Said with a look of furious scorn.) You never change, do you? You're trying to conceal your swindles behind your clever words. Well, do you know what I say? You are *not* staying here in my house."

"Now don't get all heated, dear father-in-law. I didn't imagine that you'd let me stay here gratis. I'll pay my way. Besides, it will only be for a few days, because as soon as I get my promotion..."

"Promotion! What *are* you talking about?" (He says this as if he's been stung by a scorpion.)

"What do you think I mean? Ah, ever the innocent! Always the same Don Ramón, the pure unsullied maiden. Have them bring you some lime-flower tea to calm your nerves. What did you think I meant? That just because I'm not an absolute angel I shouldn't get promoted? Don't you know that, having served for two years as an official first class, I should, according to Cánovas's Law, automatically be promoted to head of department, third class? Do you, so optimistic on your own account and so pessimistic on everyone else's, do you really think I'm going to spend my life writing letters, hoping for a smile from the director general, or picking the occasional loose thread off Cucúrbitas's jacket? No, they can wave that red rag at me all they want, but I'm not going to be fooled; I'm going straight for the man holding it."

"When it comes to sheer cheek, you're quite unbeatable, but I'll say this ... precisely because you have no shame (his face purple with rage and swallowing his own bitterness) you end up getting exactly what you want. The world is yours ... As long as you get promoted, everyone else can go to hell!"

"While you, on the other hand (with cruel sarcasm), continue to lull yourself to sleep with those same sweet dreams, believing that the little angels will bring you the letter confirming your appointment and waking each morning saying 'Today will be the day,' and reading *La Correspondencia* every night, hoping to see your name on the appointments list."

"I'm telling you once and for all (wishing he had a bottle or an inkpot or a candlestick he could throw at him) that I am not hoping for anything—indeed, I'm convinced that I'll never be given another post. On the other hand, I'm equally convinced that you, you of all people, who have just defrauded the Treasury, will be rewarded for your trickery, because that's the way of the world and certainly the way of this swinish government ... Good God! To think that I should live to see such things!" (Standing up and clutching his head in his hands.)

"What you need to do (said with some arrogance) is to learn from my example."

"Oh, a fine example you set! I don't want to listen to you, I don't ever want to see you again ... Goodbye. (Leaving the room, then turning at the door.) And get this into your thick skull: I'm not hoping for anything; I'm completely resigned to my fate and I accept my misfortune with patience, and I don't expect to be given a post now or tomorrow or in the next century ... however badly we need the money. But ..."

"But what? (With a cruel laugh.) What if I were to put my foot down and insist that they appoint you?"

"What, and be beholden to *you*?"

So great was his indignation that he couldn't bring himself to say any more, for fear he might say or do something foolish; he slammed the door, setting the whole apartment shaking, and fled to his own room, where he threw himself down on his rickety old bed, like a desperate man hurling himself into the sea.

Víctor snuggled down beneath the blanket and tried to sleep, but he too was in a state of great excitement, less because of the altercation with his father-in-law than because of recent events; he simply couldn't fall asleep, and the hard sofa on which he was lying certainly didn't help. The lamp burned down so low after midnight that the room was lit by only the dimmest of lights; and in Víctor's febrile, insomniac mind, the gloom and the smell of old food lingering in the air fused to become a single unpleasant impression. He examined the dining room from end to end: the peeling, grubby wallpaper and, in some places, especially near the doors, the greasy marks left by people brushing past or Luis's small handprints and even a few of his artistic designs in pencil, not to mention the smoke stain on the ceiling immediately above the lamp and a couple of cracks that formed a huge "M" and possibly other letters too. Víctor remembered that there used to be a clock that never chimed and never showed the right time; there had also been some rather garish still lives of various kinds of melons sliced in two. The paintings and clock had disappeared, like cargo thrown overboard to keep the ship afloat. The dresser was still there, but how old and worn it was, with its faded black edges, one glass pane broken, all decorative details gone. Inside could be seen a few glasses, face down, mismatched cruet sets, a very wrinkled lemon, a coffee-grinder, some grimy tins, and a few pieces of china. The door that led out into the kitchen was covered by a heavy curtain, bearing the marks of the many hands that had touched it, and with a hole in it large enough to serve as a food hatch.

Weary of tossing and turning, Víctor sat up in that bed which felt more like a torturer's rack, and his physical restlessness turned into wild mental ramblings. He felt a need to justify himself *to* himself, to soothe his troubled conscience by putting the blame on others, and in a voice that, while not loud, was nonetheless perfectly audible, he said: "All this is mine, you fools. You are mere office mice, so off you go and gnaw at a few files, will you? I am worth more than the whole lot of you. I can get through a month's work in a single day."

Then he lay back down again, startled by his own voice. Shortly afterwards, eyes closed, brow furrowed, he summoned up in his mind, much as a somnambulist might, the matter currently obsessing him.

"Ah, municipal food taxes. The most ingenious of inventions. In order to avoid paying them, those small-town rogues would sell their souls to the devil. They really don't like it when I send them a bill. But they can't fob me off, oh no; I'll have anyone who tries to postpone payment burned alive. You have to pile on the pressure, and since like calls to like, it's the easiest thing in the world to come to an agreement with an auditor on the subject of those demand notes. Happy the town that escapes paying interest, even if it's years in arrears. Listen, Mr. Mayor, let's come to an agreement. You need some breathing room? Well, I need oxygen too. We're all God's children, aren't we? And why should the Treasury complain? Haven't I saved you more than six million that my predecessor had given up for lost? So why all this womanish whingeing? Doesn't someone who gives such great service deserve an equally great reward? Shouldn't we defend ourselves against the state's ingratitude by thanking *ourselves* for our loyal service? Rewarding good works is the basic principle of morality, the application of justice, the law, the *Ius*, to public office. An ungrateful state, indifferent to merit, is an uncivilized state . . . What I say is this: Where there is a duty to be performed, there must also be an appropriate reward. Debit and credit, that's elementary. With one hand I give the state six million that would otherwise have gone missing, then hold out my other hand to receive my commission. What did you expect, wretched, thieving, dastardly state? That you can suck up the millions and leave me with nothing but holy water to drink? That's precisely what you would have done, you bounder, if I hadn't acted in my own interests. Because, I swear that, however clever you may be, I'm much cleverer. We're two of a kind really. And what have *you* got to complain about, Mr. Taxpayer? Can't you see that I'm on your side? But we both have to breathe, don't we? And if I go under, someone else will come along and have your guts for garters.

"And that stupid boss of mine, that beast, that bandit who, in Pontevedra, dined out on the money raised for shipwrecked sailors and, in Cáceres, left the widows of dead miners without a penny to their name; that same man, who would be capable of swallowing down a whole cemetery with all its dead, *he* wants to bring a complaint against *me*! But proving something is a tricky matter, you villain, and if you decide to stick the knife in me, I'll happily hang out all your dirty washing in public, with facts, dates, and numbers. I have good friends, people with spotless reputations, who will stand up for me . . . That's what you can't forgive . . . You're eaten up with envy. That's why you're turning against me now, you thief—a thief who, having failed as a pickpocket, had no option but to join the civil service."

After a quarter of an hour, just when he seemed about to drift off, he suddenly laughed out loud and declared: "They can't prove anything against me, and even if they could . . ." Then, at last, he did fall asleep, and had a nightmare, similar to others he'd had before when in a state of moral agitation. He dreamed he was walking down a long, wide, endless corridor, whose walls were lined with mirrors that reflected his handsome figure ad infinitum. He was pursuing a woman, a very elegant woman, who was running ahead of him, her rapidly moving feet setting her silk skirts rustling. Víctor could see the heels of her boots, which, bizarrely, were . . . broken eggshells! He had no idea who the woman might be, although she was the same woman he'd dreamed of on other nights, and as he followed her, he was telling himself this was all a dream, amazed that he should be running after a ghost, but unable to stop running. He did eventually manage to catch her up, and she then turned, saying in a hoarse voice: "Why are you so determined to steal the chest of drawers I'm carrying?" And she was indeed balancing a full-size chest of drawers on the palm of one hand, as casually as if it were a coin purse. Then Víctor woke up, feeling such a heavy weight pressing down on him that he couldn't move, and filled by a superstitious terror that seemed to bear no relation to the chest of drawers, the woman, or the mirrors. It was all utterly stupid and meaningless.

Víctor's dreams made more sense once he was awake, because he had spent his whole life thinking about the wealth he didn't have, the honors and the influence he longed for, the beautiful women whose charms were not unknown to him, about elegant, aristocratic ladies whom he felt a passionate curiosity to meet and possess; and the desire to enjoy life's greatest pleasures meant that he lived in a state of permanent unrest, watching and waiting. Consumed by a desire to join society's elite, he believed that he finally held in his hands the knot at one end of the rope that others, less audacious than him, had succeeded in climbing. What was that knot? This was a secret Víctor would never ever reveal to his vulgar, lowly Villaamil in-laws.

12

THAT "FIGURE straight out of a Fra Angelico painting," otherwise known as Doña Pura, appeared early the next morning and attacked Víctor with the keen blade of her scornful indifference, a feeling that had been further aggravated by the nagging toothache that had kept her awake during the night. "Right, time to vacate the dining room. You can have a wash in my room, but we need to sweep up in here now. You'd better be quick, unless you want to get covered in dust." The second Miaow supported these words in a more persuasive manner by entering the room, broom in hand.

"There's no need to get annoyed with me, Mama. (Doña Pura really hated it when her son-in-law called her Mama.) Ever since you became the family potentate, you've become quite impossible. What a way to treat a poor wretch like me."

"That's right, make fun of me. Hardly the best way to win us over. You certainly have a good sense of timing, because you only ever put in an appearance when we're up to our eyes in debt."

"And what if I were to say that I came precisely because I felt this *was* a most opportune moment? What would you say to that? Never despise anyone, dear Mama, because sometimes a bothersome guest can, from one moment to the next, prove most providential."

"Providential, you? (Following Víctor to the room where he was to have a wash.) What do you mean? That you're just going to tighten the rope around our necks?"

"Oh, you can shout at me all you like (in wheedling tones), but remember, I'm someone who can get you stall seats at the theater."

"We don't need your stall seats. Anyway, who are you to give us free seats? For as long as I've known you, you've been even more strapped for cash than the government."

"Mama, Mama, please, don't be so insulting. Besides, the fact that I'm poor is no reason for you to doubt my good intentions."

"Oh, shut up and leave me in peace. Anyway, you can have a wash here, but be quick about it."

"I would rather see a murderer's dagger before me than a scowling face. (Grabbing her arm.) Wait a moment. Would you like me to pay for my lodging?"

And with that, he took out his wallet, and Doña Pura's eyes lit up when she saw that it was positively bulging with bank notes.

"I don't want to be a burden. (Handing her a hundred-peseta note.) Here you are, dear Mama, and please don't judge my intentions by my lack of funds."

"Now, don't imagine ... (she said, pouncing on the note as if it were a mouse) don't imagine that I would take delicacy to such ridiculous extremes, indignantly rejecting your money in grand theatrical style. We're in no position right now to have such scruples or for vulgar displays of indignation. I'll take it, of course, and I'll use it to pay off a sacred debt ... the rest, of course, will come in handy for ..."

"For what?"

"That's my secret. Who doesn't have their little secrets?"

"And does a son, a loving son, not deserve to be the depository of those secrets? You clearly don't trust me. And I thought you cared about me more than that. Dear Mama, I know you don't consider me part of the family, but I can't simply stand aside like that. You can order me not to love you and your family, but I won't obey ... Other homes I visit leave me completely cold, but not this one; and when I notice signs of financial difficulty, I can't help but suffer, even if you tell me not to ... (Placing one hand affectionately on her shoulder.) Dearest mother-in-law, I can't stand to see Papa having to do without a decent cape."

"Yes, poor man ... but what's to be done? He's been in a pretty sorry state for some time now and without a job for far longer than we expected. Only God and us women know the hardships we've suffered."

"Fortunately, there's a remedy, even if it does come from someone of whom you have such a low opinion." (Giving her another hundred-peseta note, which Doña Pura promptly accepts.)

"Thank you ... It's not that we have a low opinion of you, it's just that you ..."

"Yes, I confess, I've been a very bad man (spoken in piteous tones), and surely my acknowledging this is a sign that I'm not such a bad man now. I have my faults like anyone else, but my heart isn't made of stone, I'm not entirely insensitive, and I have learned from experience. And I may well be as bad as you think I am, but, alongside that wickedness, I have one obsession: I simply cannot allow this family, to whom I owe so much, to suffer hardship. I just can't bear it ... you can call it a weakness or whatever you like. (Gallantly giving her a third note and not even looking at the hand doing the giving.) As long as I'm earning so much as a penny, I will not allow the father of my poor Luisa to dress indecorously, or for my son to go without warm clothes."

"Thank you, Víctor, thank you." (Half-touched by his generosity and half-suspicious.)

"There's no need to thank me. Where's the merit in repaying a sacred debt? In fact, it occurs to me that you could probably use a bit more money, because I'm sure that more than a few things will have found their way to the pawnbroker's."

"You're very rich ..." (Suddenly suspecting that the notes might be forgeries.)

"No, not rich ... this is just some of my savings. There's so little to spend it on in Valencia that you find you've saved money without even noticing. And, please, don't thank me, you'll only embarrass me. That's just the way I am. I've changed a lot. No one can possibly know how it grieves me to think of what I put you through, especially my poor Luisa. (Said with great emotion, either false or real, but so beautifully expressed that Doña Pura's eyes filled with tears.) My poor dear sweetheart! If only I could atone for the pain I caused her. If only I could bring her back to life so that she could see how my heart has changed, even if we were both doomed to die that very instant! (Giving a heartfelt sigh.) When death stands between guilt and repentance, one does not even have the bitter consolation of asking forgiveness from the person one has wounded."

"That's the way it is. But don't think about sad things now. Wait, would you like another towel? And if you need some hot water, I can bring it in an instant."

"No, don't go to any trouble on my account. I won't be long, and then I'll go and fetch my luggage."

"Well, if you think of anything, just call . . . The bell doesn't work, so if you need anything, come to the door and give me a shout."

That man, so resourceful when it came to using his words and wits to torment someone with fierce sarcasm or to wound with delicate cruelty the heart's most fragile fibers, also had an amazing grasp of the art of pleasing others—when it suited him, that is. Her son-in-law's insinuating ways were certainly nothing new to Doña Pura, but this time—perhaps because they were accompanied by a cash donation, or because Víctor's flattery had reached new heights—the poor woman believed he really was a morally changed man, or on the road to becoming so. After a few hours had passed, she could no longer conceal from her spouse that she had some money, because to conceal such wealth was entirely incompatible with Doña Pura's character and customs. Villaamil questioned her as to where she had acquired what she modestly called her "resources," and when she admitted that these were a gift from Víctor, Don Ramón became very agitated and began to grind his teeth angrily, and out of his furious mouth spewed words that would have alarmed anyone who didn't know him.

"You're such a simpleton!" Doña Pura said. "What he's given me is a mere trifle. Do you honestly expect me to keep him fed and watered for free? We're hardly in a position to do that, are we? Naturally, I've given him a good talking-to, that goes without saying, and I told him that if he insists on staying here, then he has to make a contribution to the household expenses. Really, the things you come out with, saying he's defrauded the Treasury! What proof do you have? It's all in your imagination. How can you possibly know? Besides, if he had, why would he need to move in here and live at our expense?"

Villaamil said nothing. He had long since resigned himself to the fact that, in their household, his wife wore the pants. And he also knew, all too well, that when Pura got on her high horse, he had to dismount from his, mute acceptance being essential to matrimonial harmony. This was a system recommended to him when he married, and it perfectly suited his kindly, peace-loving nature. In the afternoon, Doña Pura returned to the fray, saying:

"We can use this bit of clay to stop up a few holes. And you'd better start thinking about getting yourself some new clothes. No one's going to give a job to a man who turns up at the ministry looking like a beggar, with down-at-heel shoes, a hat that looks like something straight out of the ark, and an overcoat all stained and threadbare. Believe me, no one takes any notice of anyone dressed like that; the most such a figure can aspire to is a bed in the poorhouse. And since they *will* be giving you a position soon, you'll need some decent work clothes."

"Don't go filling my head with such hopes. You have no idea how upsetting I find it to hear you speak with a confidence I don't share; on the contrary, I have no hopes at all."

"Whatever the case, whether they give you a position or not, you still need clothes. A suit and the person wearing it are almost one and the same, and if you're not decently dressed people will look down their noses at you, and then you're lost. I'll go round to the tailor today and ask him to make you an overcoat. And a new overcoat calls for a new hat, and the new hat for some new boots."

Villaamil was alarmed by such extravagance, but when Pura assumed that governmental role, there was no contradicting her. Besides, he knew she was right about the social and political value of clothes; and he knew, too, that a well-dressed candidate was already halfway to getting the job. And thus the tailor, summoned urgently, duly arrived, and Villaamil allowed himself to be measured up as sullenly and silently if he were being measured up for a shroud rather than an overcoat.

The arrival of the tailor gave Paca and her husband food for thought for the rest of the day and part of the night.

"You may not have noticed, Mendizábal, but I saw a new hat being delivered too. For as long as we've been in this house, which is getting on for fifteen years now, that's only the second top hat I've seen come through the door; the first one was for Don Basilio Andrés de la Caña, who lived on the third floor, just a few days after the arrival of Alfonso XII. You don't think there's going to be another revolution, do you?"

"I wouldn't be surprised," said Mendizábal, "because that Cánovas fellow is clearly losing his grip. According to the newspaper, there's a crisis looming."

"There must be, which means that Don Ramón's party must be on the rise. Whose party does he belong to anyway?"

"To the blessed souls in purgatory... (Bursting out laughing.) So, he's ordered a new hat and some smart clothes, has he? Well, given such wild extravagance, I'm going to go upstairs right now with these unpaid bills and see if they can pay all or part of what they owe. You have to keep a sharp eye on folk like them and catch them at the right economic moment, if you know what I mean—in that brief, rare period when they have a bit of money."

Mendizábal was looking at his dog, who seemed to be saying with his expressive face: "Up you go, my master, and don't delay, because today they're definitely in the money. I've just been visiting them, and it's like Christmas Day up there. They've even bought a chunk of Italian sausage as big as my head, and it smells divine."

And so Mendizábal set off upstairs, preceded by his dog. Usually, whenever he appeared carrying those fateful papers, Villaamil would start trembling, his manly pride cut to the quick, and Doña Pura would get a bitter taste in her mouth, all the color would drain from her lips, and her heart would overflow with anguish and despair. Both of them, each according to their temperament, would come up with a thousand reasons to convince Mendizábal of the advantages of waiting until the next month. Fortunately for them, this man-gorilla, this monster whose huge hands would touch the ground were he to bend over ever so slightly, this example of the zoological transition whose very cranium appeared to support Darwin's bold hypotheses, never ever behaved in a callous manner when carrying out the powers conferred on him by the landlord. In short, Mendizábal, whose ugly features would not have been out of place in a display case in some anthropological museum, was a benevolent, indulgent, compassionate man who understood their situation. He felt sorry for the family and was genuinely fond of Villaamil. He pressed them only in very measured, friendly terms, and when he reported back to the landlord, he would slowly scratch one small, flat ear, and out of that hideous mouth would pour merciful words of intercession, defending the tenant who was only behind with his rent because he had been suspended. And thanks to this, the equally undespotic landlord would, with sad, philosophical resignation, wait to be paid.

When Villaamil and Doña Pura were not in a position to pay, they would add a few obliging words to their excuses, flattering Mendizábal and pandering to his particular interests. Villaamil would say: "The things you must have seen in this world, my friend, and the number of tragic, fascinating events you must have witnessed..." Folding up the bills, the gorilla would say: "Oh, the true history of Spain has yet to be written, Don Ramón. If I were to write my memoirs, then you'd see..." Doña Pura would be even more adulatory: "The world is going to rack and ruin, and you're quite right when you say that it will continue to do so as long as there's freedom of worship and what people call rationalism..." Mendizábal would always end up putting the bills back in his pocket, and the lady of the house could breathe again. They had another month's grace.

But on that day, when, thanks to Providence, they were able to pay two out of the three months' rent they owed, both husband and wife rather arrogantly took a less consensual approach, and Villaamil spoke with discreet authority about modern ideals, while Doña Pura, when she saw Mendizábal putting the bills back in his pocket, said:

"Tell me, Mendizábal, where do these ideas of yours come from? Do you really believe Don Carlos is going to bring in the Inquisition and all those other horrors? You have to be a bit touched in the head to think that."

Mendizábal gave a few abrupt responses, garbled versions of what he had read in his daily newspaper, then left, muttering under his breath. Such a strange contradiction: he would always depart in a bad mood precisely on those occasions when he had managed to get some money out of them.

13

Before proceeding any further, let us evoke the sad image of Luisa Villaamil, who, at the time of this human chronicle, was dead but not forgotten. However, if we go back a few years, we will find her still alive. Let us return then to 1868, which marked the biggest political upset in Spain in the present century, as well as marking certain grave events in the unhappy annals of the Villaamil family.

Luisa was four years older than her sister Abelarda and very slightly less insignificant-looking. Neither of the two women were what you might call "pretty," but Luisa did have something of the angel in her eyes, a touch more charm, more color in her lips, was slightly fuller around neck and shoulders, and she had a tiny advantage over her sister as regards her voice and accent, the way she expressed herself. The scant attractions of the two women had not been enhanced by their equally scant education. They had been educated in three or four different provinces, changing schools at the drop of a hat, and any knowledge they had acquired, however elementary, was extremely patchy. Luisa did manage to pick up some very rudimentary French, which was barely enough (even with much consulting of the dictionary) to understand the first page of Fénelon's novel *The Adventures of Telemachus*, and Abelarda could bang out a couple of polkas on their poor, tormented piano. Out of the four girls and one boy—the fruits of Doña Pura's womb—they were the only two to survive; the others died shortly after being born. In early 1868, Villaamil was head of the finance department in a third-class provincial capital, a city of some archaeological interest, but with a small and not particularly fascinating population, a place famous for its cathedral and for the abundance of chipped pottery and lumps of Roman masonry buried just beneath the surface, and which could be unearthed with a single blow from a pickax. It was in that "backwater" that the Villaamil family had their moment of glory, because it was there that Doña Pura and her sister set the standard for fashion and elegance and where they played a prominent role at the very top of the social ladder. Then, one day, into Villaamil's office came a handsome young clerk, on the lowest salary of five thousand reales, and who had only been given the job thanks to who he knew, but then it really doesn't matter how Víctor Cadalso arrived there. He was from Andalucía, had started work in Granada, then, without a penny to his name, came to Madrid, where, after doing a thousand and one different jobs, he had found an obliging patron who launched him into the bureaucratic world much as one might lob a ball. He soon made his mark in that provincial office, and given his many physical attractions, his way with words, his natural elegance and easy, confident manner, he soon became a favorite with his boss's family, in whose "salon"—or, rather, drawing room, which was always full of guests on Sundays and public holidays—he immediately became, from the very first night, a shining star. No one could compete with him when it came to making witty remarks, often full of puns and double entendres, or to improvising ingenious games, or to arranging sessions of hypnotism, conjuring tricks, or amateur table-turning. He would recite poetry, imitating the most famous actors; he was a good dancer; he could recall all the funniest scenes from *Manolito Gázquez;* and he had a unique gift for charming the ladies and dazzling little girls. He was the "lion" of the town, the most elegant of all the elegant young men, an example to them all as regards finesse, glamor, and dress. The cream of local society would gather either at the Villaamils, at the house of the brigadier—whose wife was a distinguished, buxom lady of a certain age—or at the house of a certain individual who was the town's *cacique,* or political boss, electoral agent, and despot; but the Villaamil's household was the most refined, and the ladies of the household the most vain and pretentious. The local *cacique* had daughters of marriageable age, the brigadier had none of any age, and the civil governor was a bachelor; the town's female elite was, therefore, composed of Don Ramón's daughters, the *cacique*'s daughters, the brigadier's wife, and the mayoress, who also ran a pharmacy. They were the *grandes dames* of the town's elegant coterie, the main recipients of the compliments showered on them by the town's rather spiritless young men who still wore outmoded tailcoats and derbies; the ladies would turn up twice a year at the local bullfight to dazzle the other inhabitants with their white mantillas; they would collect money for the poor at the cathedral on Maundy Thursday, visit the bishop, generally raise the tone, and were constantly on the receiving end of that unspoken *hommage*—imitation. In those days, Milagros still retained some vestige of her beautiful voice, could still sing perfectly in tune, and had lost none of her sense of cadence and rhythm. She would still, very reluctantly—almost having to be dragged—go over to the piano and, summoning up the remnants of her art, sing a couple of brief arias, which would be greeted with wild applause. You could hear the clapping from the nearby Plaza de la Constitución, and the compliments showered on her would last all night, enlivening the dancing and the games of forfeits.

From the moment he appeared on the scene, Víctor Cadalso—a social artiste worthy of a far better stage—became the ornament of this society, and unlike Milagros, his gifts were not on the decline but at the very height of their power and vigor. And, of course, the inevitable happened: Luisa fell suddenly and hopelessly in love with him from the very first night they met, one of those explosive loves in which the two hearts appear to be packed with gunpowder ignited by Cupid's burning arrow. This usually happens among the lower classes and in primitive societies, but it can also occur in the hearts of ordinary, innocent, easily infatuated folk, when, like a thunderbolt from heaven, there appears before them a man who seems to them to be some higher being. Luisa Villaamil's sudden passion was so like Juliet's that, the day after she had spoken to him for the first time, she wouldn't have hesitated to leave her father's house had Víctor suggested such a thing. The thunderbolt was followed by a furious romance. Luisa could neither sleep nor eat. The lovers exchanged letters two or three times a day, and were constantly sending telegrams. In the evenings, they looked for opportunities to be alone, however briefly. The lovesick young woman spoke of her griefs and joys to the moon, the stars, the cat, the goldfinch, God, and Our Lady. She felt ready, if the law of her love so demanded, to perform an act of heroism or even martyrdom. Doña Pura was quick to voice her opposition to such a love, because she had her eye on the brigadier's adjutant as a son-in-law; and Villaamil, who was beginning to see something rather displeasing in Víctor's character, had to negotiate with the *cacique* to have him transferred to another province. Guided by the defensive perspicacity that love, like all great feelings, carries within it, the lovers sensed danger and, in the face of the enemy, swore eternal fidelity, resolving to be as one and declaring they would rather die than be separated, and so on and so forth. Their shared delirium led them to extremes of behavior, and any opposition only made them entwine themselves so tightly about each other that no one could untie the knot. In short: Love, as it usually does, ended up having its way. Luisa's parents were absolutely furious, but, on second thought, what could they do but make the best of the situation?

Luisa was all sensibility, love, and affection—an unbalanced creature, with no firm grasp on the realities of life. She experienced both sorrow and joy with an unhealthy intensity. She believed Víctor to be the most honorable of men, was entranced by his good looks, and completely blind to the flaws in his character. For her, people and actions were creatures of her own imagination, hence her reputation for unworldliness and a lack of discernment. The *cacique* was best man at their hasty wedding, and his wedding gift was to have Víctor's salary increased to eight thousand pesetas, for which Don Ramón and Doña Pura were deeply grateful, for, once Víctor was part of the family, they had no alternative but to support him and make a man of him. Shortly afterwards, the revolution broke out, and Villaamil, who owed his position to a close friend of the now disgraced González Bravo, lost his post. Víctor, however, had friends in high places and was promoted to a position in Madrid. The whole family moved with him, and there began another period of hardship, because Doña Pura had always had a talent for never saving a single penny and a special way of ensuring that the first of the month, which was payday, would always find her purse completely empty.

But to return to Luisa, after the wedding, she remained utterly besotted with Víctor, who, however, was far from a model husband. The poor young woman was consumed with anxiety, always finding new reasons to be worried. She spent her time eaten up by endless concerns and feelings of foreboding, spying on her husband, following him and waiting to hear him come home at night. And that scoundrel, with his God-given gift of the gab, could disarm her with a single tender word. He had only to smile at Luisa to convince her she was happy, just as one harsh word could leave her inconsolable. In March of 1869, Luis was born, leaving Luisa so weak and sickly that those watching over her could see that she was not long for this world. The boy was born with rickets, and was the embodiment of his mother's anxieties and physical decline. He was given a wet nurse, even though there were few hopes that he would live, and for the whole of his first year his life hung by a thread. And yet he seemed to bring the family luck, for only six days after his birth his grandfather was given a job with a promotion in Madrid, and Doña Pura was able to clamber out of that sea of bad debts, improvidence, and waste. Víctor slightly mended his ways. When he saw that his wife was doomed, he once again became affectionate and solicitous. The poor woman suffered attacks of either terrible sadness or febrile joy, both of which always ended in her vomiting blood. In the final stage of her illness, her fondness for her husband grew to the point where she appeared to have lost all reason, and when he wasn't there, she would call out for him. By one of those perversions of feeling that have their origin in some mental disorder, she took no interest in her son and was curt and scornful with her parents and her sister. She only had room in her heart for her ungrateful husband, her loving words were for him alone, and her eyes no longer saw the beauties that exist in the moral and the physical world, only those beauties that her overwrought passion imagined to be his.

Villaamil, who knew about the reprehensible life his son-in-law was leading away from home, began to hate him; Doña Pura was more conciliatory and allowed herself to be taken in by Víctor's treacherous words, and as long as he treated her poor sick daughter kindly and compassionately, she was satisfied and forgave him everything else. Poor Luisa's madness, for that is what it was, reached its fatal conclusion on Saint John's Eve. She died weeping with gratitude because her husband was bestowing passionate kisses on her and whispering sweet nothings. That morning, she had suffered a more than usually violent attack, leaping out of bed and demanding to be given a knife so that she could kill Luis. She swore that he was no son of hers and that Víctor had brought him home in a basket concealed under his cloak. This was a sad and bitter day for all the family, but especially for Villaamil, who—although he gave no external show of grief, remaining silent and almost dry-eyed—virtually collapsed inside, a pitiful ruin of a man, bereft of all hopes, all illusions; he shrivelled up until he was almost like a mummy, and his face took on that look of ravenous ferocity that one might see on the face of an ancient, impotent tiger.

Impelled by the need for a salary that would allow him to accumulate some savings, Villaamil went to work abroad. He was given a reasonable post, one that provided him with the occasional decent bonus, and he returned two years later with a little money saved up, but this dissolved like grains of salt in the bottomless sea of Doña Pura's mismanagement of affairs. He then made a second sortie, this time to a better post, but after a falling-out with the local governor, he returned to Spain in the dark days of the revolts in the cities of Murcia, Valencia, and Andalucía. The government—which, after January 3, 1874, was presided over by General Serrano—sent him off to the Philippines, where things looked very promising. However, a bad bout of dysentery obliged him to return to Spain with no savings and determined to take a job as a mere porter at a ministry rather than ever to cross the seas again. He found it easy enough to find work at the Treasury again, and enjoyed three tranquil years on a small salary, with the Restoration leaving him in peace, until the fateful hour when, like a bolt from the blue, he was once again suspended.

And this terrible curse fell on him when he was just two months short of retiring on four-fifths of his basic salary, which would have been that of a head of department, third class. He went to see the minister, he knocked at various doors; all his pleas for others to intercede for him proved vain. Gradually, troublesome hardship became terrifying, barefaced destitution; all resources came to an end, and he ran out of various extraordinary, crackpot schemes to support the family.

He finally reached the stage, which was terribly painful for a man like Villaamil, of knocking on the door of friendship and begging for help or for a small temporary loan. In happier times, he himself had helped out friends, some of whom had thanked him, while others had not. Why shouldn't he do the same? At least he didn't need to ponder whether or not such behavior was proper. When a man burns his hand, he doesn't pause to consider whether or not to shake his fingers. "Proper" was a hollow word now, like the words on the label of an empty bottle. Little by little, you wear down any sense of shame, just as you do the sharp blade of a file, and your cheeks lose the habit of blushing. That poor unfortunate man became a past master at writing letters invoking friendship. He would add small, pathetic touches and write in a pseudo-official style, rather like the preambles to laws announcing an increase in taxes, saying: "It is our painful duty to demand further sacrifices of the taxpayer..." That was the model, although the actual words were different.

14

JUST TO complete Víctor's biography, it is important to add that he had a sister called Quintina, who was married to one Ildefonso Cabrera, who worked for the Northern Railway; they were both good, decent people, if slightly eccentric. Since the couple had no children of their own, Quintina had wanted to bring Luis up herself, and this might have been possible had a bitter argument not broken out between Víctor and his brother-in-law over matters relating to the very measly inheritance left to the Cadalso brother and sister. The inheritance consisted of a crumbling, roofless ruin of a house in the seediest part of Vélez-Málaga, and there were violent quarrels over whether the house belonged to Quintina or to Víctor. According to Cabrera, the matter was clear, as clear as day, and to prove this he put the matter in the hands of the lawyers, who quickly buried the whole affair beneath a pile of documents, duly sealed and stamped. And all in order to prove that Víctor was a scoundrel and had illegally sold the valuable property and kept the money. Víctor treated the whole thing as a joke, saying that the fruits of his deception hadn't even been enough to buy a pair of new boots. To which Cabrera responded that it wasn't a matter of money but of what was right and proper, that he didn't care about losing out financially, what upset him was his brother-in-law's sheer effrontery; and for this and other reasons, he came to feel such a loathing for Víctor that Quintina would fear for her brother's life whenever he visited their house. Indeed, Cabrera's mood grew so violent that he very nearly fired all six bullets in his gun at Víctor. Quintina wanted the lawsuit settled and for all those quarrels to come to an end; and when her brother visited her a few days after his return from Valencia (taking advantage of the fact that her furious husband was away inspecting the stretch of railway track for which he was responsible), she made this proposal: "If you give me your Luis, I promise to pacify my husband, who is as keen as I am to bring the boy up." This was completely unacceptable to Víctor, who, however heartless he might be, would not dare to remove the boy from the care and protection of his grandparents. Quintina was determined, though, arguing: "But don't you see, those people are bringing him up really badly. I'm not so worried about him getting into bad habits, I'm just afraid they'll starve the little angel. They have no idea how to bring up children, and they've never before found themselves in such a dire economic situation. All they're good for is putting on a front and painting their faces, and all they care about is whether or not some singer or other sang well at the opera, and their house is a veritable pigsty."

The Miaows and Quintina may have been on visiting terms, but the reality was that they couldn't stand the sight of each other, because Quintina, who was a good woman (which is to say, she was nothing like her brother), was also curious and inquisitive to a fault—in short, an interfering busybody. Whenever she visited the Villaamil household, she never went into the living room, but made straight for the dining room and, on more than one occasion, even slipped into the kitchen and lifted the lids on the saucepans just to see what they were cooking. This drove Milagros absolutely wild. Quintina was always asking questions, wanting to know everything, and sticking her prying nose into everything. She gave advice no one had asked for, she scrutinized Abelarda's sewing, asked trick questions, and, in the midst of all her impertinent chatter, she would occasionally make some casually mocking, sarcastic comment.

She adored Luis with a passion, though, always making a point of talking to him and always taking him some small gift, a toy or an item of clothing. Sometimes, she would even turn up at his school and pester the teacher, asking him about the boy's progress, meanwhile telling Luis: "Don't study too hard, sweetheart. They just want to tire out your little brain. Take no notice; you have plenty of time to develop your intellect. What you need to do now is to eat; yes, eat and get fat and have fun and play as much as you like." On one occasion, seeing that the Miaows were very short of money, she suggested that they give Luis to her, but Doña Pura responded so indignantly that Quintina never again made such a proposal except in jest. After every visit, she would always have a chat with the Mendizábals downstairs in order to worm out all kinds of details about the family on the second floor: Did they pay their rent? Had they run up large debts at the local shops (although she usually garnered this information from more direct sources)? Did they come home late from the theater? Was the dullard daughter still going to marry that fool Ponce? Had the shoemaker brought them any new shoes? In short, she was an insufferable nosy parker, an inveterate meddler, and a spy always on the prowl.

Her habits were completely different from those of her victims. She never went to the theater, she was extremely orderly, and her apartment in Calle de los Reyes was always, as they say, as clean as a new pin. Physically, Quintina was no match for her brother, who had inherited all the family's good looks: She was attractive, but not beautiful; she had a slight squint and a large, ugly mouth, albeit filled with perfect teeth. The Cabreras lived quietly and comfortably, for, on top of his wages as an inspector, Cabrera earned money from a somewhat clandestine trade, which consisted of importing religious knickknacks from France and selling them in Madrid to the priests in neighboring towns and even to the clergy in Madrid itself. It was all cheap stuff, the product of modern industry, which, never missing an opportunity, was quick to take advantage of the penurious state the Spanish church had been left in after many difficult years. Cabrera had contacts in Hendaye, and he would bring them tapestries, wall lights, genuine silverware, the occasional painting, and various other pieces of old junk plundered from the once opulent and now impoverished churches of Castile. The charm of this trade—at least, according to malicious gossip—lay in the fact, although this has not been proved, that these objects could come and go across the frontier duty-free. Usually, the ecclesiastical geegaws that Cabrera imported (objects made of gilded brass, all of it false, fragile, and in the worst possible taste), were produced so cheaply and sold so well here that they would easily have borne the cost of any tariffs imposed. Early on, when they were just starting out, Quintina used to sidle into the sacristy of some parish church with a bundle under her cloak, like a smuggler, and whisper in the ear of the church administrator: "Would you like to see a really gorgeous chalice? You'll be amazed at how cheap it is. Half what you'd pay in the shops." She soon gave up her role as dealer, however, and instead received visits at home from the local clergy of Madrid and the surrounding towns and villages. Lately, Cabrera had been importing huge quantities of religious pictures to be given as prizes or at first communions, great chromolithographs of the two Sacred Hearts; and finally, by way of expanding and enlarging his business, he brought in a whole assortment of the most popular images, Saint Josephs by the gross, Baby Jesuses and Madonnas in bulk and in various sizes, all in the devotional French style and all very glossy and affected, their clothes gilded in Byzantine fashion, their cheeks daubed with pink, as if everyone in heaven wore rouge. I don't know if it was this overfamiliarity with such holy objects or simply the way she was, but Quintina was deeply skeptical. The fact is that she did her Christian duty by attending mass on the major feast days and saying the occasional prayer when she went to bed, purely out of habit, but she never went in for any hand-kissing when dealing with priests, unless, that is, she was pressing some interesting article on them or trying to wheedle out of them a tattered old brocade chasuble.

Luis would sometimes go to visit the Cabreras, where he was captivated by all those images, especially one that showed the Eternal Father with a long white beard and holding the blue globe of the world in one hand. Could this have been the origin of his strange visions? No one knows, and perhaps no one ever will. In any case, his grandmother forbade him from returning to that house full of saints, saying: "Quintina is a wicked woman who wants to steal you from us and sell you to the French." Luis took fright at this and never again visited Calle de los Reyes.

Villaamil could not stand Cabrera either, for he was not only horribly frank when giving his opinions, he was also inconsiderate and sometimes downright rude. They had once belonged to the same circle of friends who met at a particular café, but Villaamil had taken against him ever since Cabrera declared that introducing income tax into Spain would be arrant madness, an idea that would only occur to someone without an ounce of intelligence. After that, if they did ever coincide in the street, they would simply tip their hats and carry on walking. Doña Pura had still graver reasons for loathing Cabrera than his ruthless views on income tax. That "fellow" had never once offered them half-price train tickets so that they could enjoy a little summer excursion. Víctor was forever heaping insults on his brother-in-law, in revenge for the problems the latter was causing him with letters rogatory, court orders, and subpoenas. Víctor took it for granted that Cabrera was flouting the customs rules by importing all that ecclesiastical stuff and exporting various artistic bits of cloth. He was not only robbing the state but the rail company too, because when he first started his business, he would give his packages to the train drivers to deliver, and then, when those small packages became large crates and he didn't want to risk getting into trouble with his bosses, he would fill out all the necessary paperwork but would describe his luxury items as "returnable empties" or "timber." His customs declarations were often very funny. "How do you think he described a crate full of Saint Josephs?" Víctor would say. "He said they were 'kindling'!" And because he always bribed the customs officials, they let those absurd customs declarations pass, and thus bronze thuribles became "Domestic ironware," and cheap cassocks and albs became "Umbrella parts," or "Corset kits."

15

In the days that followed, Pura paid a few of the more urgent bills, brought home from the pawnshop some of the more necessary items of clothing, and, at the dining table, the family once again enjoyed the finer fare of happier days. "Modest Ophelia" spent her idle hours in the kitchen, for she was, almost with realizing it, getting a liking for the art of the great French chef Vatel—so different, goodness knows, from Rossini's art—and she took real spiritual pleasure in perfecting that art, even inventing certain dishes. When there were adequate provisions—or if you like, enough artistic material—she would be filled with inspiration and would work eagerly, singing softly to herself, out of habit and perfectly in tune, some heartbreaking fragment, like *moriamo insieme, ah! Si, moriamo...*

On the nights when the Miaows did not go to the opera, the living room would be crowded with people. Occasionally, the splendid Doña Pura would give the actors cakes and pastries, which made Villaamil's café clique believe that he must already have been given a post or, at least, have one foot inside the office door. The promised list, however, had still not been published, because the minister, overwhelmed by letters of recommendations and compromises, could not bring himself to make a final choice. Uncertainty, therefore, grew in the family, and Villaamil plunged ever deeper into his deliberate pessimism and even went so far as to say: "We're more likely to see the sun rising in the west than to see me employed again."

From the second day on from his arrival, Víctor no longer hid away from anyone. He came and went freely; he would enter the living room when other guests were there, although he never lingered, for he found such company horribly uncongenial. Meanwhile, Pura, disarmed by her son-in-law's generosity, felt sorry for him having to sleep on the hard sofa in the dining room, and so the three Miaows eventually agreed to billet him in Abelarda's room, Abelarda having been previously transferred to her aunt Milagros's room, which was also Luis's room, where "Modest Ophelia" slept alongside her sister on the very narrowest of cots. Don Ramón did not approve of these arrangements, because his one desire was to see his son-in-law sent packing once and for all. His friend Pantoja in the Internal Revenue Department had told him that Víctor was hoping to be promoted but that a complaint had been lodged against him, which could prove disastrous unless he found some sponsor to back him. The complaint was something to do with the Office for Municipal Food Taxes, or irregularities in the cash account that Víctor had opened with the various towns in the province. It seems that the towns that were most in arrears did not appear on the list of demand notes issued, and it was believed that Víctor was in cahoots with the defaulting mayors. Villaamil was also told that the distribution of taxes proposed by Víctor in the last quarter was done in such a way that the attempted fraud was blindingly obvious, and his boss, of course, had refused to approve it.

Villaamil said nothing about all this to his son-in-law. At the supper table, he was always very taciturn, whereas Víctor was very talkative, not that anyone in the family took much interest in what he said. However, he did have long conversations with Abelarda whenever they happened to be alone, or when engaged in the interesting business of putting Luis to bed. Víctor enjoyed watching his son's development and kept an eye on his frail health, one of his main concerns being to make sure Luis was well wrapped up at night and decently clothed during the day. He ordered some clothes to be made for him and bought him a very sweet little cape and a blue suit with matching stockings. Luis, who was a touch vain, could not help being grateful to his papa for making him look so smart. As regards new clothes, though, this was as nothing compared with the money Víctor began lavishing on his own person soon after his return to Madrid. Every day, the tailor would bring him some brand-new item of clothing, and his tailor was not like Villaamil's, a fair-to-middling "artist," a mere tradesman really, but one of the most famous in Madrid. And how very handsome Víctor looked in those beautifully tailored clothes, elegant but sober, which is, after all, the very essence of true elegance, with nothing too strident about the cut or the color! Abelarda would study him discreetly, slyly, admiring him and recognizing in him the same remarkable man who, a few years earlier, had so turned the head of her unfortunate sister, and she felt in her heart a vast well of indulgence for that young man, so denigrated by the rest of the family. That well might seem small if one looked no further than its unexplored surface, but if you dug and dug, you would see that it was inexhaustible, almost bottomless, like a vast, rich quarry. And what purple veins of glittering ore were to be found there, rather like veins swollen with blood or like the precious stones melted down and solidified over the centuries in the bosom of the earth! That indulgence, rising from her heart to her mind, would take this form: "No, he can't be as bad as they say he is. It's just that they don't understand him."

Víctor himself often mentioned that he felt misunderstood—not just then, but two years earlier, when he had also spent a few months with the family. How could those poor vulgar beings possibly understand a creature from a superior sphere or caste when it came to appearance, manners, ideas, aspirations, and even faults? When Abelarda went back in her imagination to the past and scrutinized her feelings for Víctor, she had to recognize that she had had those same feelings even while poor Luisa was alive. When everyone else in the household was heaping abuse on him, Abelarda would console her sister with specious arguments, defending the perfidious lover or excusing him for his faults. "Víctor is hardly to blame if women find him irresistible," she would say.

When her sister died, Abelarda had continued to admire the widower in silence. Yes, he had caused the poor woman endless sorrows and problems, but that was all because of his fatally good looks. Somehow or other, sometimes purely out of a sense of delicacy, he would find himself caught in an amorous trap or snare set by some wicked woman. But deep down he was good; he would grow more sensible with age, and all he needed was a woman with enough heart and courage to hold him steady with a combination of affection and rigor. Poor Luisa had simply been the wrong woman. How could a woman who would burst into tears for the slightest reason possibly impose such a strict regime of behavior, a woman who once fainted because her husband arrived home with his tie knotted differently from the way she had knotted it when he left?

At the time of this story, Abelarda the Insignificant found it terribly hard to conceal how flustered she felt whenever her brother-in-law spoke to her. Sometimes, a slightly mischievous, boisterous sense of pleasure would fill her heart, as if some small parasite had made its nest there and laid its eggs; at other times, it felt more like a heavy, suffocating burden. Whatever her response, her answers were always hesitant, flat, and dull.

"Are you really going to marry Ponce, that frightened little bird of a man?" he asked her one night as he was putting Luis to bed. "A fine match, my dear. How envious all your friends will be! Not every girl is so lucky."

"Oh shut up, you fool, you nasty man."

On another night, showing a sudden intense interest in the family, Víctor told her: "Look, Abelarda, don't expect your father to be reemployed. The list has been drawn up but hasn't yet been published, and his name isn't on it. I've been told as much in confidence. Needless to say, I find this quite deplorable. The poor man, so full of hopes ... because however often he says that he has lost all hope, the truth is he does nothing but hope. When he finds out, it will be a tremendous blow. Don't worry, though; my promotion is now certain; I have a lot more support than your father does, and since I will be staying in Madrid, believe me, I won't abandon the family. I've caused you all a lot of pain, and I need to salve my conscience. However much I do to help you, I will never be free from the weight of that guilt."

"No, he's not a bad man," Abelarda would think, absorbed in her own ruminations. "And all that stuff about not believing in God is nothing but bluster, he's just teasing me and amusing himself by making me angry. Because the fact is he does come out with some very strange things, things that would never occur to anyone else. No, he's not a bad person, he's clever and very talented. It's simply that we can't understand him."

Víctor never missed a chance to complain about being misunderstood. "Listen, Abelarda, what I'm saying can't seem that outrageous to you, because you do understand me a little; you're not one of the common herd—not entirely, anyway; at least you're beginning to move away from it."

When on her own, the poor young woman would always belittle herself and think, with implacable modesty: "Whatever he may say, I *am* one of the common herd, none commoner. I'm nothing to look at, not as regards my face and certainly not my figure, and even if I was good-looking, how could I show off those good looks in clothes like these, in these rags that are being endlessly cut up and remade, turned inside out. And I'm ignorant too; I don't know anything, I spout nothing but vacuous nonsense, and I haven't an iota of wit. I'm a pumpkin with a mouth, eyes, and hands. Heavens, I'm so stupid and boring! Why was I born like this?"

16

WHENEVER Víctor entered the apartment, Abelarda would gaze at him as if he had come from another very superior social world. In the way he walked, the way he behaved, dressed, combed his hair, there was something about Víctor that jarred with the Miaows' shabby home, that was at odds with their ramshackle, vulgar household. And Víctor's comings and goings were highly erratic. He would often dine out with his friends; he would sometimes go to the theater two nights running; and, occasionally, he wouldn't come back all night. He wasn't always in the best of moods; he had bouts of depression when he would hardly say a word all day, and others when he was a real chatterbox, and given that his parents-in-law completely ignored him, he had to make do with his sister-in-law. These tête-à-têtes did not happen very often, but he knew how to make the most of them, aware of the effect that his person and his words had on the troubled mind of Abelarda the Insignificant.

Luis was feeling rather ill, so much so that he took to his bed: Doña Pura and Milagros went to the theater, Villaamil to the café in search of news of that elusive list, and Abelarda stayed at home to look after Luis. When she was least expecting it, there was a knock at the front door. It was Víctor, who was clearly in high spirits and humming a tango from some musical comedy. Hearing that his son had felt ill but was now sleeping, he listened to the boy's breathing, realized that any fever, if he had one, was only slight, then sat down at the dining room table to write letters. His sister-in-law kept a stealthy eye on him; two or three times, she walked past him, pretending that she needed something from the sideboard and casting a furtive glance at what he was writing. It was clearly a love letter, given its length, the urgency with which Víctor was writing, and the febrile facility with which he wielded his pen. Alas, she couldn't read a single phrase or a syllable. When he had finished his missive, Víctor struck up a conversation with Abelarda, who had come into the dining room to do her sewing.

"Listen," he said, leaning one elbow on the table and resting his cheek on the palm of his hand. "I saw your young man Ponce today. And you know, I've changed my mind about him. He's a good match for you, a fine lad, and he'll be rich when his uncle the notary dies, because people say he'll be his only heir... I mean, we can't go along with Ruiz's philosophy, according to which the greatest happiness in life is to be penniless... If he were right, and I let myself be carried away by my feelings, I would say that Ponce wasn't the right man for you at all, that someone else would suit you better: me, for example..."

Abelarda turned pale and was so disconcerted by these words that her attempt to laugh it off failed completely.

"Really, the nonsense you come out with! Always the joker, eh?"

"You know perfectly well that I'm not joking. (Growing very serious.) One night, two years ago, when you were living in Chamberí, I said to you: 'Abelarda, I really like you. Whenever I see you, I feel my soul crumbling...' Don't you remember? And you said... well, I can't remember what you said exactly, but what you meant was that if I loved you, you would love me too..."

"You liar! Stop it! I never said any such thing."

"Did I just dream it? Well, whatever the truth of the matter, you then fell madly in love with your precious Ponce."

"Me... fall in love... Now you're just being cruel. But what if I did fall in love? Why should that matter to you?"

"It matters because, as soon as I realized I had a rival, I turned my attentions elsewhere. That's how fate works: Two years ago, you and I were almost lovers; now, though, there's no going back. I left, you left, we both left. But then, when we meet again, what happens? I'm in a very strange position with regard to you. My heart is telling me:

'Make her fall in love with you' and, at the same time, another voice, from who knows where, is yelling 'Look but don't touch.'"

"Huh, what do I care (choking back her tears), given that I don't love you one bit, nor could I."

"I know, I know...You don't need to tell me. We're in agreement on that point: that I can go to the devil for all you care. You hate me, as is only logical and natural. But the strange thing is that knowing a person hates me makes me want to love her, and I do love you, because I want to...but, on with the motley, as your papa would say."

"Honestly, the lies you tell!" (Trying to be serious, but bursting out laughing instead.)

"I'm not lying, and I never will lie to you. Regardless of whether you believe me or not, that's the truth of the matter. I love you and I shouldn't, because you're far too angelic for me. You can only be mine in marriage, and marriage, an absurd machine that really only works for vulgar beings, would be of no use to us at the moment. Whether I'm good or bad—and, let's be frank, you think I'm bad—I have a mission to fulfill, and I know that sounds rather grandiose, but I aspire to something dangerous and difficult, for which I need, above all, total freedom; I am racing, sad and all alone, towards a goal, one that I can only reach on my own. If I were in company, I would get stuck halfway. No, I must keep going. On with the motley! (Spoken very theatrically.) What draws me on? Fate, a force stronger than either me or my wishes. Better to fail than turn back. And I can't go back or take you with me. I fear I might drag you down. And if you had the great misfortune to be the wife of this wretch...(Closing his eyes and holding out his hand as if to fend off a ghost.) No, heaven forfend! I love you enough never to have you by my side. If one day... (in a singsong declamatory voice) if one day I should lose my mind and make the supreme blunder of telling you that I love you, of asking you to love me in return, then you must reject me outright; do not allow yourself to be carried away by your vast generous heart; drive me from you as if I were some dangerous beast, because you would be better off dead than mine."

"Are you just trying to upset me? (Spoken in a tremulous voice and disguising her alarm with a frustrated attempt to thread a needle.) What foolishness! I won't listen to you ... And what's all this nonsense about me killing myself or dying or going to the devil?"

"I know you don't love me. All I ask—and this is a big favor—all I ask is that you don't hate me, but that you do pity me. Leave me, because I can cope alone, greedily clinging to these ideas as a source of comfort. In the midst of my misfortunes, of which you know nothing, I have one consolation, which is to live according to my ideal and to fortify my soul with that. Your fate is very different from mine, Abelarda. You follow your path, and I will follow mine, borne along by my fever and by the speed lent me by my fever. Let us not rebel against the fate that rules us all. We may never meet again, but before we part, I will give you a word of advice: If you don't find Ponce too disagreeable, then marry him. That's all that matters, that you don't find him disagreeable. If you don't like him, if you don't find someone else less watery-eyed, then renounce marriage altogether. That is the advice of one who loves you more than you may think ... Renounce the world, enter a convent, devote yourself to an ideal and to the contemplative life. I do not possess the virtue of resignation, and if I fail to reach the place I want to reach, if my dream turns into a mere puff of smoke, then I will shoot myself."

He said this with such energy and with such feeling that Abelarda believed him, more impressed by that nonsense than by all the other nonsense she had just heard.

"Kill yourself? You wouldn't. I certainly wouldn't want that. (Catching an idea on the wing.) Wait a moment, all this stuff about despair and shooting yourself must be because of some unhappy love affair. Someone must be making you suffer. Well, in that case, I'm glad, you deserve to suffer."

"Look, my dear (changing tone), I know you were only joking, but you might be right, yes, perhaps you're right ..."

"So you do have a girlfriend." (Feigning indifference.)

"Well, not a real girlfriend ... no."

"Some love interest then."

"Call it fate, martyrdom ..."

"Oh, stop talking about fate … Just say that you're in love."

"I really don't know how to answer you. (Affecting a charming and very appropriate look of embarrassment.) If I said yes, I would be lying, and if I said no, I would be lying too. And having assured you that I love you, how could I possibly be interested in someone else? This can only be explained by drawing a distinction between one love and another. There exists a holy, pure and tranquil affection which was born in the heart, which takes over the soul and becomes the soul itself. Let us not confuse that feeling with the insalubrious ferment of the imagination, the pagan cult of beauty, the yearnings of the senses, in which there is a great deal of vanity too, if the person we love is higher up the social ladder. What does that disquiet—one of life's accidents and pastimes—have to do with the ineffable tenderness that inspires one soul to fuse with another, that inspires the will to sacrifice itself … ?"

He did not go on, because his subtle instinct realized that such excessive subtlety was beginning to sound ridiculous. For poor Abelarda, though, those ardent concepts—expressed with a certain elegant mimicry by that extremely handsome man, who, as he spoke, had such a sweet and tender expression in his dark eyes—were the most eloquent she had ever heard, and hearing them tore her soul apart. Seeing the effect he had, Víctor racked his brain for new ways in which he could continue to drive that poor troubled girl still further out of her wits. He came up with a few more paradoxical and passionate phrases, which contradicted what he had said before, not that Abelarda noticed. The deep impression made by these latest concepts wiped from her mind the impression made by the earlier ones, and she allowed herself to be dragged along by that whirlwind through a swarm of conflicting feelings: curiosity, love, jealousy, pleasure, and rage. Víctor gilded his lies with the metaphors and antitheses of a now outdated doom-laden romanticism. However, for Abelarda, this cheap, tarnished metal was pure gold, because her limited education meant that she knew nothing of the forgotten texts from which Víctor was dredging up all that drivel about fate. He returned to the charge, saying in a rather lugubrious tone:

"I can't go on talking about this. What cannot be is not. I realize that I would be much better off giving myself to you, and who knows, you might save me, but no, I don't want to be saved. I am doomed to ruin myself and to carry with me this entirely undeserved feeling, this celestial ray that I cling to as fearfully as if I had stolen it ... In me you see a pale reflection of the Prometheus of mythology. I have stolen the heavenly fire, and, as punishment, a vulture is gnawing at my entrails."

Abelarda, who had never heard of Prometheus, was most alarmed by that vulture, and Víctor, pleased with his success, continued thus:

"I am a condemned man, a reprobate ... I cannot ask you to save me, because fate would never allow that. Therefore, if I come to you and tell you that I love you, do not believe me; it is a lie, it is a vile trap I am setting for you; spurn me, banish me from your side; I do not deserve your affection, or even your compassion ..."

With deep sadness and self-denigration, Abelarda the Insignificant thought: "I am such a donkey and so dull that I can think of no response to such high-flown, deeply felt sentiments." She gave a heartfelt sigh and looked at him, feeling an intense desire to throw her arms about his neck, crying: "I love you more than you can possibly know, but take no notice of me, I don't deserve you and am worth nothing compared to you."

Clutching his head in his hands, Víctor was letting his gaze wander distractedly over the oilcloth covering the table, all the while frowning and sighing, playing the misunderstood romantic hero, something along the lines of Byron's Manfred, adapted to suit a pharmacist's apprentice or a rookie recruit. Then he looked at her with extraordinary tenderness and, touching her arm, said:

"Ah, but I'm wearing you out with these horrible misanthropic ideas of mine, which cannot possibly be of any interest to you. Forgive me, please, forgive me. I won't rest easy until you say you forgive me. You are an angel, and I know I am not worthy of you. I do not even aspire to being worthy; that would be sheer, senseless impudence. All I want now is for you to understand me ... Do you?"

Abelarda had now reached the very limits of her ability to conceal her anguish and her distress, but she still had her dignity. She would defend her heart's secret to the death; and so, in the end, in an act of supreme heroism, she gave a laugh that was more like the spasm that precedes an attack of hysteria, and said to Víctor:

"Of course I understand you...You pretend to be a scoundrel, a nasty piece of work, when you're nothing of the sort, and you do it simply in order to deceive me. Well, you don't fool me, you silly idiot...I know more than you do. I can see what you're up to. Why keep trying to make people loathe you, if you can't pull it off?"

17

LUIS'S condition worsened. He had some kind of stomach upset, a common childhood ailment and one that would have no serious consequences if dealt with promptly. Víctor, however, was worried and sent for the doctor, and even though his own presence was unnecessary—the three Miaows were all taking loving care of their young patient and, for several nights, even deprived themselves of the pleasure of going to the opera—he insisted that Luis should not be left alone and kept constant watch over his son, making sure he was warm enough in bed and regularly taking his pulse. In order to entertain Luis and cheer him up, which is something all sick children need, he brought him a few toys, and his Aunt Quintina also visited, bringing whole bundles of colored pictures of the saints, Luis's favorite playthings. Under his pillow, he managed to accumulate a large selection of trinkets and knickknacks, which he would bring out for inspection at certain times. On those first sleepless, feverish nights, Luis had imagined he was once again sitting on the steps outside the Convento de Don Juan de Alarcón or on that block of stone on the esplanade outside the Conde-Duque military barracks, but he never saw God or, rather, he only half-saw him. He would see his body, his incomparably white, flowing robes, and, occasionally, the vague outline of his hands, but never his face. Why would God not let him see his face? Luis began to feel genuinely worried, afraid that the Lord was angry with him. But why? In one of the little colored images his aunt had brought him, God was shown in the act of creating the world. So easy! All he had to do was raise one finger, and the sky, sea, and mountains appeared ... He then raised another finger and there were the lions, the crocodiles, the coiled snakes, and the nimble mouse … But that picture was not enough for Luis. True, the artist had done an excellent job, but that God was nowhere near as handsome and venerable as his friend.

One morning, when Luis's fever had gone, his grandfather came to see him in his room. It seemed to Luis that his grandfather was burdened down by some great sorrow. Before the old man even arrived, Luis had heard murmurings among the three Miaows, which seemed to him to bode ill. It was whispered that his grandfather's name had not appeared on the new list. How did they know? Luis remembered that, just as he was waking up, he had heard Doña Pura saying to her sister: "No, there's nothing … So much for all their promises. There's no doubt about it. Víctor had already told me, he found out yesterday at the ministry."

The boy immediately connected those words—which had imprinted themselves on his mind—with the look on his grandfather's face that morning, the look of a condemned man. Being still only a child, Luis was not yet adept at putting ideas together, and so, with the innocence of youth, he created strange affinities between them. If he hadn't known his grandfather as he did, he would have felt afraid of him that day, because his face was just like that of the storybook ogres who devour children. "They haven't given him a job," Luis thought, and as he thought this, he joined together two other ideas in his post-fever mind. Childish logic is sometimes terrifyingly acute, as shown by his reasoning on this occasion: "If God doesn't want to give him a job, I don't know why he should be angry with me and refuse to show me his face. I reckon I'm the one who should be angry with him."

Villaamil began pacing up and down the room, his hands in his pockets. No one dared speak to him. Luis's good spirits were then laid low by an anguishing thought: "He hasn't been given a job because I haven't been studying hard enough, because I don't know my lessons." Then his childish logic rose up in his defense: "But how could I study when I've been ill? Let him make me better, and then he'll see how hard I'll work."

Víctor came into the room having just returned home, and the first thing he did was to embrace Villaamil, thus interrupting his father-in-law's tigerish pacing. Doña Pura and Abelarda were both there too.

"You mustn't let yourself be too cast down by misfortune," said Víctor, whose sudden display of affection was received by Villaamil with great displeasure. "Men of heart, men of moral fiber will always find the necessary strength to confront adversity... The minister has once again reneged on his word, as have all those who promised to support you. May God forgive them, and may their bad consciences torment them for the evil they have done."

"Oh, leave me alone," said Villaamil, who looked as if he were about to be garotted.

"I know that a strong man like you doesn't need to be consoled by an ordinary fellow like myself, but let's consider what's happened here—namely, the natural, logical thing that happens in all societies corrupted by favoritism. What have we just seen? A family man, an honest, upright man, a worthy civil servant, who has grown old in public service, a loyal servant of the state, who could certainly teach the minister a thing or two about how best to save the Treasury, is passed over, swept out of the office as if he were mere dust. Nothing would surprise me, and certainly not this. There's worse to come, though. While committing such an injustice, those brazen incompetents blessed with neither conscience nor experience make off with the job themselves as a reward for their own ineptitude. The only possible recourse is to withdraw into the sanctuary of one's own conscience and say: 'Fine. I have no need of their approval, my own is quite enough.'"

Víctor gave voice to these highly philosophical thoughts with his gaze fixed on Doña Pura and Abelarda, who were so deeply touched they were almost on the verge of tears. Villaamil, his face deathly pale and his jaw trembling, said not a word and resumed his pacing.

"No, nothing surprises me," Víctor added, brimming with sanctimonious indignation. "The whole system is so rotten that something even more shocking is about to take place: While this man here, who should, at the very least, be made director general, is ignored and sent packing, I, a mere worthless nothing, with only the briefest of service records...yes, believe it or not, I, when I least expected it, will almost certainly be given the promotion I have asked for. This is what the world is like, what Spain is like, this is why we are learning to despise the state, and why the embers of revolution are being stirred up in our hearts. To the deserving man: disappointments; to the undeserving: sweetmeats. That's Spanish logic for you, getting everything back to front; the land of topsy-turvydom. Here I am, with not a care in the world, in no particular hurry, with few urgent needs—yes, I, who would scorn a letter of recommendation as much as I would the person who gave it to me, I will be given a job; while this family man, laden with obligations, who, given his worth and the service he has given, had such justifiable hopes, he..."

"But I *had* no hopes I tell you," said Don Ramón, interrupting Víctor abruptly and somewhat angrily and stretching up his arms until his hands almost touched the ceiling. "I never had any hopes, I never believed they would give me a job and I never will believe it. Where do you people get that idea? I never hoped for anything. How often must I say it? Anyone would think you were all conspiring to make me lose my wits entirely."

"It's not exactly a crime to hope," remarked Doña Pura. "I myself have a few hopes, now more than ever. There'll be another list of appointments. They promised you a job and they must honor that promise."

"Exactly," said Víctor, regarding Villaamil with filial concern. "Above all, though, you mustn't get upset about it. Whatever happens—given that injustice and unreason rule—if, as I hope, I am promoted, my good fortune will make up for the family's ill fortune. I owe this family so many favors, and however hard I try, I will never be able fully to repay them. I have been a bad man, but now I intend... well, I won't say to be good, because I know that would be difficult, but at least to behave in a way that will help you to forget my errors... The family will lack for nothing, not as long as I have a crust of bread."

Overwhelmed by feelings of humiliation, which fell upon his soul as heavily as if the ceiling had collapsed, Villaamil gave a loud harrumph and left the room. His wife followed him, and Abelarda, full of very different feelings to those of her father, turned to Luis and, as a way of hiding her emotions, pretended to tuck him in more securely, all the while thinking: "No, he's not a bad person at all, and I won't believe anyone who says so."

"Abelarda," Víctor said sweetly, after they had been alone for a while with Luis. "I know there's no need for me to repeat what I just said to your parents. You know me a little and understand me a little too; you know that as long as I have so much as a crumb to eat, you will not lack for food, but I do need to tell them and to prove it so that they believe me as well. They have such a very poor opinion of me. Well, one doesn't lose a bad reputation in a matter of days. And I would have to be a real monster not to offer to help you. If I didn't do so for the grown-ups, I would have to do so for my son, who has been brought up by you here in this household, for this little angel who loves you all far more than he loves me ... and quite right too."

Abelarda was stroking Luis, trying to hide the tears filling her eyes, and Luis, finding himself so showered with affection and hearing all the things his papa was saying, and which sounded to him like a sermon or a long discourse on some religious text, was so overcome with emotion that he burst into tears. Abelarda and Víctor did their best to distract him, laughing and telling him jokes and inventing stories.

In the evening, Luis asked for his school books, much to everyone's astonishment, for they couldn't understand how someone who studied so little when he was well should want to do so when ill in bed. However, he was so insistent that they brought him his grammar and his arithmetic books, which he leafed through in desultory fashion, all the while muttering: "Perhaps not now, because I can't seem to concentrate, but as soon as I can, I'll learn the whole thing off by heart and then we'll see; yes, then we'll see."

18

POOR WRETCHED Abelarda was looking so unwell that, thinking she must be ill, her mother and her aunt spoke of calling the doctor. She, however, continued life as usual, working, often for many hours a day, on altering and mending dresses. She used a wicker dummy, which at night, having migrated from the office to the dining room, resembled a real person, a fourth Miaow, or the ghost of some family member who had come from the other world to visit her progeny. Abelarda the Insignificant would practice her very clever handiwork on that dummy. At the time, she was concocting a dress out of strips of cashmere that had already been used twice before, back to front and upside down, and which she was now piecing together with some much cheaper cloth. She had learned such make-do-and-mend solutions from Doña Pura, who, when a piece of fabric could no longer stand being washed again or turned inside out, would send it off to be dyed so that it looked as good as new. Using this method, she could make a dress for almost nothing. Abelarda's most surprising skill, however, lay in the way she could transform a hat. Doña Pura's bonnet had known several different lives, which, as with all reincarnations, made it both always new and always old. In winter, Abelarda would decorate it with velvet ribbons, and in summer with lace from a discarded shawl; any flowers or pins or other adornments were gifts from their neighbors on the floor below. During the period that Villaamil had been without a post, the much-mangled wire frame of Abelarda's own hat had taken on many different shapes and styles, depending on the whims of fashion, and it was thanks to this exquisite way of disguising their indigence that the Villaamil women always managed to step out into the street dressed to the nines.

On the nights when the Miaows did not go to worship at the altar of Euterpe, Abelarda had to put up with two or three hours of Ponce's nattering on, or else help him rehearse his role in the play. Doña Pura was most displeased at having to put on a play after the collapse of all their hopes regarding Villaamil's imminent new posting, but since the play had already been announced with a flourish and a fanfare, with all the roles allocated and the rehearsals well advanced, she had no alternative but to sacrifice her pride in the interests of that tyrant Society. Abelarda had deliberately chosen a very dull role, that of the maid, who appeared as soon as the curtain went up, feather duster in hand, complaining that her master and mistress did not pay her wages and revealing that the house where she worked was the poorest in all of Madrid. This kind of farce was a particular favorite among Madrid's great wits and basically introduced the audience to a very ordinary family with a great many pretensions and more vanity than money: a wife who wore the pants and rode roughshod over her husband, an engaged couple, various cases of mistaken identity, and a dizzying number of exits and entrances—so much so that, in the end, the stage resembled a madhouse, at which point the stupid father would enter saying, "Ah, now I understand everything," and the play would conclude with a wedding and a rhyming couplet begging the audience for their applause. Ponce was the stupid father, while the part of the cocky young rake—who was the cause of all the mayhem, as well as being the life and soul of the whole play—went to Cuevas, the son of their first-floor neighbor, Don Isidoro Cuevas, a widower with a large family, who worked for the governor of the nearby women's prison and who was known locally as the prison warden. His son was very funny, always full of jokes, and the stories he told about drunks had everyone in stitches; he was also brilliant at imitating street slang and singing flamenco songs, to name but a few of his talents—all of which meant that he was in high demand at parties like those given by the Villaamil family. The role of the young lady of the house went to Pantoja's daughter (Don Buenaventura Pantoja worked for the

Treasury and was a close friend of Villaamil), and the part of the pushy mother, vulgar, loud, and bossy—the kind of role at which the actress Balbina Valverde excelled—was given to one of the Cuevas girls (there were four of them and they earned a living making hats, which they did very well). Other roles—a lackey, an old moneylender, a phoney, bankrupt marquis who turned out to be a complete fool—were distributed among the various young men in the party. Guillén agreed to be the prompter. Federico Ruiz was the director, and his only regret was that the play was not advertised on posters in the street, so that his name could appear in large letters: *Directed by the highly regarded publicist* etc. etc.

Abelarda had a very retentive memory and quickly learned her part. She attended all the rehearsals like an automaton, meekly joining in with a world that was, to her, purely secondary and artificial, as if her home, her family, her circle of friends, and Ponce were the real comedy, full of superficial, hackneyed roles...while her mind remained free, immersed in her inner life, her real life, in a drama that was exclusively hers, pulsating with interest, and which had only one player (herself) and one spectator: God.

An endless, unruly monologue. One morning, while she was arranging her hair, a spectator might have heard the following: "Goodness, I'm ugly, so very plain! No, not plain; just dull, insignificant; no spark at all. If I at least had a talent for something—but no, I don't even have that... How could he possibly love me when there are so many beautiful women in the world and when he's so superior to me, a man with a future: elegant, handsome, and genuinely intelligent, whatever the others may say. (Pause.) Last night, Bibiana Cuevas told me that the people up in the gods at the Teatro Real have given us a nickname; they call us the Miaows because, they say, we resemble three cats, yes, three china cats, the sort people keep as ornaments on their dressers. And Bibiana thought I'd be offended. Silly girl! I don't care two hoots. So we look like cats? All the better. People laugh at us. Even better. What do I care? We're just a bunch of nobodies. You're born a nobody and a nobody you will remain. I was born a nobody and will die a nobody. I will marry another nobody and have children who are nobodies, and people will call them 'the little kittens'... (Pause.) I do wonder when Papa will get a job. When I think about it, though, that doesn't matter either; it's all the same. With or without a job, it's all the same. My home has been pretty much like this all my life. Mama's a hopeless housekeeper, so is my aunt, and so am I. If they do give Papa a job, I'll be really happy for him, because then he'll have something to do, something to occupy his mind, but financially, I don't think we'll ever be free of debts and dramas or wear anything but rags. Poor Miaows! It's quite a sweet name really. Mama will be furious if she ever finds out. I don't mind though, I'm not proud. All's spent, like the family money... not that we ever had any money. I'm going to tell Ponce about that nickname and see if he finds it funny or gets all outraged about it. I'd like him to get annoyed one day, so that I could get annoyed too. To be honest, I'd like to give him a good hard slap... (Pause.) Goodness, how dull I am, how insipid! My sister Luisa was more attractive than me, although, to tell the truth, she was nothing special either. My eyes are so expressionless, or the most they say is that I'm sad, but without explaining why. It's hard to believe that behind these eyes there's ... well, whatever there is. It's hard to believe that this narrow forehead of mine conceals whatever it is that it conceals. I find it so hard to imagine what heaven must be like; I just can't picture it at all. But how easy it is to imagine hell! It's almost as if I'd actually been there ... And those people up in the gods are quite right, we do look like cats ... Especially our mouths, because we all have the same upturned lips, especially Mama. When I laugh, it's not so bad. An idea: Would I look prettier if I wore makeup? No, Víctor would laugh at me. He may despise me, but he doesn't find me ridiculous and repulsive. Oh, *am* I repulsive? I simply couldn't bear that. Anything but repulsive. If I thought I was repulsive, I would kill myself. (Pause.) Last night, he came home and went straight to his room without saying a word. It's better like that. When he speaks to me, I feel as if my heart would burst. I would be capable of committing a crime if that would make him love me. What crime? Oh, anything... anything at all. But he never will love me, and I'll be left eternally miserable and with no crime having been committed."

"Abelarda," Doña Pura said, interrupting this monologue. "When Ponce comes, tell him that we'll kill him if he doesn't get us tickets to the benefit concert for Pellegrini. If he hasn't got any, then tell him to find some. Pelligrini is bound to give tickets to the press and to the whole blessed claque. I'm sure that if Ponce went and asked Pelligrini herself, she would let him have some. She's very kind like that. Anyway, we'll all be very annoyed if he doesn't get them."

"He will," said Abelarda, who had just finished pinning her hair up in a bun. "If he doesn't, I'll never speak to him again."

Ponce came and went in their apartment as if he were one of the family, always heading straight for the dining room, which is where his fiancée was usually to be found. That afternoon, he arrived at around four o'clock, and having left his cloak and his hat on the stand in the hall, he went into the dining room, smoothing his hair. He was a skinny, rather limp young man for whom having a fiancée was rather like having an umbrella; he had aspirations to being a writer and wrote reviews for which no one paid him; he was always busy and always complaining that no one read his reviews (but then who does?); he was also a low-ranking lawyer, but a decent enough fellow, with large ears, a pince-nez, a slight squint, trousers that bagged at the knee, a mind not over-endowed with gray matter, and, in his pocket, six reales at most. He held a minor post in the provincial government on a salary of six thousand and was hoping against hope to receive the eight thousand he had been promised over a year ago . . . and which could arrive any day—today, tomorrow. When he received this increase, they would get married at once. These hopes would not have been enough for the Villaamils to accept him as a son-in-law had he not had a rich uncle, a childless notary who was ill with cancer—and since he would die within a year or possibly even a month, and Ponce was his sole heir, the Miaows saw this suitor as a real stroke of luck. According to Pantoja, who was the unfortunate uncle's friend and executor, he would leave two houses, a few thousand in cash, and his legal practice . . .

As soon as Ponce entered the dining room, Abelarda said bluntly:

"If you don't bring us tickets for Pelligrini's benefit concert, you will never set foot in here again."

"Please, dear, at least allow me to sit down and catch my breath. I almost ran here. Something really bad has happened."

"Now what's wrong?" asked Doña Pura, who tended to treat him as if he were her son. "You always come here with some problem, which always turns out to be nothing at all."

"No, listen, Doña Pura, and you too, Abelarda, listen carefully. My uncle is very ill, very ill indeed."

"Oh dear God!" cried Doña Pura, feeling her heart skip a beat.

And she bounded into the kitchen like a faun to tell her sister the news.

"He's dying."

"Who?"

"Ponce's uncle, of course, his uncle . . . don't you see? But tell me, Ponce (returning to the dining room with feline fleetness), is he really dying? You must be very pleased . . . I mean sad."

"You'll understand then why I can't go to the theater or go and see Pelligrini . . . You see how it is . . . He's bad, very bad. The doctors say he won't last more than a couple of days . . ."

"Poor man! But why aren't you there at the dead—I mean, dying man's bedside?"

"I've just come from there. Tonight, at seven, the priest will be coming to give the last rites."

Doña Pura ran to see Villaamil in his office.

"The last rites . . . don't you see what that means?"

"What? Who?"

"I mean the uncle, of course, Ponce's uncle, who's just about to breathe his last . . . (Sidling back toward the dining room.) Ponce, would you like a drop of wine and a biscuit or two? You must be so upset . . . And don't even think about the theater now . . . that's irrelevant. We wouldn't go anyway . . . out of respect for your uncle and, needless to say, we'll observe strict mourning. Are you sure you don't want any wine, or a biscuit perhaps? Oh, no, what am I thinking? We haven't any wine, but we could send for some. Are you sure you don't want any?"

"No, thank you; as you know, wine tends to go to my head."

Abelarda and Ponce started talking, with, as their only witness, Luis, who was wandering around in the dining room, occasionally stopping next to the couple and looking at them with childish amazement. They were speaking very softly…What could they be talking about? Probably the usual trivial nonsense. Abelarda was playing her part with the indolent passivity she always displayed when dealing with life's routine business. She was accustomed to chatting with the young fool, telling him that she loved him, even suggesting some ideas for their wedding. She had adopted the habit of saying yes to all of Ponce's questions, which were always very proper and correct. Her will played no part in these conversations; the external, visible woman was performing a series of unconscious actions like a sleepwalker, disconnected from the internal woman who was then free to think about more human feelings. Before the sudden arrival of Víctor, Abelarda had considered Ponce as a last resort, a probable source of support in life's vicissitudes. She would marry him in order to have a name and a position in society and to escape from the unbearable constraints of her own family life. Since the arrival of that other man, she had continued to think those same thoughts, but much as a skater, once she has launched off onto the ice, simply skates and skates without once slipping and falling. It never occurred to her to go back on her word or to refuse to marry Ponce, because having him as a husband was equivalent to having a paper fan or a safety pin or some other equally mundane, boring object. The over-eager critic felt obliged to be more than usually affectionate that day, even going so far as to fix a date for the happy event and, overcoming his natural timidity, mentioning certain particulars about their future married life. Abelarda listened to him without really listening, as if she were listening to the rain, and given that events were now moving faster, she agreed to all his suggestions with chilly, indifferent words, like someone yawning her way through the rosary without feeling one iota of religious devotion.

The doorbell rang, and Abelarda's heart gave a leap, although she managed to preserve her cool appearance. She could recognize the way he rang the bell, the sound of his footsteps as he came up the stairs, and if, between the front door and the dining room, he made some comment to Doña Pura or to Villaamil, she could tell from his tone of voice whether he was in a good or bad mood. It was Doña Pura who opened the door to Víctor, and she immediately announced to him that Ponce's uncle was dying. Unable to contain her excitement, she would have blurted out the news to the local water-carrier. Víctor entered the dining room with a broad smile on his lips, and either inadvertently or out of sheer malice, he congratulated Ponce, who was left utterly speechless.

19

"OH, FORGIVE me. My mistake. It's just that my dear mother-in-law's eyes were positively sparkling when she told me. No doubt because she's so fond of you, my illustrious friend. Affection can have that effect. Besides, you're one of the family now, and we love you, and given that we never had the pleasure of getting to know your uncle, even by sight..."

He went over to his son Luis and rubbed his face, pinching his cheeks and kissing him, then he gave him the present he had brought. It was a stamp album along with a set of different colored stamps, some of them foreign but most of them Spanish, so that Luis could amuse himself by sticking them on the relevant pages. Luis felt immeasurably grateful for this gift. He had reached the age when we begin classifying things according to their importance and making connections between our playthings and our slowly growing knowledge of life. Víctor explained how the pages in the album were arranged and showed Luis how to recognize the nationality of each stamp. "Look, this rather brazen lady here is the French Republic. This other lady wearing a crown and everything is the Queen of England, and this eagle with two heads is Germany. You put each stamp on the appropriate page, and now all you have to do is to collect lots more and fill in the gaps." Luis was delighted, his only regret was that there weren't enough stamps to cover the whole table. He soon got the idea though, and swore to himself that he would keep the album and treasure it for the rest of his life.

Víctor meanwhile butted into Abelarda and Ponce's very private conversation, for they were almost nose to nose, doubtless sharing some secret or other, like rather dull conspirators, all very lovey-dovey on his part and rather weary and indifferent on hers. Víctor verbally elbowed his way between them, saying:

"Others may be prepared to put up with such public canoodling, but I will not. Couldn't you wait until the honeymoon to begin your turtledovery? Frankly, it's an insult to other people's misfortune. One should disguise one's own happiness in the presence of the *un*happy, just as one should conceal one's wealth from the poor. Charity demands as much."

"What does it matter to you if we do or do not love each other," said Abelarda, "or if we do or do not marry? We will be happy or unhappy as we wish. That's our business and none of yours."

"Yes, Don Víctor," said Ponce in his usual colorless way, "if you're eaten up with envy, that's your problem."

"Me? Envious? Oh, I am, I don't deny it. I would be lying if I said otherwise."

"Then go rant and rage somewhere else," said Abelarda.

"Papa, Papa," said Luis loudly, determined to get Víctor's attention, even placing one hand on his father's cheek to make him turn and look at him. "What country is this one from, this gentleman with the very bushy mustache?"

"Can't you see, child? It's from Italy...Yes, I am envious. This young woman here tells me to go rant and rage, and I might well do that—indeed, I might even bite. Because when I see two people who love each other, who have solved the problem of love and ironed out all the difficulties and are currently trotting along the path to happiness all the way to matrimony, I positively die of envy. Believe it or not, I think you two have solved the problem. I see in you, the happy couple, something I will never have. You have no ambition; you're contented to lead a quiet, modest life, respecting and loving each other with none of the usual fever and madness...You certainly won't be raking in the shekels, but you'll always have food on the table. You're no saints, but are virtuous enough simply to be able to enjoy each other's company. What more could one want? Ah, my illustrious friend Ponce, you have seen her worth and chosen her...and she, the sly rascal, who looks as if butter wouldn't melt in her mouth, she has put her hand in the basket and pulled out the best and juiciest fruit. I'm very pleased for you, and why shouldn't I be? However, this doesn't mean that, like any other man, I don't feel a twinge of envy, because my situation is so different—ah, so very different. I would give everything I have, everything I hope for, for just one thing. Can you guess what that might be?"

With a sudden intuition, Abelarda could see what was coming, and she trembled.

"Well, I would give anything to be my illustrious friend Ponce. You may not believe me, but it's true. Would you care to swap places, my friend?"

"Frankly, as long as I can keep the lady, I wouldn't mind at all."

"No, no, that is precisely the problem. I would give the blood from my veins to throw my hook into the sea of life—with, as bait, a declaration of love—and catch myself an Abelarda. That is one ambition that would cure me of all others."

"Papa, Papa. (Tweaking his father's nose to make him look at him.) What's this one with a parrot on it?"

"Guatemala ... Leave me be, child. No, I aspire to nothing more. Yes, an Abelarda who would spoil me rotten, for with a companion like her I could face anything. I would marry her however impecunious she might be, however poor. As long as we had a few chickpeas, we'd be fine. I would rather share a crust of bread with her than possess all the riches in the world. Because where could one find another woman so sweet-natured, so tender-hearted, such a perfect little housewife, such a ..."

"Don Víctor, you're getting carried away. (In a failed attempt at humor.) She is my fiancée, after all, and these compliments are beginning to make me jealous ..."

"No need for jealousy. You've struck gold ... For she, she ... oh, you can be quite sure of her, my friend; she loves you body and soul. The kings and princes of the whole planet could try all they liked to drag her away from her beloved Ponce. If I didn't know that, do you imagine that I wouldn't have set my cap at her too? Charity begins at home. Why, if there were so much as a glimmer of hope, I would make off with her myself. No chance. If anyone were to suggest that she change her Ponce for another man, she would throw the kitchen sink at him. Look at that face, so enigmatic, that little smile which looks almost put on, and tell me, would anyone dare to try his luck?"

"Come now, Don Víctor," said Ponce, his mouth full of saliva, "from the way you're talking it sounds as if you did once try your luck but got nowhere."

"Pay no attention to him, silly," said a clearly very troubled Abelarda, forcing a smile but feeling closer to tears than to laughter. "Can't you see he's just trying to provoke you."

"He can try all he likes, but my Abelarda is a very reliable person, and once she has given her word, no one could make her go back on it. We understood each other from the moment we met, our characters are a perfect match, and if I am made for her, she is certainly tailor-made for me."

"Take it easy, friend Ponce. (Growing very serious, as he always did when he elevated his cruel jokes to heroic status.) You may be tailor-made for someone or other, that's not my business, but as for Abelarda, as for her..."

Ponce looked at Víctor equally seriously now, waiting for him to finish his sentence, while Abelarda gravely fixed her gaze on her sewing.

"What I mean is that she isn't tailor-made for you, and I would argue my case with anyone who took the contrary view, for the truth must prevail. She loves you, I accept that, but as for being *made* for you...well, she's made of far superior stuff, both morally and physically—yes, physically too. Should I speak more plainly? The person Abelarda is made for is me—yes, me, but there's no need for you to take offence. However ridiculous it may seem, she is made for me. You can't possibly judge her qualities as accurately as I can, because I've known her since she was a child. Besides, you haven't known *me* long enough to see that she and I are made for each other. I know what I'm saying is impossible, and I know too that it's entirely my fault if I've arrived too late, and I know that you got in ahead of me, so let's not quarrel about that. But when it comes to recognizing her true merit, when it comes to feeling profound regret that all those fine qualities will never be mine, as far as that is concerned (enunciating this phrase very formally and in an oratorical voice), ah, as far as that is concerned, I do not and cannot yield."

"Take no notice of him, just ignore him," said Abelarda to her fiancé, who was beginning to get cross.

"Don Víctor, that might well be true, but it's hardly relevant."

"No need to get hot under the collar, my illustrious friend. Don't worry, I'm a decent fellow, loyal to a fault. I recognize that you have won what I believe should have been mine (said in a pathetic voice), and I congratulate you. It was a fair fight, and it was entirely my fault that I lost. I have no complaints. We will be friends; we will always be friends. Give me that hand of yours."

"Ah, you and your jokes, Don Víctor!" said Ponce, allowing his hand to be shaken.

Víctor would not have been so free with his words had he been dealing with anyone other than Ponce, but he knew his enemy. Ponce was becoming rather annoyed, and Abelarda didn't know what to think. If it was all a joke, it seemed terribly cruel, and if true, far too frank. Ponce was reluctant to leave, presuming that Víctor would continue talking to Abelarda in the same tone, and Abelarda was, after all, his fiancée, his wife-to-be, and having that brother-in-law living under the same roof was beginning to worry him. That scoundrel Víctor, seeing how rattled Ponce was, made a point of shaking his hand extra firmly when Ponce left, saying again: "Don't worry, I'm a decent fellow, loyal to a fault. You have nothing to fear from me."

And when he turned to Abelarda, who was staring at him in dismay, he said: "Forgive me, child, but I just couldn't hold back feelings that I've been hiding from everyone. Such emotions burst forth when you least expect it, and even a master of disguise can't always keep them in. I didn't mean to mention it, and I don't know what came over me. I was so consumed with envy at seeing you two lovebirds! I felt so frightened to find myself so alone, and all because I arrived too late—yes, too late. Forgive me, I won't say another word. I know the subject bores and annoys you. I will be discreet."

Abelarda could contain herself no longer. She sprang to her feet, feeling a mixture of fear and an intense desire to run away and hide so as to conceal the distraught look on her face.

"Víctor," she said, angry and trembling, "I don't know what you're after, but I think you must be the wickedest man in the world."

She ran to her room and burst into tears, flinging herself down on her bed and burying her face in the pillow. Víctor remained in the dining room, and Luis, who, even in his innocence, realized that something strange was going on, refrained for a while from bothering his papa with the complex matter of those stamps. It was his father who eventually evinced an interest in that intelligent pastime, and he set about explaining the national symbols that his son didn't understand:

"This bearded king is Belgium, and that cross is the Helvetic Confederation or, in other words, Switzerland."

Doña Pura arrived home and, when she failed to find her daughter in the dining room or the kitchen, went to look for her in her bedroom, from which Abelarda was already emerging, her eyes very red, but refusing to give her mother any satisfactory reason for her distress. When Pura asked Víctor for an explanation, he said sarcastically:

"Don't be so silly, Mama. She is grieving for Ponce's uncle, of course."

20

THEY PUT Luis to bed early, and he took his new stamp album with him, falling asleep with it clasped in his arms. That night, he didn't actually have one of the funny turns that usually preceded his strange visions of the celestial old man; instead, he *dreamed* that he had, and therefore lay wanting and waiting for another amazing visitation. The mysterious personage was obviously playing truant, as poor disconsolate Luis put it, for he was eager to show the man his stamp album. He waited and waited, unsure as to quite where he was, for he could as easily have been at school as in the dining room at home or in the scribe's office downstairs. And following the wild illogic of his dream, he came up with an admirably logical idea: "Of course, how stupid of me!" he thought. "How could he come to visit me when this very evening he's being taken to Ponce's uncle?"

The following day, he was declared fit and well, but the family decided that he should stay at home for the rest of the week, for which he was deeply grateful, although still determined to do a little studying in the evenings, just a teeny-tiny bit, and to really and truly apply himself once he had returned to school. He was allowed to go downstairs to the scribe's office, and he took his stamp album with him to show Paca and Canelo. He would have loved to take it to his Aunt Quintina's, but that would not be allowed. He stayed with Paca until it was dark, when he was summoned upstairs again because his family feared he might catch a chill from the cold draft coming in through the street door. On his way back, he was pondering an idea born of his conversations with Mendizábal and Paca, an idea that, at first, struck him as somewhat bizarre, but which he came to consider as the most natural thing in the world. He was alone with Abelarda, for his grandmother and Milagros were both bustling about in the kitchen, when he decided to share this brilliant idea with his aunt. She was being vehemently affectionate, kissing him and promising to buy him an even bigger stamp album, when Luis, responding equally warmly to her show of affection, said:

"Auntie, why don't you marry my papa?"

She was left speechless, not knowing whether to laugh or get annoyed.

"Wherever did you get that idea, Luis?" she said, alarming him with the fierce expression on her face. "You couldn't have come up with it on your own. Who put that idea in your head?"

"Paca did," said Luis, not wanting to take the blame for someone else's blunder. "She says Ponce's an idiot and not the right man for you at all and that my papa is clever and handsome and is going to make a brilliant career for himself."

"Tell Paca not to poke her nose in where it isn't wanted. And what else did she tell you, what else?"

"Well . . . (Scratching around in his memory.) She says my Papa's a fine gentleman . . . that he gives her a tip whenever she runs an errand for him . . . and that you should marry my papa so that everything stays in the family."

"She runs errands for him? What do you mean? Letters? Who to? Don't you know?"

"They must be to the minister, because they're great friends apparently."

"Well, everything Paca said about poor Ponce is nonsense," said Abelarda, smiling. "Don't you like Ponce? Tell me honestly."

Luis hesitated before answering. The gifts his father gave him, and the fact that he seemed to be getting on so well with all the family, had put paid to Luis's initial wariness and caution. As for Ponce, Luis hadn't really formed an opinion about him, and so he had unquestioningly accepted Paca's view.

"Ponce's a pipsqueak. When you see him walking down the street, he looks as if his trousers were about to fall down. As for brains, well, Cuevas has more brains than him. Don't you agree?"

Abelarda laughed at these remarks and would have gone on talking to Luis on this subject if her father hadn't called out for her to come and sew some buttons on his jacket, a task that kept her busy until supper time. Doña Pura announced that Víctor would not be dining at home but at the house of a friend of his, a deputy and the leader of some small parliamentary clique. Villaamil made a few caustic comments about this, which Abelarda listened to in silence and with immense sadness. The women discussed whether or not to go to the theater that night and decided they would now that Luis was better. Abelarda said she would prefer to stay behind, and when they were alone, her mother bombarded her with questions:

"Why aren't you eating? What's wrong with you? And why that sheepish look on your face? Why don't you want to come to the theater? Now don't try my patience, girl. Get dressed this minute, because we're ready to leave."

And the three Miaows set off, leaving Villaamil alone with his grandson and his gloomy ruminations. After putting the boy to bed, Villaamil began reading *La Correspondencia*, in which there was talk of a new list of appointments.

When the Miaows returned, Víctor was already back and seated at the dining room table writing letters. Don Ramón was still reading the paper, but father-in-law and son-in-law exchanged not a single word. Then everyone went to bed, apart from Abelarda, who had bedsheets to dampen and fold ready to be ironed the next day, and Víctor, seeing her absorbed in this task, and without even putting down his pen, said:

"I've been thinking about you all day. I was afraid you might be angry after what happened yesterday. I was determined never to reveal my feelings to you, and I still haven't told you the whole truth, nor shall I, God willing. When one arrives late to the party, one should simply resign oneself and remain silent. Have you nothing to say to me? Not even to tell me off?"

Abelarda the Insignificant kept her eyes fixed on the table, although her lips were moving as if words were struggling to emerge. In the end, though, she said nothing.

"I will speak to you as a brother (said in the kindly, serious tone he was so good at affecting), because it would be wrong of me to speak to you in any other way. I am deeply unhappy...as you well know. Here I am, swept along by mad, dizzying passions; here I am, burdened with a relationship I once so foolishly sought and which I have only continued out of habit and idleness and which I now wish to end. I was hoping to do this with the aid of a certain angelic creature, to whom I thought I would commend myself first before surrendering to her body and soul, but that can no longer be. What am I to do in this situation? Plunge deeper and deeper into the swamp, become ever more lost in this labyrinth with no way out? There is no possible salvation for me. Fate is dragging me under... You cannot possibly understand this, Abelarda, or perhaps you can, with that penetrating mind of yours. Ah, if only I had known you when you were free! A thousand times I have promised myself never to speak to you about this, but the words keep spilling out of my mouth ... Enough, enough, take no notice of me. That's what I've been saying to you from the start. Take no notice of me. Spurn me. I do not deserve you. I am paying the price for the terrible follies I have committed since that angel, my poor Luisa, left me ... yes, she too was an angel from heaven, but an angel so inferior to you that there really is no comparison. Frankly (leaping passionately to his feet), when I see that such a treasure is going to be Ponce's, when I think that such a storehouse of noble qualities is about to fall into the hands of..."

Abelarda was so overcome by emotion that if she hadn't said something, if she hadn't at least opened one small valve, she would have burst.

"And what if I said ... I mean (turning pale), what if I were to tell you that I don't love Ponce?"

"Is that true?"

"What if I told you that I've never loved him and never will... what then?"

Víctor had not been expecting this response and was slightly thrown.

"Ah, I see . . . Well . . . (stammering), goodness, I feel as stunned as if I'd had a blow to the head . . . Is that true? If you say it is, it must be. Abelarda, please don't toy with me, don't play with fire. Such jokes, if jokes they be, can only bring catastrophe. Because when someone loathes a man, as you loathe me . . . (confused and having no idea which way to turn) that person should never say anything that might mislead that man as regards . . . I mean as regards the feelings of the person doing the loathing, because it might be that the loathed one . . . No, I can't put my feelings into words. If you don't love Ponce, that means you do love someone else, but that is something you must not tell me . . . What would be the point? To make me feel even more confused than I already am? (Glimpsing a way out and sharpening his wits in order to make his escape.) I won't ask you about that because I would quite simply go mad. Keep your secret and show a little respect for me and my situation. If I inspire only hatred in you, rather than actual physical repugnance, then, please, leave me be, just leave now and say not a word more. I will not offer you any advice because you would not accept it, but should you ever find yourself in an awkward situation and my counsel would prove useful to you, then you know that I am to you what you wish me to be, namely a brother, if, that is, you are kind enough to treat me as a brother . . ."

"And what if I did, what if I did need your advice?" asked Abelarda, who was looking not for a way out but for a way in, and failing to find one.

"I am at your disposal. (Again feeling lost.) If you love a man and fear your family's opposition, if you find breaking off your engagement to Ponce difficult and you need help, I am here, however painful that might be for me. (Moving closer to her.) Tell me, don't be afraid. Are you in love with a man other than your fiancé?"

"That's a lot to ask . . . I mean, to expect me to confess . . . just like that. (Resorting to coquetry to get out of this uncomfortable situation.) Anyway, who asked you to butt in?"

"I'm one of the family...I'm your friend. I could be more than that if you wanted, but I'm a latecomer and therefore out of the game. If you wanted to tell me your secret, so much the better. That way, I would suffer less. One question: Does the man you love love you?"

"I haven't said anything about loving anyone...I don't think I've even mentioned that...But just suppose that I had, it's still none of your business. You're such a meddler. Besides, I wouldn't love anyone who didn't return my feelings. What a mess I would be in then!"

"So your love *is* requited. (Pretending to be angry.) How can you say that to my face?"

"I haven't said a thing."

"It's what you implied though. Anyway, I don't want to be your confidant. So *does* he love you?"

"I don't know...(Allowing herself to be carried away by her own irresistible spontaneity.) I haven't been able to find out yet."

"And I suppose you want me to find out for you. (Sarcastically.) Abelarda, I don't do that kind of thing. No, don't tell me who it is, I don't need to know. Is it someone I know? No, don't tell me his name, not unless you want to end our friendship. I say this as someone who has certain feelings for you...feelings that I would prefer not to define just now, being a man weighed down by his own cruel destiny"—Víctor had picked up this and similar philosophies from certain novels he had read—"a man forbidden from speaking of his own sufferings, and since I must not love you, and since I cannot be yours or you mine, I must not torment myself further or allow you to torment me. Keep your secret, and I will keep the part of it that I think I know. Had fate not intervened, I would yet try to cure you by plucking that love from your heart and replacing it with mine. Alas, I am not the master of my own will. That feeling (striking his breast) will never leave my heart and become a reality. Why urge me to reveal it? Leave it inside me, silent, buried, but still alive. Do not tempt me, do not provoke me. So, do you love another? No, I would prefer not to know. Why inflame an incurable wound? And to avoid further conflicts, tomorrow I will leave this house and never enter it again."

Abelarda could not conceal the pain these words caused her. Her poor brain lacked the necessary reasoning power to combat that infinitely resourceful, inexhaustibly inventive monster, so practiced at playing with serious, profound feelings. Stunned and bewildered, she was about to surrender her secret and offer herself up, defenseless and ridiculous, to Víctor's brutal sarcasm, but she managed to calm herself, to recover a little equilibrium, and say with feigned indifference:

"No, no, there's no need for you to go. Or have you made it up with Quintina?"

"Me? Don't be absurd! Why, only yesterday, Cabrera almost put a bullet in me. He's an animal, that man. Don't worry, I'll find somewhere else to live."

"No, you must stay here."

"Promise me then not to say another word about this."

"I haven't said a thing, you're the one who keeps going on about it, saying that you love me, but can't love me. What am I supposed to think?"

"As my final proof that I do love you, but shouldn't (said with stinging wit), I am going to give you these words of advice: Turn your eyes back to Ponce..."

"Thank you."

"Yes, turn your eyes back to the illustrious Ponce. Marry him. Be sensible. If you don't love him, so what?"

"You're crazy. (Utterly bewildered.) Did I say I didn't love him?"

"You did."

"Well, I take it back. What nonsense. If I did say it, I was only joking, just to draw you out and keep you talking."

"You're a very wicked woman then. I thought you were better than that."

"Well, do you know what I say? (Starting violently and angrily to her feet.) You are utterly irksome and unbearable with your...your enigmas; I can't stand the sight of you. It's my own fault for listening to all your jabber. Goodnight. I'm going to bed, and believe me, I will sleep like a log."

"Intense hatred, like intense love, can keep a person awake."

"Not me ... you nasty, stupid man ..."

"You go to sleep then, while I will lie awake thinking of you ... Goodnight, Abelarda. See you tomorrow."

And a minute after his victim had disappeared (she went to her room and immediately locked the door like someone fleeing a murderer), the pitiless wretch, a diabolical smirk on his lips, also took himself off to bed, thinking the following bitter, cruel words: "If I'm not very careful, she'll shamelessly declare her love for me. And the girl is both ill-natured and quick-tempered. And so common and stupid too. All of which would be forgivable if she were at least pretty. Ah, Ponce, what a bargain you're getting, a real basement bargain, a pest of the first order, best thrown on the rubbish heap."

21

EVEN THOUGH the Villaamil family's hopes, so cruelly nipped in the bud, were beginning to bloom again with renewed vigor, the long-suffering Don Ramón, ever true to his system of hoping in despair, still insisted that all such hopes were dead and gone. This pessimism, however, was completely at odds with the frenzied letter-writing and string-pulling in which he engaged, in the hope that this might prod the decidedly indecisive minister into action. "All this waiting for some new vacancy to appear is sheer nonsense," he would say. "I know perfectly well that when they want to do something, they will do it regardless of whether there are any actual vacancies and regardless of the law too. I'm not a complete idiot. I've seen it a thousand times; some party leader enters the ministry, knife in hand, demanding a nice fat post for someone or other. The minister immediately summons the head of personnel, who says: 'But there is no vacancy, sir...' 'Well then, make one.' And bam, there it is. No sooner said than done. But what big name, what hypothetical patron, is going to enter the minister's office and demand fiercely: 'I'm not moving until you give Villaamil a job'? Poor wretch that I am, I'm being left ever further and further behind. With this confounded Restoration—which is just the epilogue of an equally accursed revolution—all kinds of new people have emerged, and wherever you look, you won't see a single familiar face. When a Claudio Moyano, an Antonio Benavides, or a Marqués de Novaliches turns to you and says: 'My friend, we're being retired,' that's basically the end of the world. Mendizábal is quite right when he says that politics has fallen into the hands of a bunch of good-for-nothings."

In the afternoons, to distract himself from his sorrows and to sniff out any new nominations—which he still affected to believe he himself would never receive—he would go to the Treasury, in whose offices he had many friends of various ranks. There he would spend long hours chatting, hearing about all the latest rules and regulations, smoking the occasional cigarette and acting as a guide to the new, inexperienced clerks who would consult him on some obscure point of office procedure.

Villaamil felt a deep affection for the great pile that was the ministry; he loved it in the way a faithful servant loves the house and family whose bread he has eaten for many a long year; and during the grim days of his suspension, he would visit it with a mixture of respect and sadness, like a dismissed servant who keeps returning to the place from which he was expelled, dreaming that one day he will be hired again. He would walk through the main gate, along the vast corridor separating the two courtyards, then slowly ascend the monumental staircase wedged in between walls so thick they could as easily have belonged to a feudal castle as to a prison. On the stairs he would almost always meet some old colleague of his. "Hello, Villaamil, how are you?" "Oh, you know, surviving." When he reached the first floor, he hesitated between visiting Customs & Excise or the Treasury, because he had many acquaintances in both; on the second floor, though, he invariably opted for the Internal Revenue Department or Estates. The porters would all greet him, and Villaamil, being an affable fellow, always exchanged a few words with them. If he arrived late, he would find them carrying a shovelful of leftover embers from the stoves in the offices, and whose last remnant of warmth served to feed the braziers in the porters' lodges; if he arrived early, they would be taking documents from one office to another, or carrying trays bearing glasses of water and sugar lumps. "Hello, Bermejo, how are you?" "Not too bad, Don Ramón, but very sorry not to see you here every day." "How's Ceferino?" "He's been moved to the Tax Office. And poor old Cruz has snuffed it." "Oh no! But I saw him only the other day looking perfectly healthy. What a world we live in, eh? There aren't many of us old guard left. When I started working here, when

Don Juan Bravo Murillo was in charge, Cruz was already 'in post'…
But you just have to turn your back for a moment… Poor old Cruz,
I'm so sorry."

His best friend among many good friends was Don Buenaventura
Pantoja, of whom we have already heard a little, for he was the father
of Virginia Pantoja, one of the regular performers in the Miaows'
domestic theater. Don Ramón's favorite place to visit was the office
of that excellent old colleague, whose boss he had once been; he would
sit down on the chair nearest his desk and, if Pantoja wasn't there,
flick through a few papers, and if he was there, the two would almost
instantly plunge into a conversation full of bureaucratic gossip.

"Have you heard?" Pantoja would say. "Today they've appointed
two new officials, first class, *and* a head of department, all hot from
the oven. Yesterday, that nonentity"—and he would name some famous politician—"was here, and of course everything was done at
the speed of light. As I always say, when they really want to do something, they don't bother to consult the underlings."

"Oh dear," said Villaamil with a painful sigh that ruffled the
sheaves of paper nearest to him.

That afternoon, it took Don Ramón a long time to reach Pantoja's
desk. Friends and acquaintances appeared at every stage of his visit.
One would emerge clutching bundles of files tied up with official
tape; someone else would rush past him, late and afraid the boss
would tell him off. "Good to see you, Villaamil. How are you?" "Oh,
not too bad." Pantoja's office was part of a huge room divided into
smaller rooms by partition walls about six feet tall. The various departments all shared the same ceiling, and crisscrossing that vast space
were the long black horizontal pipes that suddenly headed off at right
angles wherever they penetrated the walls. This space was filled with
the strident clamor of bells, the distant voices of department heads
endlessly calling for their subalterns. This was the hour of the latecomer, when the early birds were enjoying a late breakfast or drinking
coffee brought in from the street, and so, rather than the kind of silence
required for intellectual work, it was all slamming doors, laughter,
the clatter of china and coffee pots, shouts and impatient voices.

Villaamil entered one of these rooms, greeting people to right and left. There was Guillén, the lame official, third class, a close friend of the family, a regular at the local café, and prompter for the play they were planning to put on. He was also, more to the point, the uncle of Luis's friend and rival, the Joker, and he lived with his sisters, who owned the pawnbroker's. Guillén was known for his biting, mocking sense of humor and his ability to make fun of absolutely anyone. While in the office, he would write comic sketches, often crude and smutty in nature, as well as the occasional spine-chilling melodrama that would never see the footlights; he would also draw caricatures and pen satirical verses about the many ridiculous people in the ministry. Then there was a junior clerk, barely sixteen and the son of the treasury chief, who already earned five thousand reales. He was sharp as a tack and very good at taking messages from office to office. There was also Espinosa, an official, second class, an elegant young man, with a very casual air about him, neatly parted hair, many frills and furbelows in the way he dressed, and just as many errors in his spelling; he was a good lad, who never took offence at Guillén's tedious jokes. However, the most unusual character was a fellow named Argüelles y Mora, an official, second class, and a perfect parody of a gentleman from the days of Felipe IV: slightly built, a *madrileño* born and bred, he had a gaunt, sallow face, a dyed mustache and goatee, and a long mane of hair. To complete the look, he wore a short, black cape, which could have been a reject from Quevedo's wardrobe, and a broad-brimmed hat thick with grime. It was a shame he didn't wear a ruff, but even without one, he was the very image of a town governor or bailiff. In his youth, he'd had pretensions to being handsome, witty, and elegant, but his shoulders were already beginning to stoop, and his face, with its dyed mustache, had the pitiful look of someone existing on a very Lenten diet. He also played the trumpet in a theater orchestra. His colleagues referred to him as the *pater familias*, because in every bureaucratic conversation he would make a point of mentioning the many mouths he had to feed on his measly salary of twelve thousand reales (after tax). There were a few other employees, some silently working away at their respective desks, all keeping a deferential distance from the head of department's desk, placed near the window that gave onto the courtyard.

Close by were the stands where the officials hung their cloaks and hats, although Guillén always kept his crutches with him. In between the desks stood rickety shelves and cabinets of the kind only ever seen in offices, some old and looking as if they had been disinterred from the quartermaster's stores—as they very probably had—others new but still somehow unlike any furniture used outside the bureaucratic world. Every desk was piled high with bundles of documents tied up with red tape; the paper in some—documents containing the hopes of several generations—was yellowing and dusty, with a whiff of the cinerary urn about it, while in others, the paper was still clean and new, with fresh writing in the form of marginal notes and illegible signatures. These were the more modern examples of the vast, ongoing dispute between the people and the Tax Office.

Pantoja had been summoned to the director's desk and so wasn't there. Another colleague said:

"Have a seat, Don Ramón. Would you like a cigarette?"

"Now let's see what you lot are up to? (Going over to Guillén's desk and picking up a piece of paper.) Aha. 'An original drama in verse.' The title? 'My Stepsister's Stepdaughter.' So, that's how you idlers spend your time, is it?"

"Oh, have you heard the latest, Don Ramón?" said the elegant Espinosa, taking a sip of coffee. "Cañizares—you remember him, don't you, he worked in Estates and we used to call him the Simpleton—well, he's just had his salary raised to twelve thousand. Another example of barefaced favoritism!"

"Fourteen years ago, he worked in my office on a salary of five thousand," said Argüelles, the *pater familias*, shaking his fist, his face becoming a compendium of all the world's sorrows. "He was so stupid that the only job we could give him was fetching wood for the stove, and he wasn't even any good at that. As thick as a plank, he is. I was earning twelve thousand then, the same as I earn now. Do you call that justice? Wouldn't we be better off collecting dung from the streets than serving the great whore that is the state? I think we can all agree, can't we, that there is, quite frankly, no shame left in the world."

"My friend," said Villaamil with a sad, stoical sigh, "we just have to accept it. You're talking to a man who, when he was in the provinces, had the current director working under him on just six thousand reales. He was in Monopolies and frankly, he couldn't even stick a label on a cigar box."

"You don't have to tell me," said Argüelles. "My father wanted to get me a job as a clerk in a shop, and I got all uppity because I thought it was beneath me; well, when I think of that now, I feel like tearing out the little hair I have left. That was in 1851. Not only would I not even hear of becoming a clerk in a shop, I joined the civil service, which I considered to be a gentlemanly profession, then, to make matters worse, I got married. What a fool I was ... And then, *piano, pianino*, along come nine children, a mother-in-law, and two orphaned nephews. And I'm supposed to provide for them all. And I do, gentlemen, but only thanks to the extra money I earn as a trumpeter. In 1864, my salary went up to twelve thousand reales, and there it has stayed. Do you know who got me that twelve thousand? The actor, Julián Romea, who happened to have some very useful contacts. I'll never get another raise now. I've spent fourteen years in this job, and I don't even bother asking for a promotion anymore. What would be the point? I'd have to threaten them with a gun first ..."

The laments of that trumpeter and *pater familias* were always listened to with great delight. At this point, though, Pantoja returned, and, just as when Aeneas was about to describe the fall of Troy, *conticuere omnes*: they all fell silent. He was wearing a scarlet beret, embroidered with what resembled golden artichokes and adorned with a rather fetching frayed tassel. He had on a very worn brown coat, trousers that bagged at the knee and were short enough to reveal the tops of his new and still unpolished boots. After greeting his friend, he sat down at his desk. Villaamil moved closer, and they talked. Pantoja never once forgot his duties, however, and continued to issue orders to his troops. "Listen, Argüelles, be so kind as to write to the Provincial Finance Department and ask them to ... And Es-

pinosa, fetch me that report on the debit and credit account of…"
Meanwhile, with an expert hand, he untied the tape on a bundle of
documents, which he then proceeded to disembowel. He was equally
skilled at tying the bundles up again, almost caressing them as he
moved them around on his desk or placed them on the shelf.

There was about this man's face a certain spiritual inertia. He had
a broad, smooth forehead, as expressionless as the cover of one of
those account books that has yet to be assigned a label. His nose had
a very broad bridge, which meant that his eyes were so wide apart
that they appeared to have quarreled and to be looking around quite
independently of each other. It was hard to tell where his large mouth
ended, although his ears would know, and his pursed lips seemed to
struggle to open whenever he had to speak, as if they had been expressly
made to be sealed discreetly shut.

Morally, Pantojo was the very model of entrenched traditionalism.
The term "honest functionary" was as much a part of his persona as
his baptismal name, Buenaventura. He was frequently quoted and
named, and to say "Pantoja" was to evoke the very image of morality.
A man of few needs, he lived obscurely and without ambition, con-
tenting himself with a promotion every six or seven years and never
greedy for special privileges or fearful of being suspended, for he was
one of the few who, given their practical, meticulous, painstaking
knowledge of office matters, would never be out of a job. He had
come to consider his bureaucratic longevity as a tribute to his honesty;
indeed, this idea had become a rather exalted feeling, even a supersti-
tion. He was a genuinely honest soul whose worldview was so very
narrow that he became alarmed if he heard someone speak of any
millions that did not belong to the Treasury. Any large sums of money
other than those included in the state budget sent a shiver down his
spine; and if the ministry ever came up with a project involving large
industrial companies or banks, the word *skullduggery* would immediately leap to his lips. He never visited the Treasury without a feeling of horror, as if he were in the presence of some terrifying abyss or
chasm in which lurked danger and death, and whenever some high-
up banker entered the Treasury or the Secretariat, he would tremble

for the wealth of the Exchequer, of which he believed himself to be the guard dog. According to Pantoja, only the state should be rich. All other wealth was the product of bribery and corruption. He had always worked in the Internal Revenue Department, and during his long, assiduous career, he had cultivated in his soul a distinctly unhealthy delight in pursuing the laggardly or deliberately evasive taxpayer, a delight that had something of the cruel enthusiasm of the hunter, for he took an ineffable pleasure in seeing both great and small fighting off their pursuer only to succumb at last, legs thrashing, to the superior skills of the huntsman. According to Pantoja's fixed opinion, in any conflict between the Internal Revenue Department and the taxpayer, the Internal Revenue Department was always right, and this belief was evident in his decisions, which never recognized the rights of the private individual over the state. For him, Property, Industry, even the taxpayer himself, were organisms or instruments of tax evasion, something destructive and revolutionary, whose sole object was to question the immortal rights of the one entity that was the owner and proprietor of everything—namely, the nation. Pantoja never owned anything more than his clothes and his furniture; he was the son of a porter who had worked at the so-called Sala de Mil y Quinientas at the Royal Council, he had been brought up in an attic apartment above the Royal Courts of Justice, and had never left Madrid; all he knew of the world were offices, and for him life was an uninterrupted succession of small services to the state, for which he received, as a reward, his daily bread and some stew.

22

AH, YES, where would the world be without stew? And where would wretched humanity be without salaries? A salary was the only form of earthly goods that accorded with Pantoja's moral principles; for, filed away in his soul was a lofty disdain for all other sources of wealth. He found it very hard to concede that any rich man could possibly be honest, and he viewed large businesses and bold entrepreneurs with religious horror. To acquire a vast fortune in the space of a few years, to move from poverty to opulence was simply impossible to achieve by licit means. For such a thing to happen, one would inevitably have to dirty one's hands and make off with what rightfully belonged to that eternal victim, the primary proprietor, the state. Pantoja could forgive the millionaire who had inherited his fortune and did nothing more than spend it, but he still thought him far from saintly, since, while he, the heir, hadn't actually engaged in thievery, his parents had, and responsibility, like money, is passed from generation to generation.

When he saw one of them arriving and going into the minister's office, some representative of the Rothschilds or another fabulously wealthy family, Spanish or otherwise, he would think how very beneficial it would be to have all those gentlemen sent to the gallows since they only visited the ministry in order to scheme and plot. Pantoja would share these and similar ideas with the other café habitués, and although his very narrow views made him the object of many caustic remarks, he would never back down. Whenever talk turned to the Treasury, Pantoja would immediately brandish his little flag bearing this simple, affirmative motto: Bureaucracy good, politics bad. Down with big business, down with speculation, and down too with those foreigners who only come to Spain to exploit us and run off with the wampum, leaving us poor as church mice. Nor did Pantoja conceal his sympathy for high import tariffs, believing that free trade merely protects foreign industry.

At the same time, he held that landowners are merely in the bad habit of complaining, given that people in Spain pay less tax than anywhere else, because Spain is essentially the natural home of the fraudster, and politics is the art of covering up fraud and, whether silently or violently, plundering the Treasury. In short, Pantoja had only two or three ideas, but they were as deeply carved into his *intellectus* as if they'd been hammered in with mallet and chisel. He had little to contribute to the conversations with his friends at the café, for he never spoke ill of his bosses or criticized the Ministry's plans, never spoke out of turn or revealed anything that should remain secret. There lurked in the depths of his brain a kind of communism of which he himself was unaware. The helter-skelter politics of recent years has done its best to eliminate such civil servants, but there are still a few examples, however scarce.

Pantoja was meticulous, conscientious, and incorruptible as regards his work and remained the implacable enemy of what he called "the private individual." He never found issue with the Treasury, for the Treasury was his paymaster, and he wasn't there to serve the enemies of "the house." As for certain very obscure cases, grown cobwebbed with antiquity and very hard to resolve, he always felt they were best left unresolved, and when, inevitably, the deadline imposed by law was reached, he would immediately consult the self-same law to find the ruse he needed to plunge the case back into obscurity. To draw a line under one of those disputes was tantamount to admitting that the Administration had failed, an admission of defeat and even dishonor. As for his probity, one need hardly say that he immediately sent packing any agents who offered him bribes or inducements to dispatch some business or other promptly and favorably. They knew him well enough not to approach that porcupine whose spines would bristle at the mere presence of "the private individual"—that is, the taxpayer.

In his domestic life, Pantoja was the very model of a model. No household was more methodical than his, no worker-ant harder working than his wife. They were the complete opposite of the Villaamils, who, during clement weather, spent all of Don Ramón's salary and were then left with nothing to eat. Pantoja's wife lacked Doña Pura's fatal itch to put on airs and graces, to pretend to be superior to her means and social position. Señora Pantoja had been a maid (working, I believe, for Don Claudio Antón de Luzuriaga, to whom Pantoja owed his first appointment), and her humble origins inclined her to a life lived in shy, modest obscurity. They never spent more than two thirds of Pantoja's salary, and their children were brought up both to love God and to feel a superstitious dread of worldly pomp and luxury. Despite the close friendship between Villaamil and Pantoja, the former never dared go to the latter with his frequent economic woes; he knew him as well as if he had given birth to him and was perfectly aware that the honest fellow neither asked nor gave and that begging and munificence were both equally incompatible with his nature, which was like a strongbox that opened neither to give nor to receive.

Once seated at his desk, with Villaamil beside him on the nearest chair, Pantoja pushed back his skullcap—for the slightest movement sent it sliding forward over his gleaming pate—and said to his friend:

"I'm glad you dropped by today. The report on your son-in-law's case has just come in. I haven't really had time to read it yet, but it doesn't look good. He blatantly omitted two towns from his last report on tax arrears, and his figures for the last quarter look very fishy indeed."

"My son-in-law is a scoundrel, as you well know. He's sure to have been up to some mischief or other."

"And the director told me yesterday that he's always out and about, dining with friends and spending money like water; and the number of hats and ties he owns is quite astonishing, the rascal's really quite the dandy. Tell me something: Does he live with you?"

"Yes," said Villaamil tartly, feeling his cheeks grow red with shame, for he knew that, by giving in to Pura, he too was wearing clothes bought with Víctor's money. "But I'm hoping he'll leave as soon as possible. I'd sooner die than receive anything from him."

"Because...well, I'm glad to have the opportunity to tell you this...his presence under your roof reflects badly on you—that and the fact that he's your son-in-law—because some people think you're on his side."

"Me? On his side? (A look of horror on his face.) How can you say such a thing?"

"I'm not the one saying it, I wouldn't dream of doing so. But the people here...well, you know how many rogues there are around, and when there are evil rumors flying about, those rogues are always the first to hang an innocent man out to dry."

"Víctor may be my son-in-law, but I find his shenanigans so appalling that if it were in my power to prevent him going to prison, I wouldn't lift a finger to stop it. Imagine that."

"Oh, don't worry, he won't be sent to prison, even if he deserves it. He is fully equipped with a lightning rod *and* a parachute. These times are so corrupt that it's precisely ne'er-do-wells like your son-in-law who always rise to the top. You'll see, they'll bury the report, give him the all-clear, and offer him the promotion his cronies have arranged. He's one of the most shameless devils I've ever known. He was here only yesterday, and of course he went straight in to see the undersecretary, and because he has the gift of blarney and the looks to go with it, the undersecretary—I was told this by someone who was there—welcomed him with open arms, and the two of them were chatting away for more than half an hour."

"Did he see the minister too?" (Said in a most disconsolate voice.)

"That I don't know; but I do know that a deputy from the province where that gem of a son-in-law of yours once worked popped in to recommend him. And that deputy's the kind who the more he gets the more he wants, and he never leaves here without snaffling a few big appointments—I mean really big, and precisely because he's in the opposition, he gets away with it."

"Do you think they'll give Víctor a promotion?" (In a deeply anxious tone.)

"I can't be sure of anything."

"And what about mine, do you know anything about that?" (In an even more anxious tone.)

"The head of personnel isn't giving anything away. Whenever I mention you to him, all he says is 'We'll see' and 'I'll do my best,' which is tantamount to saying nothing at all. Oh, while we're on the subject, after speaking to the undersecretary, Víctor apparently slipped in to see the head of personnel—Espinosa's brother told me this—who showed him what vacancies there were in the provinces, and your little son-in-law said very arrogantly that wild horses wouldn't drag him back there."

"My friend," said Villaamil with a look of pained bewilderment on his face, "I want you to remember what I'm about to say. You'll see for yourself, and if you doubt my words, let's have a bet on it. They'll give Víctor his promotion and give me nothing at all. Anything else would be only fair and reasonable, and reason and fairness have long since gone out of the window."

Pantoja again adjusted his skullcap, which was his way of scratching his head. Then, with a deep sigh—which just managed to escape his lips, for they only ever opened to utter solemn words—he offered his friend this by way of consolation:

"We don't yet know whether they'll be able to ignore that complaint about Víctor, although his protectors are clearly keen to do so. If I were you, I'd continue to pester the director, the undersecretary, and the minister, but I would also look for some useful strings to pull among the high-ups."

"Oh, I keep pulling, but to no effect."

"Well, keep on pulling, man, until you get something. Cozy up to the big fish, whether they're currently ministers or not; go and see Sagasta, Cánovas, Castelar, the Silvela brothers, regardless of their political stripe, because the way you're going about it now, and given how things are, you're never going to get anything. Pez won't be any help, nor will Cucúrbitas, because they're both so burdened down with other commitments; and besides, they'll only find places for their personal coterie, their protégés, their chambermaids, or even their barbers. People like them, who happily served both the Glorious Revolution *and* the Restoration, are up to their necks in water, because now they not only have to look after the current contingent but must take care not to neglect their previous colleagues, who are howling with hunger. Pez has appointed someone who took part in the uprising as well as others who flirted with the federalist movement. He can't allow himself to forget that the republicans kept him on at the Revenue Department and that the supporters of Amadeo I came very close to making him a minister, nor that the moderates from the days of Sister Patrocinio awarded him the Grand Cross."

Villaamil listened glumly and with downcast eyes to this sage advice and could not deny that it was all very reasonable. While the two friends chatted away, totally oblivious to what was going on elsewhere in the office, that wretch Guillén was using his pen to make a comic portrait of Villaamil, and once he had finished the caricature and was satisfied with it, he wrote underneath: "Señor de Miaow, pondering his plans for the Treasury." He handed the drawing to his colleagues to give them a laugh, and his quick sketch passed from desk to desk, momentarily relieving the boredom of the poor unfortunates condemned to the perpetual slavery of the office.

When Pantoja and Villaamil were talking in general terms about their work, their two voices were never in harmony, for they held wildly differing opinions, for whereas Pantoja's views were narrow and exclusive, Villaamil took a more generous view of things and had a systematic plan, the result of his studies and his experience. What enraged Pantoja was his friend's enthusiasm for income tax, which would mean doing away with individual taxes on land, industry, and consumption. A tax based on a declaration that relied wholly on the pride and good faith of the taxpayer made no sense at all in a country where you almost had to string a man up before he would pay his dues. Simplifying matters in general went contrary to that honest fellow's nature, for he enjoyed having plenty of staff and fostering as much confusion and as much red tape as possible. Another reason he felt wary of that mania for getting rid of all those different taxes was that he feared they might get rid of him into the bargain. The two men kept up a heated discussion on the subject until two o'clock, when they finally ran out of breath. And when Pantoja had to leave, summoned by the director, Villaamil was left alone with the subalterns, who were still amusing themselves at his expense, especially that mischievous fellow Guillén, who said:

"I say, Don Ramón, why don't you publish your plan so that the whole country can read about it?"

"Don't talk to me about publishing plans. (Pacing up and down the office in agitated fashion.) As if this vile country would take any notice. The minister has read my plan, and the director looked it over too, but nothing came of it... And that isn't because it's hard to understand, for in the memoranda I wrote, I made a special effort to be (a) simple, (b) clear, and (c) brief."

"Oh, I thought your memoranda were very, very long," said Espinosa gravely. "Given that they cover so many points..."

"Whoever told you that? (Getting angry now.) Each memorandum covers one point and I make just five points, which is quite enough. I wish now that I'd never bothered putting them in writing at all. Blessed are the foolish..."

"...for they are on heaven's payroll...Well said, Don Ramón," remarked Argüelles, shooting a malevolent glance at Guillén, whom he detested. "I had an idea too, but I never spoke about it. I would have been better off composing a trumpet solo."

"Quite right. You concentrate on playing the trumpet and forget about sorting out the Treasury, which, given the way things are now, is clearly going to the dogs. Look, my friend, Argüelles (stopping beside his colleague's desk, his cape pushed back over his shoulder, and gesturing expressively with his right hand), I have devoted my many years of experience to that plan. I might be right and I might be wrong, but I'm definitely on to something, of that there can be no doubt. (Everyone was listening intently.) My work consists of five memoranda or treatises, each with a title to make it more easily understood. First point: *Morality*."

"Excellent. Make way for morality, which should always be given first place."

"It is the basis of administrative order. Morality above and below, left, right, and center. Second point: Income tax."

"Now there's the crux of the matter."

"Do away with taxes on land, industry, and consumption. I would replace it with a tax on income, with a very small municipal surcharge, all very simple, very practical, and very clear; and I set out other ideas on how to collect the tax, how to oblige people to pay, to investigate non-payment, what fines to impose and so on. Third point: Additional import tariffs. Because such tariffs are not only a form of taxation, they're a way of protecting national industry. I suggest a fairly high tariff so that our own factories can prosper and so that we all wear Spanish cloth."

"Far superior to Holland cloth...Don Ramón, Bravo Murillo was a babe in arms compared with you. Go on..."

"Fourth point: Overhaul of the national debt. I bring together all the bonds that are currently out there under different names—three percent consolidated, deferred, debenture bonds and treasury bonds, mortgages, and so on—and exchange them for a single four percent bond...and no more headaches for us."

"You know more than the Jew who invented the Treasury, Don Ramón."

(A chorus of congratulatory remarks. The only one who didn't join in was Argüelles, who preferred not to laugh at Guillén's jokes.)

"It's not a question of me knowing a lot (he said modestly), it's just that I view these administrative affairs as if they were my own, and I would like to see this country set off along the right path. This isn't science; it's a matter of goodwill, application, and hard work, Work being my fifth and final point. Now, have you been paying close attention? No, neither have they. But that's their choice. The day will come when Spaniards have to go barefoot and even the richest will have to beg for their bread—not for money, mind, because no one will have any. That's the way we're heading. Now, I ask you: What possible reason could there be for them to reappoint me head of

Administration? None. So, you can look as hard as you like, but that's something you will never see. Good day."

He left with his shoulders bowed, as if he could not bear the weight of his own head. Everyone felt sorry for him, apart from the pitiless Guillén, who was always quick to come up with some label to pin to his back once he had gone.

"I've written down the five points in the order he said them, and, gentlemen, it's pure gold. Come and have a look. What a joke! Here's the list of the four points: 'Morality, Income tax, Additional import tariffs, Overhaul of the national debt, Work.' Put the initials together and they spell MIAOW."

An explosion of laughter echoed round the room, making it sound more like a theater than an office.

23

AFTER that long dialogue with Víctor, Abelarda continued to feel deeply troubled, but the poor woman tried very hard to conceal her state of mind from her mother and her aunt, and with great success. She had noticed that since making those incomprehensible declarations, Víctor had grown very taciturn. He avoided being alone with her, barely looked at her, and addressed not a single word to her. He appeared to be brooding over some delicate personal matter. After a while, though, it seemed to Abelarda that his mood improved and that he kept shooting her languid, amorous looks, to which she could not help but respond with equally fiery albeit fleeting glances. Víctor would speak to her when the rest of the family were present, but not when they were alone together. They seemed, then, like two people who love each other but dare not declare themselves, and she was waiting for the sudden, unexpected explosion that would inevitably happen, as if the laws of time and space had already chosen the moment to conjoin the orbits of those two beings seemingly compelled to meet. It was during this time that Abelarda the Insignificant began going to church more often. The Villaamil family's religious practices were normally confined to attending Sunday mass at the Convento de las Comendadoras, but while Don Ramón rarely missed a service, Doña Pura and her sister occasionally did, either because they didn't have the right clothes, or because they had things to do, or for some other reason. Abelarda, though, was eager to fortify her spirit with religion and to spend more time in church, thinking; she found consolation in looking at the altars and the sacrarium where God himself is kept, in listening devoutly to mass and contemplating the saints and virgins in their flowing robes. These innocent consolations soon prompted another sweeter and more efficacious idea—that of confession, for she felt an urgent, pressing need to tell someone the secret filling her heart. She was afraid that if she didn't, that secret would, spontaneously and indiscreetly, slip out one day when she was with her parents, and the thought terrified her, because her parents would be furious if they knew. Who could she confide in? In Luis? He was still only a child. It had even occurred to her (idiotically) that she might reveal her secret to that kindly fool Ponce. Finally, though, her resurgence of religious feeling brought its own solution, and the very next morning, she went to the confessional and told the priest what was happening to her, adding details that the priest really didn't need to know. Afterward, Abelarda felt immensely relieved and ready to face whatever might happen next.

As it was Lent, there were services every evening at that church and on Fridays at the churches of Montserrat and Salesas Nuevas. The family were rather taken aback at the frequency with which Abelarda was now attending church, and Doña Pura could not help commenting impertinently: "Well, better late than never!"

Ponce, however, was extremely pleased and indeed almost enthusiastic about his fiancée's devotions, for he was one of the more Catholic young men of the present generation (although, as tends to be the case, more in word than deed), and this helped to soothe Doña Pura's anxieties. The illustrious Ponce occasionally accompanied Abelarda to church for the evening service, despite her repeated requests to be allowed to go alone. He would usually wait for her afterwards and then they would return home together, discussing the preacher much as, on the previous night, they had discussed the singers at the Teatro Real. If Abelarda went to the church earlier in the day, she would go with Luis, who soon grew very fond of these excursions. The boy would spend some time listening devoutly to the service, but would then grow bored and wander about the church, gazing up at the standards of the Order of Saint James hanging in Comendadoras, peering through the large iron grille at the nuns, or inspecting the altars full of wax votive offerings. Luis felt less at home in Montserrat (the church belonging to the old convent that is now the women's prison) than he did in Comendadoras, which is one of the most beautiful and spacious of Madrid's churches. He found Montserrat, in comparison, cold and bare and the saints shabbily dressed; even the services seemed dull; what's more, in the chapel on the right as you went in, there was a huge, dark figure of Christ wearing only a loincloth, his mane of real hair as long as a woman's and his body covered in gobbets of blood. Luis found this figure so disturbing that he would only dare to look at it from a distance and would never have gone into the chapel itself for love nor money.

On his restless meanderings around the church, Luis more than once sat down on a solitary bench, feeling the beginnings of the malaise that usually preceded one of his strange visions. Before he drifted off, he sometimes told himself that he would be sure to see "the man with the white beard" there in the church, since this was, after all, one of his houses. But when he closed his eyes, mentally summoning up that extraordinary visitor, no visitor appeared. Occasionally, though, he thought he spotted the august old gentleman coming out of the sacristy door and somehow disappearing into the altar, as if he had slipped into it through an invisible crack. It also seemed to him that the Lord himself came out, attired in a priestly robe and embroidered chasuble to say mass—*to say mass to himself*—which Luis thought very strange indeed. However, he wasn't sure if this was true; he might well have been mistaken; indeed, he had major doubts about it. One evening, in Montserrat, listening to the priest saying the rosary with about two dozen women and more than a hundred female prisoners in the choir giving the responses, Luis could feel himself being lulled to sleep by the intense murmur of their voices. The church was so poorly lit that it seemed to be all mystery and shadows, shadows made still denser and darker by the gloomy cadence of the prayers. From where Luis was sitting, he could see one arm of that Christ figure, as well as the ceiling lamp lighting it. He was so filled with panic that he would have run out into the street if he could, but he couldn't even stand up. He tried to overcome this torpor and kept pinching his arms, saying: "No, no, if I fall asleep, and that long-haired Christ sits down next to me, I'll just die of fright." Fear and his sterling efforts to remain awake finally drove off the unhealthy torpor.

Whenever his friend and schoolmate Silvestre Murillo, the sacristan's son, appeared, the church of Montserrat provided him with both good and bad experiences, for Silvestre initiated Luis into some of the ecclesiastical mysteries, explaining all kinds of things that Luis didn't understand—for instance, the reservation of the Holy Sacrament, the difference between a gospel and an epistle, why Saint Roch has a dog with him and Saint Peter a bunch of keys: in short, displaying a liturgical erudition that was a wonder to hear. "The host, for example, carries God inside it, and that's why the priests wash their hands before picking it up so as not to get dirt on it, and *dominus vobisco* is like saying: *Watch out, be good*." When they visited the sacristy, Silvestre would show him the vestments, the unconsecrated hosts (which Luis regarded with superstitious respect), as well as the parts of the special altar that would soon be erected for Easter, along with the pallium and the drapery for the cross; and in the casual way Murillo showed him these things and explained them, he revealed a certain skepticism that Luis did not share. Murillo could never persuade him to enter the chapel of the long-haired Christ, even when he told him that he had actually held that hair in his own hands while his mother was combing it and that the "Gentleman" was very kind and had performed all kinds of miracles.

Given how impressionable the minds of children are, and how quickly and energetically their nascent will adapts itself to those impressions, it was hardly surprising that his visits to the church awoke in Luis the desire and intention to become a priest, as he told his grandparents over and over. Everyone laughed at this precocious sense of vocation, and even Víctor was highly amused. However, Luis assured them that, for him, it was either becoming a priest and taking mass or nothing, because he was filled with enthusiasm for all the priestly tasks, including preaching and sitting in the confessional and listening to women's sins. He said this with such charming naiveté that everyone laughed, and Víctor used Luis's words as an opportunity to speak to Abelarda the Insignificant alone for the first time since their earlier, much-pondered conversation. No other adult was present, and the only person who could hear them was Luis, but he was completely immersed in his stamp album.

"While I would not, like my son, say that I wish to be ordained, I have, for some time now, felt an intense need to believe! Whatever you may think, Abelarda, that feeling comes from you (he gave her a long, lingering, tender look), from you and the influence your soul has over mine."

"Well, why don't you just believe then, no one's stopping you," retorted Abelarda, who felt more capable of speech that evening and was hoping to gain some greater clarity from him.

"What stops me are my banal, routine thoughts, the false ideas acquired while out in society, and which, together, form a kind of dense undergrowth very hard to root out. What I need is an angelic teacher, someone who would love me and show some concern for my salvation. But where will I find such an angel? If one does exist, she's not for me. I am a poor, unfortunate wretch. I can see goodness almost within my grasp, but I dare not approach. You are blessed indeed if this feeling is beyond your comprehension."

Abelarda felt now that she had the strength to deal with this matter, because, thanks to religion, she could even confess her secret to someone who should not hear it from her lips.

"I wanted to believe and so I believed," she said. "I sought consolation in God and I found it. Shall I tell you how?"

Víctor, who was sitting at the table clutching his head, suddenly sprang to his feet and declared with the voice and gestures of a consummate histrion:

"No, don't speak. You will only torment me, not console me. I am a reprobate, a sinner...."

He had carefully prepared these superficial phrases, gleaned willy-nilly from various novels, ready to be brought into use at the first opportunity. As soon as he had said them, though, he remembered that he had arranged to meet some friends at the local café and immediately looked for a way of cutting the thread that his sister-in-law had begun to spin between them.

"Abelarda, I must go, because if I stay a minute longer...well, I know what will happen, I will tell you what I must not tell you... not yet at least. Allow me to leave. I am going for a walk—an aimless, wandering, feverish walk through the streets of Madrid, thinking about what cannot be mine... not yet at least...."

He gave a sigh, then another. He left Abelarda feeling confused and puzzled, trying to fathom the meaning of that "not yet at least," words that evoked happy horizons.

That night, before supper, Víctor came back full of good cheer and embraced his father-in-law, who, aghast at such familiarity, was on the point of saying: "Unhand me, sir!" But Víctor soon explained the reason for his good mood. He had been at the ministry that afternoon, and the head of personnel had told him that Villaamil's name would be on the next list.

"Oh, not that again!" exclaimed Don Ramón angrily. "When will you stop mocking me?"

"He's not mocking you," said Doña Pura, filled with sweet hopes. "If he says that, it's because he knows it's true."

"Yes, whether you believe it or not, it's true."

"Well, I refuse to believe it," declared Villaamil, stabbing the air with his right index finger. "And I won't allow anyone to laugh at me, all right? Since when have you bothered to go to the ministry to ask about me? You go there on your own business, to wheedle a promotion out of them, and they'll give it to you too, of that I'm sure. How could they not?"

"Well, I'm telling you (said with great energy) that I may well have gone there on other occasions with that intention, but today I went there—in the company, I should say, of two very influential deputies—purely and simply to intercede on your behalf, to praise you to the heavens to the head of personnel, having first sounded out the minister. I'm not telling you this to earn your gratitude; besides, there's no particular merit in what I did. And just as sure as the sun will rise each and every day (very solemnly), I said to my friends, who support my demands: 'Gentlemen, before you even think of promoting me, I beg you to reinstate my father-in-law.' And I repeat that I did not do this in order to be thanked by anyone. It's the very least I could do."

Doña Pura looked absolutely radiant, and Villaamil, his pessimism shaken, resembled a combatant who, suddenly stripped of his defenses, stands naked and unarmed before the enemy's guns. He struggled to regain his pessimistic aplomb. "Sheer nonsense . . . And even if it were true that Tom, Dick, and Harry had all recommended me, does that necessarily mean they will reinstate me? Leave me in peace and plead your own case, because you only have to open your mouth and they'll give you a promotion, whereas I could pester the whole human race to death and still get nothing."

Abelarda did not say a word, but her heart was filled with gratitude toward Víctor, and she felt proud to love him, telling herself that there could now be no possible doubt about how genuine his feelings were. How could that fine, noble voice ever utter anything but the truth? While they were eating, the debate continued, with Villaamil stubbornly insisting that the upper ministerial echelons would never take pity on him, while the whole family valiantly argued the opposite. Then Luis came out with the sentence that became famous in the family for a whole week and was repeated ad nauseam, celebrated either as a priceless example of childish wit or as one of those flashes of wisdom that can sometimes descend from the divine mind to that of certain beings in direct communication with the divinity. The mixture of enchanting innocence and arrogant aplomb with which Luis said these words only added to their charm:

"But Grandpa, don't be so silly. Why do you keep asking and asking those men from the ministries, who are mere nobodies, and who never take any notice of you anyway? Ask God, go to church, pray, and you'll see, God will give you that new post."

Everyone roared with laughter, but these inspired words had a very different effect on Villaamil. His eyes almost filled with tears, and he thumped the table with the handle of his fork, saying:

"This little devil knows more than any of us, and more than the whole world."

24

VÍCTOR left immediately after dessert, which consisted, as it happens, of some very fine Alcarria honey, and afterward, Doña Pura scolded her husband for the rude incredulity with which he had received his son-in-law's news.

"Why wouldn't he want to help you? We shouldn't always think the worst of people. Besides, if Víctor hadn't bothered to put in a word for you, he certainly should have."

"Of course," said Abelarda, ready to offer up a passionate panegyric to her brother-in-law, whom she couldn't understand when it came to matters of love but whose much-vaunted reputation as a cad she believed to be slanderous.

"Are you women really such innocent fools," said Villaamil, growing furious, "that you believe anything that lying cheat tells you? I bet you anything you like that, far from recommending me, he went there with some story that would have doused any faint desire the head of personnel might possibly have had to reinstate me..."

"Honestly, Ramón!"

"Papa, please! How can you say such things?"

"It's just unbelievable that, after all these years, you still don't realize that that man (growing ever angrier) is the most evil, treacherous creature under the sun. To make him all the more terrible, God—who in his wisdom chose to make a few other dangerous animals alarmingly beautiful—only gave Víctor that sweet look, that tender smile, and the gift of flattery with which to deceive those who don't know him, so that he could befuddle, fascinate, and then devour them afterward. He's the most monstrous..."

Villaamil stopped, realizing that also present in the room was Luis, who should not have to hear such an "apologia." Víctor *was* the boy's father after all. And the poor child was staring at his grandfather with terrified eyes. Abelarda, as if her very heart were being plucked from her piece by piece, felt, first, a desire to burst into tears, then a brutal impulse to contradict her father, to cover his mouth, or to heap insults on his venerable head. She stood up and went to her room, pretending that she was looking for something, and from there she continued to hear the murmur of conversation. Doña Pura was timidly denying what her husband had said, and he, once Luis had left the room—summoned to the kitchen by Milagros to wash his face and hands—repeated his barbarous, implacable, bloodthirsty anathema against Víctor, adding that he wouldn't have any dealings with him for all the tea in China. Villaamil said this with such feeling and conviction that Abelarda felt she might go mad there and then, thinking that the only solution for her wild grief would be to leave the house, run to the viaduct in Calle de Segovia, and throw herself off. She imagined the brief moment before she plunged into the abyss, her petticoats flying up around her, her head about to crack open on the paving stones below. How wonderful! Followed by the sensation that she was becoming mere mush, nothing more. All her troubles over.

Shortly after this, the select crowd who occasionally gathered in that elegant mansion began to arrive. Milagros, having finished in the kitchen, lit the oil lamp in the living room. She smoothed her clothes, leaving the old lady they employed to do the dishes alone, for while our "Modest Ophelia" may have happily embraced every branch of the culinary arts, she drew the line at the coarse business of washing up, and she entered the "salon" looking pleasingly well turned out. Abelarda took longer to appear, and when she did, her face was so thick with powder she resembled a miller's daughter, and all that powder failed to disguise her cadaverous complexion or the dark circles under her eyes. Virginia Pantoja, along with her mother and the other ladies, observed her in silence, saving any comments for later. However, they did all say privately to themselves: "Goodness, she *is* looking old!" Also present was Salvador Guillén, who had come to introduce his colleague from the office, the elegant Espinosa. As soon as these guests began arriving, Villaamil left the house, cursing such gatherings, and instead spent a few hours in the café discussing the imminent crisis or assuring them that, as sure as two and two make four, there definitely would be a crisis. Pantoja usually went with him, returning afterward to fetch his family, and on the way, they would mull over the same eternal, inexhaustible, insoluble subject. As an expert on bureaucratic life and the mysterious psychological energies that determine the rise and fall of civil servants, Pantoja was drawing up a new plan of campaign for his friend. While he should, of course, continue his search for a dynamic patron among those with political influence, he must also keep pestering the minister and the head of personnel; he must become their shadow, watching their every move, attacking them when they least expected it, and even making the ultimate demand: "A letter of recommendation or your life." Yes, terror was always the best weapon—after all, ministers, undersecretaries, and heads of personnel were human too, and in order to live and breathe freely again, they would end up giving the bothersome wretch whatever he wanted, simply to have him out of sight and out of mind. While acknowledging that this advice made genuine human and political sense, Villaamil loathed the fact that he had now sunk low enough to become what he had so often despised in others: an importunate pest and an unrelenting beggar.

Víctor did not usually stay for such domestic gatherings, but that night, he returned home earlier than usual and went into the living room, provoking admiring glances from Virginia Pantoja and the Cuevas girls. He was so superior in every way to the men they usually saw there! Guillén detested him, and since the feeling was entirely mutual, the two men would fire double-edged comments at one another, to the great amusement of the other guests.

The following day, before lunch, when Víctor, Doña Pura, Abelarda, and Luis were in the dining room, Luis having just returned from school, Víctor said to Doña Pura:

"Why on earth do you invite that vile cripple into our home? Don't you realize that he only comes here to amuse himself watching you, so that he can tell tales about you back in the office?"

"Are we so very odd," said Doña Pura casually, "that a lame duck like him would bother coming here just to laugh at us?"

"He's a poisonous toad who only has to see something slightly less grubby than himself to start drooling with envy. When Papa goes to see Pantoja in the office, what do you think Guillén does? He draws a caricature of him. There's already quite a collection of them being handed around among those other idlers. Yesterday, for example, I saw one with a caption saying: *Señor Miaow pondering his plan for the Treasury*. It had been doing the rounds from office to office until Urbanito Cucúrbitas took it to Personnel, where that fool Espinosa, the brother of the dandified fellow who was here last night, pinned it to the wall as a joke to make visitors laugh. When I saw it, I really hit the roof, and we nearly came to blows about it."

Doña Pura was so indignant she could barely breathe or speak.

"Well, I'll tell that reptile never to set foot in my home again. And what did you say he called my husband? The *nerve* of the man..."

"They're only calling him by the nickname the people at the theater have given to the whole family," said Víctor, sweetening this cruel remark with a smile. "It's a very silly nickname if you ask me."

"You mean they call *us* the Miaows?" the two sisters exclaimed, red-faced with rage.

"Oh, don't take it too seriously, it's not worth it. It's common knowledge that when you take your seats up in the gods, everyone says: 'Ah, the Miaows are here.' Ridiculous, really."

"And you have the cheek to laugh at their joke!" cried Doña Pura, picking up the first thing that came to hand, which happened to be a bread roll, and aiming it at her son-in-law's head.

"Now, now, don't take it out on me, Señora; I didn't invent the nickname. If I were to accompany you one night, and a member of that vulgar crew dared say it in my presence, well, I can tell you, one blow from me and he wouldn't have a tooth left in his mouth."

"Oh, you really think you're something, don't you? (Swallowing her rage.) You're all talk, you are. It's just lucky you're not the only person we have to defend us..."

The anger of the two sisters was as nothing in comparison with the fury filling little Luis's mind when he heard that Guillén called his grandfather names and held him up to ridicule; he said to himself: "This is all the fault of the Joker, and I'm going to give him what for, because that cow of a mother of his, Guillén's sister, she was the one who came up with the blasted nickname in the first place and then told that poisonous toad of a scoundrel brother of hers, who then spread it round the office."

He was so furious that, when he went back to school, he was clenching his fists and grinding his teeth. If he had met the Joker in the street, he would have really gone for him and "punched him right in the face." He ended up sitting next to him in class, where he jabbed him with his elbow, saying:

"I don't want anything to do with you, you creep. You're no gentleman, and your family aren't gentlemen either."

The Joker did not respond but rested his head on his arm and closed his eyes as if overcome by sleep. Luis noticed then that his friend's face was very red, his eyelids puffy, and that he was breathing heavily through his mouth or making snorting noises as if to unblock his nose. However hard Luis jabbed him with his elbow, he couldn't shake him out of that leaden torpor.

"What the heck's wrong with you? Are you ill?"

The Joker's face was red hot. The teacher came over to him and, seeing the state he was in and that it was impossible to get him to sit up, took a closer look at him, felt his pulse, then placed one hand on his forehead.

"You're ill, child. Run along home and have them put you to bed and cover you up so that you can sweat it out."

The Joker staggered to his feet and, with a grim look on his face, wobbled out of the room. Some of his classmates watched him enviously because he was being allowed home before everyone else. Others—among them Luis—thought he was just putting it on, a comedy act so that he could get out of school and spend the afternoon playing in the Retiro Park with the ragtag and bobtail of Madrid, because the Joker was very sharp, a born liar, and no one could beat him when it came to inventing stories and practical jokes.

The following day, Silvestre Murillo reported that the Joker was ill with typhus, that he had it so bad that if his fever didn't go down that night, he would die. There was some discussion outside school as to whether to visit him or not. "You might catch it." "It's not catching, stupid." "Who are you calling 'stupid'?" "You." Finally, Murillo, another boy they called Slowcoach, and Luis went to visit the patient. The house was only a short distance from the school and had a lamp outside and a pawnbroker's sign. They went boldly up the stairs, still arguing over whether or not typhus was catching, and Murillo, who was doing most of the talking, encouraged his friends by declaring roundly:

"Oh, don't be so wet. Do you really think you're going to die just by going inside their apartment?"

They rang the bell and a woman opened the door, but when she saw those small and insignificant visitors, she ignored them and left them standing there, not even deigning to respond to Murillo's question. Then another woman came into the hall and said:

"What do you young monkeys want here? Ah, have you come to ask after Paquito? Well, he's a lot better this afternoon..."

"Show them in," came a female voice from inside. "See if my little boy knows them."

As they went in, they saw the pawnbroker's office, in which sat a gentleman wearing a skullcap and spectacles who (thought Luis) resembled a government minister, then they walked through another large room full of clothes—whole seas and oceans of clothes—before finally reaching a room replete with neatly folded cloaks, each in its own numbered box, and there was the patient, with, beside him, two nurses, one sitting on the floor, the other standing beside the bed. The Joker had been horribly delirious all night and part of the morning, but for the moment, he was quieter, and the fever had not yet returned.

"Sweetie," said the woman or lady beside the bed, and who must have been his mother, "your little friends have come to ask how you are. Would you like to see them?"

The poor boy gave a groan, as if he were about to burst into tears, which is the sound sick children make to indicate what they find disagreeable or troublesome, which tends to be absolutely everything.

"Look, here they are. They're obviously very fond of you."

Paquito turned over in bed and, propping himself up on one elbow, shot his friends a look of glassy astonishment. His eyes, though red and puffy, were very dull, his lips so dark they looked almost black, and there were two wine-red spots of color on his cheeks. Luis felt a mixture of pity and instinctive terror that made him keep a safe distance from the bed. His classmate's fixed, lifeless gaze frightened him. Of the three friends, Paquito clearly only recognized Luis, because all he said was "Miaow, Miaow" before slumping back on his pillow. His mother gestured to them to leave the room, and they meekly obeyed. In the next room, they came across two of the Joker's younger brothers, all grubby faces and ragged trousers, wearing filthy pinafores and with holes in their shoes. One of them was dragging a rag doll by a piece of string tied around its neck, and the other was playing with a legless horse, yelling like a desperado, "Come on, gee up, gee up!" When they saw the three boys, they ran over to them, wanting to make friends, but Murillo, acting the grown-up, told them off for making so much noise when their brother was ill. They stared at him, uncomprehending. They had no idea what he was talking about. From the pocket in his pinafore, the younger child took a piece of much-chewed bread, sticky with saliva, and bit into it. As they walked back through the living room, the man who looked like a government minister was examining two embroidered shawls a woman was showing him. The three friends greeted him with exquisite courtesy, but he did not answer.

25

LUIS RETURNED home that afternoon in a pensive mood. He didn't feel as sorry for his classmate as he should have, because that nincompoop had insulted him, throwing that shameful nickname in his face, and in front of other people too. Children are implacable in their resentments, and friendship puts down no real roots in them. Nevertheless, and even though he could not forgive his rude school-mate, he decided to pray for him thus: "Make the Joker get better. It won't be that difficult. You just have to say, 'Arise, Joker,' and that will be that." Then, remembering that his friend's mother, the same lady who had been standing by the bed looking so upset, had been the one to invent that cruel nickname, all his acrimonious feelings returned. "She's not a lady," he thought. "She's just a woman, and now God is punishing her for giving other people nicknames."

That night he was very restless; he slept badly, waking again and again, his brain struggling anxiously with a very strange phenomenon. He had gone to bed hoping to see his kind friend with the white beard; however, despite him having all the usual symptoms, his friend did not appear. What Luis found painful was that he kept dreaming that he could see him, but this wasn't the same as actually seeing him. Anyway, he wasn't satisfied, and his mind continued to grapple with this absurd, difficult thought: "No, that's not him, because I'm not really seeing him, I'm just dreaming that I can see him, and he's not talking to me, I'm just dreaming that he's talking to me." He moved from these febrile ponderings to this: "Anyway, he wouldn't be able to tell me off now for not studying hard enough, because today I actually knew my lesson. The teacher even said: 'Very good, Cadalso.' And the whole class was simply flabbergasted. I explained all that stuff about the adverb and only stumbled over one word. And when it came to the manna falling in the desert, I knew that too, and the only thing I got wrong was about the Commandments, when I said they were written on a table instead of a tablet." Luis was exaggerating his success in class that day. True, he had known his lesson better than usual, but there was no real reason for such self-congratulatory rhetoric.

Both inhabitants of that narrow room had a bad night, for Abelarda did nothing but toss and turn on her hard bed, unable to sleep, or only for a few brief moments, before she was shaken awake by strange shiverings that prompted her to utter words the sound of which startled even her. Once she said: "I'll run away with him." And then a sighing voice answered: "With the one who had the cigar rings." When she heard this, she sat up in bed, terrified. Who had spoken those words? All was silence in the room, but shortly afterward, the voice spoke again, saying: "He's punishing you for being naughty, for giving people nicknames." Finally, Abelarda's mind grew clearer, and she returned to reality, recognizing her nephew's soft voice. She turned over then and fell asleep. Luis was half murmuring, half moaning, as if he wanted to cry but couldn't. "I did know my lesson, I did." And later: "Don't lick my stamp with your black tongue...You see? That's what you get for being naughty. Your mama isn't a lady, she's a woman..." To which Abelarda responded: "That tarted-up woman who writes to you isn't a lady, she's a hideous old cow. Silly man, and yet you prefer her to me—me, who would die for you...Mama, Mama, I want to be a nun." "No," Luis was saying, "I know you didn't give the Commandments to Señor Moses on a table, but on a tablet... All right, two tablets...The Joker's going to die. His father will wrap him in an embroidered shawl...You can't really be God because you haven't any angels...Where *are* the angels?"

And Abelarda: "I've already stolen the key to the front door. I want to escape. Fancy waiting for me out in the street on a cold night like this...Just listen to that rain!"

Luis: "There's a mouse coming out of the Joker's mouth, a black mouse with a very long tail. I'll hide under the table. Papa!"

Abelarda out loud: "What? What is it, Luis? What's wrong? Poor little thing... it's those nightmares of yours again. Wake up, love, you're talking nonsense. Why are you calling for your papa?"

Luis was also awake now, although he was still not thinking very clearly: "I'm not asleep, Auntie. There's this mouse, but my papa has caught it. Can't you see my papa?"

"Your papa isn't here, silly. Go to sleep."

"Yes, he is; look, over there. I'm awake, Auntie. Are you?"

"Wake up properly, sweetheart. Shall I turn on the light?"

"No... I'm sleepy. It's just that everything is so very big, everything, and my papa was in bed beside me, and when I called to him, he picked me up."

"Look, dear, lie on your other side and then you won't have bad dreams. Which side are you lying on now?"

"My left side. Why is everything so huge, so big?"

"Lie on your right side, my love."

"I'm lying on the side of my left hand and my right foot. Do you see? This is my right foot, but it's so big. That's why the Joker's mama isn't a lady. Auntie..."

"What?"

"Are you asleep? I'm going to go to sleep now. The Joker isn't going to die, is he?"

"Of course not. Don't even think such a thing."

"Tell me something else. Is my papa going to marry you?"

In the cerebral turmoil brought on by the darkness and by insomnia, Abelarda could not respond as she would have in the clear light of day and with a clear head, which is why she allowed herself to say:

"I'm not sure, I'm really not at all sure... Possibly..."

Shortly afterward, Luis murmured "Good," as if he were pleased with her answer, then fell asleep. Abelarda, though, didn't sleep another wink all night, and the next day she woke very early with a thick head, heavy eyelids, and in a very bad mood, wanting to do something new and outrageous, to start an argument with someone, even if it was the priest whose mass she intended to hear, or the altar boy who would assist him. She duly went to church, where she had many very bad thoughts, such as running away from home for no particular reason, marrying Ponce then deceiving him, becoming a nun and inciting the other nuns to mutiny, making a mock declaration of love to Guillén, beginning her role in the play and then withdrawing halfway through, leaving them all high and dry; poisoning Federico Ruiz, throwing herself over the balcony from her seat in the gods at the Teatro Real and landing in the stalls at the high point of the opera ... and other such wild notions. However, sitting there in the calm, silent church and hearing three masses one after the other gradually calmed her nerves, allowing normal thoughts to return. When she left the church, she felt rather alarmed and even amused by all that extravagant nonsense. She could understand throwing herself over the balcony at the theater in a moment of despair, but why poison poor Federico Ruiz? Whatever for?

When she arrived home, the first thing she did, as had become customary, was to ask whether Víctor had gone out or not. As it happened, he had, and Doña Pura said with undisguised glee that her son-in-law would be lunching elsewhere. Her resources had been dwindling as quickly as that salt-dissolved-in-water we call money. It was so strange! The moment she changed a five-peseta piece, all five pesetas were gone. And she could already see, fast approaching, the terrifying boundary that separates scarcity from utter penury. Familiar specters were gazing across at her from beyond that boundary and pulling mocking faces. They were her terrible lifelong companions—debt, beggary, and pawnage—determined to follow her to the grave. She had already put out feelers to see if Víctor would give her a means of cutting loose from those ghastly companions, but as soon as she so much as hinted at this, Víctor had pretended not to understand, which was a sign that his wallet no longer contained the treasures of happier days. She had also noticed that on a couple of occasions now, shoemakers or tailors had come to see him, expecting to be paid, and Víctor had put them off, either telling them to come back another day or promising he would go and see them shortly. This intimation of hard times ahead made Doña Pura very nervous indeed.

That afternoon, Doña Pura and her sister went to visit some friends.

Milagros charged Abelarda with sorting out the kitchen, but the overwrought young woman—on finding herself alone, because Villa-amil had gone to the ministry and Luis to school—forgot all about the pots and pans and went into Víctor's room, intending to rummage around, investigate, and generally make close contact with his clothes and other possessions. In undertaking this forbidden inspection, Abelarda the Insignificant felt a stimulating mixture of curiosity and profound spiritual delight. Just being able to examine his clothes and explore every pocket, even if she found nothing of any interest, was a pleasure she would not have exchanged for other more obvious, less dubious ones. For, while handling his shirts, she fantasized about moments of intimacy that her vivid imagination invested with every appearance of reality. She dreamed of performing noble acts, like looking after her man's clothes, whether he was her husband or not, eager to make some small repair, a loose button or a lining come unstitched, and meanwhile recognizing his smell, even though he was always very clean and elegant, and enjoying being able to savor it from closer up than when her family and other people were around. On the few occasions that Abelarda had been able to indulge in such orgies of fantasy and recondite sensations, her rummagings in his pockets had shed no light on the mystery she felt enfolded Víctor's existence. In his trouser pocket she sometimes found a few coins of different values, tram tickets and theater tickets; and in his jacket or frock coat, a note from the ministry perhaps, or some mundane letter. When she finished, she was always careful to return everything to its proper place, so that he wouldn't notice she had been there, and then she would sit down on the trunk to ponder. There had been no space in Víctor's room for a chest of drawers or a wardrobe, which meant that he kept all his other belongings in that same trunk, as if he were merely spending a few days at an inn. What drove Abelarda to despair was that she always found the trunk locked, for she would love to have been able to examine its contents with hands and eyes. What secrets would that mysterious piece of luggage hold? She had tried several times to open it with different keys, but in vain.

Then, believe it or not, on that very day when she sat down on the trunk, she heard a metallic clink. She looked and saw that the keys were in the lock! Contrary to his usual cautious, prudent habits, Víctor had forgotten to take them with him. Seeing the keys and lifting the lid happened almost simultaneously. Inside, the top layer was full of clutter. There was a battered soft felt hat, various shirt collars and cuffs, cigars, a box of writing paper and envelopes, under-wear, a few knitted items, folded-up newspapers, and cravats, some old and some brand-new. Abelarda studied all this for a while with-out touching anything, making sure, as curious people and thieves always do, that she knew exactly where everything went, so that she would be able to put each item back in the same place. Then she moved that one layer aside and began exploring the second layer. She didn't know quite where to begin. At the same time, what prevailed over any other ideas was the assumption that Víctor was involved with some very upper-class society lady of the highest rank. She would soon know everything; she was sure now to find irrefutable proof. This expectation so dominated Abelarda that, even before she found the corpus delicti, she thought she could smell it, because, in her investigations, smell was perhaps her keenest sense. "Ah! I thought so! What's this? A bunch of violets." And as she carefully picked up an item of clothing, she found beneath it a faded, highly scented posy. She continued her explorations. With all the force of a guiding light or a mysterious omen, her instinct, intuition, or whatever it was was leading her down into those disorderly depths. She carefully removed a few more objects and placed them on the floor, then carried on searching here and there, until her febrile hand alighted upon a bundle of letters. Aha! Finally, she had found the key to the secret. Well, it was sure to be there, wasn't it? She picked up the bundle, and just holding it in her hand filled her with fear at her own discovery.

She could already make out a few words without removing the rubber band, because the letters had no envelopes. The first thing that jumped out at her was the coronet on the letter heading, and since she knew nothing about heraldry, she had no idea if this indi-cated a marchioness or a countess . . . Abelarda thought then how very wise and perspicacious she had been. Yes, she had been quite right when she assumed that the mysterious person with whom *he* was involved would be someone from the upper echelons of society. Víctor had been born to inhabit the higher spheres of life, just as the eagle is born to soar up to the heights. It was absurd to think that such a man could descend to the banal, shabby spheres that she inhabited, and reasoning thus, she managed to persuade herself that Víctor's incomprehensible, obscure language and behavior were only incomprehensible and obscure because she was too dim, and her understanding of life too crude for her to be able to grasp how very superior a man he was.

The hour had come. She didn't know where to begin. She would have liked to read the whole bundle from beginning to end, but time was pressing, and her mother and her aunt would soon be back. She quickly read one letter, and every sentence was like being stabbed with a knife. There was a refusal to break off the relationship, excuses offered in response to some jealous accusation; the letter was full of saccharine terms that Abelarda had only ever read in novels; it was all elegant turns of phrase and declarations of eternal love, hopes for future happiness, plans to meet again and sweet memories of past encounters, as well as the careful precautions required to avoid suspicion, and, finally, more outpourings of love. But however hard Abelarda looked, nowhere could she find a name, the name of that shameless hussy. The signature did not help either; sometimes it was some conventional expression, like "your sweetheart" or "your babykins"; and sometimes just a scrawl... But as for a name, not a trace. Had she had time to read all the letters carefully, she would have been able to work out, by various hints and references, who that "babykins" was, but Abelarda could not linger; it was getting late, someone was knocking at the door... She had to put everything back in its place so that Víctor would not notice that someone had been ferreting about in there. She did this quickly and went to open the door. She could not forget the imagined face of that hated lady, not then nor in the days that followed. Who could she be? Abelarda the Insignificant thought she was sure to be some gorgeous, terribly chic woman, capricious and confident, as Abelarda assumed all upper-class women were. "She must be so pretty! And the perfumes she'll use!" she would say to herself all the time, in words of fire that leaped from her brain to sear themselves on her heart. "And the clothes she must have, the hats, the carriages!"

26

THERE'S our friend Don Ramón, once again heading off to Pantoja's office. He doesn't intend to speak about his plight—about the terrible, heartrending situation he finds himself in—but, without meaning to, he does, for everything he says drifts unerringly toward that eternal subject. It's the same with passionate lovers, who, regardless of what they're talking or writing about, always end up speaking of love. That day, in his friend's office, he found a man engaged in a heated discussion. He was a gentleman from the provinces, one of the enemies of the Administration, to whom the "honest functionary" referred scornfully as "private individuals"; the man was a wholesale vintner who also ran a retail business, and the Treasury, having caught him out, was making him pay taxes on both businesses. The man protested that he was in the process of closing his shop and concentrating solely on his warehouse. The matter had been passed to Pantoja to resolve. There was this "private individual" complaining about having to pay tax on two businesses—and what did Pantoja do? He told him that he'd have to pay *three* lots of tax. The man, of course, was spitting fire and said such dreadful things about the Administration that he almost got himself thrown out in the street. Villaamil realized that the man was quite right. Unlike his friend Pantoja, he had never been the arch enemy of the "private individual," but he dared not say anything because this would risk him falling out with the "honest functionary." In his feeble moral state, he even supported the Administration's resident Draco, saying: "Of course you must pay, in your three roles as retailer, wholesaler, and maker of wines."

Finally, the unfortunate man left, singing as loudly as a nightingale in mating season, and when Villaamil and Pantoja were left alone, the former immediately asked:

"Has Víctor been back? How's the case against him going?"

Pantoja did not respond at once; indeed, he looked as if his lips had been sewn together. He was busy opening letters, inside which he could hear the rustle of sand stuck to the now dry ink, and to ensure that not a single grain would be lost, the "honest functionary" was carefully tipping any grains into the sander on his desk. This was an old habit of his—reusing the sand or pounce powder used in another office—and he performed it with meticulous care, as if he were guarding the interests of his mistress, Senōra Treasury.

"Believe me," he said at last, allowing his lips to open and shielding them with one hand so that the other clerks would not hear. "They won't do anything to your son-in-law. The complaint is nothing but hot air. Believe me, I know what I'm talking about."

"Influence can get you anything," said Villaamil grimly. "It can absolve criminals and even reward them, while loyal men die."

"And it's not political influence that turns the world upside down and makes a mockery of justice . . . there are other forms of influence that overturn far more apple carts."

"What are they?"

"Petticoats," said Pantoja so softly that Villaamil couldn't hear him and had to ask him to repeat the phrase.

"Oh well, what else is new? But tell me, do you think that's the case with Víctor?"

"Well, my nose certainly thinks so. (Mischievously tapping the side of his nose.) I have no proof, but I've been in this place for so long now, Ramón, that I can smell things like that . . . I may be wrong, of course, and time will tell, but last night in the café, Ildefonso Cabrera, Víctor's brother-in-law, was telling us a few tales about what Víctor has been getting up to . . ."

"Scandalous!" cried Villaamil, clutching his head. And in the midst of his Catonian indignation at the ignominious thought of those poisonous petticoats, he was wondering why there were no beneficent petticoats, which, by favoring decent men like him, could be of service to the Administration and to the country.

"That rogue knows what he's doing. Mark my words: They'll bury that complaint..."

"And then on with his promotion! On with the motley!"

The bell rang, summoning Pantoja to the director's office. As soon as he had gone, the other clerks rushed over to Villaamil.

"Villaamil, my friend, neither you nor I are going to prosper until our lot get into power, and 'our lot' are the petroleurs."

"Yes, if only they could get into power tomorrow," said Don Ramón, his jaw quivering and his eyes at their fiercest and most carnivorous.

"This is no joking matter, because things are looking very bad. There's a crisis looming."

"Oh, I wasn't joking. This is no time for jokes. I wish the whole of Madrid would rise up tonight and we could have the Paris Commune all over again and set everything ablaze. I'm telling you, our friend Job was just a spoiled child who only complained out of habit. Bring on Saint Petroleum! They can't take more from us than they already have. No one can be worse than this lot."

"Have you heard the latest? They say they're going to cede the Balearics to Germany... And they want to lease out Customs to some Belgian company, with, as an initial downpayment, a few old railway bridges."

"I can almost see it now, my friend...That might be a joke elsewhere, but it's a serious matter here. Don Antonio may be a shrewd enough fellow, but frankly, you'd never know it. I reckon almost anyone could do a better job than him."

"Of course," said Argüelles, smoothing his waxed mustache. "What if we were to form our own ministry, with Villaamil as first minister. And our elegant colleague Espinosa would go to the Foreign Office and sort out the diplomatic service."

"Terrific stuff! And we'll put Guillén in charge of the War Office!"

"Good grief, a cripple in the War Office! He'd be better off in the admiralty."

"Yes, then he could use his crutches as oars."

"And he does resemble a turtle," said Argüelles, who could never resist getting a dig in at Guillén. "And for me, the Home Office."

"Agreed. Then you can appoint your whole caravan of children as temporary staff, including the babes in arms."

"*And* issue a royal edict commanding that the trumpet must be played at all funerals. But what about the Treasury, gentlemen?"

"The Treasury must go to Villaamil, along with the post of first minister."

"And what shall we give to the excellent Pantoja?"

"Why, *he* should have the Treasury of course," said Villaamil, who, while taking none of this banter seriously, was letting the joke run simply to enjoy a little light relief from his own anguished thoughts.

"That would be disastrous. What would become of income tax?"

"Ah," said Villaamil with a wan smile, "I had forgotten about that."

"No, definitely not Pantoja, because if he was in charge, he'd put a tax on the fleas on your back. Long live income tax, the dogma of the new cabinet, and long live the overhaul of the national debt."

"That," said Villaamil, grown serious now and yawning, "is something Pantoja might allow me. Now come on, gentlemen (like someone returning to his senses and springing to his feet), you have work to do, and so do I. Back to work!"

He moved on to the Estates Office (on the same floor to the right), where Francisco Cucúrbitas was second in command, and from there, he went to drop like a bomb on the Personnel Department, where he had various acquaintances, among them a man called Sevillano, who sometimes kept him up to date on any real or possible vacancies. Then he went down to the Treasury, before making a brief visit to the postal services section, although not without first having his usual chinwag with the porters outside each office. In some he was received with a slightly frosty cordiality, in others his frequent visits were beginning to grow tiresome. No one knew what they could possibly say to give him hope, and those who had told him to keep on pestering were beginning to regret their kindly advice, now that the advice was being practiced on them. Villaamil was at his most persistent and annoying in the Personnel Department. The head of that department—a slippery individual and a nephew of Pez's—knew Villaamil, although not well enough to perceive the man's many excellent qualities beneath his guise as an importunate petitioner. And as Villaamil's visits multiplied, Pez grew extremely brusque and made it clear that he did not wish to talk to him at all. Villaamil was a very sensitive soul and found such rebuffs horribly painful, but absolute necessity obliged him to make the supreme effort and brazen it out. Nevertheless, he sometimes came away feeling very low and saying to himself: "I can't do it, I just can't. I can't play the role of obdurate mendicant." As a consequence, he would stay away from the Personnel Department for a few days, until the tyrannical law of necessity reimposed itself in brutal terms; pride rose up against simply being ignored, and—like a starving wolf who, regardless of danger, sets off across the fields and, undaunted, approaches the farmhouse in search of an animal or a man—Don Ramón, hungry for justice, would return to the Personnel Department, braving all rebuffs, all surly faces and even surlier responses. The person who received him most warmly and encouragingly, gladly offering his help, was Don Basilio Andrés de la Caña (Tax Office). Villaamil would return home from such excursions exhausted in mind and body. His wife would do her best to interrogate him, but he stood firm in his pose of studied dignity, insisting that he had only gone to the ministry to smoke a cigar with his friends and that, since he expected nothing and had no hopes of being reappointed, the family should prepare themselves for a little trip to the poorhouse rather than building castles in the air. Doña Pura would respond by saying that if he wasn't doing anything to get reappointed, then *she* would have to get to work, asking Señora de Pez, Carolina de Lantigua, to intervene on his behalf, because even cats know that when political string-pulling fails, you have to resort to the petticoat brigade.

"No, no, she's not the kind of petticoat brigade that makes and unmakes fortunes," said Villaamil in a tone of profound skepticism, knowing the bureaucratic world as he did. "Carolina Pez is an honest woman, and therefore of no use in such matters. Besides, the Carolinas of this world have no influence anymore; they simply bumble along. There is even talk of dropping them completely. Imagine that: people who have drunk from every udder and survived the Glorious Revolution *and* the arrival of our little King Alfonso... But the sweetmeats they enjoy should rightfully be for us, the loyal servants who are left here howling at the moon. In fact, there are already murmurings against them. I'll go further: The Administration needs loyal servants, servants who identify with the politics of monarchy; and jobs cannot be held in perpetuity—if they were, where would it all end? There's the head of personnel, Pez's nephew, selling his protection to those men who sacrificed their jobs rather than serve under the wretched Republic. This is a scandal without equal, and there's sure to be trouble, and, just as surely, Spain will go to the devil. So, you see how it is? You can't expect much from the Pez family, whether in petticoats or pants. Anyway (returning to his theme, which he had forgotten about in the heat of the discussion), with or without their help, I won't get anything. La Caña is the only one looking out for me now. He would do something if he could, but I have hidden enemies who are working in the shadows to destroy me. Someone has clearly declared open war on me. Who that might be, I don't know, but the traitor exists, you can be sure of that."

At around this time, early March, the unhappy family again began to notice the symptoms of "nomoneyitis." There was one week of terrible penury, barely concealed from their closest friends and borne by Villaamil with stoical dignity and by Doña Pura with that valiant equanimity of spirit that always saved her from despair. The remedy arrived unexpectedly and from the same source as on another equally painful occasion. Víctor was in the money again. When she least expected it, Doña Pura was surprised by new offers of cash, which she did not hesitate to accept, without making any philosophical inquiries as to where it had come from. She felt it would be indiscreet to tell her husband that she had seen Víctor's wallet bulging with notes. How her eyes had lit up! She pocketed the coins along with any concerns as to their provenance. If he still had no job, where had he found all that money? And even if they had given him a new appointment... There must be some secret donor... But why bother probing such a possibly dangerous enigma? She disliked prying into other people's lives.

Víctor was once again dressed to the nines. He had ordered more clothes; he had a box in different theaters on various nights, as well as in the Teatro Real; he often gave the family little presents, and his generosity went so far as to invite the three Miaows to the opera—in a box, no less.

All this provoked genuine indignation in Villaamil, because it was an insult both to his own poverty and to public morality. Doña Pura and her sister laughed off the invitation, because even though they were longing to go to the opera, they lacked the finery required for such a very public event. Abelarda refused point blank. There was a huge row about it, and Doña Pura came up with a few ways of getting around the enormous practical difficulties created by her son-in-law's invitation. Here is one of the ideas invented by the chimerical brain of that figure straight out of a Fra Angelico painting. As mentioned before, her friends and neighbors, the Cuevas, made ends meet by making hats. Once, when the Miaows managed to nab three press seats at the Teatro Español, Abelarda, Doña Pura, and Bibiana Cuevas donned the best hats their friends had in their workshop, each having first adorned her own according to her personal taste. Why not do the same on this occasion? Bibiana wouldn't object. And, as it happened, she had three or four real gems, one for Marchioness A, another for Countess B, and each prettier and more elegant than the last. They could easily disguise the hats, given the endless supply of pins, clasps, ribbons, and feathers in the workshop, and even if the rightful owners were present in the theater, they would never recognize the hats in their new disguise. As for their clothes, they could sort something out there too, again with the help of their friends, perhaps getting hold of a cloak or two brought from a shop to try on; and since Víctor had promised to provide them with new gloves, going to the theater was no longer an absolute impossibility. Not many women would be able to conceal their "brokeitis" so very stylishly!

27

ABELARDA would have nothing to do with such shenanigans, saying that she would rather die than be seen in a box at the opera like that, and so the whole idea was dropped. They had to make do with seats in the front row of the gods one night when the theater was putting on Meyerbeer's *L'Africaine*, and this unusual sight caused a murmur to run through the audience. "The Miaows sitting in the front row!" Such a thing hadn't been seen in ten years. All the seats in the center and on both sides were packed to the gills. The Miaows were known to that audience as regular fixtures up in the gods, but always in the back row on the right-hand side, near the exit. On nights when they were absent, it felt as if there were an empty space, as if the frescos on the ceiling had suddenly disappeared. They were not the only regulars in the gods, for innumerable people and even whole families occupy those same seats for all eternity, generation after generation. These worthy and tenacious dilettanti form the mass of the knowledgeable public who can bestow or withhold musical success and who are the archive of all the operas sung there in the last thirty years and of all the artists who have trodden those glorious boards. Groups, cliques, and somewhat cozy coteries are formed there; friendships are made, as well as countless marriages, for it provides the perfect atmosphere and opportunity, in between tender arias and duos, for all kinds of billings and cooings and meaningful glances.

From their front-row seats, the Miaows smiled at their friends on the right-hand side and in the center, and other members of the audience up in the gods kept shooting them looks and such comments as: "Doña Pura's very sylph-like tonight! But she looks as if she used up the whole of her powder box on her face." "And there's her sister with the velvet ribbon round her neck. If all three of them did the same, they'd only need a little bell each to complete the picture." "Have a good look through your opera glasses at the youngest Miaow, it's just unmissable. She's wearing the exact same coffee-and-cream outfit her mama wore last year. And the few ribbons she's sewn onto it look just like the ones you get round cigar boxes." "Yes, you're right." "And the other one, the one who used to be a singer until her voice broke—well, she's wearing the dress she must have worn at the Liceo Jover when she played Adalgisa." "Yes, you're right. It's a Roman tunic complete with a Greek key pattern border and everything. Very classical!"

"Tell me, Guillén," people were murmuring in another circle of friends where the wretched cripple usually held court, "have they given the poor father of your Miaow lady friends a job? Because it certainly seems like it, if they can afford to splash out on front-row seats."

"No, not unless they've found him a post at the madhouse. The family is just about scraping by at the moment, something at which the good gentleman is a past master."

Having seen the opera numerous times before, Abelarda was paying more attention to the audience, anxiously surveying stall seats and boxes, watching all the ladies walking down the center aisle wearing lavish cloaks, dresses with long trains, and then rustling their way along to their seats in rows already occupied. The theater was gradually filling up, although the boxes didn't fill up completely until the end of the first act, when Vasco da Gama, frustrated with the retrograde bigwigs of the Inquisition, finally had his say. At this point, Queen Mercedes appeared in the royal box, with Don Alfonso behind her. The usual ladies—all familiar figures to the audience— entered during the second act, kept their cloaks on until the third, and applauded mechanically whenever everyone else did. The Miaows—who knew by sight all of these elegant society folk, their fellow subscribers—commented on them just as they were commented upon when they took their seats. Seeing those people almost every night, they had come to feel as if they really did know them, as if they were on friendly terms with those ladies and gentlemen. "Ah, there's the duchess, but no sign of Rosario yet... María Buschental will be here soon, and her friends are sure to turn up too. Oh, look, there's María Heredia... But how pale Mercedes is looking—so pale! And there's Don Antonio in the ministers' box, along with that man Cos-Gayón... who deserves to be shot by the way."

After much searching, Abelarda the Insignificant finally located her brother-in-law in the second row of the stalls. He was wearing tails and looking as elegant as the very best of them. What a strange thing life is! Who would have thought that that man resembling a duke, the handsome young man chatting nonchalantly away with his neighbor in the stalls—who happened to be the Italian ambassador— was, in fact, an obscure, unemployed clerk with lodgings in the house of poverty, in a shabby, humble room and who kept his clothes in a trunk? "Isn't that Víctor?" asked Doña Pura, turning her opera glasses on him. "He certainly fancies himself. If only they knew... He looks every inch a prince, but then men like him are ten a penny in Madrid. I don't know how he does it—where he gets those fine clothes, stall seats in all the theaters, magnificent cigars. There he is, chatting away as if to the manner born. Goodness knows what nonsense he'll be telling that poor man next to him, but then foreigners are so innocent, they'll believe anything."

Abelarda didn't take her eyes off him once, and when she saw him gaze up at one of the boxes, she would follow the direction of his gaze, thinking this would reveal his secret lover. "Which of them could it be?" she was thinking. "Because it must be one of them. Is it that one dressed in white? It could be. He seems to be looking at her, but no, he's looking away now. Could it be one of the singers? No, what am I thinking, it wouldn't be a singer. It'll be one of those elegantly dressed ladies in the boxes, and I intend to find her out." She would fix on one woman for no particular reason, merely following her instincts; then rejecting that hypothesis, she would fix on another woman, then another, reaching the conclusion that none of them were his lover. Víctor showed no particular preference as to who he gazed at in the boxes or the stalls. It might be that the two of them had agreed not to look at each other openly and thus betray their secret. He also glanced up at the first row in the gods and waved at the family. Doña Pura nodded for a full quarter of an hour in response to that greeting rising up to the poor Miaows from the noble depths of the theater.

In the intervals, a few friends—fellow subscribers to the gods— came to greet them, pushing their way through the crush. Federico Ruiz was one of them, and he and all of them wanted to know what Milagros thought of the soprano singing the role of Selika for the first time that night. The Miaows did not leave until Selika had met her end beneath the manchineel tree, for they never missed a single note, and only left their seats when the curtain came down for the last time. As they wended their way slowly down the broad staircase packed with people, several close friends came over to them—among them Guillén—as well as a few of those female friends who had made such cruel fun of them when they first took their seats in the front row.

When they returned home, they found Villaamil still awake. Víctor had not yet come home and did not do so until very late, when everyone was sleeping—everyone but Abelarda, who heard his key in the door and, getting out of bed to peer through a crack in the door, watched him go into the dining room and then into bed, having first drunk a glass of water. He was cheerily humming to himself, the collar of his jacket turned up, a silk scarf casually tied around his neck, his felt hat looking very worn and battered. He was the very image of the elegant man about town.

The following day, he caused the family a good deal of work, asking for help with various minor repair jobs: sewing on a button, doing a delicate bit of darning, or making some adjustment to his shirts. Abelarda, though, dealt with it all very diligently. At lunchtime, Doña Pura came home announcing that the pawnbroker's son had died, something Luis confirmed, but more as if it were a piece of gossip than a cause for grief, an attitude proper to the heartless age of childhood. Villaamil intoned a grand funeral oration for the poor child, declaring that it is fortunate to die in childhood and thus avoid all the sufferings of this vile life. The ones who really deserved our compassion were the parents, who are stuck having a terrible time, while the child flies off into the sky to join the glorious battalion of angels. Everyone agreed with these thoughts, apart from Víctor, who listened with a wry smile on his lips, and when his father-in-law withdrew, and Milagros went to her kitchen and Doña Pura resumed her busy comings and goings, he confronted Abelarda, who was still at the table, and said:

"Blessed are those who believe! I would give anything to be like you, going to church and spending hours and hours there, taken in by all the theatrical effects they use to cover up the eternal lie. As I see it, religion is a magnificent robe in which they clothe the void so that we don't feel too terrified. Isn't that what you think?"

"Of course I don't!" exclaimed Abelarda, offended by the sly tenacity with which he chose to wound her religious feelings whenever he found an opportune moment. "If I did, I wouldn't go to church, because that would make me a complete hypocrite. You shouldn't say things like that to me. If you don't believe, that's your problem."

"But being an unbeliever doesn't make me happy. I deplore it, and you would be doing me a huge favor if you could convince me that I'm wrong."

"Me? I'm not a professor or a preacher. Belief comes from inside. Doesn't it ever even enter your head that there might be a God?"

"It used to, before. But that idea has long since flown."

"Well, what can I say? (Taking him seriously.) And don't you think that, when we die, we'll be called to account for our actions here on Earth?"

"Who's going to do that? The worms and maggots? When departure time rolls along, Mother Matter will take us in her arms; she's a very decent person, but she has no face, no will, no conscience, nothing. We disappear into her, dissolve entirely. I accept no medium terms. If I believed what you believe—namely, that somewhere up there, I don't know where, some white-bearded Judge exists, who either forgives or condemns and hands out passports to heaven or hell—I would enter a monastery and spend the rest of my life praying."

"That would be the best thing you could do, you fool." (Taking the napkin from Luis, who was staring at his father with wide, astonished eyes.)

"Why don't you do the same?"

"Who knows, I might one day. So be careful. God will punish you for not believing in him. He'll strike you with his hand, and it's a very heavy hand, you'll see."

Just then, Luis, who was most disturbed by his father's crude comments, could not contain himself, and with childish determination, he picked up a piece of bread and hurled it at his progenitor's face, yelling:

"You beast!"

Everyone laughed at this, and Doña Pura rained down kisses on her grandson, urging him on:

"Yes, you tell him, sweetheart. He's a very naughty boy. He only says he doesn't believe because he knows it will annoy us. What a treasure my little grandson is, eh? He's worth his weight in gold. He knows more than a hundred scholars. He's going to be a priest and climb up into the pulpit to give his little sermons and say his little masses. We'll all be old wrecks by then, but the day our Luis first says mass, we can kneel down before him so that he can give us his blessing. And the humblest of us all, positively drooling with pleasure, will be this idle fellow here. And then you'll say to him: 'You see, Papa, you did believe in the end.'"

"What a fine, talented son I have!" said Víctor, leaping joyfully to his feet and kissing his son, who turned away to avoid such a show of affection. "And I love him all the more for it! I'm going to buy you a velocipede so that you can ride around in the little square opposite. Your friends will be *so* jealous!"

For a moment, the promise of a velocipede upset all of Luis's ideas, as he calculated with crude egotism that his desire to become a priest and serve God and even become a saint was in no way at odds with owning a precious velocipede and being able to speed by under the very noses of his classmates, who would all be green with envy.

28

THE FOLLOWING morning, when his wife returned from doing the shopping, Villaamil shared with her a very interesting conversation he'd had. He was in his office writing letters, and when he heard her come in, he whispered mysteriously to her to join him, then, closing the door, said: "Not a word of this to Víctor, because the swine might just ruin it for me. Now, while I still don't hold out any real hope, I did make some progress yesterday. I have won the support of a very influential deputy. We had a long conversation last night. And just so that you know the whole story, I'll start at the beginning. My friend La Caña introduced me to the man. I told him my past record, and he was quite astonished when he learned of my suspension. Then I dropped into the conversation my ideas on the Treasury, and do you know, he feels exactly the same. He shares my views completely: that we should try new, simpler methods of taxation, relying on the good faith of the taxpayer and economizing on the way we collect taxes. Anyway, he promised me his total support. He's a very important man and, it seems, they never refuse him anything."

"Is he on the opposition?"

"No, he's very much on the government side, but being something of a rebel, he's always making life difficult for the government. He's someone who cares only for the good of the country. Whenever he stands up to speak, the ministerial benches tremble because he can demonstrate, point by point, how and why agriculture is ruined, industry dead, and the whole nation plunged into desperate poverty, which is, of course, as plain as day. Anyway, the government, who see him as their accuser, are afraid of him—terrified really—and they'll give him whatever he wants. He gets appointments by the dozen . . . We've agreed that I'll let him know today if there's a vacancy, as hinted at by Sevillano and Pantoja. I'll go to the ministry as soon as I've had lunch, find out whether or not there's a vacancy, and if there is, I'll write to him at home or in congress, depending on the time of day. He's given me his word that, this very afternoon, he'll speak to the minister, who is currently extremely grateful to him for agreeing not to stand up and demand an explanation about some very dubious government contract. The minister would give him David's harp if he wanted it. Do you understand?"

"Yes, yes, of course I do (radiant with happiness), and it sounds to me as if, this time, no one's going to take our cake away from us."

"I'm still not what you'd call confident, no, not at all, and as you know, I always prefer to expect the worst. Anyway, here's my plan: I'll go to the ministry; you keep Luis at home this afternoon, and have him wait here, because I'll need him to deliver the letter. I won't see the man himself, because Víctor is insisting that he and I go and see the head of personnel together this afternoon, and I want to go with him just to throw him off the track. Do you see? Best not to let the wretch know which way the wind is blowing."

Springing to his feet in a state of high excitement, he began pacing up and down the narrow room. His overjoyed wife left him alone, and despite his advice to give nothing away, her daughter and her sister could tell from her face that she had been the recipient of good news. She was one of those people who treasure up inside them a whole arsenal of spiritual weapons against life's sorrows and who have the ability to transform facts, reducing them down and assimilating them, thanks to an ability to sweeten everything, just as the bee changes everything it sips into honey.

Luis, then, had the whole day off school, because, in the morning, the teacher had arranged for them all to go to poor Joker's funeral. And Luis was one of those chosen to hold one of the ribbons draped over the coffin, possibly because, thanks to his father Víctor, he was the best dressed. His grandmother had made him wear his confirmation suit complete with gloves, and he did look very smart and dapper and took great pleasure in being so well turned out, his contentment quite unaffected by the sad reason for such sartorial elegance. Paca kept kissing him and saying how very grand he looked before he set off to the pawnbroker's house, followed by Canelo the dog (who was also keen to have a finger in the pie, so to speak, although it was unlikely that he too would be given a ribbon to hold). As they turned into Calle del Acuerdo, Luis met his Aunt Quintina, who smothered him in kisses, heaped praise on his elegant appearance, smoothed any creases in his jacket, and straightened his collar so that he would look even more handsome.

"This is all down to me, you know, because I was the one who told your father to buy you some new clothes. It would never have occurred to him. His mind's always on other things. By the way, sweetheart, I've been trying once again to persuade your papa to have you come and live with me. What's wrong? Why the long face? You'd be much better off with me than with those pretentious Miaows . . . You should see the lovely things I have at home, you really should! There are some Baby Jesuses holding a little globe of the world in one hand, and they look just like you, not to mention some simply gorgeous cribs . . . You really must come and see them. And now we're waiting for some miniature chalices to come in, some exquisite monstrances, and a few chasubles . . . so that good little children can play at saying mass; as well as saints the size of toy soldiers and loads of candlesticks and lamps to light and put on pretend altars. You really must come and see, and if you come, you can do whatever you like, because it's all there for you to play with. You will come, won't you, sweetie?"

Luis listened wide-eyed to these descriptions of sacred toys and nodded, although he was all too aware of the difficulty of seeing and enjoying such wondrous things when his dear grandmother wouldn't even let him set foot in his aunt's house. They had reached the home of the deceased, and Aunt Quintina, after kissing him and pinching his cheeks, left him in the company of the other boys, who were already there and making far too much noise for such a sad occasion. Then— some out of envy, others because they couldn't resist making fun of everyone—started teasing their friend Luis about his classy outfit:

his blue stockings and his equally blue gloves (which, it should be said, were far too tight around his fingers). He wouldn't let the other boys touch him, though, determined to defend his spotless sleeves from attacks by those envious ragamuffins. There followed a discussion as to whether or not they should go up and see Paco Ramos dead, and among those who voted yes was Luis, whose curiosity was pricked because this was the first time he had ever done such a thing.

As it turned out, the sight of the poor dead boy made such an impression on him that he nearly fainted. He felt an intense pain in the pit of his stomach, as if a part of it were being torn out. Poor Joker seemed bigger somehow. He too was dressed in his best clothes, and his hands, holding a posy of flowers, were folded on his chest; his face was very yellow, with purple blotches, and his almost-black lips were slightly parted, revealing his two front teeth, large and white, and again larger than they had been in life...Luis recoiled from this horrific sight. Poor Joker! So still, when he had always been so lively; so silent, when he had never stopped making a racket, always laughing and talking; so serious, when he had been the very embodiment of mischief, always messing around in class! In the midst of this emotional turmoil—Luis could not have said with any certainty if it was sadness or fear—an idea elbowed its way through his other feelings; it was the voice of egotism, which speaks louder in childhood than the voice of pity. He thought: "Well, he'll never call me Miaow again now." And this realization seemed to lift a weight from his shoulders, as if he had solved a difficult problem or successfully fended off some danger. As he went back down the stairs, he tried to overcome those queasy feelings by repeating to himself: "Now he'll never call me Miaow again. Just let him try!"

Shortly afterward, the blue coffin was carried downstairs and placed in the hearse, and in order to watch the funeral party leave, several women appeared on the various balconies, including that of the pawnbroker's establishment. Guillén emerged into the street, his eyes red with crying and so grave-faced that he looked like a different person. It was he who arranged everything and distributed the ribbons, entrusting one to Luis. Then he climbed into the carriage, alongside the teacher with his rattan walking stick and faded hat, the shopkeeper from next door, wearing a clean collarless shirt and no tie, and an old man unknown to Luis. They set off. Luis sensed that his own clothes made quite an impression and felt a pleasant flicker of pride. He felt very pleased with his role as one of the bearers of the ribbons, thinking that the funeral wouldn't have been half so splendid if he had not been chosen. He glanced around looking for Canelo; however, as soon as Mendizábal's very sensible dog realized that this was a funeral—a grim occasion conducive to grim thoughts—he had turned and trotted off in another direction, thinking that it made more sense to see if he could meet some elegant, susceptible lady dog in the local area.

In the cemetery, curiosity—more powerful than fear—prompted Luis to try and see everything. Two men lifted the coffin down from the carriage and then raised the lid . . . Luis could not understand (until a friend explained) why those brutes, having first covered his friend's face with a handkerchief, then sprinkled quicklime over his body . . . . Watching these rituals, Luis felt a tight knot in his throat. He peered between the legs of the older people in order to see, to see more. The really strange thing was that the Joker kept so still and silent while that dreadful thing was being done to him. Then the lid was closed again. How terrible to be locked inside! They gave the key to Guillén then slid the coffin into a hole, pushing it right in, toward the back. A bricklayer started bricking up the hole. Luis kept his eyes glued on the man as he worked. When it was done, he let out a huge sigh, as if he had been holding his breath for a long time. Poor Joker! "Well, people can call me Miaow all they want, but *he* won't ever do that again."

When they left, his classmates again began teasing him about his dapper appearance. Someone hinted malevolently that they would push him into a ditch, from which he would emerge in a truly frightful state. A few filthy hands did touch him with an intention that was all too easy to divine, and Luis—his fingers imprisoned in those gloves, numb and incapable of movement—didn't know how to react. Finally, though, he managed to free himself by taking off the gloves and stuffing them in his pocket. The other boys dispersed before they reached Calle Ancha, and Luis continued on with the teacher, who left him at the door of his house. Canelo was already back from his lewd little jaunt, and together they went upstairs to lunch, for the dog had already sensed that new supplies of food had arrived.

"Where are your gloves?" Doña Pura asked Luis when she saw him come in without them.

"It's all right, I didn't lose them. They're in my pocket."

At around three o'clock, Villaamil arrived looking very flustered and went straight to his office, where, with his wife standing beside him, he wrote a letter; she was delighted to see him in such a state of healthy excitement, a sign that something was actually going to happen.

"Right. Ask Luis to deliver this letter and wait for a response. Sevillano tells me that there *is* a vacancy in the Treasury, and I need to know whether the deputy will ask them to give it to me or not. We must strike while the iron is hot. I've arranged to meet Víctor, and I want to be there, just to put him off the scent. This is a very delicate business I'm engaged in, and I need to proceed with the greatest caution. Give me my hat and my cane, because I'm off out again. May God look favorably upon us. Tell Luis not to come back without an answer. He should give the letter to the porter and wait in the room on the right as you go in. I'm not hoping for anything, but I need to pull out all the stops, every one of them..."

Followed by Canelo, Luis set off at around four o'clock carrying the letter and still wearing his funeral outfit (minus the gloves), because his grandmother thought this was the ideal occasion on which to show it off. He didn't need to be told how to get to the congress, for he had been there before on a similar mission. The walk took him twenty minutes. Calle de Florida-Blanca was crammed with carriages, which waited in line after dropping off their owners at the door. The coachmen, in braided top hats and capes, chatted to each other from their respective seats, and the line stretched as far as the Teatro de Jovellanos. There was another line, this time of people, outside the doors to the building in Calle del Sordo, under the watchful eye of a few policemen just in case things should get out of hand. Having examined the scene, the observant Luis went in through the door with the glass canopy. A porter in a frock coat kindly drew him to one side while he ushered in some very grand fur-coated gentlemen, for whom the red screen door immediately opened. Luis then approached the porter again, and taking off his cap (for gold braid never failed to impress him and he knew nothing of hierarchies), he handed him the letter, saying shyly:

"I'm to wait for an answer."

The porter read the envelope and said:

"I'm not sure he's arrived yet, but he will."

Then, placing the letter in a file, he told Luis to wait in the room on the right.

There were quite a lot of people there, most of them standing by the door: men of very different types, some shabbily dressed, with a scarf about their neck, looking like rank moochers; women wearing veils and clutching rolled-up bits of paper, which were clearly petitions of sorts. Some angrily eyed the gentlemen coming in, ready to stop them in their tracks. While others of a more prosperous appearance were merely asking for tickets to the gallery, only to find they had all been taken. Luis also kept an eye on certain gentlemen who entered in groups of two or three, talking heatedly. "This must be a very big house," thought Luis, "to hold all these people." Then, grown weary of standing, he moved further into the room and sat on one of the benches in the waiting area. There he saw a table where some people were writing cards or notes, which they handed to the porters, then waited, making no effort to conceal their impatience. There was one man who had been there for three hours and might well have to wait another three, while the women sat motionless in their chairs, sighing and hoping for a response that never came. From time to time, the screen door would open and a porter would call out, "Señor So-and-So," and Señor So-and-So would spring gladly to his feet.

An hour passed, and Luis, still sitting on that hard bench, kept yawning out of sheer boredom. To distract himself, he would get up now and then and stand at the door to watch the bigwigs coming in, all the while pondering the mysterious nature of that place and what so many of these so-called gentlemen got up to in there. The congress (as he well knew) was a place where people "spoke." He had often heard his grandfather and his father saying: "Today So-and-So or What's-His-Name spoke and said this, that, and the other." And what would it be like inside? He would love to know. Yes, what would it be like? Where did they do all that "speaking"? It must be as huge as the church he went to, with a whole sea of pews, where they sat, all talking at once. And what was the point of so much chatter? Because the ministers went there too. And who exactly were the ministers? The people who governed and dished out appointments. He also remembered hearing his grandfather say, in one of his frequent bouts of ill humor, that the parliament as a whole was a farce and they were just a bunch of time-wasters. He would also occasionally speak enthusiastically about a particular speech. In short, Luis couldn't form a clear idea of the place, and his mind was all confused.

He returned to his bench, and from there he saw a man come in who looked just like his father. "My papa is here too!" When the screen door was held open for him, Luis almost ran after him, shouting, "Papa, Papa!" but it was too late, and so he stayed where he was. "Is my papa going to speak? If only Mendizábal was here, because he knows everything and always tells me really interesting things..." Just then, he felt his eyes cloud over, and an ice-cold shudder ran down his spine. So sudden and violent was the onset of the malaise that he only had time to say to himself, "It's happening, it's happening," then, head drooping, he leaned against one corner of the bench and fell deep asleep.

29

FOR A MOMENT, Luis couldn't see anything. It was all darkness, all emptiness. Then, shortly afterward, the Lord appeared, sitting opposite him—but where exactly? Behind him there was something like clouds, a luminous white mass that oscillated and undulated rather as smoke does. The Lord seemed very serious. He looked at Luis, and Luis looked at him, waiting for him to speak. It had been a long time since he last saw him, and he now felt even more respect for him.

"The gentleman for whom you brought the letter," said the Lord, "hasn't yet answered you. He read it and put it away in his pocket. He'll respond later. I've told him to give you a resounding 'Yes,' but I don't know if he'll remember. He's too busy talking at the moment."

"Talking," Luis said. "And what's he saying?"

"Many things, my friend, many things you wouldn't understand," replied the Lord, smiling kindly. "Would you like to hear all that stuff?"

"Yes, I would."

"They're all being very uppity today. It's sure to end in a huge row."

"And what about you, sir?" asked Luis shyly, still unable to bring himself to address the Lord more familiarly. "Aren't you going to speak?"

"Where? Here? Well, my child . . . I'll say . . . yes, one day I might speak. What I nearly always do, though, is listen."

"Don't you get tired?"

"A little bit, but what can I do?"

"Will the gentleman with the letter say 'Yes'? Will they give my grandfather a job?"

"I can't be sure. I've told him at least three times to do just that."

"Because the thing is (spoken confidently) I'm studying really hard now."

"Now don't get too full of yourself. You *are* working a little harder, but there's no point exaggerating when it's just the two of us talking. If you didn't spend so much time with that stamp album of yours, you'd do much better."

"I knew my lesson yesterday."

"Given your usual standard, it wasn't bad, but it's not enough, my child, it's not enough. If you want to be a priest, then you have to try harder, because, for example, if you want to say a mass to me one day, you need to learn Latin, and if you're going to preach, you have to study all kinds of things."

"When I'm older, I'll learn everything, but my papa doesn't want me to be a priest, and he says he doesn't believe in you at all and that no one can make him. Tell me, is my papa a bad man?"

"Well, he's not exactly a good Catholic."

"And what about Aunt Quintina, is she a good person?"

"Oh yes, and you should see the lovely things she has in her apartment. You should go and visit."

"My grandma won't let me. (Sadly.) That's because Aunt Quintina has got it into her head that I should go and live with her, but everyone at home—well, they'll have none of it."

"That's understandable. But what do you think? Would you like to stay where you are and be allowed to visit your aunt's house and see all those saints?"

"Oh, wouldn't I just! Tell me, is my papa inside there too?"

"Yes, somewhere or other."

"And is he going to speak?"

"Of course."

"Forgive me, but the other day, my papa said that all women are bad, that's why I don't ever want to get married."

"Very wise. (Trying not to laugh.) No hasty marriages. Besides, you're going to be a priest."

"And a bishop, unless you decide otherwise . . ."

Just then, he saw that the Lord was turning around as if to drive away something that was bothering him ... Luis craned his neck to see what it was, and the Lord said:

"Go away, be off with you and leave me in peace."

Then Luis saw, peeking out from among the folds of his celestial friend's cloak, the heads of several little ragamuffins. The Lord drew up the hem of his garment and revealed a few small boys, stark naked and with wings. This was the first time Luis had seen them, and given that he had angels with him, he could no longer doubt that this really was God. A few more began to appear among the clouds, and they were making a terrific racket, laughing and capering about. The Lord again ordered them to leave and flapped one corner of his cloak at them, as if they were flies. The youngest ones fluttered about, rising up to the ceiling (because there was a ceiling), and the older ones kept tugging at their kindly grandfather to make him go with them. Finally, the old man got rather angrily to his feet, saying:

"All right, I'm coming, I'm coming. What tiresome creatures you are! You're being positively unbearable."

But he said this in a good-natured, easy-going tone. Luis was transfixed by this beautiful sight, and he saw that one of the winged ragamuffins stood out from the others ...

Heavens! It was the Joker, the very same, not stiff and ashen-faced as he had been in his coffin, but alive and happy and really handsome. What really amazed Luis was that his classmate stood right there before him and, as impudently as you like, hissed out:

"Miaow, Miaow, pussykins!"

The respect Luis owed to God and his followers did not stop him from getting angry at this remark, and he even ventured to respond:

"You rogue, you rascal ...you learned that from your slut of a mother and your aunts, who everyone calls the harpies!"

The Lord smiled and said:

"Now be quiet all of you ... Off we go."

And he moved slowly away, herding his angels before him and shooing them along with his hands as if they were a flock of hens. But from a great distance, when the Heavenly Father was already disappearing into the clouds, that shameless Joker turned and stood legs akimbo, looking straight at his friend, a broad grin on his ragamuffin mug, pulled all kinds of faces, then stuck out his tongue as far as it would go and said again:

"Miaow, Miaow, pussykins!"

Luis raised one hand ... If he'd had a book in it, or a vase, or an inkpot, he would have hurled it at his friend's head. Then Joker skipped away, and from a distance, cupping his mouth with his hands, he let out a "miaow" so loud and long that it seemed as if the whole congress building, reverberating to that deafening meow, was about to collapse ...

A porter bearing a letter woke the boy up, although it took a while for him to come to.

"Boy, boy, was it you who brought a letter for the gentleman? Well, here's the answer. It's Señor Don Ramón Villaamil, is that right?"

"Yes, that's me ... I mean that's my grandfather," Luis said, rubbing his eyes. Then he left.

The cool air of the street cleared his head a little. It was raining, and his first thought was that his clothes would be ruined. Canelo, meanwhile, had killed time walking up and down Carrera de San Jerónimo, looking at the pretty "girls" passing by, some of them in carriages, showing off their flashy necklaces, but when Luis emerged from the congress building, Canelo was already back from his travels and waiting for his friend, hoping that he might buy some more cakes. Alas, Luis had no spare change, and even if he had, he was in no mood for eating rich food after what he had seen and given that the physical turmoil he had experienced had not yet disappeared.

What about the letter? What did the letter say? Villaamil opened it with trembling hands (while Doña Pura led Luis to his room to change his clothes), and when he read it, his heart sank. It was one of those formulaic letters written in their hundreds every day in congress and in the ministries. Lots of polite phrases, lots of vague promises that neither confirmed nor denied anything. When his wife came into the office, Villaamil cut a tragic figure, pointing to the letter thrown down on the desk.

"Ha!" she said when she had read it. "The usual flimflam. But don't worry. Go and see him tomorrow and ..."

"I tell you (spoken in despairing tones), they are merely toying with me ..."

He spent the night plunged in gloom, but the following morning, his mood had changed completely. Such abrupt shifts from despair to hope are part of the jobseeker's wearisome life. Villaamil received a brief note from the great man, asking him to visit him at home between twelve and one. Villaamil was in such a frenzy to go that he could scarcely put on his coat. "He just wants to see me to tell me some nonsense or other," he thought, clinging as ever to the worst of all outcomes. "But we must go, we must go." And off he went, leaving his wife in a state of high excitement, expecting some imminent triumph. On the way, Villaamil did his best to embrace his usual pessimistic fatalism. According to his theory, what happens is always the opposite of what one expects. That's why we never win the lottery, precisely because when we buy a ticket, we do so in the firm belief that we'll win the top prize. The expected never happens, especially in Spain, because Spaniards, traditionally, live from day to day and are always surprised by events over which they have no control. If one accepts this theory—that all plans will inevitably come to nothing— what can one do to make anything happen? Imagine the opposite and immerse yourself in the idea that the contrary of what you hope for is sure to happen. And to ensure that something doesn't happen? Assume that it will; make yourself obstinately believe in the truth of that assumption. Villaamil had always used this system with great success and could recall a multitude of examples. On one of his trips to Cuba, in the midst of a terrible storm, he managed to convince himself that he would die, removing from his mind all hope of survival, and of course the ship was saved. On another occasion, when he was once again under threat of being suspended, he steeped himself in the certainty of his misfortune; he thought only of that inevitable dismissal; he could see it there before him day and night, flaunting itself with brutal nonchalance. And what happened? They promoted him.

In short, on his way to the house of this father of the nation, Villa-amil again immersed himself in the prospect of impending disaster, thinking: "I can see it coming; this gentleman is going to give me the coup de grâce, saying: 'I'm very sorry, my friend, but the minister and I don't see eye to eye, and I can do nothing for you.'"

However, the words of that favored individual proved very differ-ent, and Don Ramón would never have dreamed that he would address him in this manner: "Yesterday afternoon, after writing to you, I spoke to your son-in-law, who told me that you would prefer a post in the provinces, which, of course, changes things completely, because it's much easier to find a post there. I'll deal with the matter today."

The pleasant surprise he felt at such words was mingled with distaste at the thought that Víctor had been meddling in this busi-ness. He returned home feeling most uneasy, because he really didn't like Víctor's person and opinions being mixed up in his affairs. Doña Pura did not share his misgivings, and the sun of her joy shone down from a cloudless sky. Yes, it would be a nuisance having to pack up and move, but they were in no position to choose, they must simply make do with what was possible and thank God for that.

From that day on, Villaamil began attending church with embar-rassing regularity. When he left the house and found the doors of the Comendadoras open, he would slip inside and hear mass if it was the right time, or if not, he would kneel there for a while, doubtless try-ing to reconcile his fatalism with Christian doctrine. Would he succeed? Who knows? Christianity teaches us: "Ask and you will receive"; it tells us to trust in God and to expect him to give us the remedy for all our ills; but a long life of anxiety prompted other ideas in Villaamil: don't expect and you will receive; don't expect to succeed and success will be yours. He must have found a way of accommodat-ing those two ideas. Perhaps he renounced his diabolical theory and returned to that consoling dogma; perhaps he surrendered all his heart's hopes to the all-merciful God, placing himself in his hands so that he would give him what was most fitting: death or life, a new position or eternal redundancy, a modest living or ghastly poverty, the happy peace of a servant of the state or the desperation of the always famished jobseeker. Perhaps he was already anticipating his heartfelt gratitude for the former and his feelings of resignation for the latter, and was determined to wait stoically for the divine decision, renouncing all anticipation of the future, the sinful habit of proud mankind.

30

RETURNING home one evening, as night was falling, and noticing that the Montserrat church was still open, he went in. The church was very dark. He almost had to feel his way along the central nave to a pew, beside which he kneeled and gazed up at the altar, which was lit by a single lamp. The only sounds to break the silence were the footsteps of some member of the congregation coming and going and the faint murmur of prayers, and into that profound silence Villaamil poured his own melancholy prayer, an absurd mixture of piety and bureaucracy…"However hard I search my conscience, I cannot find a sin terrible enough to merit such a cruel punishment. I have always worked for the good of the state and always striven to defend the Administration from those who would defraud it. I have never ever been involved in or condoned any untoward business, never. You know that, Lord. There are my account books from when I was in charge of the audit. Not a single wrong entry, not one erasure. Why such injustice from all these wretched governments? If it is true that you give us all our daily bread, why do you deny me mine? I'll go further: If the state is supposed to treat everyone equally, why does it abandon me? Me! When I have served it so loyally. Do not disappoint me now, Lord. I promise I will not doubt your mercy as I have at other times; I promise not to be pessimistic, but to place all my hopes in you. Now, dear Father, please touch the heart of that weary minister, who is a good man, but constantly bombarded by letters and recommendations."

After a while, tired of kneeling, he sat down, and his eyes, accustomed now to the darkness, began to make out the vague shapes of altars, images, and people, a few old ladies crouched around the confessionals, mumbling prayers. He did not expect the happy encounter that happened about half an hour later when, as he sat fidgeting about on the hard wooden pew, his grandson suddenly appeared before him.

"Goodness, I didn't see you there. Who did you come with?"

"With Aunt Abelarda, but she's in the other chapel. I was waiting for her here, and I fell asleep. I didn't notice you arrive."

"Well, I've been here a while," said Villaamil, giving him a hug. "Do you just come here for a siesta? That's not good, you know. You might catch a chill. Your hands are frozen. Let me warm them up."

"Grandpa," said Luis, cupping his grandfather's face and tilting it slightly to one side. "Were you praying that you would be given a job?"

Don Ramón was in such a troubled state that, on hearing what his grandson said, he went from laughter to tears in less than a second. Luis, however, didn't notice his grandfather's eyes welling up and merely sighed loudly when he heard this reply:

"Yes, my dear. As you know, we should pray to God when we are in need."

"Well," Luis blurted out, "I've been telling him that every day, and he hasn't done a thing."

"You've been praying too? What a sweet boy you are! The Lord only gives us what is best for us. And we have to be good, because otherwise we're lost."

Luis gave another deep sigh as if to say: "That's the problem, isn't it? Being good, I mean." After a long pause, the boy again cupped his grandfather's face in his hands to make him look at him and murmured: "Grandpa, I knew my lesson today."

"Really? Well, I'm pleased."

"When will they put me in the Latin class? I want to learn how to say mass. But you know, I don't like this church, and do you know why? See that chapel? Well, inside it is a very frightening 'gentleman' with long hair. I wouldn't go in there for all the tea in China. When I'm a priest, I'll certainly never say mass in there."

Don Ramón burst out laughing.

"You'll gradually lose your fear and find that you'll even be able to say mass to that long-haired Christ."

"I'm already learning to say mass. Murillo knows all the Latin words, and when to ring the bell, and when to lift the priest's train."

"Look," said his grandfather, ignoring what Luis had just said. "Go and tell your aunt that I'm here. She won't have seen me either. And it's time we were all going home."

Luis went off to deliver the message, and the sound of his footsteps struck a happy note in that gloomy silence. Abelarda, who was kneeling on the floor, turned round, then stood up and joined her father.

"Have you finished?" he asked.

"Almost." And she continued her murmurings, her eyes fixed on the altar.

Villaamil put a lot of store by his daughter's prayers, which he thought were for him, and so he said:

"Don't hurry, pray as long as you need to, we have time. It's true, isn't it, that a great weight seems to lift off our hearts when we tell our woes to the only person who can console us?"

These words rose up spontaneously from the depths of his soul. The time and place were right for that sweetest of acts, that flinging wide the doors of the soul and letting out all its secrets. Abelarda was in a similar psychological state but felt a still more urgent need to unburden herself. She could not possibly have remained silent at that point, and as soon as she spoke, confidences—which, in another time and place, she would never have allowed herself—would inevitably flow from her lips.

"Ah, Papa!" she said. "You can't imagine how unhappy I am."

Villaamil was startled by these words, because as far as he was concerned there was only one source of unhappiness in the family— his suspension and his agonizing wait for a new appointment.

"Of course," he said glumly, "but now . . . now we must have faith . . . God will not abandon us."

"Well," said Abelarda, "he's certainly abandoned me. Such terrible things happen to us. God sometimes makes mistakes . . ."

"What are you saying, child? (Very alarmed.) Mistakes? God?"

"I mean that sometimes he fills a person with feelings that make her very unhappy, because what's the point of loving someone if things aren't going to work out?"

Villaamil did not understand. He looked at her to see if the expression on her face would explain these enigmatic words. In the gloom, though, she was barely visible. And Luis, standing before them both, understood not a word of their conversation.

"To be perfectly honest," said Villaamil, seeking some light in all this confusion, "I have no idea what you mean. What is it that's making you so unhappy? Have you quarrelled with Ponce? I find that hard to believe. Why, only last night in the café he was telling me how he couldn't wait to get married. He doesn't want to put it off until his uncle dies, although, frankly, the poor man's pretty much at death's door."

"No, no, that's not the reason," said Abelarda, her heart in her mouth. "Ponce hasn't upset me."

"So…"

They both fell silent, and after a brief pause, Abelarda looked at her father. A cruel feeling was bubbling up inside her, a desire to wound her kindly father by saying something very unpleasant. How to explain this? The only possible explanation can be her sudden rejection of the upsurge of piety in her troubled mind, which, searching in vain for what was good, rebounded instead toward what was bad, a feeling in which she took momentary pleasure. Her state of mind (related to the nervous disorders that often afflict the female organism) bore some relation to the cerebral state that provokes acts of infanticide; and, in this case, that mysterious wave of anger broke over her poor, wretched, much-loved father.

"Haven't you heard?" she said. "Víctor's been given a new post. At midday today, just after you left, someone knocked at the door. It was his letter of appointment. And he happened to be at home. They've promoted him and appointed him something or other in the Finance Department here in Madrid."

Villaamil was utterly stunned, as if someone had delivered a hammer-blow to his head. His ears buzzed … he felt as if he were going mad and asked her to repeat what she had just said, which Abelarda did, in a voice vibrant with cruel parricidal rage.

"It's a really good job," she added. "He's very pleased, and he said that if they fail to give you a post, he could—temporarily of course and just to keep you occupied—give you some minor position in his office."

For a moment, the unfortunate old man felt as if the whole church were falling in on him; indeed, a great weight was pressing down on his heart, stopping him from breathing. At the same instant, Abelarda, now recovered from the mental storm that had so clouded her reason and her daughterly feelings, bitterly regretted the deadly blow she had just dealt her father and tried, as quickly as possible, to pour balm on the wound.

"They're sure to give you a new appointment soon. That's what I've been praying to God for."

"Me? Them give *me* an appointment! (With pessimistic fury.) God only protects scoundrels. Do you really think I expect to get anything from the ministry or from God? They're one and the same ... It's a farce from top to bottom, nothing but nepotism and corruption! Where does all this humility and praying get us, when here I am forever overlooked and ignored, while that halfwit, that liar, that schemer..."

He struck his head such a blow with the palm of his hand that he frightened Luis, who stared at his grandfather in astonishment. Then Abelarda felt a resurgence of that parricidal malice along with an instinctive need to defend the passion filling her soul. However misguided, life's great mistakes—and its most profound emotions— are great survivors, refusing point-blank to perish. Abelarda came to her own defence by defending Víctor.

"No, Papa, he's not a bad man (spoken with great feeling), not at all. You and Mama are so wrong about him! You have a very super-ficial view of him, you don't understand him."

"And what would you know about that, you silly girl?"

"Well, I do know. None of you understand him, but I do."

"*You* do?" And as he said this, a terrible suspicion entered his mind, only adding to his confused state. Then, regaining his composure, he told himself: "No, that's impossible, that would be absurd!" However, seeing how worked up his daughter was, seeing the wild look in her eyes, that cruel suspicion returned.

"Oh, so you understand him, do you?"

While resisting having to penetrate the mystery, it nonetheless drew him dizzyingly down as if into a great abyss, which grew deeper and more terrifying the more he peered into it. He did a rapid review of certain previously inexplicable things his daughter had said or done; he made connections, recalled words, gestures, incidents, and finally had to admit that this was a very serious situation indeed. So serious and so contrary to his own feelings that even the mere idea that it might be true terrified him. He wanted, rather, to forget about it or pretend that it was a mere surmise with no reasonable basis in fact.

"Come along," he murmured. "It's late, and I have things to do before I go home."

Abelarda knelt to say her final prayers, and Villaamil, taking Luis's hand, walked slowly over to the door, without genuflecting this time, and without looking at the altar or even remembering that he was in a holy place. Together they walked past the chapel of the long-haired Christ, and when Luis tugged at his grandfather's arm to keep them as far away as possible from that alarming figure, Villaamil grew annoyed and said sharply:

"He won't eat you, silly."

Finally, the three of them left the church together, and on the corner of Calle de Quiñones, they met Pantoja, who stopped to tell Don Ramón about Víctor's outrageous promotion. Abelarda continued on home. As she went up the dimly lit stairs, she heard someone else coming down. She would have liked to hide, an impulse driven by a sense of shame and fear provoked in turn by some mysterious presentiment. Her heart was warning her that something strange was about to happen, the natural, inevitable result of previous events, and this imminent encounter made her tremble. Víctor saw her and stopped a few steps above the landing, where she had paused when she saw him approaching.

"Have you been to church?" he asked. "I'm not eating supper here tonight by the way. I've been invited out."

"Good," Abelarda said, unable to think of a more ingenious, spontaneous response.

Víctor then bounded down the four steps separating them and, without a word, grabbed Abelarda round the waist and, leaning back against the wall, drew her to him. Abelarda allowed herself to be embraced, putting up no resistance at all, and when, with feigned passion, he kissed her forehead and her cheeks, she closed her eyes, resting her head on the chest of that handsome monster like someone enjoying a much-needed rest after laboring long and hard.

"This was inevitable," said Víctor in the emotional tones he was so good at mimicking. "We've never spoken clearly before, but now we understand each other. My love, I will sacrifice everything for you. Are you prepared to do the same for this poor wretch?"

Abelarda said yes merely by opening her lips.

"Would you leave home, family, everything to follow me?" he said in a fit of infernal inspiration.

The poor fool said "Yes," out loud this time, and with a firm nod of the head.

"To follow me, never to be parted?"

"I would follow you wherever you go, I wouldn't hesitate..."

"And soon?"

"Whenever you want... now even."

Víctor thought for a moment.

"My love, this can all be done without causing any scandal. But we must part now; I think I can hear someone coming; yes, it's your father. Go upstairs now. We'll talk later."

When she heard her father's footsteps, Abelarda woke from that brief dream. She went on up the stairs, trembling with emotion and without looking back. Víctor continued slowly on down the stairs, and when he passed his father-in-law and Luis, he didn't say a word, and nor did they. By the time Villaamil reached the second floor, Abelarda had already knocked at the door, wanting to get inside before her father saw the look of criminal excitement on her face.

31

ABELARDA the Insignificant spent the whole night in a state verging on madness, her mind divided between wild joy and sepulchral gloom and intermittently filled by a piercing sense of mistrust. She had surrendered her will so unconditionally, without demanding that he do the same and end that affair with the unknown woman, doubtless one of those awkward relationships difficult to break off. *Would* he break it off and end all his previous love affairs? That's what he should do. And she was quite within her rights to say so. But there had been no time for any of that, no time to give or ask for the necessary explanations. It had struck like lightning, that exchange, that mutual abandonment of wills. It would be good to clarify the situation as soon as possible, to drive away all fear of duplicity and cast aside the lady who wrote those letters. Once this was done, Abelarda would give herself wholly to the man who had so absorbed her heart and soul; she would renounce all liberty and would be his in whatever fashion or under whatever conditions he wanted, with or without scandal, with or without honor.

While he was eating, Villaamil kept a close eye on his daughter, his face taking on its most characteristically tigerish qualities. He ate without appetite, as if he had speared on his fork a piece of palpitating, half-alive flesh, moaning and quivering in excruciating pain. Doña Pura and Milagros didn't dare mention Víctor's new appointment. They were both sullen and glum and funereal, and Abelarda ended up becoming part of that silent chorus of sepulchral figures. There was nothing on at the theater that night. Don Ramón shut himself in his office, and the three Miaows went into the living room where the illustrious Ponce and the Cuevas girls were gathered. Abelarda veered between being taciturn and brooding and feverishly talkative.

At midnight, the meeting drew to a close, and everyone went off to bed. The house lay in silence, with Abelarda awake, waiting for Víctor so that they could say what they needed to say and pour out their souls one to the other, like wine from glass to glass. One o'clock struck, then one thirty, and still the gallant lover did not appear. Between two and three, the unfortunate young woman was in a highly febrile state that filled her mind with the most bizarre nonsense. He must have been murdered ... Or could it be that the embrace, the kiss, and that declaration of love on the stairs had been a foul mockery ... She rejected this idea as simply too absurd and quite beyond the usual bounds, according to her, of human wickedness. Then she thought (by then it was already half past three) that having already found out that her lover was leaving her, or on hearing from his own lips the sad words of farewell, the fashionable woman with the fancy letter heading was plotting some ghastly revenge and had invited him to supper and was in the act of poisoning him, filling his glass of sherry with the poison of the Borgias. The foolish girl mixed these strange suspicions with a thousand other scenes familiar from operas: the curses the mezzo-soprano heaps on the tenor, because he has spurned her for the soprano; the vile tricks the baritone comes up with to dispatch his hated rival; the sublime constancy of the tenor (by now it was four o'clock), who, succumbing to the dastardly tricks of the bass and the contralto, dies in the arms of the soprano, while exchanging a promise with the soprano that they will love each other in the next world.

At five, Víctor had still not returned. By then, Abelarda's mind was a volcano that erupted from her eyes in feverish sparks and from her lips in spiteful, loving, furious monosyllables. During his time with them, that "superior man" had only twice stayed out all night, and the first time this happened, he had returned at around ten in the morning in a deplorable state, revealing in his manner, his words, and even his clothes, the excesses of a night spent feasting with some distinctly dubious people. If only this is what had happened now! But no, something bad had happened. Between that tender encounter on the stairs and his inexplicable absence lay an enigma, a mystery, possibly a misfortune or even an atrocity, which, in her bewilderment, the poor young woman could not comprehend. Six o'clock and still nothing. She burst into tears, and no sooner had she laid her head on her pillow than she was up again, sitting on a trunk or pacing the room, like a caged bird hopping from perch to perch.

Daybreak, and still no sign of him. The first person Abelarda heard moving about was her father, who went into the kitchen then back to his office. Eight o'clock. It would not be long before Doña Pura left her "fine feather mattress." Even if Víctor did return, it would no longer be possible for the sorrowful maiden to speak to him alone, and so she lay down, not in order to sleep or even to rest, but so that her mother would not find out that she had been awake all night. It was gone nine when the night owl arrived, looking much the worse for wear. Doña Pura opened the door to him and said not a word. He went to his room, and Abelarda, emerging from hers, could hear him blundering about in that narrow space, with barely enough room for bed, chair, and trunk.

"If you're going to church," said Doña Pura, taking a few coins from her purse, "buy four eggs on the way back, will you. And take Luis with you. I'm not going out. I have a headache. And your father, understandably, is extremely upset. Fancy giving that ne'er-do-well a job and leaving an honest man like your father out in the street, a man who knows more about the Administration than the whole ministry put together! What a government, eh, what a government! And then they're surprised when there's a revolution. Yes, buy four eggs. Frankly, I don't know how we're going to get through the day. Oh, and bring me that black braid for my dress and some hooks and eyes."

Abelarda went to church, and when she returned with her mother's shopping, she found her mother, her aunt, and Víctor in the dining room, engaged in a furious argument. The loudest voice was Víctor's:

"But, my dear ladies, is it my fault that I should be given a job before Papa? Is that reason enough for everyone in this house to turn on me? I've half a mind to chuck that letter of appointment out of the window, because family harmony comes first. Here I am doing my very best to win your affections, to make you forget all the pain I've caused you, and now here are my mother-in-law and her sister ready to pluck out my eyes because, Lord help us, the minister has decided to give me a post. Well, ladies, you can bite and scratch as much as you like, and I won't complain. Call me every name under the sun, and I will only love you all the more."

"As if we didn't know," said Doña Pura in viperish mode, "that you have loads of influential contacts in the ministry and that, if you really tried, Ramón would already have been reappointed!"

"Goodness me, Mama," replied Víctor, genuinely taken aback "How can you be so naive? How can you say that in all seriousness? That I...Well, I clearly have quite a reputation in the family. And what if I were to swear that I have put more effort into trying to get Papa reappointed than I did for myself? No, even if I swore that was so, you still wouldn't believe me. But whether you believe me or not, I swear that's the truth."

Abelarda took no part in the quarrel, but in her mind, she sided with her brother-in-law. At this point, Villaamil came into the room, and Víctor went straight over to him and said:

"You're a reasonable man; now tell me, do you believe, as these ladies do, that I have plotted or schemed or intrigued to get the powers-that-be to give me a job rather than you? Because that's the story they're burning my ears with at the moment, and frankly, it hurts me to be treated like a Judas with no conscience. (Spoken in a noble, wounded tone.) Don Ramón, I have been totally loyal to you. It's hardly my fault if I have been given preferential treatment. Do you know what I will do now? And may I be struck dead if I'm lying. I will cede my post to you."

"No one is suggesting any such thing," said Villaamil with a serenity he only achieved by doing considerable violence to himself. "Give *me* a post! Do you really think anyone is thinking of doing such a thing? What they've done is only natural and logical. Somewhere or other you have some very good sponsors, male or female. I have no one. Good luck to you."

And with that, he went back into his office and shut the door, leaving Víctor out in the corridor, somewhat confused and with a response on his lips he dare not give. He returned to the dining room, where he again tried to get around Doña Pura, trying to win her over with wheedling expressions of affection.

"Can there be anything worse than being so woefully misunderstood! I devote myself to this family, I make sacrifices for it, I embrace all its misfortunes as if they were mine and share with them my limited means, but it makes no difference. I am and always will be a bothersome guest and an unwanted relative. Patience, patience..."

He said this with practiced guile, as he picked up a piece of paper and went over to the dining table to start writing. As he sat down, he saw his sister-in-law standing looking at him, her right hand resting on her chin in a fond, attentive, pensive pose, similar—beauty apart—to the famous statue of Polyhymnia among the other ancient Muses. One didn't need to be particularly sharp to read in both her eyes and face words such as these: "What are you doing there just ignoring me? Don't you realize that I'm the only person who understands you? Turn to me and take no notice of the others. I've been waiting for you all night, you ungrateful man, but your mind is on other things. What happened to your plan for us to run away? I'm ready. I'll go just as I am."

Seeing her in that pose and reading her thoughts in her eyes, Víctor realized that he had a debt to settle with her. He hadn't given a thought to the encounter on the stairs the previous night, or if he had, only as a very paltry incident, like an inconsequential student prank. When he thought of it now, his first feeling was one of annoyance, as if suddenly remembering that he had to make some tiresome duty visit. However, he instantly composed his face, for in his wide repertoire as emotional histrion, he had a beautiful mask for every occasion, and making sure that his mother-in-law was nowhere to be seen, he adopted the tenderest of expressions, glanced up at the ceiling, then at Abelarda, and the following brief exchange took place:

"My love, I must talk to you, but where and when?"

"This evening...at the Comendadoras church...at six o'clock."

And that was that. Abelarda ran off to tidy the living room, and Víctor started writing, scornfully throwing off his mask and thinking something along these lines:

"The silly fool can't wait to know when it's her turn to ruin herself...Wouldn't you like to know? Well, it's not going to happen."

32

RIGHT on the dot, Abelarda entered their chosen meeting place, the church of the Comendadoras. The dark, silent church was perfect for that mysterious rendezvous. Anyone seeing her arrive would have been astonished to see her there, wearing her finest clothes, her Sunday best. She had only put them on once her mother had left the apartment at five. She sat down on a pew, praying feverishly and distractedly, and fifteen minutes later, Víctor arrived. To begin with, he couldn't see a thing and had no idea where to go. Abelarda went over and touched his arm to serve as his guide. Hand-in hand they took a seat near the door, in a rather secluded spot in the darkest part of the church, at the entrance to the Chapel of Sorrows.

Despite the skill and confidence with which he usually handled even the most awkward situations, it took a while for Víctor to choose his words, uncertain quite how to broach the subject. Finally, determined to keep things brief, and mentally commending himself to his guardian devil, he said:

"I must begin by asking your forgiveness, my love; yes, forgiveness for my... my imprudent behavior. The love I feel for you is so deep, so overwhelming, that last night, unthinkingly, I wanted to carry you along with me through the many perils that await me. You must be quite furious with me, and I can understand that, because to propose such a thing to a woman of your qualities and in the way that I did... But I was blind, mad, I didn't know what I was doing. What must you think of me? I deserve your scorn. Suggesting that you should leave your parents, your home, to follow me—me, an errant comet (recalling phrases he had read years before and shamelessly plagiarizing them), flying through space, with no fixed destination, not even knowing where that impulse comes from or where my mad flight will take me! I will fall and fail. But I would be an utter villain, Abelarda (taking her hand), the most monstrous of monsters, if I allowed you to fall and fail with me...you, who are an angel; you, who are the jewel of your family...Oh, I beg your forgiveness and would go down on my knees to obtain it. I have gravely offended your dignity, I abused your innocence by proposing such an outrageous thing, the child of an impulsive mind...so please, forgive me, and accept my honest excuses. I love you, yes, I love you, and I always will, but my love is hopeless, because I cannot aspire to possessing such a...such a gem. I would be spitting in the face of God were I to aspire to such a thing..."

Abelarda could not really understand all this verbiage so contrary to what she was expecting to hear. She looked at him and then at the nearest image, a Saint John the Baptist carrying his usual lamb and flag, and she kept asking the saint if all this was real or a dream.

"You're...you're forgiven," she murmured, breathing hard.

"Do not be surprised, my love," he went on, now fully in control of the situation, "if, in your presence, I grow timid and unable to express myself clearly. You mesmerize me, leave me speechless, make me keenly aware of my own insignificance. Forgive my bold behavior last night. Now I want only to be worthy of you, to imitate your sublime serenity. You are showing me the path I should follow, the path of the ideal life, with my every action perfectly aligned with the divine law. I will imitate you—that is, I will try to imitate you. For, O incomparable one, we must part. Were we to stay together, your life would be at risk and so would mine. We are surrounded by enemies who are watching us, spying on us. What can we do? We must separate here on Earth, only to meet in the lofty sphere of thoughts and ideas. Think of me, for you will always be in my thoughts..."

Feeling deeply troubled, Abelarda kept shifting about on the pew as if it were covered in thorns.

"How could I forget that, when all the family turned against me, you alone understood and consoled me? Ah, that is something that could never be forgotten, not in a thousand years. You truly are sublime, while I am a mere wretch. Abandon me, then, to my sad fate. I know you will pray for me, and that consoles me. Were I a believer and could prostrate myself before that altar or another similar one, if I could pray, I would pray for you. Farewell, my love."

He tried to take her hand, but Abelarda withdrew it and turned away.

"Your scorn is like death to me, although I know that I deserve it...Last night, I treated you disrespectfully, coarsely, indelicately, and yet you say that you forgive me. Why then turn away from me? Ah, I know my presence wounds you, that you find me loathsome... And I deserve that, I know I do. Farewell. I am paying for my sins, for, as you see, I keep trying to leave you but cannot bring myself to do so...I am nailed to this wooden pew...(Growing impatient and gabbling now in order to finish quickly.) Will you remember me in your future life? I have a word of advice: Marry Ponce, but if you do not, then enter a convent and pray for him and for me—for this... sinner...You were born for the spiritual life. You have a great soul, too large for the narrow world of matrimony or the prosaic life of the family. I can't go on, my dear, because I can barely think; I'm spouting nonsense now. Courage...I must make the supreme effort... Farewell, farewell."

And like a soul borne away by Satan, he left the church, muttering under his breath. He was in a hurry and congratulated himself on having paid off a very bothersome debt. "Damn it!" he said, looking at his watch and quickening his pace. "I thought I'd get it over with in ten minutes, and it took me twenty. And that other lady has been waiting for me since six o'clock! But I can't help feeling sorry for the poor hopeless little fool. They're going to have to put her in a straitjacket—or, rather, a straitcorset."

And what was Abelarda doing or thinking? Well, if she had seen the devil himself climb into the pulpit and deliver a sermon accusing the faithful of not sinning enough and telling them that if they continued in that vein, they would never gain their place in hell—well, if Abelarda had seen that, she wouldn't have felt half as astonished as she did now. The monster's words and his swift exit left her frozen, incapable of movement, her brain congealing under the impact of that encounter, like a hot substance that sets very quickly after being poured into a cold mold. It didn't even occur to her to pray—whatever for? Nor to leave—where would she go? She was better off staying there, still and silent, rivaling in immobility Our Lady of Sorrows and Saint John the Baptist with his pennant. The former was standing at the foot of the cross, stiff and austere in her widow's weeds, her heart pierced by several small silver daggers, her hands clasped so hard that the fingers fused to become a tight bundle. Christ, much larger than the image of his mother, was spread out on the wall above, touching the ceiling of the chapel with his crown of thorns and reaching out his incredibly long arms. Beneath him were candles, the attributes of the Passion, wax ex-votos, a grimy offertory box with a rusty padlock, the altar cloth spotted with candle wax, and the altar table repainted to resemble marble. Abelarda was looking at all this, but without seeing the whole, only the tiniest details, fixing her eyes here and there like a needle that pricks but doesn't pierce, while her soul was filled by the gall of the vinegar-soaked sponge.

Two very serious events occurred at the same time, either one of which could have decided the future life of that insignificant, overwrought young woman. Just two and a half hours after the incident we have just described came another no less important one. Ponce, talking to Doña Pura in her living room, with no other witnesses, was expressing his annoyance with her and her husband because they had not yet fixed a date for the wedding.

"But it's as good as settled, my dear. Ramón and I want nothing more. How about a date in early May? The Festival of the Crosses on the third, perhaps."

Shortly before, Doña Pura had explained her daughter's absence, saying that she had caught a terrible chill that evening in the church. She had come home with her teeth chattering and with such a high fever that her mother had immediately sent her to bed. This was the truth, but not the whole truth, for Doña Pura said nothing of her amazement at seeing her daughter return so unusually late and wearing a dress she didn't normally wear on an evening visit to the local church. "Those are your very best clothes; fancy wearing them in a place where no one will see you and possibly staining that gorgeous cashmere worth fourteen reales on those greasy, dusty, filthy pews." She also failed to mention that her daughter had not responded coherently to anything she had said. This, her chattering teeth, and her lack of appetite had prompted Doña Pura to send her straight to bed. She wasn't quite sure what to make of it and was anxiously trying to understand what lay behind some other rather odd behavior she had noticed in her daughter of late. "Whatever the reason," she thought, "the sooner we marry her off, the better." She said something along these lines to her husband, but Villaamil was so gloomy and downhearted that he didn't deign to say a word in response.

Abelarda, who was pretending to be asleep so that no one would bother her, watched Milagros putting Luis to bed; however, Luis stayed awake for some time, tossing and turning. When they were alone, Abelarda told him to be quiet. She didn't want to be disturbed; it was late, and she needed to rest.

"But Auntie, I can't sleep. Tell me a story."

"Look, I'm in no mood for stories. Leave me in peace or else . . ."

Usually, when her nephew couldn't sleep, Abelarda, who adored him, would soothe him with fond words, and if that wasn't enough, she would go over to his bed and, by singing to him and tucking him in, would eventually succeed in making him drift off. That night, though, she was so beside herself with rage that she felt real loathing for the poor lad; his voice grated on her, and for the first time in her life she thought: "What do I care if you fall asleep or not, if you're good or bad, or if you go to the devil."

Luis, accustomed to his aunt showering him with affection, would not give up. He was determined to have a chat, and in a wheedling voice he said to her:

"Auntie, have you ever, by any chance, seen God?"

"What are you talking about, you silly boy? If you don't shut up, I'll come over and . . ."

"Don't get angry, Auntie...I haven't done anything wrong. I do see God, if you must know; I can see him whenever I want. But tonight, I can only see his feet...covered in blood they are, nailed to the cross and tied with a piece of white rope, like the feet of that long-haired Christ in Montserrat church...and it really frightens me. I don't want to close my eyes because...well, I've never seen his feet before, only his face and hands...and the reason this is happening to me is because I committed a big sin...because I told my Papa a lie, I told him I wanted to go and live with my Aunt Quintina. And it was a lie. I only want to go there for a little while, just long enough to see the saints. I don't want to live with her, though. Because going off with her and leaving you all here would be a sin, wouldn't it?"

"Shut up, will you, I've had enough of your foolishness. You can see God, can you, you silly ass? Of course, there he is, just so that you can see him, you idiot."

Shortly afterward Abelarda heard Luis sobbing, and, strangely, instead of pity she felt such an intense dislike for him you could almost describe it as loathing. That snotty little boy was a fool, a fraud, always leading the family up the garden path with his nonsense about being able to see God and wanting to become a priest; he was a hypocrite, a liar, a sneak...not to mention ugly and sickly, not to mention spoiled rotten...

This hostility toward the poor child was similar to the feeling of hatred for her own father that had welled up in her heart just the previous night, a hatred that went against her own nature and was doubtless the product of one of those epileptic auras that can subvert a woman's primary feelings. She didn't know why such monstrous feelings had set seed in her mind, and she watched them grow and grow by the minute, taking a kind of unhealthy pleasure in watching them become ever stronger. She hated Luis; she hated him with all her heart. The boy's voice got on her nerves and drove her frantic.

Still sobbing, Luis went on talking:

"I can see his legs all stained with black blood, I can see his knees with huge dark bruises on them, Auntie...I'm so afraid. Quick, come over here!"

Abelarda clenched her fists and gnawed at the sheets. That plaintive voice stirred her whole being, and a red wave rose up inside her, a wave of blood that rose and rose and clouded her eyes. The child was a lying, wheedling impostor, brought into the world to torment her and the whole family... However, her habit of tenderness kept her rage in check. She made as if to leap out of bed, go straight over to Luis, and give him a sound beating, but immediately stopped herself. Ah, if she laid hands on him, she wouldn't be content with giving him a good hiding... she would strangle him, yes, she would. Such was the fury searing her soul and such was the thirst for destruction in her burning hands!

"Auntie, now I can see that little skirt thing all covered in blood, lots of blood... Please, light the lamp or I'll die of fright; get rid of him, tell him to go away. It's the other God I like, the handsome grandfather, with no blood on him, just a very fine cloak and a very white beard..."

Abelarda could hold back no longer and she jumped out of bed, only to stay standing, frozen to the spot, not out of pity, but because of a memory that dazzled her mind with its vivid light. One sad night, her dead sister had done exactly as she had just done. Yes, Luisa had also had those sudden bursts of loathing for her child, and one night when she heard him crying, she too had jumped out of bed and made as if to pummel him with her fists, mother transformed into wild beast. Fortunately, they had managed to restrain her, because if they hadn't, heaven knows what would have happened. And there was Abelarda repeating the same words her dead sister had said, calling the poor child a monster, a fiend from hell, come down to earth as a punishment and a curse on the family.

This memory led her to realize how similar the cause and the effect were, and she thought with horror: "Am I mad like my sister? Dear God, is this madness?"

She got back between the sheets and lay listening to Luis's sobbing, which eventually seemed to stop, as if sleep had finally overcome him. A considerable time passed, during which she too appeared to doze off, but then she started awake again, filled by the same vengeful rage at its most intense. The memory of her sister no longer held her back; there was nothing in her mind to correct the idea or, rather, the crazed belief that Luis was a bad person, a loathsome freak, a vile creature who should be exterminated. He was to blame for all the ills bearing down on her, and once he had been erased from the world, the sun would shine more brightly and life would be happy. That boy represented all that was perfidious in human nature: treachery, mendacity, dishonesty, bearing false witness.

Profound darkness reigned. Barefoot and in her nightdress, Abelarda threw a shawl round her shoulders and advanced, feeling her way...Then she drew back, looking for some matches. And at that moment, it occurred to her to go to the kitchen in search of a sharp knife. To do so, she needed light. She lit the lamp and looked at Luis, who was now sleeping deeply. "The perfect opportunity!" she thought. "He won't scream now or try to struggle...I'll have my revenge on you, you fraud, you clown, you buffoon...Try telling me now that you can actually see God...As if there were such a God." After observing her nephew for a while, she left the room, filled with resolve. "The sooner the better." The memory of the boy's sobs and all that guff about being able to see God's feet only further fueled her rage. She went into the kitchen, but couldn't find a knife. Then, in a corner, she spotted an axe for chopping firewood, and that seemed to her a far better tool for the "job," more reliable, more efficient, more cutting. She picked it up, practiced making a few chopping movements, and, once satisfied, returned to her bedroom, her shawl over her head, the lamp in one hand and the axe in the other. No more outlandish or more alarming figure had ever been seen in that apartment. However, as she opened the glazed door into the bedroom, she heard a noise that made her start. It was the sound of Víctor's key turning in the lock. Like a thief caught redhanded, she extinguished the lamp, entered the room and crouched down behind the door, hiding the axe behind her. Even though she was in total darkness, she feared that Víctor might see her as he walked past on his way to the dining room, and she hunkered right down, because the fury that had dictated her last actions suddenly changed into a feeling of horror tinged with feminine embarrassment. He passed by, lighting his way with a match, went into his room, and immediately shut the door. Silence returned. Through the two glazed doors came the feeble light of the candle that Víctor lit before going to bed. Ten minutes later, it went out, and all was darkness again. But the poor woman still did not dare to light her lamp; she felt her way to her bed, hid the axe underneath the chest of drawers next to it, and slipped in between the sheets, thinking: "Now is not the moment. The boy would scream and he, Víctor... Well, I'd like to give him the ax blow of the century, but one blow wouldn't be enough, nor would two or a hundred, or even a thousand blows. I could chop away all night and still not be done."

33

OUR UNFORTUNATE friend Villaamil had not been able to rest easy since the bitter moment when he learned of his son-in-law's promotion, and to make matters worse, his ministerial sponsor would now have nothing to do with him. Villaamil would leave the house immediately after lunch and spend the day visiting office after office, recounting his misfortunes to anyone he met, describing the appalling injustice he had suffered, not, of course, that it had taken him by surprise, because he had never expected anything else. It was true that—driven by cruel necessity, and beginning to sense that his self-imposed pessimism was becoming a hindrance—he would occasionally remove his pessimism like someone removing a mask, and say in plaintive tones:

"Cucúrbitas, my friend, I will take anything. My proper rank is that of head of Administration, third class, but if they were to give me a post as a first- or even second-class clerk, I would take it, yes, I would, even if it was in the provinces."

He told the same old story to the head of personnel, to any influential friends who visited him at home, and, by letter, to the minister and to Pez. To Pantoja he confided:

"Although it would be a great humiliation, I would even accept a post as clerk, third class, simply to get out of this wretched situation. Then, it will be as God decrees."

Or he would suddenly rush off to see Sevillano, of whom more later, who worked in Personnel and who would say to him pityingly:

"I know, I know, but you must calm down. We know what the situation is... but you really must try and calm down."

He would then turn his back on him.

Little by little, Don Ramón began to behave in ways that went entirely counter to his true nature, pestering everyone and losing all sense of what might be deemed reasonable behavior. After watching him go from office to office, hassling various friends and even the porters, Pantoja said to him confidentially:

"Do you know what that wicked son-in-law of yours said to your deputy? He said you were mad and would be incapable of undertaking any post in the Administration. He actually said that, and the deputy repeated it in the Personnel Department in the presence of Sevillano and Espinosa's brother, who came and told me."

"He said that? (Dumbstruck.) Oh, I can well believe it. That man is capable of anything..."

This news completely unhinged Villaamil. His tireless, stubborn persistence and the increasingly desperate look in his eyes began to alarm his friends. In some offices, they did their best not to respond or answered very brusquely so that he would give up and clear off. But he was immune to all snubs and slights, his pride having added another layer to his already thick skin. In the absence of Pantoja, Espinosa, and Guillén, the other employees would tease him mercilessly.

"Villaamil, have you heard what's going on here? The minister is going to present to Parliament a bill introducing income tax. La Caña is looking into it."

"So, he's stolen my idea! My five memoranda lay sleeping on his desk for more than a year. You see what one gets for burning the midnight oil to come up with a plan that will revive this moribund Treasury, this land of petty thieves, this government of numbskulls who, when they're down to their last peseta, make off with someone else's ideas. Oh really!"

And then he would race off, hurtling down the stairs to the Tax Office (in the courtyard on the left), eager to give his friend La Caña a stern telling-off. Half an hour later, he could be seen panting his way back up the same weary staircase to visit the Treasury or Customs & Excise. Sometimes, before going in, he would harangue the porters with an account of his long administrative record.

"When I first entered the service, Espartero was still regent and Señor Surrá y Rull was the minister, oh, he was an excellent man and very well regarded. It seems like only yesterday that I climbed those stairs. I had on a pair of checkered trousers—they were fashionable then—and a top hat, which I was wearing for the first time. Not a soul from those days is left, because poor Cruz, who I met here on that very day, departed this world two months ago. What a life, eh? Don Alejandro Mon gave me my first promotion, he was a good man and full of energy! He would arrive at eight in the morning and set the troops to work, that's why he achieved as much as he did. The real early bird, though, was Don Juan Bravo Murillo, while the number one night owl was Don José Salamanca, who would keep us Secretariat folk here until two or three in the morning. Tell me, do any of you remember Don Juan Bruil, who, by the way, made me clerk, third class? What a man! He had a temper on him though. Mind you, our friend Madoz was prone to fly off the handle too. A real firecracker. In 1857, I had a director who would never do a favor for a living soul or even see anyone unless they happened to be a woman asking for help. Skirt-chasing has been this country's downfall."

The porters humored him for as long as they could bear it, but they too grew weary of him and would invent urgent errands just to escape. The good man, having spoken at length, would go inside then, and in Customs & Excise or in Estates, there would always be someone—like Urbanito, Cucúrbitas's son—who would invite him to a coffee just to get him talking and amuse himself listening to Villaamil's litany of impassioned complaints.

"This is happening to me because I'm a decent fellow, because, if I'd wanted to, I could have revealed a few things I know about certain high-ups, if you know what I mean. Because if I'd been like other men who go to the newspapers with tales of scheme A or plot B . . . well, things would be quite different. What can one do, though? One can choose not to be decent and discreet, but if it's simply not in one's nature . . . A scoundrel is a scoundrel from the cradle up. It wasn't even worth my while writing those five memoranda setting out a

hat... then there are the cravats you wear. If they ever reappoint me, I'll wear something similar... Anyway, like I say, I would be happy with a post as clerk, third class, or anything really; what matters is getting my name back on the payroll and being someone again, so that I don't feel that even the walls here are weeping when they see me walk into the office... You're an essential worker here, Francisco, so do it for God and for your sons—three of whom are already in post on five thousand, not to mention Urbanito, who earns twelve thousand. If my wife were more like Pez's wife—namely, more fish than frog*—I wouldn't be in the position I am today. It's as if you have it in your blood, and when your kids are born and utter their first cry, instead of giving them their mother's milk to drink, you give them Paragraph A, Section 8 of the Budget. Anyway, I must go; put in a word for me and drag me out of this hole I've fallen into. I don't mean to trouble you, because I know how busy you are, but then I'm pretty burdened down as well. Goodbye, goodbye."

Don't go thinking that our man then went out into the street. Drawn irresistibly upward, he made the wearisome ascent up to the Secretariat, where he arrived panting and out of breath. One day, he met with a novelty. The porters, who usually opened the door for him, wouldn't let him in, trying to disguise with kind words the order they had been given to keep him out.

"Don Ramón, go home and rest, a little nap will clear that mind of yours. The boss is busy and isn't receiving anyone."

Villaamil was most annoyed by such an order and even protested, saying that it couldn't possibly apply to him. His cloak slipped from his shoulders and swept the floor as he paced back and forth, and the porters even had to put his hat back on, for it had fallen from his venerable head.

"Don't worry, Pepito Pez, I'm going," he said, breathing hard. "So, this is how you repay the person who was once your boss and covered up your many faults. Ingratitude sprouts in the most unexpected places. After doing you a thousand favors in the past, here you are

*Pez, in Spanish, means "fish."

treating me like a dog. An all too human logic ... Anyway, now we understand each other. Farewell! Ah (turning round at the door), tell your head of personnel, Señor Don Double-Dealer, that you and he can go and pull up weeds."

34

UP THE stairs he went again, to the second floor, to Pantoja's office. When he arrived, Guillén, Espinosa, and some other nincompoops were tittering over the drawings Guillén had put together—a series of crude cartoons depicting Villaamil's life from birth to death, each one accompanied by a coarse, vulgar couplet, a vain attempt at wit. Argüelles, who disapproved of Guillén's coarse jokes, left the group and got on with his work. Guillén said that Villaamil had been born in Coria, the traditional birthplace of fools (which was a gross historical error, for he had, in fact, been born in the province of Burgos); that he had been begging for a position even in his mother's womb; and that his umbilical cord had been tied off with a piece of red tape. This illustrated history said, among other things, "No swaddling clothes for Baby Miaow / only letters of appointment," and further on, "When he cries and hollers for the breast / to his lips instead a budget they pressed." Then, when he reached maturity: "Overwhelmed by feelings of love without measure / he marries Doña Pura, that feline treasure"; and soon after they are married, the troubles begin. The ramshackle Villaamil household was described in these elegant lines: "Whenever they're short of meat and rice / they go on the hunt for a few resident mice." However, it was in his depiction of Villaamil's sublime work on taxation that the inspired coupleteer reached new heights: "In his indefatigable search for facts / Miaow invents the income tax ... He presents his plan to the relevant minister / who sees it all as rather sinister ... And, having listened to Miaow's self-INCOMIUM / he sends him off to the insanatorium." At the end, the poet threw in these flattering lines: "He sustains his grim and miserable existence / by dint of beggary and sheer persistence," and he even imagined the hero's glorious death: "They finally give him his paltry ration / and the poor man dies of sheer jubilation ... And when he dies, all the cats intone / a Miaowful setting of Psalm 51 ..."

On seeing Villaamil approach, his colleagues hurriedly tried to conceal the abominable document, but their failure entirely to repress their hilarity revealed both the joke and its cause. Poor Don Ramón had noticed before that his presence in the office (whenever Pantoja wasn't there) provoked a resurgence among those idlers of a pressing need to make fun of others. That day, their sudden silences, their words accompanied by knowing looks, the comic gravity with which they greeted him, all revealed to him that his person and possibly even his misfortune were motives for much cruel mockery, and knowing this cut him to the quick. His pride was wounded by both the tangle of ideas beginning to form inside his head and by the anger he felt at all his many tribulations; he was growing embittered, his innate meekness mutating into peevishness and his peace-loving nature into thin-skinned susceptibility.

"Let's see, let's see," he grumbled as, scowling, he joined the group. "It seems you were talking about me. What are those bits of paper Guillén is at such pains to hide? Let's be clear, gentlemen. If one of you has something to say to me, then say it to my face. I've noticed that there seems to be a conspiracy in this office to slander me, to ridicule me, to turn our bosses against me, to represent me to the minister as some kind of grotesque—as a ... And I want to know who the swinish conspirator is, damn him!" (Throwing back his cloak and bringing his fist down hard on the nearest desk.)

They all froze and fell silent because they weren't expecting Villaamil to behave with such dignity. Argüelles was the first to see this change of temperament as evidence of some kind of mental disturbance. Along with his loathing for Guillén, he felt intensely sorry for his friend, and putting his arm around his shoulder, he begged him to calm down, adding that, in his presence, no one would dare malign such a respectable person. This reasoning did not reassure Villaamil, however, because he could see that wretch Guillén still smothering his laughter, his face pressed against his desk, and, filled with rage, Villaamil went over to him and said in a hoarse, tremulous voice:

"I'll have you know, you vile cripple, that no one laughs at me. I know you've written some stupid verses and scrawled a few drawings ridiculing me. I heard the people in Customs & Excise talking about them—about how they show me telling the minister about my plan for income tax and him packing me off to the madhouse."

"Me? But Don Ramón, really..." said Guillén in a timid, cowardly voice. "It wasn't me who did the drawings, it was Pez Cortázar in Estates, and then Urbano Cucúrbitas passed them around."

"Well, whoever it was, the perpetrator of this trash is an utter swine whose proper place is in a pigsty. They insult me because they see how low I have sunk, but is that the behavior of gentlemen? Come on, tell me. Is that what decent people do?"

The good man turned and sat down, utterly drained by his efforts. He continued muttering, though, as if talking to himself:

"It's as if they were determined to use every means possible to destroy me, to discredit me, to have the minister think me odd, deluded, idiotic."

He kept uttering the deepest of sighs, his chin buried in his chest, and he remained like that for a full fifteen minutes without saying a word. The others were silent, grave-faced, occasionally exchanging serious, possibly pitying glances, and for a while, all that was heard in the office was the scratching of Argüelles's pen. Then the sound of squeaky boots announced the return of Pantoja. Everyone pretended to be busily working when he arrived, carrying bundles of papers. Villaamil did not look up to see his friend and didn't even seem to notice his presence.

"Ramón," said Pantoja fondly, calling to him from his desk. "Ramón, whatever's wrong?"

And uttering another huge sigh, like someone waking from a dream, Villamil finally stood up and walked unsteadily over to his friend's desk.

"Come now," Pantoja said, removing a sheaf of papers from the nearest chair so that his friend could sit down. "You're behaving like a child. Everyone's talking as if you were beginning to lose your wits. Get a grip, man—and above all (growing slightly annoyed), whenever the talk turns to tax plans and drawing up new budgets, you must stop spouting this nonsense of yours about income tax . . . That's all very well for newspaper articles (said in a scornful tone), or in the café with a few foolish ne'er-do-wells, the kind who waste a lot of breath on the country's budgets but never pay their tailor or their landlady. You're a serious man, though, and you can't really believe that our tax system, the fruit of long experience . . ."

Villaamil sprang from his chair then, as if a very sharp thorn had thrust up through the seat, and this sudden movement cut short Pantoja's sentence, which he was doubtless going to conclude in true administrative fashion, more suited to an official document than to a human utterance. Kindly Pantoja was utterly astounded to see his friend's face—jaw trembling, eyes flashing, a look of frenzied rage— and he was even more astounded when he heard him say these furious words:

"Well, I maintain—yes, on Christ's head I maintain—that only bureaucratic donkeys . . . no, worse, only tricksters and cheats would stick to the present system . . . Because only someone with cobwebs for brains could fail to recognize and proclaim that income tax, or whatever you choose to call it, is the only rational and philosophical way forward for the tax regime . . . I would go further and say that you here listening to me now, starting with you, Pantoja, are nothing but a bunch of ignoramuses, administrative pests, like woodworm or phylloxerae, gnawing away at and devouring everything, like the complete and utter idiots you are. And, if he pressed me, I would say the same to the minister, because I don't want a letter of appointment or a post or a pension or anything; all I want, above all else, is the truth, good governance, and the reconciliation . . . compagination . . . and harmonization (tapping the tips of his index fingers together) of the state's interests with those of the taxpayer. And the fool, the wretch, who says all I want is a new job can meet me man to man out in the street, or in Plaza del Dos de Mayo, or in Pradera del Canal, at midnight and with no witnesses . . . (Bawling out these words so loudly that clerks from the nearby office rushed in.) Needless to say, you take me for a mere nobody because you don't know me, because you haven't seen me defending justice and the law against those villains intent on trampling both. I do not come here to beg for some despicable, rotten little post somewhere; I don't care two hoots about the Administration, about you, or the director or the head of personnel or the minister ... all I'm asking for is order, morality, economy ..."

He looked wildly about him, and finding himself surrounded by so many faces, he raised his arms, as if urging on a seditious mob, and uttered a savage cry of "Long live balanced budgets!"

With that, he stumbled out of the office, his cloak trailing behind him. Pantoja, scratching his head with his cap, watched him compassionately, genuinely upset.

"Gentlemen," he said to his colleagues and to the other curious onlookers gathered there. "Let us pray for our poor friend, who has clearly lost his wits."

35

It was shortly before eleven o'clock the following morning—which was, moreover, the last day of the month—that Villaamil could be seen laboring up the ministry's narrow staircase, stopping every few steps to catch his breath. When he arrived at the entrance to the Secretariat, the porters, who had seen him leave the previous afternoon in the lamentable state described above, were amazed to see him looking so calm now, apparently restored to his usual mild, modest self, a man incapable of raising his voice to anyone. They were suspicious of such meekness, though, and when Villaamil sat down on the bench, which was as hard and narrow as a church pew, and held up his feet to the nearby brazier, the youngest of the porters went over to him and said:

"What are you doing here, Don Ramón? You should be at home resting; there's no need for you to be wandering around in these parts."

"You may well be right, friend Ceferino. I should stay safe at home and leave these gentlemen here to sort things out as they think best. What business is it of mine? True, the state has to pay for any broken windows, and one cannot view such wastage with indifference. Do you happen to know if the final budget has been shown to the minister? Ah, you don't. Well, why should you? You're not a taxpayer. Well, let me tell you, the new budget is even worse than the current one, and all they do in these offices is create an endless stream of nonsense and stupidity. Not that I care. I'll just sit quietly at home, watching the country collapse around me, a country that could be swimming in gold if it so chose."

Having concluded this peroration, Don Ramón remained alone,

thinking, his chin resting on his hand. A few clerks he knew walked past, but since they didn't speak to him, he said nothing. He was perhaps pondering the solitude that was growing around him and the speed with which he had been abandoned by those who had once been his colleagues and who had, until recently, called themselves his friends. "The reason," he thought with admirable insight, "is that my misfortunes have made me somewhat eccentric, and the pain of my situation does make me say things one would not expect from a totally sane man; indeed, they run completely counter to my character and to my... ah, what's that pesky word... ah, yes, my idiosyncrasy. Well, so be it."

He was distracted from these thoughts by a friend who came straight over to him as soon as he saw him. It was the paterfamilias Argüelles, swathed in a black cloak—or, rather, a sixteenth-century-style half-cape—and with his usual slouch hat, waxed mustache, and neat goatee beard jutting out above his high collar. Before going up to the Tax Office, he usually dropped in at the Personnel Department to unburden himself to a friend there who told him all the news and fed his hopes of an imminent promotion.

"What on earth are you doing here, my friend?" he said in the tone of voice one tends to reserve for the gravely ill. "Shall we have a coffee together? No, coffee might disagree with you. You need to take care of yourself, and if you'll take my advice, you would be wise not to come back to this den of iniquity for some days."

"Where shall we go then?" asked Villaamil, standing up.

"To the Personnel Department. We can have a little chat with Sevillano, who will update us on the day's appointments. Come on."

And they headed off down a long, rather gloomy corridor, which turned first to the right and then to the left. As they walked down that mysterious passageway full of twists and turns, Villaamil and Argüelles could have been mistaken for caricatures of Dante and Virgil, seeking, by hidden signs, the entrance to or exit from the infernal places they were visiting. Given Don Ramón's simple, plain appearance and ample cloak, it was easy enough to see him as a burlesque Dante; as for Virgil, one would have to replace him with

Quevedo, that parodist of the *Divine Comedy* (although Argüelles bore a closer resemblance to Quevedo's *The Bailiff Possessed* than to the great Quevedo himself). Neither Dante nor Quevedo, on their respective fantastic journeyings, could have even dreamed of anything like that labyrinth of offices, the cacophonous clamor of bells being rung in every part of that vast mansion, the opening and closing of screens and doors, the footsteps and throat-clearings of clerks on their way to their desks, doffing cloaks and hats—nor anything that could compare with the to-and-fro of dusty bundles of paper, glasses of water, spadefuls of coal, or with the tobacco-filled air, the orders passed from desk to desk, and the bustle and buzz of those hives where the bitter honey of the Administration is made. Villaamil and his guide entered an office in which there were just two desks and one person, who, at that moment, was changing his hat for a purple corduroy beret and his shoes for slippers. This was Sevillano, an official in the Secretariat, a good fellow, although getting on in years, and a popular figure among his colleagues, with a reputation for being very astute. He greeted Villaamil rather cautiously and studied him closely.

"Oh, surviving," said the eternally unemployed Villaamil in reply to Sevillano's routine inquiry, then he sat down on a chair by the desk.

"No news about my case," said Argüelles, using a formula that was, at once, a question and a statement.

"None," said the rather vain Sevillano, who, by coming and standing in front of the desk, appeared to be motivated by a desire to show off his embroidered slippers and his dainty feet. "Well, nothing to speak of. No one has put your name forward, nor do they seem likely to."

"I can't say I'm surprised," said Argüelles, removing his cloak and hat as if wishing to compete with Sevillano's slippers by revealing his long, curly hair. "That wretched man Pantoja has let me down three times now, and I'll be blowed if he doesn't do it a fourth time. I'll put up with anything as long as that repulsive midget Guillén doesn't get in ahead of me. If they promote him before me, if a children-laden paterfamilias who does all the hard work in the office sees himself overtaken by that worthless creature who wastes his time drawing cartoons . . . (Turning to Villaamil seeking his agreement.) Am I right? Does it seem fair to you that, after all my years in the job, they still feel it's too soon to give me a promotion, and yet they'll give it to that cripple, who is not only a bad man but an even worse friend, and who, besides, can't even make an accurate copy of a document?"

"It is precisely because he's so useless," said Villaamil in the most lugubrious of voices, "that his career is assured."

"If they promote him ahead of me," declared Argüelles, stamping his foot, "I'll raise merry hell, I'll go to the minister and I'll say . . . well, I'll . . . . I'll certainly give him a piece of my mind. Promoting him over me would be tantamount to insulting me to my face or spitting at me. Such injustice makes a man's blood boil, makes you feel like throwing all morality out of the window and joining forces with Judas. That worm Guillén, with his jokes and his doggerel and all his other bits of garbage, has become very popular here. People laugh at his stupid remarks . . . And it's true that we're all to blame for letting him get away with it . . . But I promise you, Don Ramón, he's not going to show any more of his stupid drawings to anyone, not when I'm there. I'll tell him what's what, I'll tell him . . ."

Argüelles stopped speaking, thinking he saw some signs of over-excitement on Villaamil's face; however, the old man was listening serenely, apparently unconcerned by the thought of those coarse jokes.

"Leave him be," he said. "For my part, I have learned how to rise above such silliness. You will recall that, yesterday, when I found out they were making fun of me, I didn't say a word. One must treat such things with scorn, nothing more. Afterward, in the street, I bumped into Cucúrbitas's son, Urbano, the one who works in Customs & Excise, and he told me that Guillén had shown off his cartoons there as well. Besides, they're utterly stupid. They're not even funny. According to them, when I was a baby, payslips were used instead of diapers, and I went to the minister with my idea about income tax . . . Well, I would like to ask Guillén, what has it got to do with an ass like him whether I did or didn't do that? What does he know about matters far beyond the understanding of a puny little runt like him. Then he calls *me* a sponger, which is a vile slander; because if, in the difficult straits in which I find myself, necessity forces me to ask for help from a friend, that doesn't make me a parasite. No, one must bear these calumnies with great patience and not give the calumniator the pleasure of hearing one's complaints, because the knowledge that he has hit home will only puff him up still more. Scorn and indifference are the best response, and may he vomit up poison until his soul shrivels into nothing... Ha! I will not reward such ignoble creatures with so much as a glance. And to think that I have welcomed that man into my home, because he often comes to visit us—yes, he flatters my family, drinks my wine, and appears to love us all as dearly as if we were his brothers and sisters. The monster! I'll go further and say that Pantoja is partly to blame, because he allows Guillén to waste good office time coming up with that rubbish ... I know those daubs as if I had actually seen them, because Urbano didn't stint on detail. You know, people think that boy is a fool, but I reckon he has a lot of talent, and his memory is second to none. He also told me that Guillén based the nickname 'Miaow' that he gives me in those cartoons on the initial letters of my five memoranda. And I accept the name, because that 'M,' that 'I,' that 'A,' that 'O,' and that 'W' are the equivalent of INRI, the odious sign they placed above Christ on the cross ... Now that I have been crucified among thieves, let them, to complete the picture, write above my head the five letters with which they mock and scorn my great mission."

36

SEVILLANO and Argüelles had initially listened to him with some respect, but as soon as they heard these comments, they hesitated between pity and laughter, with pity prevailing in the form of this response from Sevillano:

"You're quite right to despise such idiocy. There's nothing more despicable than making fun of a worthy gentleman fallen on hard times. They tried to show me those stupid drawings too, but I refused to look at them. Now, if you like, we can have some coffee."

The office boy came in then, bearing a tray. Villaamil politely refused the offer, but the other two men sat down to savor the brimming cups of a beverage that is the joy and consolation of office life.

"I have to say," said Don Ramón, with all the serenity of a man in full control of his faculties, "that one can grow inured to injustice, can become accustomed to life's blows and to the idea of some nonentity, some louse, getting ahead of you. Spanish logic never fails. The scoundrel takes precedence over the honest man; the ignoramus over the expert; and the decent civil servant always remains firmly at the bottom of the ladder, grateful that, as a reward for his services, they at least allow him to keep his job . . . I don't know, perhaps that's also a logical consequence."

"If they promote him ahead of me, I'll kick up a stink, a really big stink," said the paterfamilias in between sips of coffee. "Loud enough for the whole School for the Deaf to hear me."

"They'll hear you and say nothing, because there's no alternative but to resign yourself to your fate. Here's my reasoning. (Drawing his chair closer to the coffee-drinkers.) Who is sponsoring you? No one, and I say no one because no woman is sponsoring you."

"That is true."

"Exactly. Whenever I hear of some particularly absurd appointment, I ask, 'Who's the woman?' Because it's a proven fact that when some nobody overtakes another really useful employee, you only have to listen closely to hear the rustle of skirts. For example, I bet I know who asked for that cripple Guillén to be promoted. It was his cousin—the widow of that army fellow, the one who's in the Philippines—Enriqueta, a big, buxom woman and a very flighty piece by all accounts; indeed, it's said that she may or may not have had an affair with our illustrious head of department. Now on whose door, do you think, does that lout Guillén usually go knocking? Our friend Argüelles here, with all his kids in tow, will be left howling with hunger, while Guillén climbs further up the ladder."

Sevillano confirmed mad Villaamil's sour observations, although when Villaamil made such apposite points, he didn't appear to be mad at all; and Argüelles smoothed his pomaded hair and twirled his mustache before tugging so hard at his goatee beard that he nearly pulled it out by the roots.

"I've been saying the same thing for years, damn it. To get anywhere in this dastardly Spanish state of ours, you have to be utterly shameless. And given that our friend Villaamil is on such good form today, let us tell him something he doesn't know. Who do you think recommended that not only should the complaint against Víctor Cadalso be buried but that he should also be given a promotion?"

"There must be some woman involved, some impressionable young society lady, because Víctor is a past master at seducing the ladies."

"He was initially sponsored by two deputies," said Sevillano, "but however much wind they blew into his sails, they got nowhere until pressure came from above…"

"But according to what Ildefonso Cabrera told me, that scapegrace," said Don Ramón, growing heated, "is in cahoots with marchionesses and duchesses and all kinds of high society ladies…"

"Oh, pay no heed to that, Don Ramón," said Argüelles. "After all, your son-in-law is really just a social climber. There are no truly elegant young men, as there were in my day. You can forget all about those imagined conquests, because his sole source of support is a neighbor of mine. On the second floor of my house lives a marquis ... I can't remember his title, but he's from Valencia and has some Moorish-sounding name like Benengeli. Now this marquis has a twice-widowed aunt living with him ... a mere child you might say ... My wife, who is past fifty now, swears that when she was still in diapers (my wife, you understand), she knew this woman in Valencia, and she was al-ready married then. In short, she must be over sixty if she's a day, and although she was doubtless once a handsome woman, no amount of makeup can save her now, and no potion can give her back her looks."

"And my little son-in-law has seduced this 'innocent' creature."

"Not so fast. It's public knowledge in Valencia that this old shark became infatuated with Víctor, and he ... well, I suppose he fell for her too, fully aware, it goes without saying, of what he was getting into. They came to Madrid together and carried on their affair here. I don't need anyone to tell me this, because, given that the marquis and his family won't let the fellow in the house, I see him out in the street, waiting for the old dear. She sets off in her carriage, dressed to the nines, all puffed up and pleased with herself, lots of fake curls and a face with more paint on it than a Raphael portrait ... She stops on the corner of Calle de Relatores, where that terror of all young ladies climbs in, and off they go who knows where ... And according to the footman, who lives in the attic room, top left, the old trot re-ceives a letter almost every day and immediately sends her little one a three-page answer ... The footman posts the letters for her and tells me that the name and address on the envelope is none other than 13 Calle de Quiñones, second floor."

"Well, I would have to be a babe-in-arms to be surprised by that," declared Villaamil, half amused, half scornful. "And that old hag has come here, to this temple of the Administration (growing indignant), to burden the state with the ignominy of her recommendations in favor of that reprobate!"

"No, she has never come here, she doesn't need to," said Sevillano.

"She has plenty of strings to pull in the ministry and has no need to actually set foot here."

"She just has to put in a word with some bigwig and a note arrives here almost at once."

"So, she's the sort who never asks but only commands."

"Precisely. Do this . . . and it's done. What we need is a good lightning conductor to stop those bolts from the blue, a minister with character. But where will we find such a messiah? (Slapping his knee hard.) This damned Administration is a real son of a whore, and it's impossible to have dealings with it without sullying oneself. But for those who have children, Argüelles, what can they do but prostitute themselves? You need to find yourself a nice plush frock coat, because you've still got your looks. You would only have to smarten yourself up a bit and you'd have conquests by the dozen . . . and you might catch a really big fish . . . Go on, lad. Why, if I were twenty years younger . . ."

Sevillano was laughing, and Argüelles was preening himself, his vanity flattered, twirling that awful dyed mustache of his. Villaamil's words had, it seemed, not fallen on stony ground, because age had not cured Argüelles of his Don Juanesque pretensions.

"Frankly, gentlemen," he declared in the tones of a man of the world, "I have never liked the idea of love as a negotiating tool. Love for love's sake, I say. I wouldn't take on a creature like Víctor's bit of stuff if you paid me. She's as old as the hills, and every inch of her is fake, believe me."

"There's no room for squeamishness here, it's up and at 'em!" said Villaamil, who had been seized with a fit of giggles. "This is not the moment to be turning your nose up at anything. But our paterfamilias here is very fussy. He only likes tender young maidens."

"I know you're only joking, but you're quite right. From fifteen to twenty are the prime years; after that, other fools can have them."

"Come now, what if you were to find a sweet young thing like Víctor's lady friend, because she's sure to have plenty of shekels and there would be no empty pockets while she's around . . . I realize now that my son-in-law, having spent all the money he filched from that

Excise swindle of his, has been spending the old dear's war chest...
Goodness (slapping his knee again), we live in an age so immoral that
we don't even have the right to feel embarrassed, because the dung,
the wretched layer of dung on our faces, won't even let us blush!"

He got up to leave. Argüelles sighed and waved a farewell to Sevillano, who had started back at work before they even left.

"Let's go to the office," said Argüelles, wrapping his cape around
him and taking his friend's arm as they headed off along the corridors.
"Otherwise, that beast Pantoja will scream at me for being late. What
a life, eh, Don Ramón, what a life! By the way, did you notice that
while we were talking about Víctor's protectress, Sevillano didn't
utter so much as a peep? That's because he has found his own ancient
mummy—yes, didn't you know? The widow of that fellow Pez y
Pizarro, who was head of Lottery Funds in Havana, the cousin of
our friend Don Manuel. Even the dogs in the street know that...
anyway she protects him, and wangles him a little promotion every
two years."

"What? (Stopping and staring at him in an appropriately Dantesque
pose.) So, Sevillano... I must admit I'd often thought he was rising
up the ranks rather fast. Why, I was head of department when he was
just starting out on a salary of five thousand..."

He made the sign of the cross, and then together they continued
on to the Tax Office. Pantoja and the others started when they saw
poor Don Ramón, fearing a repetition of the previous day's scene.
However, Villaamil's calm voice and the relative serenity of his face
reassured them. Without so much as a glance in Guillén's direction,
he went and sat next to Pantoja, to whom he said from behind his
hand:

"I'm fine today, Ventura. I had a good night's sleep, cleared my
head, and I feel almost contented today—no, really, positively beaming with contentment."

"Just as well, my friend, just as well," said Pantoja, looking Villaamil
in the eye. "But what brings you here?"

"Oh, nothing, just habit. I feel happy today... see, I'm laughing.
(He laughs.) This may be the last time I come here, although I have

to say that this place amuses me; I mean it, one sees things here that could make one . . . die laughing."

Work finished earlier than usual because it was payday, the fortunate day that brings to a happy close all the usual end-of-the-month anxieties, opening up a whole new era of hope. On payday, there is more light in the rooms of that "cooperative," the air is purer, and the hearts of the unhappy laborers in the land of public finance take on an indefinably jolly and diaphanous quality.

"You'll all be getting your pay today," said Villaamil to his old friend, interrupting for a moment his hail-fellow-well-met demeanor.

You could tell from the sound of footsteps, the ringing of bells, the sense of movement and animation in the offices, that the operation had begun. Work stopped, documents were tied into bundles, desks were closed and pens abandoned among the jumble of papers and the grains of sand that stuck to sweaty hands. In some departments, officials and clerks were already filing into the cashier's office as their names were called, and there they had to sign a receipt before receiving their money. In other departments, the cashiers sent a messenger around with the sacred cash in a bowl, in silver coins and small bills, along with the necessary receipts. The head of that section was then in charge of distributing the payments and making sure everyone signed a receipt.

37

IT IS A known fact that when Villaamil saw the porter arrive bearing that bowl of money, he became very excited, his highly improbable bonhomie only increasing and finding expression in these celebratory words:

"Come on, come on, cheer up! Here at last is the holy advent... the culminating moment of the month... Saint Moneybags himself... You'll be living high on the hog with a fortune like that..."

Pantoja began distributing the money. All took their full pay, apart from one of the junior clerks, to whom Pantoja handed an IOU issued to a moneylender, saying:

"Debt cancelled."

And Argüelles received only a third of his wages, the rest being held back. He scowled as he took the money and signed the receipt with an angry flourish; only then did the great Pantoja take his, slowly and ceremoniously putting the notes in his wallet and stowing the coins safely in his vest pocket. Villaamil kept his eyes fixed on the whole operation and only looked away when the last coin had disappeared. His jaw was quivering, his hands shaking.

"You know," he said to his friend as he stood up, "we could go for a stroll. As you can see, I'm in such a good mood today. It's all been most entertaining..."

"No, I have to stay in the office for a while longer," said Pantoja, wanting to be rid of his calamitous friend. "I need to go to the Secretariat."

"Goodbye then. I'll be off. I really am so very happy... and on the way, I'll buy some pills."

"Pills? Yes, that's what you need."

"Indeed! Goodbye until the next time. Long life to you, gentlemen, and good health. I'm pleased to say that I myself could not be feeling better…"

Like tributaries swelling a mighty river, the multitudes pouring forth from every office flooded down the broad staircase. On the second floor, Revenues and Estates were discharging their personnel, who, heading downstream, immediately joined forces with the numerous flocks of men emerging from the Secretariat, the Treasury, and from Customs & Excise. The stairs were almost overwhelmed by this human torrent, which made a tremendous racket as it flowed on down, the sound of heavy footsteps mingling with all the cheerful, sparkling, payday chatter. In Villaamil's ears, these vast murmurings blended with the clink of coins recently put away in pockets and purses. The metal of those coins, he thought, must still be cold, but would soon warm up on contact with the body and even melt away once in contact with life's many inevitably pressing demands. On reaching the vast hall separating the entrance from the stairs, one could see the courtyards to right and left filling up with staff from the Tax Office, the Subtreasury, and from Postal Services, and those various streams became one before they reached the street. Faded capes abounded, more so than threadbare overcoats, but there were also some that were spanking new, as well as a few gleaming top hats that stood out among the throng of battered black derbies tinged with verdigris. The clatter of footsteps was deafening, but above that noise, Villaamil could still hear the tinkle of five-peseta coins. "Today," he said to himself, giving a heartfelt sigh, "almost all the wages were paid out in brand new five-peseta pieces and a few two-peseta coins bearing Alfonso's head."

As these tributaries flowed out into the street, the noise gradually stopped and the building was left empty, deserted, full of the thick dust raised by those departing feet. Yet still they came, more laggardly detachments of the office multitudes. Altogether there were three thousand of them, three thousand salaries of diverse amounts, which the state was putting back into circulation as a roundabout way of returning to the taxpayer part of what had been so pitilessly taken from him. The joy of getting paid, a feeling natural to humankind, lent the pack a rather pleasant, reassuring appearance. They were no doubt an honest, anodyne mob who had had enough of the horrors of revolution and were on the side of order and stability, a populace in overcoats, whose sole political idea was to secure and defend the food on their table; a bureaucratic proletariat, the ballast of the good ship Government, a mass born out of the hybridization of the people with the mesocracy, the cement that binds and solidifies the architecture of government institutions.

Villaamil was just drawing his cape more tightly about him against the cold air when someone tapped him on the shoulder. He turned and saw Víctor, who helped him fasten the cape about his neck.

"What's up...why are you laughing?"

"It's because...well, because I feel very contented today...for reasons that are none of your business. Can't a man be happy if he wants to?"

"Yes, but...Are you going home?"

"That too is none of your business. Where are you going?"

"Upstairs, to collect my certificate of appointment. I'm in a good mood today as well."

"Have they promoted you again? I wouldn't be surprised. There seems to be no stopping you. I don't know why they don't just appoint you minister and be done with it. You'd better make the most of it while there's still a good supply of old hags."

"Don't mock. The reason I'm in a good mood is because I have finally reconciled with my sister Quintina and her brute of a husband. He's going to keep that cursed house in Vélez-Málaga, which wasn't worth a bean, and pay the costs, while I..."

"Et cetera, et cetera. That's another thing that matters to me about as much as knowing if there are fleas on the moon. What do I care about your sister Quintina or about Ildefonso, or about what you get up to or whether you're reconciled with them or not?"

"It's just that..."

"Go on, run upstairs and leave me alone. Who do you think you are, anyway? You go your flower-strewn way, and I'll go mine. I'll tell you this, though: I don't even envy you your good luck . . . that's because I would always prefer honor without ships to ships without honor. Goodbye."

Without giving Víctor time to respond to these gnomic words, and once again wrapping his cape tightly about him, he set off out into the street. Before he reached the gate, though, someone tugged at his cape, accompanying that tug with these friendly words:

"Villaamil, my friend . . . oh, sorry, would you rather be alone?"

It was Urbano Cucúrbitas, a burly spring chicken of a fellow with sparse fair hair, long legs, a prominent Adam's apple, and a rather self-satisfied air; indeed, he resembled the precocious progeny of that gallinaceous breed known as Cochin chickens; he was wearing an elegant checkered suit, a very stiff high collar, and a pale-colored derby; he had enormous hands and feet, was spotlessly clean, and his smiling mouth revealed even his molars, which one might have called wisdom teeth had he had any wisdom.

"Hello, Urbanito. Have you picked up your wages?"

"Yes, I have it here (tapping his pocket and making the coins jingle), mostly in pesetas. I'm just going for a stroll along the Castellana."

"In pursuit of some new conquest, eh? You lucky man. The world is your oyster. And how cheerful you look! Well, I too happen to be in a good mood today. Now tell me, what about your little brothers, did they all receive their little salaries too? Blessed are the children to whom the state gives suck, be it from the nipple or the bottle. You'll get on well, Urbanito; I think you're very clever, contrary to what other people say, for they think you very stupid. No, I'm the stupid one. Do you know what I deserve? The minister should call me into his office, put a pair of ass's ears on my head, and make me kneel there for three hours, because I've been a complete imbecile, having spent my entire life believing in morality and justice and balancing the budget. I should be forced to run naked through the streets, to be given insulting nicknames, Señor de Miaow for example, and have caricatures made of me complete with doggerel verses that would make even the walls snigger...Not that I'm complaining, mind. As you see, I'm quite content, I'm even laughing...I find my own imbecility absolutely hilarious."

"Look, Don Ramón. (Placing both hands on his shoulders.) I had nothing to do with those cartoons. I confess that I did smile a little when Guillén brought them into my office, and I won't deny that I was tempted to show them to my father, and indeed I did..."

"I'm not expecting any explanations from you, dear boy."

"No, let me finish...My father was so angry he almost hit me. Anyway, when Guillén heard what my father had to say, he shot out of our office and hasn't been seen since. I think it was just a silly passing joke, and you know how much I respect you, and that it's pure nonsense to take the initial letters of the titles of your five memoranda and make a ridiculous, meaningless word out of them."

"Careful now, my young friend. (Looking him in the eye.) I agree that the word *Miaow* is pure nonsense, but I can't accept that those five letters are not of profound significance..."

"Really?" (Perplexed.)

"Because one would have to be either very stupid or without an ounce of decency not to acknowledge and agree that the M, the I, the A, the O, and the W mean the following: My...Ideas...Accommodate...Omnipresent...Worlds."

"I see. Anyway, as I was saying, Don Ramón, take good care of yourself."

"Although there will be those who maintain...and I would not dare to contradict them...there will be those who maintain, perhaps with some justification, that the five mysterious letters mean this: Minister...Implacable...Administrator...Of...the World."

"That seems to me a very wise interpretation, and very intriguing too."

"What I say is this: We need to examine all possible versions, because one person will say one thing, another something else, and it's quite hard to decide who is right. I would advise you to consider the matter carefully and to study it, because that's what the government pays you to do, but no need to go into the office every day, or, if you do, you need only stay for a few hours in the afternoon...And make sure your brothers study it too, with the baby's bottle of the appointment letter still in their mouth. Goodbye, and remember me to your papa. Tell him I have been crucified for the crime of imbecility on the shameful cross of idiocy and that he has been chosen to stick the lance in my side while Montes will hand me the sponge soaked in vinegar at the precise moment that I pronounce my five last words, saying: 'Miserable...Ignominious...Annihilated...Overwhelmed...Wasted.' And by 'wasted,' just so you know, I mean 'brought to decay or ruin' or smeared with all things fetid and repellent, which symbolize idleness and joblessness, or call them principles if you will."

"Don Ramón, are you going home now? Would you like me to go with you? I can call a cab."

"No, my dearest boy, you go for your little walk. I'll make my way home *pian pianino*. I have to buy some pills first...there's a pharmacy not far away."

"I'll come with you...and, if you like, we can go and see a doctor first..."

"A doctor! (Roaring with laughter.) Why, I've never felt better in my life, never stronger. Don't talk to me about doctors. With those little pills..."

"You really don't want me to come with you?"

"No. Not only do I not want you to, I beg you not to. Everyone has their little secrets, and the act, however seemingly insignificant, of buying a certain medicine can make one feel rather shy and embarrassed. And embarrassment, my lad, appears when you least expect it. How do you know that I am not some young—I mean, old rake? You take your way, and I will take mine to the pharmacy. Goodbye, you clever boy, you ministerial baby; enjoy yourself while you can; only appear at the office in order to collect your wages, seduce as many young women as possible—but always aim high, mind, go for the ones with money, and when a complaint is brought against you at work, just kick up the very devil of a fuss...Goodbye, goodbye... you know how very fond I am of you."

The burly youth headed off down Calle de Alcalá, and Villaamil, after first making sure no one was following him, set off toward Puerta del Sol, but before he reached there, he entered what he called the pharmacy—namely, the firearms shop at Number 3.

38

DURING that time, Doña Pura and her sister noticed something odd about Villaamil's manner, behavior, and language, for while he seemed excessively lazy and indifferent about relatively important matters, he threw himself with an almost brutal energy into other seemingly trivial affairs. Regarding fixing a date for Abelarda's wedding and sorting out certain details essential to such an important event, Don Ramón said not a word. Not even his future son-in-law's handsome inheritance (for God had now carried off his uncle the notary) drew from him a single enthusiastic hyperbole of the kind that poured forth from Doña Pura's mouth. On the other hand, the most minor thing became an event of enormous importance, and if his wife accidentally slammed a door (given how strained her nerves were), or if she used a copy of *La Correspondencia* to make curling papers, he would kick up a fuss that would last most of the morning.

It should also be noted that Abelarda seemed completely uninterested in the formal arrangements for her wedding, but Doña Pura attributed this to the proper modesty of a demure, well-brought-up young woman whose will was always at one with her parents' will. Given the family's dire financial straits, preparations for the wedding would be limited, almost nonexistent—just some new undergarments, the fabric for which had been purchased thanks to a donation from Víctor, although no mention of this was made to Villaamil for fear of upsetting him. I should say that, ever since that scene in the church of the Comendadoras, Víctor had barely made an appearance in the Villaamil household. He only very rarely slept there and had all his meals elsewhere. The usual evening guests continued to come, apart from Pantoja and his family—whose visits became less and less frequent, for reasons Doña Pura could not fathom—and Guillén, who vanished completely, much to the delight of the three Miaows. The repeated absences of Virgínia Pantoja greatly delayed rehearsals of the play, and Abelarda forgot all her lines; for these reasons and given Doña Pura's lack of enthusiasm for parties as long as the problem of her husband's suspension remained unresolved, all theatrical plans were shelved.

The ever-reliable Federico Ruiz would spend an hour or so there in the evenings, always apologizing profusely to the Miaows for taking up their time when he knew how busy they must be with the wedding preparations ... Ah, those wretched preparations, and how many castles and towers did Doña Pura's fertile imagination build on those fragile foundations! One morning, Ruiz arrived all out of breath, followed by his wife, both of them brimming with happiness, drunk on joy, wanting their friends to share in their good fortune.

"I have come," he said breathlessly, "so that you may congratulate us. I know how fond you are of us and how glad you will be to know that I have been given a commission."

Both Federico and his wife were embraced by each of the three Miaows. And sensing happiness in the air, kindly Villaamil emerged from his office and, before Federico could even tell him the gladsome news, Villaamil took him in his arms, saying:

"A thousand thousand congratulations, my dearest friend. Richly deserved, none more so."

"Thank you, thank you very much," said Ruiz, locked in the tight embrace of Villaamil's huge arms as he pressed him urgently to him. "But please, for heaven's sake, don't squeeze me so tight, you'll crush me ... Don Ramón—ouch, you're hurting me ..."

"Ramón," said Doña Pura, surprised and rather afraid, "what way is that to embrace a friend?"

"It's just ..." stammered Villaamil, "It's just that I want to congratulate him properly ... to congratulate him heart and soul, so that he will remember me and remember how very happy I am at his success. And what exactly is the commission?"

"A small commission right here in Madrid ... and that's what's so very fortunate about it…anyway, I have been asked to ponder and propose improvements in the way the natural sciences are currently being taught…and to make sure any improvements are put into practice."

"Oh, excellent! I don't know why it didn't occur to them to do that sooner. And to think that this wretched country has existed all these years without knowing how the natural sciences are taught! Fortunately, my dear Ruiz, we are about to find out. Our wise government has a real talent for choosing its staff…That's why the nation is positively bursting with pride. That little commission of yours will really hit the spot, I'm sure. We need more such ideas to save our poor, oppressed homeland. Anyway, I'm very, very glad. I'll go further, Señor Ruiz; if you are to be congratulated, then so is the whole country, which must be over the moon knowing that someone is finally going to carry out such a study. Isn't that so? Now, with your permission, I will get back to work. A thousand million congratulations."

Without waiting for Federico to respond to these enthusiastic words, Villaamil turned and went back into his office. Ruiz and his wife, and the Miaows too, were bewildered by this wild, exaggerated way of offering his congratulations, but they said nothing. The happy couple then left to continue their visits, spreading the good news and enjoying to the utmost this harvest of congratulations. And the little commission was not the only reason for Ruiz to be happy that morning, for the mail had brought him another unexpected pleasure: no more and no less than a diploma from a Portuguese society set up for the express purpose of rewarding those who realize heroic acts when putting out fires, as well as those who write articles propounding the best theories about this vital service. According to the diploma, every member of said association had the right to use the title "Fireman, Savior of Humanity," and to wear a very striking uniform replete with glittering braid. The nomination was accompanied by a drawing of the splendid jacket. Ruiz was overflowing with pride at his new commission (on which depended Spain's scientific future), his status as honorary fireman, as well as the stunning livery he intended to wear on the first solemn public occasion that presented itself.

That afternoon, Luis went for a walk with Paca, and on his return, he sat down to study at the dining table. After Abelarda's extraordinary—not to say bizarre—fit of rage on the famous night described above, her brain appeared to have recovered, to the point that a beneficent, restorative state of forgetting had, it seemed, removed from her mind all traces of the event. She only recalled it in the way one might recall, when still bleary with sleep, a stupid nightmare that fades with the light and the realities of the day. She kept herself busy preparing her trousseau, and Luis, weary of studying, was amusing himself stealing and hiding her reels of cotton.

"Now listen, little one," said his aunt, not in the least put out, "if you don't stop your little tricks, I'll give you a clip on the ear."

Instead, she gave him a kiss, and he grew still bolder, coming up with more tricks, all of which were, of course, perfectly innocent. Doña Pura was helping her daughter with her cutting out, and Milagros was working away in the kitchen, all smeared with grease and wearing her floor-length leather apron. Villaamil was still shut up in his lion's den. This was the scene when the doorbell rang, and who should appear but Víctor. Everyone was surprised, because he didn't usually arrive at that hour. He said not a word and went straight to his room, where he could be heard washing and taking clothes out of his trunk. He had doubtless been invited to some elegant supper somewhere. So thought Abelarda, making a special effort not to look at him or even to glance at the door to his tiny room.

The strangest thing, though, was that, soon after the monster's arrival, she, poor creature, suddenly felt stirring in her soul the same terrifying agitation she had felt on that other night. That sense of mental upheaval exploded like a bomb, and in the very same instant, her blood began to boil, bitter hatred made her lips draw tighter, her nerves vibrate, and in the tendons of arms and hands she felt a brute desire to grasp, to squeeze, to tear into pieces whatever was most dear to her, most beloved, and most helpless. It was at this critical moment that Luis had the very bad idea of tugging at the thread she was tacking with, making the cloth pucker...

"You'd better behave yourself, child, or else," shouted Abelarda, her whole body electric with emotion, her eyes flashing. Nothing worse might have happened if the silly boy, eager to play the scamp, had not given another tug at the thread, and then all hell broke loose. Not even realizing what she was doing—like a mindless mechanism receiving an impulse from some hidden source—Abelarda reached out one hand, seemingly as hard as iron, and, with her first blow, caught Luis full in the face. The slap was loud enough to be heard in the street. As Luis drew back, the chair he was sitting on wobbled and fell to the floor with a crash.

Doña Pura let out a scream:

"Oh, my poor little boy. What *are* you doing, woman?"

And Abelarda, blind and wild, pounced on her victim, clutching at his chest and throat with furious fingers. Just as caged, idle beasts instantly recover their ferocity with the first blow they deal their keeper, and cast off the apathetic sloth of captivity at the first sight and scent of blood, so Abelarda—throwing Luis to the floor and digging her nails into him—was no longer a woman, but a monstrous being created out of thin air by this crazed, unwholesome perversion of her feminine self.

"I'll throttle you, you little wretch! I'll kill you, you liar, you fraud!" she was shouting, grinding her teeth, then groping blindly on the table for scissors to stab him. Fortunately, she couldn't find them.

Doña Pura was so terrified that she froze, unable to step in and prevent the imminent disaster, instead uttering anguished, desperate screams. Milagros rushed in, followed by Víctor in his shirtsleeves. The first thing they did was wrench poor little Luis from his aunt's grasp—which proved fairly easy, because once the initial impulse was over, Abelarda's strength rapidly ebbed away. Her mother tried to help her up, but Abelarda remained on her knees, still convulsed with rage and utterly distraught, muttering in a trembling, broken voice:

"That wretch...that good-for-nothing...he wants to destroy me...yes, me, and the whole family..."

"But whatever's wrong, child?" cried her mother, apparently ignoring the brutal assault that had just taken place, while Víctor and

Milagros were examining Luis to see if he had any broken bones. The boy burst into tears, his face scarlet, his breathing labored.

"Good God, what a dreadful thing to do!" Víctor murmured grimly.

And it was precisely then that Abelarda entered a new phase of her crisis. She let out a tremendous roar and started gnashing her teeth; her eyes rolled back, and she dropped down as if stone dead, then began writhing about and panting. Villaamil entered the room at that moment and was horrified by the scene that greeted him: his daughter having a fit; Luis crying, his face all scratched; Doña Pura unable to decide who to help first; the others too stunned to speak.

"It's all right," Milagros said at last and ran off to fetch a glass of cold water to sprinkle on her niece's face.

"Are there no smelling salts?" asked Víctor.

"Child, child, whatever's wrong?" said Villaamil to his daughter. "Do try to come to your senses."

They had to hold her down so that she wouldn't hurt herself with her incessant, violent kicking and flailing. At last, calm came on as quickly as had the attack. She began to sob loudly, struggling to breathe as if she were suffocating, and copious tears marked the final stage of that terrible fit. However hard they tried to console her, that river of tears was unending. They carried her to bed, where she continued to weep, pressing her hands to her heart. She appeared not to remember what she had done. Between them, Villaamil and Víctor had managed to calm Luis, convincing him that it had all been rather a bad joke.

Suddenly, Villaamil—jaw twitching, gaze furious, face ashen—planted himself before his son-in-law and yelled:

"This is all your fault, you meddler. Leave my house this instant. I only wish you had never entered it."

"So, I'm to blame, am I? It's my fault, is it?" Víctor responded brazenly. "I always thought you were a bit soft in the head..."

"The fact is," said Doña Pura, emerging from the next room, "nothing like this ever happened before you came here."

"Oh, not you as well. Anyone would think you were doing me a favor by letting me stay here. And there I was thinking I'd been helping you to fend off starvation. If I do leave, where will you find a better lodger?"

Faced by such insolence, Villaamil could find no words to express his indignation. He stroked the back of a chair, tempted to pick it up and bring it down hard on his son-in-law's head. He managed to restrain himself and, putting a very tight rein on his rage, said in the hollow intonation of a precentor:

"Enough niceties. From this moment on, you are no longer welcome here. Pack up your belongings and clear off; no excuses and no delay."

"Don't worry, I'm going. I've hardly been living in the lap of luxury here."

"Luxury or not (almost bursting with outrage), leave now! Go and live with one of the grotesque creatures protecting you. Why do you need this poor, unfortunate family? You'll find no letters of appointment here, no government posts, no references—pure nothing, as someone once said. And we are happy in our poor but honest lives. Can't you see how happy I am? (Clenching his teeth together in a broad smile.) You, on the other hand, will find no peace when you reach the pinnacle of your glorious, dishonorable ascent. Out in the street with you. And I, Señor de Miaow, hope never to set eyes on you again."

Víctor livid; Doña Pura alarmed; Luis again on the verge of tears; Milagros scowling.

"Fine," said Víctor with the cool air he always adopted when about to make some particularly wounding remark. "I'll leave. I've been wanting to for a while, and the only reason I didn't was out of charity, because I can be a support here, not a burden. This time, though, the break is final. I will take my son with me."

The two older Miaow women stared at him, terrified. Villaamil clenched his teeth still more fiercely.

"What do you expect? After what has just happened," added Víctor, "do you really expect me to leave my own flesh and blood in your care?"

The logic of this argument left the Miaows of both sexes nonplussed.

"Don't be so silly," said Doña Pura, hoping to come to some agreement. "Surely you don't think such a thing will happen again. And where exactly will you go with your son? Besides, the little one doesn't want to leave us."

She was almost in tears. Then Milagros said:

"No, the boy definitely isn't leaving."

"Isn't he?" said Víctor with brutal resolve. "Come on, get my son's clothes and put them with mine."

"But where will you take him, you fool? Whatever can you be thinking of?"

"Oh, I have a plan. His Aunt Quintina will bring him up far better than you can."

Overwhelmed by grief, Doña Pura broke out in a cold sweat, her heart beating painfully hard, almost as if she too were about to have a fit. Villaamil was turning round and round on the spot as if being whirled about by an inner cyclone; then he stopped still, legs spread wide, arms outstretched, echoing the figure of Saint Andrew nailed to the cross, and he roared out as loudly as his lungs would allow:

"Take him then . . . take him, and may the devil go with you! You crazy, cowardly women, do you not know what MIAOW stands for? Mortification . . . Immolation . . . Abasement . . . Opprobrium . . . Waste."

And bumping into the walls as he went, he ran into his office. His wife followed, fearing that he was about to hurl himself from the balcony into the street.

39

"I won't give in, I won't," Víctor said to Milagros, when they were left alone. "I'm taking my son. Surely you understand that, after what happened today; I wouldn't be able to live in peace if I left him here."

"For heaven's sake, my dear," responded "Modest Ophelia," hoping to bring him round to her view. "That was just a piece of nonsense. It won't happen again. Don't you see, the child is our one consolation in life. And if you take him away..."

She stopped, overcome by emotion and trying to disguise her sadness, for she knew all too well that, if the family appeared too keen to keep Luis, that would be motive enough for the monster to insist on taking him from them. She thought it best to leave this delicate issue in the diplomatic hands of Doña Pura, who always used a combination of firmness and gentleness when dealing with her son-in-law. When Doña Pura went into her husband's office, she found him slumped in an armchair, clutching his head.

"What do you think we should do?" she asked in a bewildered voice, for she hadn't yet had time to make a decision.

Imagine her great, no, her immense surprise when her husband looked up and said these implausible words:

"Let him take the boy. It will be painful in the extreme to see Luis leave here, but what can we do? There's no point in getting all worked up, in fact... in fact, the boy would be better off with Quintina than here with... *you three*."

When she heard this, Doña Pura gazed in silent astonishment at her husband's troubled face. Hearing such an outrageous statement only confirmed her suspicions that he was beginning to lose his sanity.

"He would be better off with Quintina than with us? You're not in your right mind, Ramón."

"And leaving aside what would be best for the boy (somewhat softening his cruel words), Víctor *is* his father and has more authority over him than we do. If he wants to take him away..."

"He won't want to! Of course, he won't. I'll sort things out with the rogue..."

"I won't say another word to him; I won't demean myself by having anything more to do with him. (Sinking into despondency, the force of his rage now subsided.) I would simply leave him to do as he pleases. He has the authority, after all. And in that case, we must simply hold our tongues and suffer."

"You're telling us to hold our tongues and suffer (both horrified and determined), when that vile fellow wants to take from us our only joy? No, Ramón, you are clearly not right in the head. Víctor will take the boy, but it will have to be by force, by tearing him from us, and not without us first ripping off the blackguard's ears."

"Well, my view is that it's best not to argue with such a fellow... I think that if I ever do see him again, I'll probably bite him. Indeed, I feel a kind of physical urge to bite someone, anyone. I'm telling you, Pura, the Administration is in a disgraceful state, and one can no longer speak of the men in the Treasury as being honest and long-suffering. And as for balancing the budget—not a chance. Given the rabble who are beginning to invade the place, that's quite impossible."

"Why mention the Administration now (growing excited), what on earth has that got to do with anything? Oh, Ramón, you're really not yourself! What do I care about honest, long-suffering men... they can go to hell for all I care. Look at yourself in the mirror and open your eyes as wide as possible..."

"They're wide open already! (Meaningfully.) And what horizons I see before me!"

Seeing that any agreement was impossible, Doña Pura again took up the matter with Víctor, who had still not left. Contrary to her belief, he remained utterly immovable, standing by his decision with a tenacity worthy of a far better cause. Both Miaows were in a state of real anguish, and Abelarda, realizing she was the origin of the conflict, lay on her bed sobbing her heart out. Doña Pura had to split herself in two, tending to her daughter's needs and arguing with Víctor, coming and going between them but unable to overcome either the affliction of one or the implacable obstinacy of the other. She had never seen Víctor cling so stubbornly to a decision, nor could she find the reason for such cruelty and determination. To do so, she would need to have known what had happened the previous day in the Cabrera household. On appeal, Cabrera had won the long-drawn-out dispute over the crumbling house in Vélez-Málaga, with Víctor being condemned to reimburse the value of the property and pay all legal costs. The irreconcilable Ildefonso had already placed the noose about Víctor's neck and was preparing to pull it tight by insisting on those repayments and pitilessly, remorselessly pursuing him and hounding him. However, the wily Quintina took advantage of the judgement to satisfy her own maternal ambitions, and by cajoling Ildefonso, by flattering and generally buttering him up, she succeeded in persuading him to approve the following agreement: The whole matter would be buried; Ildefonso would pay the legal costs (but keep the house, of course). And Víctor would hand over his son. Ildefonso saw his chance, and although taking the child from the care and protection of his grandparents left a bad taste in his mouth, he forced himself to swallow it down. After all, it would merely be a matter of having to put up with an awkward scene in the Miaow household, with Pura and possibly Milagros lashing out at him, and Villaamil taking a bite too. This was clearly what lay behind Víctor's determination to have Luis change households and families.

Ponce arrived in the thick of all this turmoil, with Milagros and Pura running back and forth between an inconsolable Abelarda and an inflexible Víctor, meanwhile stopping en route to see Luis, who had also resumed his sniveling. Ponce could not have come at a worse moment, and his mother-in-law-to-be, greatly put out by his visit, hustled him into the living room, saying:

"That rogue Víctor has played a cruel trick on us. What happened here today was a genuine tragedy. He has decided to take the boy from us, uprooting him from the home and family where he has always lived. We are all incredibly upset. When Abelarda realized that the villain was going to take the boy from us, she collapsed, fell into a faint. We put her to bed, but she won't stop crying. Really, you have no idea!"

In the end, since Abelarda was lying on her bed fully clothed, they allowed Ponce to go in and see her. She wasn't crying now, but her eyes were burning and her limbs limp. The illustrious Ponce took a seat at the head of her bed, squeezing her hand and even allowing himself the ineffable pleasure of kissing it—only, of course, when her mother wasn't in the room, her mother having first told her daughter the version of events she had given Ponce.

"What wickedness," said Ponce to his beloved. "He's like a beast from the apocalypse."

"You don't know just how wicked he is," responded Abelarda, staring hard at her fiancé while he dabbed at his eternally moist eyes. "God has never sent a blacker soul into this world...Can you imagine such evil? Wanting to take Luis from us, the source of all our joy, our happiness, the child who has lived with us ever since he was born. He owes his life to us, because we have cared for him as if he were the very apple of our eye. We nursed him through measles and whooping cough, never stinting in our love. And his father rewards us with this despicable act of ingratitude. You know what a softie I am; in fact, I'm so cowardly and inoffensive that I even feel sorry for a poor flea when I kill it. Well, if I could lay my hands on that man, I would slice him in two with a knife, so there!"

"Calm down, pussycat," said Ponce in honeyed tones. "You're overwrought. Try not to think about it. You do love me, don't you?"

"Of course I do," said Abelarda, firm now in her decision to throw herself off the viaduct—in other words, to marry Ponce.

"Your mama will have told you that we've fixed a date now: the third of May, the Festival of the Crosses. That seems such a long way off, and how slowly the days and nights pass!"

"Oh, it will soon come round...One day follows another," said Abelarda, staring up at the ceiling. "And every day is the same."

The discussions between the two Miaows and Víctor carried on until, finally, he left—in evening dress—and neither the diplomacy of one nor the plaintive pleadings of the other had managed to soften Víctor's hard heart. All they achieved was to postpone his removal of Luis until the following day. When Villaamil heard this, he came out of his office and addressed his son-in-law with these curt words:

"I promise, I give you my word, that I will take him to Quintina's house myself. There's nothing more to say. There's no need for you ever to come back here."

The monster responded by saying that he would return that night to change his clothes, adding benevolently that taking his son away from his grandparents did not mean that they could not visit him, for they could go to Quintina's house whenever they liked, and he would be sure to tell his sister so.

"How terribly gracious of you," said Doña Pura scornfully.

And Milagros:

"Me? Go *there*? You've got a nerve!"

There is an important factor missing in our consideration of this grave situation: We do not know how Luis felt about it: if he would happily change families, or if, on the contrary, he would resist with the implacable determination proper to that innocent age. As soon as the monster had left, Doña Pura set about urging the boy to resist, assuring him that Aunt Quintina was a very bad person, that she would lock him up in a dark room, that her house was full of huge snakes and poisonous insects. Luis did not believe a word she said, because this was far too tall a tale for a child his age to swallow, an age when a child is beginning to know something of the world.

That night, no one had any appetite, and Milagros returned the dishes to the kitchen untouched. Villaamil only opened his mouth to dismiss the horrific picture his wife had painted of the Cabrera household:

"Pay no attention, child. Aunt Quintina is a very kind woman and will look after you and spoil you rotten. There are no toads and no snakes there, only the loveliest things you can imagine, saints so real you half expect them to speak, beautiful images and superb altars and all kinds of other things. You'll be very happy there."

When they heard this, Pura and Milagros were astonished, unable to understand how Luis's grandfather could, so shamelessly, so spine-lessly, have gone over to the enemy's side. How could he possibly support Víctor's wicked idea, even defending Quintina and depicting her home as some kind of childhood paradise? If only the family had more money, because the first thing they would do then would be to summon an expert on mental illnesses so that he could study Villa-amil's head and explain what exactly was going on inside!

40

LUIS HAD no appetite either, and even less appetite for studying. While his aunt —now completely recovered from her savage outburst, and having only a very vague recollection of what had happened—was helping to put him to bed, she kept showering him with kisses and caresses, which he received rather warily, as Doña Pura equally warily looked on. That night, Milagros also slept in their room, just in case.

Luis soon fell asleep, but woke in the middle of the night feeling all the warning signs that he was about to have one of his visions. His Aunt Milagros tucked him in again and spoke soothing words, then lay down beside him to calm his fears. The first thing Luis saw as he drifted off was a large empty space in some indeterminate location whose horizons melded seamlessly and apparently interminably with the sky, because everything looked the same, both near and far. He couldn't tell whether this place was the earth or the sky, and then it occurred to him that it might be the sea, which he had only ever seen in paintings. But it couldn't be the sea, because the sea has waves that rise and fall, and that surface was more like glass. Far off in the distance, very far off, he could see his friend with the white beard approaching at a leisurely pace, gathering his cloak around him with his left hand and using his right hand to lean on a big stick or staff like the sort used by bishops. Even though he was still some way off and was walking very slowly, he soon reached Luis's side, clearly pleased to see him. Then he sat down—but where, if there was no rock or chair to be seen? It was all very amazing, because behind the Lord's shoulders, Luis could see the back of one of the armchairs in his own living room, but most astonishing of all was that the kindly grandfather then leaned toward him and stroked his cheek with his precious hand. On feeling the touch of the very fingers that had created the world and everything in it, Luis felt an intensely pleasurable shiver run through him.

"Now let's see," said his friend. "I have come from the other side of the world simply in order to have a chat with you. I know some very strange things have been happening. There's what your aunt did for one . . . which seems quite extraordinary given how very fond she is of you . . . Can you understand it? No, I can't either. I can assure you that, when I saw what she did, I thought I must be imagining it. Then there's your papa, determined to carry you off to live with your Aunt Quintina. Do you understand the reason for all this?"

"Well . . ." said Luis shyly, astonished that he should have any ideas of his own when in the company of that fount of eternal wisdom. "I think it's all the fault of the minister."

"The minister!" (Surprised and amused.)

"Yes, sir, because if that man had given my grandfather a post, everyone would be happy and none of this would have happened."

"You sound to me like a very wise young man."

"My grandfather is furious because they won't give him a post, and so is my grandmother, and my Aunt Abelarda too. And my Aunt Abelarda can't stand my papa, because my papa told the minister *not* to give my grandfather a post. And because she doesn't dare confront my papa, because he's stronger than her, she took it out on me. Then she started crying . . . Tell me, is my aunt a good person or a bad one?"

"I would say she's a good person. Remember that she only laid into you like that because she really loves you."

"Well, she has a very funny way of showing it. I can still feel where she dug her nails into me. She's been angry with me ever since the day I said she should marry my papa. Didn't you know that? My papa loves her, but she can't stand the sight of him."

"That certainly is very strange."

"It's true though. One night, my papa told her he was madly in love with her, that he had it really bad . . . that he was a condemned man and all kinds of other things . . ."

"What are you doing eavesdropping on what grownups are saying?"

"I was just there in the room..." (With a shrug.)

"The things that go on in your house! I'm beginning to think you're right though. The wretched minister is to blame for everything. If he had done as I said, none of this would have happened. In that great mansion full of offices, would it have been so very difficult to find a little corner for your poor grandfather? But you see, they take no notice of me, and then things go wrong. I know they have all kinds of other matters to attend to, and that whatever I say just goes in one ear and out the other..."

"Well, make them give him a job now. You just have to go there and tell them, and thump the minister's desk with that stick of yours."

"They'll take no notice. If it was just a matter of thumping a desk, there would be no problem, but however hard I thump, they still ignore me."

"Darn it (emboldened by the vision's benevolent attitude), when *are* they going to give him a job then?"

"Never," declared the Father serenely, as if that "never" were a word intended to console rather than to induce despair.

"Never? (Unable to understand how this could be said so calmly.) Then we're done for."

"Yes, never. What's more, I should tell you that this was my decision. Because what use are worldly goods? No use at all. You'll have heard that often in sermons—well, now you're hearing it from my lips, and I know all there is to know. Your dear grandfather will not find happiness on this earth."

"Where then?"

"Don't be silly. Why, here by my side. Surely you realize that I want to bring him to live with me here?"

"Ah! (Opening his mouth as wide as he could.) That means my grandfather is going to die."

"Yes, because really, child, what is the point of your grandfather continuing to live in this evil, ugly world? He's no use to anyone now. Do you think it's acceptable for him to carry on living only to have other people laugh at him, and to have his daily requests for a new post passed over by some minor minister?"

"But I don't want my grandfather to die."

"Of course you don't, and quite right too ... but you see, he's getting old and would be far better off here with me than with you, his family. Do you understand?"

"I do. (Agreeing purely out of politeness, but not entirely convinced.) So ... is Grandpa going to die soon?"

"That's the best thing he can do. Warn him. Explain to him that you've spoken with me and that he needn't worry about writing any more letters of appointment and can tell the minister to go fish, and assure him that he'll know no peace until he's here with me. What's wrong? Why are you frowning? What don't you understand, you ninny? I thought you were planning to become a priest and devote your life to me. Well, in that case, you'd better get used to such ideas. Have you forgotten what it says in the catechism? You'd better learn it by heart then. This world is a vale of tears, and the sooner you leave it the better. All this, and all the other things you'll learn by and by, that's what you'll be preaching from my pulpit when you're older, in order to convert sinners. You'll make the ladies cry, and they'll say: 'Our little Father Miaow has a real way with words.' You do still want to be a priest, don't you, and learn a few bits and pieces of the mass, a little Latin, and so on?"

"Yes, sir ... Murillo has already taught me lots of things: what 'alleluia' and 'Gloria Patri' mean, and I know what you have to sing when the priest raises the host and what to do with your hands when he reads from the holy Gospel."

"Well, you already know a lot then, but you must apply yourself to your studies. You'll see all the stuff the priests use in the services at Aunt Quintina's house ..."

"Yes, they want to take me to live with Aunt Quintina. What do you think? Should I go?"

At this point, Luis was so charmed by the frankness and kindness of his friend, who was now stroking his cheek, that he felt confident enough to respond in kind, and, first timidly, then as if it were the most natural thing in the world, he began tugging at the vision's beard, and the vision did nothing to stop him nor did he appear annoyed and say as Villaamil had said to Víctor: "Who do you think you are?"

"As for whether or not you should go and live with the Cabreras, I will say nothing. You want to go there to see all those ecclesiastical playthings, but at the same time, you fear being separated from your grandparents. Do you know what I would advise? When the moment comes, just follow your instincts."

"And what if my Papa drags me off there without giving me time to think?"

"I don't know. I don't think he'll do that. If you really can't decide, then just do what your grandfather tells you to do. If he says 'Go to Aunt Quintina's house,' then go."

"And if he tells me not to?"

"Then don't go. Forget all about those ecclesiastical toys, and do you know what you should do instead? Tell your friend Murillo to give you another quick Latin lesson, and have him explain the mass properly and about the priest's vestments as well: how to put on the cincture and the stole, how to prepare the chalice and the host for consecration ... because Murillo's very well informed, and he could also teach you how to take the viaticum to the sick and what prayer to say on the way."

"Hm ... Murillo does know a lot, but his father wants him to be a lawyer. How stupid! He reckons he'll get to be a minister and marry a really pretty girl. Isn't that disgusting!"

"Yes, it is disgusting."

"The Joker used to have some wicked ideas too. One afternoon, he told us he was going to find himself a sweetheart and go gambling. What do you think of that? And he smoked cigarette butts and used bad language."

"He's lost all those naughty habits here."

"Where is he, by the way? He's not with you today."

"They're all in detention. Do you know what they did this morn-

ing? The Joker and a few other young scamps who are always up to
something or other, well, they stole the world—you know, the one I
usually carry around in one hand—and they started rolling it along
the ground, and before I knew it, it had fallen in the sea. I had the
devil of a job to get it out. Luckily, it's not a real world; there aren't
any people on it, so it was no big disaster. I gave them all a good hiding. They won't forget that in a hurry. I'm keeping them locked up
for the rest of the day..."

"I'm glad. Serves them right. But where do you lock them up?"

The celestial person, still allowing Luis to tug at his beard, smiled
at him as if not knowing quite what to say.

"Where do I lock them up? Let's see...where do you think?"

A child's curiosity is implacable, and woe to anyone who provokes
it and doesn't immediately satisfy it! Luis's tugs on the Lord's beard
must have become too violent, because his kindly old friend had to
put an end to such familiarity.

"Where do I lock them up? Hm, you want to know everything,
don't you? Well, I lock them up...wherever I want to. What business
is it of yours?"

With those final words, the vision vanished, and Luis slept until
morning, tormented by a need to know where those boys had been
locked up...Where the devil *would* he lock them up?

41

Víctor did not return that night but arrived early next morning to repeat the cruel sentence he had imposed on Luis, refusing to surrender to Doña Pura's threats or to the tears of Abelarda and Milagros. In the face of such sadness, Luis rebelled, refusing to put on his clothes or shoes and bursting into tears; and heaven knows what would have happened without the discreet intervention of Villaamil, who came out of his room to say:

"Since we must part with him, let's not torment the poor child or upset him unnecessarily."

Víctor was astonished to see his father-in-law being so reasonable and was very grateful to him for those soothing words, which would allow him to carry out his plan without having to resort to violence and without any unpleasant scenes. Seeing that they had lost their case, Milagros and Abelarda withdrew to Villaamil's office to weep. Pura retreated to the kitchen, cursing the Cabreras, the Cadalsos, and all other races hostile to her peace of mind; meanwhile, Víctor was helping his son put on his boots, intent on removing him from that place promptly before any fresh complications arose.

"Just you wait," he was saying to Luis, "you'll see some lovely things at Aunt Quintina's: magnificent saints, as big as the ones in the churches, and other smaller ones you can play with; Madonnas in gold-embroidered cloaks, with a silver moon at their feet and stars all round their head. Really lovely, you'll see. And there are other nice things too: candlesticks, Christs, missals, monstrances, thuribles..."

"And can I light the incense and swing one around so that it gives off a smell?"

"Yes, my dear. It's all there for you to play with and to learn. You can even take the saints' clothes off and see what they look like underneath, then put their clothes back on again."

Villaamil was pacing up and down the dining room listening to all this. When he saw that Luis, after that initial burst of enthusiasm about the thurible, was once again growing despondent at the thought of leaving home and saying, "I want Grandma to take me and to stay with me there," he realized that he needed to join in the process of persuading Luis that all would be well. Stroking Luis's head, he said:

"And there are miniature altars too with matching candles and chandeliers, as well as monstrances and embroidered chasubles—oh, and a really gorgeous ciborium, bits of cloth to drape over the cross, and all kinds of other beautiful things . . . for example . . ."

He didn't know how to continue, but Víctor stepped in to help his faltering imagination, adding:

"And a silver aspergillum so that you can sprinkle holy water everywhere, and a Paschal Lamb . . ."

"A live one?"

"No . . . I mean, yes, yes, a live one."

To cut short this painful situation and hasten the critical moment of departure, Villaamil helped Luis on with his jacket, but he hadn't even finished buttoning it up when—oh, dear God!—a furious Doña Pura appeared and hurled herself at Víctor, poker in hand, saying:

"Murderer! Leave my house this instant! You're not going to steal this little gem from me! Leave now or I'll split your head open!"

And the moment the other Miaows heard her angry voice, they appeared too, singing the same song. In short, things were turning ugly.

"Given that you won't let him go willingly, then you'll have to do so unwillingly," said Víctor, stepping back out of the reach of the three furies' nails. "I'll bring in the law. He's not going to stay here, so you'd better . . ."

Villaamil intervened again, saying in a conciliatory voice dredged painfully up from the very depths of his sorrowing heart:

"Calm down, calm down. We had it all arranged until you women arrived and ruined everything. Go to your rooms."

"You're a useless idiot," said his wife, blind with rage. "Yes, you're to blame, because if you had taken our part, between us we would have won the battle."

"Be quiet, you fool, I know all too well what I have to do. Now leave this room, all of you."

But seeing how concerned his aunts and his grandmother were for his welfare, Luis again began to dig in his heels. Pura's one desire was to scratch out her son-in-law's eyes, and the whole affair looked set to end badly. It was fortunate that Villaamil was in such a reasonable mood that day and so in control of himself and the situation that he seemed like a different man. Somehow or other, he managed to impose his authority.

"Look, as long as you're here, we'll get nowhere," he said to Víctor, nimbly snatching him from between the bull's horns (that is, from Doña Pura's claw-like fingers). "Go now, and I give you my word that I will take my grandson to Aunt Quintina's. Leave it to me . . . Don't you trust me?"

"Oh, I trust you, but I'm not entirely convinced that you can subdue these madwomen."

"I'll make them see reason, don't worry. Now leave and wait for me at Quintina's house."

Having succeeded in reassuring his son-in-law, he then turned his eloquence on his family, using every ounce of ingenuity to make them see how impossible it was to prevent the boy from leaving.

"Don't you see that if we resist, the judge himself will come and take him away?"

The dispute lasted for half an hour, and in the end, the Miaows seemed resigned, although not convinced—never that.

"The first thing you have to do," he said, wanting to get them out of the way before the actual moment of departure, "is to go into the living room singing very softly. I'll talk to Luis. He won't stop loving you simply because he's going to live with Quintina! Besides, his father has promised me that he'll bring him to see us every day and will spend all Sunday with us..."

Abelarda was the first to leave, weeping as bitterly as if she were leaving someone in their death agony so as not to see them die. Then Milagros left, and, finally, Pura, who would never have given in had her husband not subdued her with this final argument:

"If we insist, the judge will come here this very afternoon. Imagine the scene. Let us drain the bitter cup and leave it to God to punish the scoundrel who has made us drink it."

Alone with Luis, Villaamil came close to losing his forced but precarious composure and bursting into tears. He swallowed that bitter gall, mentally addressing the heavens with these words: "Terrible though it is to part with him, Lord, he will definitely be better off there, much better... Come on, Ramón, courage, and don't lose your nerve." However, he had not reckoned with his grandson, who, hearing his aunts sobbing, again changed his mind, and when the cruel moment of departure arrived, he became distressed, saying:

"I don't want to go."

"Don't be silly, Luis," said Villaamil in an admonishing tone. "Do you really think we would make you leave us if it wasn't for your own good? Now, nice, obedient boys always do as they're told. And words really can't convey what wonderful things await you at Aunt Quintina's."

"And can I actually pick them up and do what I like with them?" asked Luis with a greedy urgency revealing the boundless egotism of childhood.

"Of course! You can even break them if you like."

"Oh, no, I wouldn't break them. You mustn't break church things," said Luis rather earnestly.

"Fine, then let's go. We'll leave very quietly so that they don't hear us and make a fuss... Anyway, you'll see, there's a really beautiful baptismal font as well. I've seen it myself."

"A font... what, with lots of holy water in it?"

"It holds as much water as the kitchen sink. Come along. (Picking him up.) It's best if I carry you."

"And is that font for baptizing people?"

"Of course! You can play with it as often as you like, and you can learn how to christen a baby, ready for when you're a priest."

Villaamil crept down the corridor to the hall, carrying his grandson in his arms, and when, during that dangerous voyage, Luis kept up a stream of questions, making no attempt to lower his voice, Villaamil gently covered his grandson's mouth with his hand and whispered in his ear:

"Yes, you can christen babies, as many babies as you want, and there are mitres small enough to fit your little head, and golden copes, and a staff, so that you can dress up as a bishop and hand out blessings to us all..."

With that, they went out of the front door, which Villaamil did not close so as not to make any noise. Then he hurried down the stairs like a thief escaping with stolen goods, and once he reached the foot of the stairs, he breathed more easily and put his load down on the ground, unable to carry him any further. He was not exactly strong and was unused to lifting weights, even one as light as his little grandson. Afraid that Paca and Mendizábal might make some tactless comment, he dispensed with any salutations. Paca was about to say something to Luis about how sorry she was to see him leave, but Villaamil was too quick for her, saying, "We'll be back," and stepping out into the street in a flash.

Fearing that Luis would again have second thoughts, Villaamil felt obliged to come up with more persuasive deceits and tricks:

"You'll have lots of artificial flowers to put on the altars, it would take you a whole year to see them all... and then there are candles in every color... and votive lights... And there's an amazing Saint Ferdinand dressed in armor like a warrior, and a Saint Isidore with a pair of oxen that look just like the real thing. And the little altar where you can say your masses is even prettier than the one in Montserrat..."

"Is there a confessional too?"

"Indeed there is, and a very fine one too, with a grille so that the ladies can confess their many sins. You're going to be very happy there, and when you're a little bit older, you'll be a priest in no time at all and know as much as Father Bohigas in Montserrat church, or the chaplain in Saletas Nuevas, who's about to become a canon."

"Will I become a canon too, Grandpa?"

"No doubt about it. And a bishop too, and you might even become pope."

"The pope's the one in charge of all the priests, isn't he?"

"He is. Oh, and there's a miniature Holy Week float made out of at least a thousand parts, with loads of statues and all in white like sugar paste. It looks as if it's come straight out of a cake shop."

"Can you eat it, Grandpa, can you?" asked Luis, so intrigued by these things that his home, his grandmother, and his aunts had vanished from his thoughts.

"You bet you can! Whenever you get tired of playing, you can take a bite," said Villaamil, getting slightly confused now, because his imagination was fast running out of steam and he didn't know what else to say.

He was walking briskly along Calle Ancha, with Luis taking three steps to his one, clinging, or, rather, hanging on to his grandfather's hand. Then Don Ramón suddenly stopped and turned, heading instead for the upper part of the street, to the Hospital de la Princesa. Luis noticed that they were going the wrong way and said impatiently:

"But, Grandpa, aren't we going to Aunt Quintina's house in Calle de los Reyes?"

"Yes, my dear, but we'll take a short walk first so that you can get a bit of sun."

The mind of the poor, distressed old man suddenly took a step back, energetically rejecting the very idea of giving up his grandson and letting him change families. Meanwhile, Luis was chatting away, asking endless questions and tugging at his grandfather's arm whenever the answers were not immediately forthcoming. Villaamil answered evasively, in monosyllables, because all his thoughts were turned inward. Head down, staring at the ground as if he were counting the cracks in the paving stones, he was trudging up the hill, dragging Luis with him—not that Luis noticed his grandfather's anguish, or his trembling lips, or his mumbled comments. "Isn't what I'm about to do a crime, or even two crimes? Handing over my grandson and then . . . Last night, after thinking long and hard, both things seemed absolutely right, with one seeming the natural consequence of the other. Because if I am suddenly going to cease to live, Luis would be better off with the Cabreras than with my family . . . Because I think my family would bring him up badly, carelessly, giving in to all kinds of whims and fancies . . . not to mention the danger of him living close to Abelarda, who might suffer a relapse one day. I don't like the Cabreras, but they seem proper, orderly folk. How different from Pura and Milagros! What with their music and their other obsessions, they're no use at all. That's what I thought last night, and it seemed the most sensible idea any human mind could ever have come up with . . . So why have I changed my mind now and feel like taking the boy back home with me? Would he be better off with the Miaows than with Quintina? No, no . . . Am I losing confidence in my plan to save us all, one that would give me both freedom and peace? Are you giving in to the temptation to carry on living, you coward? Does your body still feel drawn to life's pleasures?"

Tormented by such cruel doubts, Villaamil gave a huge sigh, and sitting down at the foot of the railings where the hospital backs onto Paseo de Areneros, he took Luis's hands in his and looked at him hard, as if trying to find the solution to that terrible conflict in his grandson's innocent eyes. Luis was burning up with impatience but didn't dare to hurry his grandfather, in whose face he saw such sadness and weariness.

"Tell me, Luis," said Villaamil, folding him in a fond embrace. "Do you really want to go and live with Aunt Quintina? Do you think you'll be happy with her? Do you think the Cabreras will give you a better upbringing, a better education than at home? Tell me frankly."

Now that the question had entered pedagogical terrain, and setting aside the allure of those ecclesiastical playthings, Luis didn't know quite how to answer. He looked for a way out, and finally found one:

"I want to be a priest."

"Yes, I understand that you want to be a priest, and I approve ... but what if I wasn't here, and Pura and Milagros go to live with Abelarda when she marries Ponce; who do you think you would be better off living with?"

"With Grandma and Aunt Quintina together."

"That's not possible."

Luis shrugged.

"And aren't you afraid that, if you were to stay where you are, my daughter might get all worked up again and try to kill you?"

"She won't do that," said Luis with admirable wisdom. "She's getting married now, and she won't hit me again."

"So, you're not afraid. And where would you prefer to live, with Aunt Quintina or with us?"

"I would prefer you all to live with my aunt."

Villaamil had already opened his mouth to say, "Look, my dear, the stuff I told you about little toy altars was pure drivel. We've been lying to you simply so that you would agree to leave home," but he stopped himself, waiting for Luis to come up with his own primitive idea, born of innocence, as to how to solve this dreadful problem. Luis climbed onto his grandfather's knee, and placing one hand on Don Ramón's shoulder to steady himself, he announced:

"What I want is for Grandma and Aunt Milagros to come and live with Aunt Quintina."

"And what about me?" asked Villaamil, astonished at being left out of the equation.

"You? Well, I'll tell you. They won't give you a post, you know. Not now, not ever."

"How do you know this?" (His heart in his mouth.)

"I just know. Not now, not ever. Besides, you don't need one."

"How do you know that? Who told you?"

"Well, I ... All right, I'll tell you, but promise not to say a word to anyone else. I see God ... I sometimes fall into a kind of sleep, and then he stands before me and talks to me."

Villaamil was too taken aback to speak. Luis went on:

"He has a white beard, he's about your height and wears a really lovely cloak. He tells me all about what's happening...he knows everything, even what we boys get up to at school..."

"And when have you seen him?"

"Often. The first time was outside the Convento de Don Juan de Alarcón, then somewhere near here, then at the congress and at home...I start off feeling as if I were going to faint, then I begin to shiver, and then along he comes and we start chatting...Don't you believe me?"

"Oh, I do believe you...(said with intense feeling) how could I not?"

"And last night he told me that they won't ever give you a job, and that this world is a very bad place, and that you're too good for it, and the sooner you go up to heaven the better."

"How funny. He's said the same thing to me."

"Do you see him too?"

"No, I don't actually see him...I'm not pure enough to deserve such a blessing, but he does speak to me now and then."

"Anyway, that's what he told me, that you should die soon so that you can rest and be happy."

Villaamil was utterly astonished. His grandson's words were like a divine revelation, irrefutably true.

"And what does the Lord say to you?"

"That I must become a priest...which is exactly what I want... and that I must study Latin hard and learn everything as quickly as possible..."

Don Ramón's mind was inundated—if that is the word—with a sense of categorical certainty, with no room for even the smallest shadow of a doubt, a certainty that laid out neatly before him the ideas he must now put into action with unswerving determination.

"Come along, my dear, let's go to Aunt Quintina's house," he said, getting up and taking Luis's hand.

He walked there as quickly as possible, not bothering this time to fill Luis's mind with overblown descriptions of toys and other sacred-cum-recreational thingamajigs. When he knocked at the door of the Cabrera house, Quintina herself came to open it. Villaamil sat down on the bottom step and covered his grandson with kisses before handing him over to Quintina and escaping without so much as a word of greeting. When he thought he heard the boy whimpering, he quickened his pace and set off down the street as fast as his poor legs would carry him.

42

IT WAS nearly midday, and Villaamil, who had not yet eaten any breakfast, suddenly felt hungry. He headed off to Plaza de San Marcial, and when he reached the slopes of the hill once known as Príncipe Pío, he stopped to gaze down at Campo del Moro and the distant boundaries of Casa de Campo. It was a splendid day, the sky an impeccable, burnished blue, the sun bright and piercing—one of those precociously summery days when the heat feels more importunate because the trees still have no leaves. The horse chestnuts and the poplars were beginning to come into leaf, but the plane trees were scarcely in bud; and the pagoda trees, the honey locusts, and other leguminous trees were still completely bare. A few Judas trees already bore pink blossom, and the privet hedges were showing off their lush new shoots rivaling the evergreen euonymus. Villaamil observed how the various arboreal species wake from their winter sleep at different times and took pleasure in breathing in the warm air rising up from the Manzanares river. Forgetting his hunger, he wandered on to La Montaña, walking through the newly planted garden in the middle, before circling around the barracks until he could see the mountains—clear blue spotted with white, like a splash of watercolor paint spreading naturally over the paper, the work of chance rather than the artist's brush.

"How beautiful!" he said to himself, loosening the clasp on his cloak because he felt too hot. "It seems as if I were seeing this for the first time, and as if those mountains, those trees, and this sky had only just been created. It's true that in my wretched existence, full of work and travails, I've never really had time to look up or ahead. I've always had my eyes lowered, staring down at the filthy, worthless ground; at the rotten Administration, devil take it; and the lousy faces of ministers, directors, and heads of personnel, may they rot in hell. But how much more interesting is a patch of sky, however small, than the face of Pantoja, or Cucúrbitas, or the minister himself! Thank God I can finally experience the sheer pleasure of contemplating nature, because all my sorrows and all my problems have ended, and I no longer need to worry about whether or not they're going to give me a post; I'm a new man, and I finally know what independence is, what it means to be alive, and I couldn't care one jot about any of them; I envy no one and I am…yes, I am the happiest of men. Right, time to eat, then, on with the motley!"

He clicked the fingers of both hands flamenco-style and, once again wrapping his cloak about him, headed for Cuesta de San Vicente, walking almost the whole length, peering into all the shop windows. He finally stopped outside an expensive-looking tavern, murmuring: "This looks like a good place. In you go, Ramón, treat yourself." No sooner said than done. Shortly afterward, Villaamil was seated at a round table with, before him, some bone-handle cutlery, a plate of lamb stew that smelled utterly divine, a jug of wine, and a good chunk of bread. "How delightful it is to be here," he was thinking as he got stuck into his stew, "free, with no commitments, without a thought for my family…because, I'm pleased to say, I have no family; I'm alone in the world, alone and master of whatever I do. How delightful, how extraordinarily pleasurable. The slave has cast off his chains and doesn't give two figs for what other people might think, and as his former oppressors parade past, he regards them as complete nonentities. Goodness, but this stew tastes good! That silly creature Milagros has never cooked anything as delicious—well, she's only capable of doing two things: curling her hair, and singing and miaowing at the top of her voice, '*Morriamo, morriamo…*' She sounds like a dog yelping when someone steps on its tail…But this stew really is delicious. They certainly know how to cook in this place! And the innkeeper seems a good sort too, and those green oversleeves really suit him, as do his carpet slippers and that leather cap. He's far more handsome than Cucúrbitas and even Pantoja! And this wine is good too, cool and with a bite to it. Delicious. All this is the effect of my new-found freedom, no longer having to give a damn about anyone, my head clear of anxieties and sorrows, because I've left any loose ends tied up: My daughter's going to marry Ponce, who's a good lad with a decent income; my grandson has gone to live with Quintina, who will do a far better job of bringing him up than his grandmother... and as for her and her useless sister, well, Abelarda and her husband can look after them... In short, I no longer have to provide for anyone; I am free and happy and independent and, like the Romans, can fling wide the doors to Hannibal! Yes, this is true happiness! I no longer have to decide which poor Christian I must write to today, asking for a small loan. What a relief to put an end to so much ignominy! My soul feels larger, more expansive... I can breathe more freely, I have regained my young man's appetite, and I feel like shaking the hand of everyone I see and telling them how very happy I am."

This was as far as he had got with his soliloquy when three young men entered the tavern, presumably having just arrived on the train, each with a knapsack on his back, a cane tucked in his belt, and dressed in peasant-fashion—all of them wearing espadrilles, but each with a different hat, for one wore a round one, the other a beret, and the third a silk scarf tied around his head.

"What fine-looking lads!" thought Villaamil, gazing at them, rapt, while they, noisy and insolent, were asking the innkeeper for something to take the edge off their huge appetite. "Could they be young farmworkers, who have left the obscure poverty of their villages to come to this land of Babel, to find a job that will give them a veneer of respectability and the air of decent folk? Poor unfortunates! I will do them the great favor of opening their eyes to reality!"

Without further ado, he marched straight over to them, saying:

"Young men, consider what you are doing while there's still time. Return to your cabins and your meadows, and flee the vile abyss that is Madrid, for it will swallow you up and make you unhappy for the rest of your lives. Listen to the advice of someone who has your interests at heart, and go straight back to the countryside."

"What's he saying?" said the brighter of the three, picking up his jacket and slinging it over his shoulder. "Devil take the old fellow! We're this year's recruits, and if we don't report for duty, they'll shoot us..."

"Oh, I see, well, if you're soldiers, that's a different matter entirely. Defending the country and all that. I did my bit too, you know. I joined a company of volunteers when that rogue Gómez was advancing on Madrid. I will tell you, though, not to listen to what your officers preach at you, and to rise up and rebel at the first opportunity, boys. Scorn that great whore, the state. You do know what the state is, don't you?"

The three lads laughed, revealing healthy white teeth: They were doubtless vastly amused by this scarecrow standing before them. Since none of them knew what the state was, Villaamil had to explain:

"Well, the state is humankind's greatest enemy, destroying anything it can lay its hands on. Be very careful... Stay free and independent and pay no heed to anyone."

One of the young men took the cane from his belt and brought it down so hard on the table that he almost broke it in two, meanwhile shouting:

"Landlady, we're starving out here. In the name of Suleiman the Magnificent, bring us some meat!"

Villaamil was amused by this lively show of wit and filled with admiration for their youth and their hot blood. The innkeeper asked them to wait and then set before them bread and wine to stave off their hunger. Villaamil then paid his bill, and the innkeeper—already intrigued by his unusual manner, and assuming that he was slightly touched—ran over to offer him a glass of wine. Don Ramón gratefully accepted this kind offer, and taking the glass and raising it aloft, he drank to "the prosperity of the tavern," while the recruits bellowed:

"Here's to Madrid, five minutes' rest, and some food! Long live Nastasia, Bruna, Ruperta, and all the girls from Daganzo de Arriba!"

And when Villaamil bade a very gracious farewell to the innkeeper and praised the excellent service and the perfect seasoning, the innkeeper said:

"There's nowhere like it in Madrid. Remember the name: *The Lord's Vineyard*."

"Ah, I'm afraid I won't be back. Tomorrow I'll be far away, my friend. Gentlemen (turning to the young men and doffing his hat to them), look after yourselves. Thank you and enjoy your meal. And don't forget what I told you . . . stay free and independent . . . be as free as the air. Look at me. I don't care two hoots about the state. Goodbye."

He left, dragging his cloak behind him, and one of the young men ran over to the door, shouting:

"Hey, Grandpa, hold on tight or you might fall over! Grandpa, come back, you've left your wits behind!"

But Villaamil heard none of this and continued on, looking for the path that would lead him back to La Montaña. He found it at last, crossing an empty building site and another one fenced about ready for construction to begin, and finally, after taking many a wrong turn and avoiding ditches and gullies, and trudging through the shifting soil of garbage dumps, he again reached the square outside the barracks and walked round it, not stopping until he reached the bare slopes that led from the Argüelles district down to San Antonio de la Florida. There he sat on the ground and, feeling very hot from the sun and the wine he had drunk, took off his cloak.

"What a lovely peaceful lunch I had today! I haven't felt so happy since, as a youth, we saw off that General Gómez fellow. I wasn't free physically then, but I was in my mind, just as I am now, and I was never worried about whether I'd have enough money to buy food at the market. Having to go shopping every day is what makes life so unbearable . . . Look at those little birds, prettily pecking about. Do they worry about what they'll eat tomorrow? No. That's why they're happy, and now I am like them: so contented that I would start chirruping if I knew how, and would, if I could, fly from here to Casa del Campo. Why does God not make us birds rather than human beings? We should at least be given the choice. No one would choose to be a man and have to go grubbing around for jobs and spending money on jackets and ties and all the other paraphernalia—which, as well as being bothersome, cost a small fortune. Look at them; just look at those birds, not a care in the world, just grabbing whatever they can find and eating their fill. Not one of them will be married to a bird called Pura, who has no idea, and never has, of how to run a household, or the least notion of saving money..."

Seeing the sparrows just a few yards away, hopping closer, cautious yet bold, to see what they could find on the ground, Don Ramón took from his pocket the bread he hadn't eaten at lunch, and crumbling it up, he threw it to the little birds. They all flew off when he moved his hands, but soon returned and, having discovered the bread, fell on it like wild things. Villaamil smiled and took pride in observing their greed, the graceful way they fluffed out their feathers and hopped nimbly about. The slightest noise, the faintest shadow or hint of danger sent them flying, but their frantic appetite quickly brought them back to the same place.

"Don't you worry, eat, eat," he was saying to them in his mind, entranced and motionless, so as not to scare them. "If Pura had been like you, things would have been very different, but adapting to reality is quite beyond her. Is there anything more natural than confining oneself within the limits of the possible? There are only potatoes to eat; well, then, potatoes it is. If things get better and you can stretch to having a partridge for supper... then partridge it will be. But no, she wants partridge every day. This is why we've had thirty years of problems, thirty years of fear and anxiety; when there was food to be had, we scarfed it down as if we absolutely had to finish the lot; when there wasn't, we lived on debts and loans. That's why, whenever I was given a post, we already owed a whole year's salary. We were locked in that perpetual cycle, uttering prayers—'To thee do we send up our sighs'—and gazing at the stars...

"Thirty years. And they call that living. 'Ramón, why don't you ask this or that friend? Ramón, whatever are you thinking of? We're not chameleons who can live on air. Ramón, you're going to have to pawn your watch, the little one needs boots... Ramón, I may have no shoes, and I can survive like that for a few more days, but I really cannot do without gloves, because we have to attend the benefit concert for La Furranguini . . . Ramón, tell the cashier to advance you five hundred reales; it's your birthday, and we have to invite so and so . . . Ramón . . .' And I wasn't man enough to tie my wife up and put a gag on that mouth of hers, which should have been the mouth of a mendicant friar, given how naturally she took to begging! Fancy putting up with that for thirty years! Now, though, thank God, I have found the courage to step out of my chains and become myself again. Now I am I, which no one can deny, and I have finally learned to do what I did not know how to do: to reject Pura and all those like her and to dispatch them to the back of beyond."

Unable to restrain his enthusiasm and good cheer, he thumped the ground so violently that the sparrows fled.

43

"Now DON'T be silly...no one's going to hurt you. Who do you take me for? Some heartless minister stealing the daily bread from a family man in order to give it to some good-for-nothing? Because you too are fathers and have small children to feed. Don't get alarmed, and eat up your crumbs...Believe me, if I had been married to a different woman—to Ventura's wife, for example—I would never have ended up in this situation. Ventura's wife, who my wife makes fun of because she says Scettish not Scottish, is worth a hundred Puras. With Pura, there's never enough money; not even a director's salary would be enough. What ruined us was her outrageous arrogance, all those visitors and theater tickets and baubles, and her way of looking down her nose at others, as if she were in some way superior. Fear not, little ones; it's safe to approach, because I still have a few crumbs left. As for Milagros, you will, I'm sure, agree that, although good-hearted and simple, she is just as useless as her sister. That fellow who jumped into the water because of her was quite right, because if he hadn't jumped and was now tied to her for life, he would have drowned a hundred times over and lived to tell the tale, which is the worst thing that can happen to a poor Christian. Those two sisters have had me spend the better part of my life with a noose around my neck, growing gradually tighter and tighter. No one could accuse me of treating them unfairly, because ever since I married...No, now it occurs to me that when I went to Señor Escobios to ask him for his daughter's hand, that worthy doctor in the Fourth Cavalry Brigade should have given me a good, hard slap to bring me to my senses. Ah, how grateful I would have been later on. Go on, eat, eat; there's no hurry, we're not here to take people's bread away from them. As I was saying, from the day I married until now, I have been at the mercy of those two harridans, their lack of substance and their profligacy, and they can't say that I was ever anything but meek and mild, the soul of patience, nor that I'm abandoning them and leaving them in poverty, because the only reason I feel able to regain my freedom is that I know now that they will be protected by Ponce, who is a saint and will keep them fed and clothed, which is precisely why his uncle the notary left him all *his* crumbs. Ah, illustrious Ponce, what a task awaits you! It's not going to be easy. If you're not careful, they'll bankrupt you...evaporate you, volatilize you, suck you dry. That's your affair, though. I've done my bit...I've carried my cross for thirty years; now someone else can carry it...it's a job that requires young shoulders...and it's a heavy weight, my friend Ponce, as you'll find out. To be frank, my daughter may not be very bright, but she's worth her mother and her aunt put together, plus she at least has some idea of order and prudence and is far less likely to boast...But keep your eye on her, Ponce, because if I know anything about women's feelings and affections, my Abelarda is about as fond of you as she would be of a toothache. I'm still convinced that Víctor, the sly dog, turned her head...Anyway, marry her soon, and if the Miaows are happy and learn what they failed to learn in my time with them, I will be very happy and will even applaud from up high, yes, I will."

Villaamil spent the afternoon immersed in such thoughts as these, which were far longer and more diffuse than they appear here. He occasionally moved to a different place, ruthlessly trampling, as he did so, one or two of the shrubs that the city council had planted on that bare piece of land. "The city council," he said to himself, "is the son of the county council and the grandson of that pig of pigs, the state, so one need have no scruples about trampling the whole wretched lot of them; indeed, it is our right. Like fathers, like sons. If I had my way, I wouldn't leave a tree or a streetlight standing...My revenge if you like...Then I would lay into the buildings, starting with that swinish ministry, razing it to the ground...leaving it as flat as the flat of my hand. Then I would leave not a railway, bridge or warship alive and would even smash to smithereens the cannon in the fortresses."

He wandered about that godforsaken place, hat in hand, receiving on his bare head the full force of the sun's rays, which, as the afternoon progressed, beat ferociously down on the earth and all that was on it. He was wearing his cloak slung loosely about him now and had every intention of taking it off, only deciding not to because he thought it might be useful that night, for however short a time. He paused on the edge of the steep bank near Cuesta de Areneros, above the new potteries in Moncloa, and pondering the precipitous slope, he thought serenely: "This seems like a good place, because I would go rolling down here like a lost sheep. Then let them come and find me if they can, unless some goatherd finds me first ... A good place, and yes, convenient too, whatever others might say."

He must have felt, however, that this was not, after all, the right place to carry out his rash intentions, because he continued walking, going first down and then up, inspecting the terrain as if he were intending to build a house there. Not another living soul to be seen. The sparrows were already retreating to the rooftops down below or to the trees in Calle San Bernardino and Paseo de la Florida. Suddenly, the poor man felt an impulse to remove the gun from his pocket and take aim at those innocent birds, saying: "So, you scoundrels, you rogues, once you've eaten my bread, you simply leave without so much as a goodbye. What would you say if I were to put a bullet through you? Because not one of you would escape. And I'm a very good marksman! Just be thankful that I need to keep all my bullets, because otherwise you would pay with your lives, the whole lot of you ... I do actually feel like killing everything that lives, as a punishment for how badly humanity and nature *and* God (said in a furious voice) have treated me—yes, yes, they have all behaved in the most scoundrelly fashion ... They have all abandoned me, which is why I now adopt the motto I invented last night, literally: *Murderous* ... Ignominious ... Arbitrary ... Overweening ... World ..."

With this refrain singing in his brain, he continued to walk, moving ever farther off until, when night had fallen, he found himself on the heights of San Bernardino from where he could look down over Vallehermoso and the formless mass of Madrid's houses, crenellated with towers and cupolas and swarming with lights amid the darkness ... His homicidal, destructive thoughts had subsided, and the poor man had returned to his topographical concerns: "This would be an excellent place, but then again, the excise officers might spot me, and they're stupid enough to try and stop me doing what I want to do and must do ... No, onward to the Cementerio de la Patriarcal, where there will be no importunate people poking their noses into what is none of their business, because I want the world to realize one thing and one thing only: namely, that I don't give a damn whether they balance the budget or not, and that I thumb my nose at income tax and the whole vile Administration. The people who find my body will realize not only this but also that I really don't care whether my remains end up being thrown on a dunghill or are carried to the Pantheon of the Kings at El Escorial palace. What matters is my soul, which will fly up into what is known as the empyrean, high up somewhere behind those shining stars that appear to be winking at me, calling to me ... But this isn't yet the moment. First, I want to go back down to that cesspit of a city, Madrid, and tell a few home truths to those vulgar Miaow women who have made my life such a misery."

His hatred of his family—which had begun to stir into life inside him in recent days and which occasionally burst forth in the form of a mad frenzy or a violent rage—now exploded, making him clench his fists and grind his teeth and hurry on, a wild and sinister figure, his hat slipping off his head and his cloak dragging along the ground. By now, it was pitch-black night. He strode purposefully toward the esplanade outside the Conde-Duque barracks, then, as he approached the Plaza de las Comendadoras, he slowed his pace, moving more stealthily, more cautiously, keeping in the shadows and constantly changing direction. After making his way down an entirely empty Calle de San Hermenegildo, he turned toward Plaza del Limón, walked back around the Plaza de las Comendadoras, and finally ventured across Calle de Quiñones, where he looked up at the balconies of his apartment, first making sure that Mendizábal and his wife were nowhere to be seen. Crouched on the corner of the dark, silent, solitary square, he kept gazing at the house, watching to see if anyone came or went. Would the Miaows be going to the theater that night? Would Ponce and their other friends be arriving to spend the evening there? In the midst of all this mental turmoil, he was still able to keep one foot in reality, believing that it was certain and inevitable that Pura, alarmed by her husband's absence, would dispatch all the family friends to look for him.

Lurking there on the corner, like a thief or a murderer listening for the footsteps of an unwary passerby, Villaamil craned his neck to watch without being seen. Strictly speaking, his body was in the Plaza de las Comendadoras and his head in Calle de Quiñones, his flaccid and prodigiously elastic neck bent around the corner itself. "Here's Ponce rushing back from somewhere. They've probably been to Pantoja's house, to the café, to all the other places I usually frequent...This other man, huffing and puffing along, looks to me like Federico Ruiz. He has doubtless come from the police station or the morgue...where he went to make inquiries. Poor things, what a lot of trouble they're being put to! And how I enjoy seeing them so busy and imagining how upset the Miaows must be...Too bad—and you, Doña Pura from Hell, it's your turn to swallow the hemlock now, the hemlock I've been swallowing for thirty years without a murmur of complaint. Ah, now someone else is leaving and coming over here. It looks like it's Ponce again. I'll hide in this doorway. Yes, it's him... (Watching Ponce walk across Plaza de las Comendadoras.) I wonder where he's going. Perhaps to Cabrera's house. What a lot of work I'm causing you. Was there ever such a fool? No, you won't find me, you won't catch me, you won't deprive me of my glorious, blessed freedom. Even if you were to turn the whole world upside down, you would never find me, you fools! What do you want? (Shaking his fist at some invisible being.) Do you want me to return to the clutches of Pura and Milagros so that they can continue to blight my life with their incessant requests for money, with their profligacy, their imprudence and their pretensions? No, I'm up to here with it; my bitter cup is full... If I were to continue living with them, a fit of madness might come upon me one day, and I would kill them all with this gun... yes, with this gun (closing his fingers around the grip of the gun in his pocket). Therefore, it's best if I kill myself, thus freeing myself and going straight up to God in heaven. Ah, Pura, my suffering is over. Sink your claws into another victim. You have Ponce now with all that nice fresh money; you can gorge yourself on him. I won't care. How I will laugh! Because, dear Ponce, Doña Pura is a real fiend, and as soon as she has some money in her hand, it's time for a party, at which the food and the clothes must all be of the finest quality, without a thought for where she will find tomorrow's crust of bread... Oh, dear God, how I have sometimes envied the most humble of artisans, the most wretched of beggars; whereas now, free and unfettered, I wouldn't change places with the king himself. No, I wouldn't, and I say that from the bottom of my heart."

44

EMERGING from the doorway and resuming his spying. "There's the Cuevas boy, looking very worried and in a tremendous hurry. Where will he be off to? Go on, search hard, my boy, search hard, and Doña Pura will reward you with a glass of muscatel . . . And that silly billy Milagros will be at her wits' end, because the poor thing really does love me . . . Well, that's only natural given that she's lived with me all these years and eaten my bread . . . And if we're being absolutely fair, Pura loves me too . . . in her fashion, of course. And although I once loved them both, now I loathe them. What would I say to the two of them—well, to the three of them really, because my daughter weighs on me too . . . They are like three dead weights sitting here in the pit of my stomach, and whenever I think of them, my blood seems to turn to molten steel and the top of my brainbox feels as if it were about to explode . . . The three Miaows, damn them! Whoever came up with that nickname was spot on. No, no more living with madwomen. And whatever came over that poor daughter of mine, falling for Víctor, of all people! Because if I'm not mistaken, she really did love him. Dear God, what stupid women! Being taken in by a ne'er-do-well because of his pretty face . . . when he, of course, despises her; of that there's no doubt . . . Well, I'm glad. It serves her right. Take your medicine, you little fool, and come back for more, then marry Ponce . . . Frankly, even if I wasn't going to end it all to save myself from further misery, I should do it just so as not to have to witness any more such goings-on."

When he saw a light on in his office, he grew angrier: "There'll be no theater for you tonight, Doña Pura. Just as well then that you have to stay at home. Too bad! I can see you already trying to work out where to find the money for your mourning clothes. Not that I care. Get it from wherever you like. You could sell my skin for a drum or my bones for buttons. Magnificent, admirable, dee-lish-ous!"

As he was thinking this, he spotted Mendizábal standing in the doorway opposite and realized, to his horror, that Mendizábal had seen him. He felt terribly alarmed and worried when he saw his neighbor eyeing him suspiciously. "The creature has recognized me and is coming after me," thought Villaamil, keeping close to the wall as he retreated into Plaza de las Comendadoras. Before he did so, he took another look, and Mendizábal really was following him, like a hunter quietly pursuing his prey, trying not to startle it. Wrapping his cloak about him, a terrified Villaamil began running as fast as he could, imagining he could hear the other man's footsteps behind him and that a huge arm was about to reach out and grab him by the scruff of the neck. He was genuinely frightened. Fortunately, there was no one else around, because if there had been, and Mendizábal had cried out "Stop that man!" then Villaamil's precious freedom would have ended right there. He fled with remarkable speed across Plaza del Limón, past the barracks—successfully avoiding the sentry's beady eye—and as he was heading down Calle del Conde-Duque, he glanced back to see that, although Mendizábal was still following him, he was lagging some way behind. Without even pausing for breath, Villaamil made his way to the deserted esplanade and, before his pursuer could catch him up, hid behind a pile of flagstones. Removing his hat and peering very cautiously through a gap in the stones, he saw the man-gorilla looking very lost, glancing to right and left, but concentrating more on Paseo de Areneros, where he thought his prey must have gone. "So, you obscurantist, you want to catch me, do you? You won't succeed though. I know more than you do, you ugly monster—uglier than hunger itself, and more reactionary than Judas. As you know, I have always been a liberal and would rather die than live under a despot. Go to hell, you die-hard traditionalist, you'll never throw your chains around me ... I shit on your absolutism and on your inquisition. Fie on you, you Carlist, liberticide beast, for I am free, a liberal and a democrat, an anarchist and a petroleur, and I will do what I damn well like..."

Although he had now lost sight of the ugly gorilla, he still didn't feel entirely safe. And aware of Mendizábal's herculean strength, he knew that once the fellow had him in his grasp, he wouldn't easily escape, and so to avoid such an encounter, he hunkered down in the shadows behind the various piles of blocks and flagstones. Safe in the thick darkness, he again caught sight of Mendizábal, who, having despaired of finding him, was apparently returning home. "Farewell, you dolt, fanaticism's henchman, oppressor of the people... Look at that face, those arms, that body! It's a miracle you're not walking on all fours. Go on, keep searching, then you can go boasting to Doña Pura, saying that you saw me... Rogue, reactionary, savage, may the demons carry you off down into hell!"

When he thought it safe to do so, he went back into the streets, always afraid that Mendizábal might still be pursuing him, and he took not a single step without first looking around him. He imagined his pursuer could emerge from any doorway or be lurking on every dark corner, watching and waiting, ready to pounce, lithe as a monkey and brave as a lion. As he left Callejón del Cristo and turned into Calle de Amaniel, there, all of a sudden, was Mendizábal talking to some women. Fortunately, he had his back to Villaamil and so didn't see him. Finding himself thus trapped, Villaamil had a flash of inspiration, which was to enter the first open door he came to. He found himself in a tavern. Once he had recovered from the shock, and in order to justify his abrupt arrival, he went straight over to the bar and ordered a glass of red wine. While he waited, he observed the other clientele: two sergeants, three civilians in short jackets, and four very rough-looking whores. "What pretty, elegant young women!" he thought as he peered at them over his glass. "I'm almost tempted to pay them a compliment or two, I, who, since I led Pura to the altar, haven't made a single flattering remark to another woman. It must be the rejuvenating effect of freedom, my youth resuscitated. Goodness, my whole body is tingling. Fancy a man spending thirty years never once thinking about another woman! How odd. I think I might have another glass of wine....Thirty virtuous years should allow one to kick over a few traces...Another glass, please. (Addressed to the innkeeper.) Hm, I've taken a real liking to those young ladies, and if it wasn't for their good-for-nothing escorts, I would make some remark that would show them what a difference there is between dealing with a real gentleman and keeping company with mere worms and raw recruits. I should strike up a conversation with them, even if only to allow time for Mendizábal to move on...God save me from that proud ultramontanist, that factionalist! Still, I do like those girls—especially the one with her hair caught up in a topknot and wearing a red cloak...She's looking at me too, and...Steady on, Ramón, such adventures can prove very dangerous. Calm down now, and have another glass of wine to pass the time. Landlord, another glass..."

The party left, and thinking very quickly, Villaamil said to himself: "I'll tag along behind them, and if the villain's still out there, I'll slip away with those gallants and their ladies." And this is what he did, following after the young girls—for so they seemed to him—and their soldier companions. Mendizábal was no longer to be seen in the street, but Don Ramón, still on edge, stayed as close as he could to the riffraff, thinking: "If that orangutan does attack me, these brave soldiers will fight him off...You'll be fine, Ramón, don't worry...No one can take away that child of heaven: your sacrosanct liberty."

As they neared Plaza de las Capuchinas, the cheerful band headed off along Calle Juan de Dios. He heard the cackling laughter of those brazen women and the men's curses and coarse language. He gazed after them with a mixture of sadness and envy: "Oh happy age, free from worries and free from care! Long may it last. Commit every folly you can think of, young ones, and every possible sin as well, and laugh at the world and its obligations, until black care arrives and you become enslaved to earning your daily bread and maintaining your social position."

With these words, all other accessory and incidental ideas vanished, leaving only the single, dominant idea, that of his terrible psychological state. "It must be very late, Ramón. Hurry up and put an end to yourself, for that is God's will." He remembered his dear grandson

Luis then, for he was once again in Calle de los Reyes. He stopped outside the Cabreras' house, and looking up at the second floor, he mumbled these words into his cloak: "My dearest boy, Luis, the purest and noblest member of the family, a child truly worthy of your mother, whom I will see very soon: How are you getting along with those people? Do you miss us? Don't worry, you'll soon grow used to your new home; they are good people, orderly and frugal, they'll do a fine job of bringing you up and will make a man of you. Don't regret having come here. Look at me, your loving grandfather; I even have a notion to pray to you, because you are a saint in the making and will surely be canonized ... I can see it now. It was from your innocent lips that I received confirmation of what had already been revealed to me ... and ever since I heard your words, I have ceased to hesitate. Farewell, angelic boy, your grandfather sends you his blessing, or, rather, asks for your blessing, because you are a little saint, and on the day that you give your first mass, there will be such joy in heaven ... and on earth ... Farewell, I must hurry. Sleep, and if ever you are unhappy and someone takes away your liberty, you know what to do. Simply leave this place ... for there are many ways ... and you know where to find me. Ever yours."

He spoke these last words as he walked toward Plaza de San Marcial, adopting the easy, unhurried pace of a man heading home having completed the day's tasks. He once again found himself on the slopes of La Montaña, in places beyond the reach of any street lighting, and where the uneven terrain put him in danger of plunging into the earth rather earlier than planned. At last, he came to a halt on the edge of a newly dug embankment, where the soil was still so soft and shifting that anyone venturing onto it would have sunk in up to his knees, not to mention run the very real risk of rolling down into its invisible depths. He was suddenly assailed by a painful thought, born of his long habit of always expecting the worst and viewing everything from the most pessimistic of angles. "Now that I can already see both an end to my enslavement and my imminent entry into Eternal Glory, fate is about to play another dirty trick on me. This wretched instrument (taking out his gun) will probably fail me and I'll be left half dead, half alive, which is the worst thing that could possibly happen, because then they would take me back to those damn Miaow women. What a poor unfortunate wretch I am! Yes, that's what will happen, I can see it now. I only have to wish for one thing and the very opposite will happen. Do I want to kill myself? Well, then, vile fate will arrange it so that I continue to live."

However, the logical process that had always served him so well in life, the system whereby he would imagine the opposite of what he wanted in order to get his wish, inspired these thoughts in him: "I will imagine that I'm going to bungle the shot, and if I imagine it well, focusing my mind on it, then I won't bungle it. Always imagine the opposite of what you want. So, I will imagine that I don't die and am taken home. Oh dear God, going back to Pura and Milagros and my daughter, with their constant visits to the theater and the constant lack of money, having to go badgering people for a loan...or for a job, always pestering friends...I can see it all too clearly: This stupid gun is no use at all. Did that shameless armorer sell me a dud? Let's try...no, it won't work...but just in case, I commend myself to God and to my beloved little saint, Saint Luis Cadalso...no...the wretched thing is useless...Shall we take a bet on it? Oh, how those horrible Miaow women will laugh! Now, yes, now...I bet it won't work."

The shot rang out in the solitude of that dark, deserted place. Villaamil was hurled headfirst into the shifting soil, then rolled straight down into the abyss, remaining conscious just long enough to be able to say: "Ah...it did..."

OTHER NEW YORK REVIEW CLASSICS

For a complete list of titles, visit www.nyrb.com.